PLAYIN' HARD

ALSO BY
WHITNEY D. GRANDISON

The Gilded

Hold You Down

Away from the Sun

Knights Series

A Love Hate Thing

Arlington High

The Right Side of Reckless

WHITNEY D. GRANDISON

wattpad books

wattpad books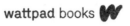

An imprint of Wattpad WEBTOON Book Group

Published in Canada by Wattpad WEBTOON Book Group, a division of Wattpad WEBTOON Studios, Inc.

36 Wellington Street E., Suite 200, Toronto, ON M5E 1C7 Canada

www.wattpad.com

First Wattpad Books edition: April 2025

ISBN 978-1-99885-432-5 (Trade Paper original)
ISBN 978-1-99885-433-2 (eBook edition)

Library and Archives Canada Cataloguing in Publication information is available upon request.

Printed and bound in Canada

1 3 5 7 9 10 8 6 4 2

Cover design by Saniyyah Zahid
Typesetting by Delaney Anderson

To the beautiful, strong, intelligent, powerful, majestic, courageous, unstoppable Black girl

&

Uwe Stender for always and always and always believing in this story

1

CREE

Amid the fruit-scented air that permeated the restroom, two girls hovered above the sinks. One was crying and the other was consoling her. In between Girl One's sobs, I could just make out what she was upset about. Apparently, she'd gone and hooked up with Tremaine Dickenson and he'd quickly dismissed her afterward, giving her a gold bracelet as a walking away present.

Girl One's sobs increased and it took a lot to not scowl at my reflection as I washed my hands. Hell, at least he'd given her something before serving her walking papers. What was there to cry about?

"It's like he . . . *used* me." Girl One turned and faced her friend, showing her tear-drenched face. She was pretty, and from the look of her figure, she definitely fit the Baller's Club type.

At Moorehead High, the Baller's Club was the cause of many female meltdowns. The club consisted of four boys who played on either the basketball or the football team. Tremaine Dickenson was one of them, along with Marcus Hamilton, Chris Casey, and DeAndre Parker. Together they went through girls like they went through Jordans. You'd think others would catch on and wise up, but some people at Moorehead were just that obtuse.

Finally having heard enough, I rolled my eyes and left. The girl's sobs were indicative of the full-blown breakdown she would endure. She'd brought it on herself, though. What Tremaine had done was nothing new, and she'd subjected herself to becoming smashed and passed as soon as she took the shit that came out of his mouth seriously. There was just no point in offering up sympathy for the naïve.

I know that sounds tough, but if you walk up to a ride that has a reputation for spinning, why get mad when you step on and it spins? Anyone with sense and eyes could see the Ballers for who and what they were: four walking BEWARE OF DOG signs.

Along the way to my fifth period Honors English class I stopped to pick up my best friend, Troiann Nguyen, at her locker. Troiann was a tiny little thing, only five one, taking after her Vietnamese mother instead of being tall like her Black father. She was gorgeous with her brown-sugar complexion and big, almond-shaped eyes.

"You will never guess the train wreck I just witnessed," I told her.

She gave me all of her attention, leaning close. "What's up?"

I chuckled and shook my head. "I just saw one of Tremaine's latest victims crying in the bathroom. Apparently, he ended things after hooking up."

Troiann shook her head as well. "They never learn."

After having watched the same repeat dozens of times, it was clear they didn't. "At least she got a bracelet out of it."

"For real?" Troiann was taken aback. "What was she crying for, then?"

"Beats me." I shrugged as we headed into our class.

Speak of the devil. Tremaine stood across the classroom laughing about something with DeAndre. There was no denying that their group was good looking and dressed to impress, with perfect haircuts and groomed—if any—facial hair. They stood out among the male population at Moorehead High.

Apart, they were each unique in their own way. Tremaine was the major heartbreaker, collecting shattered hearts like Thanos and his Infinity Stones. Star wide receiver on the football team, he was tall, dark skinned, handsome as ever, and could finesse his way into girls' pants with little to no effort.

Chris was the wild one. Rumors constantly featured him and his latest debauched escapade, which proved my instincts right in keeping my distance. Not to mention that time his Instagram profile came across my feed and I noticed his bio read *Your Mom's Favorite White Boy*. It made me snort even as I continued to scroll.

Marcus was more low key than Tremaine or Chris. He was as gorgeous as his friends, with light-brown skin and the softest look-ing coils on his fade haircut, and he was built like a machine after years playing tight end. Girls frequently said he was nasty work, that he came on sweet but once he slept with you, he ghosted you.

And then there was DeAndre.

With his broad chest and shoulders, height, and smooth brown complexion, he was beautiful. A work of art not even the ink stain-ing his skin could ruin. Yet there was always a look of indifference written across his face. An unreadable mask I couldn't decipher. He fit right in with the Ballers due to his athletic prowess, but in other ways he seemed different. Tremaine and Chris could be wild and cut up in class, with Marcus sometimes chiming in, but DeAndre was more reserved. Sometimes he came off more *man* than *boy*.

Between them there was wealth, status, and a sprinkle of tat-toos. Equal parts alluring and foreboding.

Most importantly, the Ballers Club played it smart. Not only did they dominate the sports teams they participated in, they also were academic all-stars.

Other athletes at our school wore their varsity jackets with their letters as badges of honor. Not the Ballers. They went against the grain and wore bomber jackets instead. DeAndre wore maroon, Tremaine black, Marcus navy blue, and Chris olive green. It was corny and flashy, but admittedly unique.

I caught sight of Tremaine in his customary black bomber jacket as he talked with *another* girl on the other side of the classroom, and rolled my eyes.

"Don't worry, they gon' get theirs one day," Troiann said as we took our seats.

We lived in the real world. Karma didn't exist and good didn't always conquer evil. It was futile to wish failure upon the boys. The only thing to do was stay as far away from them as possible.

"Take notes, Troy, you can't domesticate a wild animal, and when it comes to the Ballers, you can't turn an asshole into Prince Charming."

Troiann snickered. "You're a mess."

Our teacher, Mr. Ventura, stepped into the room and immediately went over to his desk upon the bell ringing. He pressed a button on his MacBook and a somewhat familiar tune played. It was upbeat and old school. As soon as the male singer began singing and spelling out the word *love* it came to me. *The Parent Trap*! That's where I knew the song from.

Mr. Ventura leaned back against his desk and let the song play, a broad smile on his face as he nodded along. When it was over, he hit a key on his Mac and turned to face us, grinning even more. "Now that's a jazzy tune."

Going further, he went over to the smart board and wrote down *LOVE* boldly, underlining it three times.

"Let's talk about l-o-v-e." He sounded enthusiastic about it, almost as enthusiastic as he was about Jane Austen. He sat on his desk. "Who wants to start?"

No one in the class budged.

"Don't all raise your hands at once." Mr. Ventura attempted a joke—which no one laughed at. "Well, come on, what's your opinion? I know we're all sixteen and seventeen, but we've got minds by now, right?"

Jael Reed raised her hand and Mr. Ventura quickly motioned her to speak. "I think love is an amazing feeling." She looked at her boyfriend, Ben, and blushed.

Give me a break.

I was no expert on the subject, since I'd never actually been in love, but something told me it was more than just a simple feeling.

I raised my hand to speak up.

"Yes?" Now Mr. Ventura was ecstatic more of us were participating. The smile on his face was almost pitiful, he was so geeked.

"From my perspective, love is not a feeling. Love is a verb, it's all about action. What good is a feeling if you're not acting on it? After all, 'Faith without works is dead,'" I stated, using a quote from a Bible verse my grandmother had once taught me.

"That's a good thought, Miss Jacobs. Anyone else agree?" Mr. Ventura asked, searching the room.

To my surprise, DeAndre raised his hand. "I disagree. Love is not just a verb, it's a noun, an adjective—it's more than just action, speaking from experience."

He spoke as if he had a heart or had been in love. The Ballers Club didn't even date girls long enough to comprehend the idea of actual feelings, let alone love. "And what experience is that?" I practically blurted out.

DeAndre turned, questioning my nerve to challenge him. "Life."

I looked elsewhere. "Whatever."

Mr. Ventura whistled loudly. "Looks like we've got ourselves a good debate going. Who else wants to join in?"

Others joined in on the discussion, some siding with DeAndre and some siding with me.

My cell phone vibrated in my pocket and I pulled it out, finding a text from Troiann.

> That boy can't even spell love

Instantly I felt better having my best friend on my side.

> The only four-letter word significant to them is BALL

Troiann let out a small snort and did her best to compose herself.

Mr. Ventura cleared his throat, gathering my attention. "No cell phones, Miss Jacobs."

"Right, sorry." I glanced at Troiann, only to find DeAndre watching me. Instead of looking away when he was caught, he just kept on, as if to see if I'd shift focus first.

Everything was a game to the Ballers. I didn't want to play or get anywhere near their web, but I couldn't give DeAndre the satisfaction of seeing me give in.

Mr. Ventura called the class to order and I turned away, peeking back once more to catch DeAndre smirking and shaking his head. Tremaine reached over and slapped him five.

I gritted my teeth.

From then onward I refused to waste another thought on DeAndre Parker or the Ballers Club.

Screw them and their egos.

Troiann was anxious to get to lunch. The girl ate like a horse and would never turn down free food. "Hurry up, CJ, before the line's hella long," she whined as she stood in the row of desks next to me, all ready to go. The bell had just rung and she was acting like it was a race to get down to the cafeteria.

"Oh, gee, we wouldn't want to miss our chances at greasy mystery pizza, now would we?" I asked as I stood and shot Troiann a teasing smile.

"Anything tastes good when you're hungry."

"When are you *not* hungry?" I turned to lead the way out of the room but was stopped by the sight of Tremaine and DeAndre waiting at the end of the aisle.

I wanted to hold my head high and walk right by them, even though it seemed like they were locking me in.

Nevertheless, I tried it anyway, making my way down the aisle as if they weren't there.

They didn't budge, and there was no slipping by because they were both *huge*, especially Tremaine. DeAndre was closest, standing directly in my way as I came to a stop in front of him. He was wearing a Billionaire Boys Club T-shirt, and even that made him appear arrogant. For that I continued my glare from his shirt to his brown eyes.

DeAndre met my sneer with a smile as he stuck his hand out. "Cree Jacobs, right?" he asked, as if I was some stranger and not a girl he'd been in school with since the fourth grade.

I nodded, offering nothing in response or shaking his hand.

"I just wanted to thank you for that interesting discourse we had in class. It's always good to have a debate every once in a while." The more he smiled, the more condescending his whole approach became.

"Yeah," I replied. "It's always interesting."

7

"Love is such a debatable topic, but I'm sure you know that. We're all entitled to our opinions."

"Right."

"So you agree?"

"With what?"

"That we're all entitled to our own opinions on love."

He was confusing me. I couldn't tell what his point was and why he was blocking me from leaving.

"I just don't think it's a good thing to equate sex with love," I said. That was all DeAndre and his friends did. How would they know anything about real relationships or love anyway?

DeAndre blinked and his smile broadened. "Now *that* is a completely different argument, Cree. Sex and love are sometimes mutually exclusive, and other times, they go hand in hand."

I snorted. "How would you know?"

Confusion took over DeAndre's face. "What's that supposed to mean?"

I crossed my arms, not holding back the truth. "I've heard about you and your friends, DeAndre."

Mr. Ventura had stepped out into the hall, and a few of our classmates lingered, watching the show DeAndre was putting on.

DeAndre looked over at Tremaine, and they shared the same grin. He turned back to me, touching his chest. "I'm flattered. Nice to know our reputation precedes us. Now what was it that you heard about us? Our charity basketball games, donating to the local food bank, or our Vintage Fire clothes drive?"

I wrinkled my nose, not impressed. "I'm not fooled by your façade. I've seen all of you in action. You're all just bad boys who do occasional good deeds."

"Some might substitute *bad* for *fun*."

"Some are stupid and naïve."

"Some are just stuck up."

"Oh really?"

"Exactly."

Chuckles echoed in the room. Our peers were enjoying DeAndre's cool persona and my growing aggravation. What did he even want?

"You're a dog, DeAndre," I let out.

DeAndre shrugged, showing he didn't care. "Of a high pedigree."

"There isn't a high pedigree for mutts."

My jab rolled off him as he took a moment to size me up slowly. When he was finished, he narrowed his eyes, appearing quizzical as he asked, "Are you a feminazi?"

Appalled, I scoffed. What more, I pushed him out of my way, done with the whole conversation. He wasn't worth the loss of brain cells in the effort it was taking to get through to him.

"Didn't mean to offend you, I just picked up on that 'I hate dudes' vibe." He spoke from behind me, causing his audience to snicker some more.

Instead of responding on my way to the door with Troiann in tow, I raised my middle finger, letting my feelings for him be known loud and clear.

I hate the Ballers Club.

2

DEANDRE

Two girls stood at our lunch table outside in the quad as Chris and Tremaine entertained them.

It was April, and the snow and cold had finally left Akron, Ohio, making eating outside appropriate on days when the weather was nice like this.

Our table was facing the windows, and as I looked inside the cafeteria, I caught sight of Cree walking with Troiann.

I liked to think I knew girls well. I could tell what they were all about within the first five minutes of speaking to them. I could tell whether they were the headstrong type, the emotional type, the clingy type, if they moaned in bed or liked it rough. It wasn't that hard figuring them out, but then there was Cree Jacobs, the only exception. Every baddie needed her anthem, and every good girl needed a choir. And it was more than obvious what type of girl Cree Jacobs was—on the surface.

With her soft-looking brown skin, thick natural coils, and familiar pretty face, I didn't know her all that well—and she damn sure didn't know *me*.

That didn't stop her from clearly having a problem with me.

During our discussion after class, I was surprised to find that she smelled good, like coconut, and not like venom, like I'd suspected. Being up close to her, I'd briefly admired her lips: the top one brown, the bottom pink, full and plump looking yet twisting into an angry sneer the moment I opened my mouth.

At six foot two, I had several inches on her, but that didn't stop her from standing strong in her contempt against me. Cree had the sharpest gaze I'd ever seen. Lethal brown eyes. Shit could cut you to stone if you were the type to fold under pressure.

I watched as Cree and Troiann searched for a spot to sit down and eat. She moved gracefully, as if she was walking on air. *Angel* suited her well, especially with that holier-than-thou, uppity shit she was pulling in class.

Never before had I noticed her, but when our opinions clashed in class, Cree walked right onto my radar. I hadn't any qualms against her or her opinion until she started throwing jabs. She had basically called me a disease-ridden dog, and that was disrespect I could not tolerate.

People hated on me and my friends mostly because they weren't invited to kick it with us. And to be honest, I'd hate me, too, if I wasn't involved in the shit me and my boys got into. We did our schoolwork and extracurricular activities, and then we had our fun on and off the court or the field.

To some we were heartless assholes because we didn't make it a habit to wife or cuff a girl, but we were just being realistic. There was no way in hell any of us were interested in the long term—we were in high school.

In our eyes, one night was all you got; two if you was bad enough.

Only simpleminded people believed in that happily ever after shit anyway.

The more I sat and watched Cree, the more pissed off I became at her words.

Who was she to judge me?

Troiann hadn't even said a word. I guess it also went to show that Cree had no clue her best friend was sleeping with my best friend. None of us were guarded when it came to the girls we messed with, and it was no secret Marcus was getting it in with Troiann.

In that way, Troiann Nguyen was a walking weapon I could keep in my back pocket.

The sound of clapping pulled me from my staring.

Chris slapped Tremaine's chest. "Yo, Tyra's bad as hell."

Tremaine agreed. "People say she looks like Kelly Rowland."

I shook my head at that claim. She looked more like a member of Poverty's Child than anything.

"Real talk, I'm just lookin' for a tutor," Chris said, a near-desperate look in his blue eyes. "My pops gon' kill me if I fail geography."

Dude knew every Future lyric yet couldn't memorize the shit we were learning in class.

"Good luck with that. Y'all wanna go to After Hours tonight?" Tremaine asked.

"Yeah, we can get into something," I told him.

After Hours was the local nightclub. It was eighteen and over, with a few all-ages nights, but we never got carded. If we weren't at After Hours, sometimes we hit Inferno, a strip club Chris had connections to. His cousin was a bouncer and a big fan of our football and basketball, and he usually let us sneak in.

I let the boys discuss the evening's endeavors as I once again found myself watching Cree. She was definitely a virgin, or else she wouldn't have been up on my case about *my* sex life.

A french fry landed on my tray, distracting me. "You *still* on

Cree Jacobs?" Tremaine asked. "Let it go, you win some and you lose some, Dre."

A scowl marred my face. "I don't lose."

Chris craned his neck to get a good look at Cree. "What happened?"

Tremaine explained our clash in and after Ventura's class. "And she was just being stuck up." Tremaine was sitting on the tabletop next to Chris, but he leaned over and slapped Marcus's shoulder. "Yo' girl was even there."

Marcus looked down at his tray. "She's not my girl."

Cap.

It was bullshit and we all knew it.

"Anyway, Cree was all 'you got STDs' and walked away, leaving Dre stuck in his feelings."

The more Tremaine talked, the more annoyed I became. I had let Cree off easy.

I sat up and pushed my tray away, leaning my elbows on the table. "I get plenty of girls. Who's Cree Jacobs?"

"One girl you can't have," Tremaine said matter-of-factly.

His use of the words *can't have* set me off. I was a Parker, there wasn't much I *couldn't* have. If there was one thing in life that came to me easily besides basketball, it was definitely girls.

Lifting a brow, I looked over at Tremaine. "It wouldn't be that hard to show her what's up."

Tremaine snorted and waved me off. "Cree would never give you any."

"You'd really have to shoot ya shot then," Chris added.

"It don't even matter. Dre couldn't get the box if he were a gynecologist," Tremaine remarked, making the boys laugh. It would be sorta funny, if it was true.

They sounded like amateurs. "I can get her without even touching her."

Marcus looked skeptical. "Is that right?"

"Yeah, it is," I said. A mindfuck was just as good as a regular fuck. "Give me Troiann's number."

Marcus slid away from me then asked, "Why?"

"I need to ask her a favor."

"Nah, man, leave her outta this."

I shook my head. "It's time to see which team she's playing for."

"Cree's her *best* friend, Dre," Marcus said, almost whining.

Yeah, he'd caught feelings all right.

I held my hand out expectantly. "I'm a 'dog,' Marcus, and doggie wants the kitty."

Begrudgingly, he handed over his phone and I found Troiann's number and typed it into my own phone.

I was just talking shit. I hadn't any real aspirations to teach Cree a lesson, but I did want to get under her skin. I'd never done a thing to her to warrant all that attitude. It was only fair I returned the favor.

"Hello?" Troiann answered her phone, sounding curious at my unknown number.

"Hey," I said with faux peppiness. "It's DeAndre."

In the cafeteria, I watched Troiann scowl as she stood from her lunch table and headed toward the girls' restroom. "What?" she hissed into the phone.

Rolling my eyes, I said, "That's not a nice way to greet someone."

"I don't like you."

I picked at a nail, thinking nothing of her comment. "That's how you feel?"

"That's how it is. I'm hanging up now."

"Do that and Cree's going to get a cute little picture of you and Marcus," I said casually, thinking of the adorable home screen image Marcus had of them cheek to cheek.

Troiann's shock was palpable through the phone. "What do you want?"

I grinned. *Too easy.*

"I'm glad you see things my way," I said. "Now, here's what we're going to do . . ."

3

CREE

It was just my dad and me—and now Loraine, his wife. My mother had passed away during my birth, so for most of my life it was just my father and me. Occasionally my father's sisters would come around, but for the most part, we were pretty much a duo.

By day my father was a carpenter, and by night he would be all about me—at least that was how things used to be before Loraine. He met her when he was building a new section for the elementary school where she taught. Friendly conversation turned into a date, which turned into a relationship, and that eventually turned into marriage.

I was fifteen when I lost my father to Loraine. I knew it was wrong of me to feel that way, but it was like my father was all about her. No more did he attempt to teach me about fixing cars, no more did he tell me stories about his day.

But I suppose my actions didn't help either. I stayed away from home a lot while he was courting Loraine. My aunt Kathy ran a ballet studio, and I spent a lot of summers learning to dance from her, though my style was more contemporary. With Loraine in the picture, I danced nearly every day, perfecting my craft.

I'd gotten a job at Henry's, the local grocery store, to help around the house and to have some extra cash of my own. It also helped me avoid my father and Loraine.

As I stood in the prepared foods section of Henry's after school, cooking food and dealing with the public was the last thing I wanted to do after failing to get my earlier run-in with DeAndre Parker out of my head.

Troiann had done her best to distract me from the situation during the rest of the school day, but there was no forgetting the words exchanged with DeAndre. I still couldn't get over how he'd felt the need to corner me.

Really? *Are you a feminazi?* What a dumbass.

If I *had* to define myself, I would call myself a womanist before anything. I owed this to my late paternal grandmother. She was an artist and had painted portraits of Black women as works of art: goddesses, mothers, oceans, stars, constellations, and galaxies—she painted Black women as everything. Black women were the universe, Mother Nature. And we had to take care of Mother Nature. It was because of my grandmother that I was extra concerned about the well-being of the Black woman.

DeAndre could just go fuck himself.

I was running around preparing for the dinner rush, doing my best to make the most of my workday, when I looked up and noticed the last person I needed to see standing in front of our hot case.

DeAndre peered up at our menu, but his stance read like more of a model's pose. Nola, my co-worker, instantly stopped telling me some story about her and her boyfriend when she noticed one of Moorehead High's top dogs standing in our grace.

When her jaw metaphorically hit the ground at the sight of DeAndre's handsomeness, I knew she'd be a goner if he laid some charm on her. I hated to admit it, but when those perfect lips of his were forming a smile *or* smirk, he was stunning. Throw in the perfect amount of hair on his chin that balanced his look just right with the ease of whichever words flowed from his mouth, and I could see why so many melted in his presence.

DeAndre tore his gaze from the menu and slid it over to me, tilting his head momentarily as he took me in.

"Chicken?" he said, sounding bored.

I nodded. His question was an odd one; the smell of fried chicken saturated the entire area.

"What deals y'all got?" he asked.

As if coming out of her standing coma, Nola went and stood in front of me. "We got a four piece, eight piece, twelve piece—"

"Eight piece," DeAndre said, still staring at me.

"Jojos? Mashed potatoes? Any sides?"

DeAndre shook his head.

"You paying here or up front?"

He shrugged. "It's whatever." He moved over to where he could see me better. "'Sup, Cree?"

"Hey."

"I bet the chicken is good if you made it."

"Why do you say that?"

"I get the feeling all things have to be up to your standards if you make them."

Was it a jab? I wasn't sure. Something I'd noticed about DeAndre was that he wasn't entirely boneheaded. He had a rather smart way of insulting people.

"Well, I did make it. I hope you like it."

"I'm sure I will."

"Good."

"Great."

We stood there, him just staring at me, and me trying to figure out his angle.

"Anything else, DeAndre?" I prompted.

"I bet you and your boyfriend have the most intellectually stimulating conversations."

Now I could see what he was doing. He was making fun of me.

I crossed my arms. "I'm not stuck up, and I don't intend to turn every conversation into a debate."

"Word?" He still looked and sounded bored, annoying me to the core.

I gritted my teeth. "Yes."

He dug in his pocket and gathered his phone, returning a text, it seemed. "I've got a party I'm throwin' Friday night. If you down to have a good time, come through."

If I said no, then I would still look salty, but if I said yes, I would have to ingratiate myself and actually go to one of *his* parties.

It was a challenge a large part of me didn't care for.

Nola handed DeAndre his chicken and he briefly examined the box before thanking her and turning back to me.

"See you around, Cree." There was something wrong with the smile on his face and the way he spoke.

My phone vibrated in my pocket, pulling me away from watching DeAndre's exit.

I looked over at Nola, finding her staring after DeAndre as if in a trance. To think she had a boyfriend waiting at home.

"Nola, I'm going to take my break, okay?" I said.

She nodded and went back to work.

I headed into the backroom after clocking out for break and found a missed call from Troiann.

She had perfect timing. I needed her to talk me out of going to DeAndre's party. Even though I only had fifteen minutes, I called her back.

"Cree?" Troiann asked as she answered her phone.

"Guess who just showed up here?" I cut to the chase.

"Who?"

"DeAndre."

"Did he apologize?"

"Not in so many words, but he invited me to some party at his house this weekend. Not happening, like *ever*."

"Why not? I hear the Ballers throw the best parties."

Was she serious? "Troy! This is the same guy who tried to embarrass me in fifth period, remember?"

"So go to his house, enjoy the free stuff, and leave," Troiann reasoned. "It'll only get worse if you avoid him."

She wasn't making any sense. We hated the Ballers Club, why would we go out of our way to go to their events? Beyond that, I didn't negotiate with terrorists.

"Not happening."

Troiann sighed. "I don't think that's a good idea, but anyway, I was calling to see if you wanted to go to After Hours tonight."

It was Tuesday. A *school* night, and I got off at nine. I would smell like chicken, garbage, and a little bit of chlorine, plus I wanted to head over to the studio to put in a half hour of dancing before going home for homework and bed.

"It's a school night, Troy."

"So, come on, you need to go out and relax. Please." I could just picture her doing her famous baby-like pout, the one that always got her in my good graces and had me saying yes to whatever she asked.

"I won't even have time to pick out something to wear," I said.

"I'm at The Closet right now. I'll find you something."

I scowled. "You can't shop for me. I don't browse the juniors' section."

Troiann clicked her tongue. "I know your size, CJ, whatever.

I'ma find you something cute, you're going to go home and shower, and I'll come over around ten, got it?"

There was just no getting out of this.

"Fine," I huffed. "I gotta go, 'bye."

Troiann had been my best friend since the sixth grade, and I knew she had my best interest at heart. It was the only reason I was letting her drag me out to a nightclub on a school night.

—

The beat to some catchy rap song turned up to the max had the club jumping and my heart pounding hard against my chest.

Troiann's cousin had supplied the fake IDs, and the girls were definitely using them to the fullest. I sat at the bar, putting on a casual grown-up and sexy act as I prepared to order a drink from the bartender, who kept giving me the eye. Part of me wondered if he was onto me, but I only wanted another Sprite, so it wasn't like he would catch me slipping.

Troiann and her cousin, Minh, were drinking some fruity drinks while they sat on either side of me. Even with the loud, lively atmosphere of After Hours and my best friend beside me, I just wasn't feeling the club.

Troiann nudged me with her bony elbow. "Come on, Cree, lighten up, we in here."

I forced a lopsided smile on my face. "I'm just not feeling this."

Minh's eyebrows pushed together. "What's wrong with you?"

Troiann faced her cousin. "This boy sorta got on her nerves."

"So?" Minh asked.

Troiann took a sip of her drink and went on to explain the situation further. "At our school, there's this group of boys called the Ballers Club. They're four fine brothas—"

"Chris is *not* a brother," I corrected, noting that Chris was the only White one of the bunch.

Troiann rolled her eyes. "Tell him that. Anyway, two of them play basketball and the other two play football. They're hot, they got money, and they get girls."

"Whoa," Minh said, taking a quick sip of her drink.

"Right." Troiann agreed. "Now, today in class DeAndre and Cree got into a little disagreement and he tried to clown her."

Minh patted my arm. "Sorry, C."

"He wasn't that bad," Troiann said. "Out of all the boys, he's one of the ones who isn't so terrible."

Isn't so terrible? She had to be kidding.

"Troy, he's one of them, of course he's terrible," I said.

Troiann faced me, appearing skeptical. "Of course because he's a Baller I'd avoid him like the plague, but when it comes to DeAndre, excluding today, I don't think he's as bad as the others. He's sort of . . . *mysterious.*"

DeAndre Parker, mysterious? "Guys like DeAndre are easy to figure out. They think because they listen to The Weeknd and Drake and post pictures with text on them on Instagram they're deep, when in reality they just like overrated music and clichéd bullshit. Come on, Troy, don't give in to the hype."

"True." Troiann agreed. "But we haven't really spoken to DeAndre besides today. We don't really know him, which is a good reason to head to his party."

"I know their type. If you're not smoking weed, getting drunk, partying, or having sex, you're lame to them. I don't need that kind of pressure around me, Troy, no."

Troiann shook her head. "You know *of* them, you don't even really *know* them, CJ. I don't condone what I see, but I won't place a label on the entire product without getting to know it."

It seemed like my best friend was almost defending DeAndre, which made no sense.

"Wait." Minh held up a hand, leaning close. "Are you talking about DeAndre Parker? As in, one of Darrel Parker's fine-ass sons?"

Troiann wagged her finger, fighting a smile. "That'd be the one."

I groaned. "Whatever, let's just drop it, okay? Aren't you here to ogle boys or something?"

A blush spread across Troiann's face. "Why?"

"Because the last time I checked, my best friend was all about boys."

Troiann swiveled around on her stool and faced the near-packed dance floor. "Yeah, boys, right. Looks like there are a lot of options to choose from tonight."

Minh turned as well, her mouth quickly falling open in an *O* shape. "Shit, do you see that dude in the burgundy sweatshirt?"

Soon, the two of them linked arms and headed to the dance floor to flirt.

I wasn't in the mood to dance in such a packed space, and I wasn't in the mood to drink alcohol either.

The bartender caught my eye once more. He was handsome, young, but not anything I was interested in.

I had to thank Troiann for supplying such an attention-worthy dress for me to wear for the evening. It was black, it was short, and it clung to my figure. When it came to my body, I had just enough in the front and just enough in the back—too much to really be a dancer by some standards. That was another reason my father didn't want me taking dance seriously; he saw what it did to some girls, saw the eating disorders, saw the thin frames. He said he was raising a healthy young woman and didn't want me subjected to the harsh pressures that came with that profession. So, for me, dance was just a hobby instead of a potential career.

As the bartender continued to sneak glances at me, I knew it had everything to do with the dress and nothing to do with my age.

"What can I get for you?" he asked as he finally came over.

Oh, hell, if you can't beat 'em, join 'em, right? "A Panty Wetter," I said, taking a chance and making up a drink that sounded like something you'd get from a bar.

"Coming right up." He nodded and headed over to his supply of alcohol.

Shit, they were real?

A chill ran down my spine, as I sensed someone was behind me, too close.

"Rookie," DeAndre whispered in my ear as he came around and sat beside me, smirking at my nerves.

He sat wearing a simple black T-shirt with black jeans. A gold chain hung around his neck, a gold watch was on his wrist, and there was even gold in his black Parkers. I had to admit, the Ballers knew how to present themselves.

Still, I moved farther away from him. "Am not." *Are to.*

My action made DeAndre chuckle. "Damn, Cree, so every time we run into each other it's gotta be World War III?"

"You tell me, DeAndre."

"Class was class, aren't we both over that?"

If he was willing to put it behind us and let things return to the status quo, that was fine by me. "In *my* defense, I had just watched one of Tremaine's girls crying about him in the restroom."

"In my defense…" DeAndre gestured to himself. "…I'm not Tremaine."

I hated to admit it, but DeAndre had a point. He didn't seem as harsh and careless as Tremaine was.

Troiann also had a point the more I thought about it. I couldn't think about what DeAndre's niche was. He played basketball like Chris, had a few tattoos like the others, and his father had played in the NBA. But when it really came down to DeAndre Parker, I wasn't sure *who* he was.

A smile hung in the corner of his mouth. "What? Why you starin' so hard?"

Busted. "I'm not."

The bartender handed me my drink and I slid him a few bills, thanking him.

The drink tasted sour, fruity, and strong. There was no missing the alcohol.

Doing my best to keep my face straight, I swallowed it and went back to my Sprite.

I could feel DeAndre watching me, forcing me to look from my Sprite to his eyes. "I'm a nice person, Cree. I look out for people I admire. Take right now for example—I know something your eyes aren't ready to see just yet."

Him and his riddles. "Not interested," I told him, even though I kinda *was* curious.

DeAndre smiled and pivoted the conversation. "So you wanna dance or what?" he asked, gesturing to the dance floor where—ironically enough—the newest Drake song was playing.

He was not Patrick Swayze and I was not Jennifer Grey, and we were not about to dirty dance on the dance floor.

Calmly, I shook my head. "No."

"There are a lot of girls in here, and I'm only gonna ask you one more time before I take advantage of it."

"So?"

"Cree, I don't want you."

"Okay."

"I just want a simple dance, that's all. No strings attached."

I wasn't entirely sure about his approach. "It's too hot in here and I already feel sweaty as it is. I—"

"I can tell."

"Screw you, DeAndre."

"We could do that, but according to you, I'm dirty, and I wouldn't wanna taint your purity."

So what, I was a virgin. Even Troiann had lost her virginity before me. It wasn't like being a virgin was something to be ashamed of, though. "Cool."

DeAndre seemed to be suppressing a smile. "You amuse me, Cree."

What was that even supposed to mean?

I wanted to cross my arms but that would've only brought attention to my cleavage.

"Am I really not supposed to be *offended*?" I asked.

DeAndre shook his head. "Nah, I'm just sayin', I could be good to you in a fun way, but bad where it counts. Good girls like you, you deserve the best. I like to run solo for a reason."

He was saying all the right words, but I still didn't trust him. "Then why are you still running game?"

DeAndre grinned, standing from his stool. "Why do you assume you're worthy of my game?"

He didn't even let me reply as he walked away, disappearing into the mass of bodies filling After Hours. Goose bumps prickled all over my skin, an aftereffect of the conversation I'd had with DeAndre, where once more he left me feeling befuddled.

4

DEANDRE

We should've gone to Inferno. After Hours was a dud, and I wasn't in the mood anymore after talking to Cree.

I headed home to call it a night after an hour of putting up with the heat wave and the perfumed scent of sweat and body spray that was the club. The boys and I parted ways and I drove off on my own. I wasn't even in the kitchen door before my cell rang.

Troiann's name and number flashed across the screen, and I could already tell what she wanted.

"Yeah?" I answered as I shut the door behind me.

"You made your point, now leave me and Cree the hell alone!" The call ended before I could even reply.

I shook my head. Hadn't she learned by now that I didn't take disrespect too kindly?

My phone rang again, and this time it was Marcus.

I let out a chuckle. Yes, he was whipped.

"Yeah?" I leaned against the counter, bracing myself for his version of telling me to leave Cree alone.

"Man, are you happy now?" he asked.

"Why wouldn't I be happy, Marc?"

"With Cree Jacobs, Dre."

My point hadn't quite been made just yet. "Can't say that I am."

Marcus sighed. "Troy was just stickin' up for her friend, I mean, you and Trey *were* cornerin' them."

Was he seriously defending some girl over me?

I had to admit, it was cute of Troiann to think that talking to Marcus would get me to leave Cree alone, as if I answered to him. Until Marcus manned up and claimed Troiann, none of what he was saying would stick. But I had to hand it to Troiann; at least she wasn't fucking with Marc for free.

"Doesn't matter, I'm enjoying this, immensely." It had been fun watching Cree squirm earlier at the club. Troiann had done well in talking her into coming out for the evening.

"Why? You're not going to get anything out of it. Cree would never give you the time of day."

I looked at my phone, making sure it was on and I'd heard right. Cree was friends with a girl who wouldn't give guys like us "the time of day." Troiann was acting all stuck up as well, but she was smashing Marcus. The same Marcus who'd hooked up with two sisters just because he could; the same Marcus who'd once had a pregnancy scare with a girl and still went about his regular routine without a care; the same Marcus who was just about money over girls like the rest of us. I was the dog yet Marcus got a pass? Bull-fucking-shit.

I got it, girls like Cree and Troiann weren't our biggest fans. But to act as though they were above us? That was straight trash. Troiann was sleeping with Marcus—whether she was a groupie or not, she had gotten down with the Club in the end.

Cree would be no different. If I was interested in "running game" on her, she wouldn't know which way was up or down after I was through with her.

"Never say never, Marcus."

"Cree would *never* give you any, so you might as well hang it up."

Closing my eyes, I shook my head. This was coming from my best friend. He knew me. How could he doubt me? "Wanna bet?"

Marcus chuckled. "Shit, bro, if it wasn't for Troiann, I'd take you up on that."

The taming of the shrew. I humored myself.

In the end, it wasn't about trying to hook up with Cree—it wasn't even like that. I just wanted to open her eyes a little. We weren't all that bad.

"Troy—"

"Is not my problem or concern," I replied. "Since when are you two official?"

"We ain't official."

Cap'n Crunch. Why else would he be considering her feelings? "So why are you hung up on her?"

"I'm just . . . having fun, Dre. Chill."

He just couldn't say he liked her.

I loosened up. Troiann was Marcus's problem, and when it came to Cree, that was my own personal business. "By the time this is all said and done, Cree's gonna be the one apologizin' to me."

"Remind me never to piss you off," Marcus mumbled with a sigh. "See you tomorrow, Dre. No more messin' with Troy, got it?"

Swallowing down the first sarcastic remark that came to mind, I instead said, "Sure thing, Marc, we'll stay out of each other's way."

I hit End and headed to the rec room, where I heard the TV on. More than likely it was my brother Devonte since my other brother Darnel was away at college. Devonte was a senior, and in the fall he'd be joining Darnel at Ohio State, making waves on their basketball team as well.

One could say basketball just ran in the family. With our dad being a retired player, it was a no-brainer what sport we'd all picked up by the time we were able to walk. Our mother wasn't in the picture, and she hadn't been since I was three, so there was no arguing when it came to our father's demands for us to push basketball before everything else.

Devonte was on the phone, sweet talking some girl as he lay back on the sofa flipping through the channels. He was saying all the right things, but his face showed he couldn't give a shit if he tried. Half a minute later he ended the call and dialed another number and started talking to another girl, saying different yet sweet things as well.

Shaking my head, I took a seat in the chair in the corner, tossing a pillow at him to signal for him to leave the TV on BET.

Devonte clicked his tongue and sighed. "Babe, ain't no other girl for me right now. It's just you, so why you mad? What, you don't trust me or something? That's foul . . ." The rest of the conversation went on with him putting himself down and playing into the role of being insecure before turning it around and telling whoever the hell he was talking to that they weren't putting enough faith in their relationship.

That was one thing I didn't do, fill girls up with lies. Honestly, the whole lying, cheating, and games bullshit felt like a waste of time. I didn't do relationships. It was in and out for me, and if a girl wasn't down for that, then I bounced—there was no time for drama.

Tremaine and the other guys didn't exactly follow in my footsteps, hence why they were the ones with the most shit flying their way. Loudmouthed girls waving their manicured nails in their faces, cocking their heads from side to side as they talked slick. That was not my style, and something I didn't want to be subjected to. It was just easier and more respectful to be blunt about it.

Devonte ended his second call and tossed his phone aside, looking over and smiling at me. "I'm too good."

More like too messy. If he was really good, he'd talk both girls into a throuple and kill the bullshit.

"Sure," I replied.

Devonte smirked, rather proud of himself. "Gotta keep it clean, Dre. Never let 'em catch you slippin.'"

I shook my head in disgust. Lying was foul and unnecessary. "I can't take you seriously when you talk this way. Do better."

Devonte flipped me the bird. "What's up with you, see anything interesting at the club?"

I thought about the girl I'd met at After Hours, the girl whose number was in my cell. As fine as she was, I probably wouldn't call.

"No," I said. "It was empty tonight."

Devonte nodded. "Yeah, that's why I stayed in. It's Tuesday, wasn't going to see much no way."

Footsteps sounded in the hall and soon we were graced with our father's presence. He was carrying a cold bottle of water from the fridge as he peeked his head in the room.

Devonte nodded toward him before standing and retreating up to his room.

My father patted his shoulder as he passed before coming and standing in the doorway, eyes on me.

"What's up?" he asked, taking a glance at the TV.

Most parents would freak out if their kid came in at midnight on a school night, but not our dad.

I shook my head. "Nothing, just getting in."

"Have a good time?"

"Not really, we should've gone to Inferno."

My father chuckled. "*Inferno?* Who lets you boys in there?"

He wasn't naïve or out of the loop. He knew about the shit we got into, but as long as my grades were up and I didn't lose on the court, he was okay with it.

"Chris has connects," I said.

"I bet that boy does. Anyway, I was on some business calls earlier, and we're gearing up for the design for the Parker 8s. I want your take on the colorways," my father said, referring to his popular eponymously named sneaker line.

I sat up, staring him square in the eye. "Are you gonna take my advice, or just go with your first instinct as always?"

My father leaned against the wall. "Okay, let's hear it."

"Baby blue and coral, orange and coral, light green and coral, purple and coral, black and coral, white and coral, no matter the leading color, coral is the undertone," I said.

My father's brows furrowed in confusion. "What's with that?"

I tapped my temple. "Gender neutral color. Girls love sneakers as much as we do, girls love ball as much as we do. Make an exclusive line of matching men's and women's shoes for the Parker 8s to match that colorway and you'll double your profits. The 'relationship goals' crowd would eat up matching sneakers."

My father stood back, ruminating on my idea. In another moment, he furnished a smile as he wagged his finger at me. "I'll see what we can do. Maybe, if this goes well, for the Parker 9s, we'll broaden the scheme and do a greenish color." He gave me a warm look, impressed with my overall idea. "Someday, Dre, after you've been in the league for a while, you'll be talkin' to your boy about how to design your latest sneakers."

Making it pro wasn't a *what-if* but a when. I was a Parker. I was born to play ball. My father was a champion. A warrior. An icon. He'd played his whole twenty-year career for the Cincinnati Chargers, number 4, acquiring five championship rings to boast about before retiring five years ago at the age of thirty-eight. After LeBron, Ohio had Darrel Parker. A fifteen-time NBA All-Star who had happily settled down in his home city of Akron.

There's nowhere else I'd rather be he'd been quoted when journalists asked him why he didn't go west or south upon retiring.

Ohio was home, especially Akron.

My father covered his mouth as he yawned. "Better get to bed, Dre, you know you gotta be up at five."

My father had his rules for us. We had to be up at five every day to run around our neighborhood. It was training. We had to be in great shape if we were going to make it to the NBA like he had.

My father ran a tight ship raising all of us on his own. We didn't whine, we didn't get emotional, and we didn't lose. We just did our best to do better. Without our mother we were three variations of our father, taking nothing from the mother who wasn't there.

People liked to think that we had it easy; that we were spoiled, rich kids. My father was rich. Not me. He gave us an allowance but it wasn't something we just got, we had to earn it. I worked my ass off on and off the court to impress him and to earn my cut of allowance. I played hard, but I worked harder.

And when it came to Cree Jacobs, I wouldn't stop until I got the big score. She thought she knew everything about me, and I couldn't wait to show her that she didn't.

5

CREE

Avoiding DeAndre after Tuesday's disagreement in class and encounter at After Hours had been easy. We kept out of each other's way all week in English and he didn't show up at Henry's. By the time Friday rolled around I was convinced I could avoid his party as well.

With one period left in the school day and the night off from work, I was up for anything. Before I could ask Troiann what she wanted to do for the night, the PA buzzed and the assistant principal came on to remind us about the upcoming talent show in a month.

"Ain't nobody trying to be in no talent show," Troiann said, waving off the announcement. "Not like anyone's got talent that doesn't involve a ball."

"Some of these people would pay to see one of the Ballers throw or bounce a ball," I joked.

Troiann chuckled. "Hell, yeah. I actually wouldn't mind seeing Marcus throw one."

I waited for the punchline but it never came. "Eww, Troy, no."

Troiann shrugged. "Marcus is cute, Cree."

Across the room Marcus sat with the rest of the Ballers Club.

All were J'd up, wearing clothes that accentuated their unique styles. Marcus was leaning back with one of his arms propped up so he could rest his head on his fist. His bulging muscles showed under his tattooed bicep.

"Get real, Troy, besides, he's facial hairfishing. We've seen the baby face beneath those whiskers." I pretended to wrinkle my nose at the thought, even though Marcus was still cute. The added moustache and hair on his chin were a nice touch, though.

Troiann cackled loudly. "Girl, stop hatin'. Dang."

Mr. Donatelli called the class to order, wanting to get back to his lesson. "Let's talk about cultural geography," he said.

There were only ten minutes left of class and he wanted to bring this up now?

I snuck a frown at Troiann, and she did her best not to laugh.

"Whether your culture's American, or not," Mr. Donatelli went on, "sometimes culture goes along with ethnic background, would you agree?"

A few of us murmured in agreement to speed things along.

Mr. Donatelli hummed, stroking his chin. "Interesting. Fashion, film, music, and language go along with culture, don't they?"

Again, we agreed.

Mr. Donatelli looked at all of us, studying each row of desks. "Let's examine African American culture."

Here we go. Despite the fact that I hated the term *African American*—I preferred *Black American*—the last thing I wanted to do was discuss the culture I was a part of. If there was one thing I knew in my short seventeen years on the planet, it was that while Black culture was popular, Black people weren't. When it came to fashion, language, and every aspect of our culture, other people had no problem copying us and going along, but when it came to us as a people, *we* weren't good enough, it seemed.

Did I want to discuss the continuous plight of my people? No.

"Let's face it, this school is predominantly African American, I would say that is the most influential culture Moorehead has."

Looking around the room filled with various shades of brown skin, there was no denying the fact.

"I see what you guys wear, hear what you listen to, how you talk—actually, that brings me to a good topic," said Mr. Donatelli. "Now the *N*-word—"

The class was in an uproar before he could get the rest of his thoughts out.

Mr. Donatelli sat back and crossed his arms. "Perhaps some of you would like to speak on it?"

All at once people started speaking, some daring Mr. Donatelli to say it, others watching with guarded eyes to see if he'd utter such an offense, and some speaking against or for it.

DeAndre raised his hand, properly gaining permission to speak. "I personally don't believe you can reclaim a slur, especially when an outsider using it can bring you down. The origin of that word will always be there, you can't paint over it. When I was a kid, I said it once and my grandmomma sat me down and told me never to say it again. She told me that people died hearing those words, people *lived* being treated like those words, and for that I just don't say it. It's about respect for the past and perseverance for the future for me."

It was times like this when he spoke so eloquently that I felt like I didn't really know who DeAndre was. Arrogant Baller or not, I agreed with everything he said.

Mr. Donatelli commended DeAndre as the bell rang. "I like that. I wanna study this more. I was going to assign a paper on a random country's culture, but given the social climate over the last few years, I have a better idea. I'm assigning a paper in pairs to discuss culture and what it means to you; what are you proud of, what are you ashamed of, where do you see yourselves going forward? Ten pages, due at the end of the grading period. It's either that or a final exam, up to you. See you Monday, class dismissed."

He was basically giving us an optional way out of studying for exams, though I was sure the paper wouldn't be that easy if he expected us to type out ten pages. *Thank god for double spacing.*

Troiann and I exited the classroom and as I was musing over the idea of a paper or an exam as we meandered down the hall, something to my left caught my eye.

On the wall hung a poster of a girl crying and holding a pregnancy test. The caption THEY TOLD ME YOU COULDN'T GET PREGNANT YOUR FIRST TIME . . . THEY WERE WRONG was at the bottom of it, along with basic facts about abstinence and safe sex.

Troiann shook her head. "Oh god, that should be every girl's fear, getting pregnant through some really bad sex."

I cringed. "What?"

Troiann looked at me. "The first time does not feel good, it ain't all sunshine and roses—at least it wasn't for me. I'm just saying it would suck to get pregnant after *that*. At least get knocked up while you're getting it good, you know?"

Getting it good? It was so easy for Troy to talk that way. Me, I hadn't gotten *it* at all. If my first time was going to suck, I definitely wasn't looking forward to it.

"It's only bad because he's too big at first, right?" I asked.

Troiann chuckled. "If you're lucky he's packing."

I cringed even more. I was going to die a virgin.

Troiann nudged me. "Hey, it isn't that bad. Look at it this way, if a woman can give birth to a seventeen-inch baby, she can take a—"

"Troy!" I thought to cover my ears. I couldn't hear any more.

"Now there's something we can agree on." DeAndre was

standing behind us, causing me to jump nervously. He had heard us?

Troiann scowled. "Eavesdropping much?"

DeAndre came between us and draped his arms across our shoulders. "I can see why any guy could want you," he said to Troiann before turning to me and flashing a smile that made me feel uneasy. "It's Friday."

Oh no.

I moved out from under his arm. "Yes, the day before Saturday."

"And the day after Thursday," Troiann replied, mirroring my motion.

"And the day of my party, you coming through, Cree?" DeAndre asked.

"Probably not, I think there's a *Love & Hip-Hop* marathon on tonight."

DeAndre's grin did not falter. He wasn't giving up just yet. "Record it, I want you to come and have a good time tonight."

"I'm sure I'd have just as good of a time fussing over the TV."

DeAndre shook his head. "You shouldn't watch shows that aren't good for you."

"How do *you* know what's good for her?" Troiann interrupted.

DeAndre slowly shifted his attention to Troy. "Why do I have a feeling there's some place you gotta be?"

They stood there, staring at each other for a minute or two, before Troiann oddly gave in.

She turned to me. "I'll call you later, 'bye."

I tried to let Troiann's departure distract DeAndre as I made a beeline for my locker, but as soon as I got to the door I found that he was right behind me.

Damn it.

Ignoring his presence as best as I could, I opened my locker, shelved my books, and grabbed my duffel bag. I had time to head to the dance studio after school and I wasn't going to miss it.

DeAndre crossed his arms and leaned against the locker next to mine. "What's in the bag, Cree?"

"Drugs," I said flatly, deciding to ignore all homework until Monday morning.

DeAndre chuckled. "And I thought we were startin' off clean."

I sighed. "It's just my dance outfit."

One of DeAndre's brows perked up. "Oh, you dance. Like ballet and shit?"

I rolled my eyes. "Contemporary dancing, mostly to R & B and hip-hop."

"Word? Let me see you dance one day."

Even if he wasn't serious, I said, "Sure."

My answer took DeAndre by surprise. "Not even nervous?"

I loved feeling people watching me move and become one with the rhythm. I loved the spotlight and the crowd's gasps and audible praise. I had done a few shows when I was younger, and *shy* wasn't in my vocabulary. "Not even a little."

"You must be good."

I shrugged and closed my locker. "I'm okay."

DeAndre rolled his eyes. "'Okay'?"

"Modesty never hurt anyone, you know. What would you say about you and basketball?"

DeAndre stood from the locker, looking past me and eyeing Armani Young as she was heading down the hall. Armani was one of the popular pretty girls all the boys in our junior class gawked at; seniors too. She was kinda mean. She was only nice to a select few, and those who did get along with her called her Ari.

DeAndre returned to me. "I'm the shit at basketball."

He *was* according to everyone at Moorehead High and the

city; him and his brothers. It was because of their father and their own skills that they held verified accounts on all social media and were rumored to have the chance to make history by being the first overall draft picks consecutively when they declared for the NBA.

"Great." I walked past him, making my way down to the first floor to go out to the bus, and of course DeAndre was right behind me.

"So, you comin' or what?" DeAndre asked. "I'm just trying to make up for class."

"I'll think about it." Without another word I crossed the student parking lot to the waiting bus without looking back.

~

I was sweaty and all I wanted to do was head upstairs to shower as soon as I entered my house. Instead, I was greeted by Loraine in the foyer and the reality that my father wasn't home.

Gritting my teeth, I went to step past her up the staircase, but Loraine surprised me by blocking my route. Locks of her long, dark hair flowed with her movement.

"Cree, what's up?" She smiled as she reached out and caressed my shoulder. I hated that after two years she was still trying to win me over. It was not going to happen. It wasn't entirely her. She was only thirty-one, young, likable, but still, everything about how things now were left me uneasy.

I shook my head. "Nothing, just going to shower."

"I hear the school's throwing a talent show."

I tugged on my duffel's strap. "Yeah, they keep trying to promote it, but I don't see it happening. No one's interested."

Loraine frowned. "Why not you? You've got plenty of talent, obviously." She stood back and gestured at my sweaty state.

"Dance is just recreation for me, nothing too serious, besides, Dad would flip."

I went to move past her but again she stepped in my way. "Your father wants you happy, Cree, and I'm sure if you wanted to pursue dance he would be more than happy as long as you are."

I could've laughed, but I did her a favor and just kept it simple with a smirk. "Trust me, Loraine, we've had this discussion. It isn't happening."

Loraine pursed her lips. "Fine, what are you up to tonight? I was thinking maybe we could . . ."

Oh no. Anything but that. Thinking on my toes, I brought up the only way out of the situation. "There's this party I was invited to. Troy wanted to go, and you know how that goes."

Loraine lit up with curiosity and excitement. "Oh really? Who invited you?"

"DeAndre Parker, it's his party."

Her threaded eyebrows shot toward the ceiling. "*Darrel Parker's* son? Ooh, you go, girl."

"Trust me, DeAndre does not see me like that. I'm—" *A good girl.* His words. Not mine. "—not 'it' for him."

Loraine waved me off. "Cree, you're way more put together than I was at your age. Now I was a late bloomer, you, you got it goin' on."

That was what relatives were supposed to say. But it meant a lot that she was trying, and boosting my esteem. "Thanks, Loraine."

"Okay." Loraine clapped her hands. "Go on and shower, and let's get you ready."

Lifting a brow, I asked, "'Ready'?"

She snuck me a clever look. "You got a party to get to, and you need to look even more gorgeous than you already are."

Of course she wanted to turn my impromptu decision to go to DeAndre's party into a bonding experience.

I was going to say no, but looking at Loraine, Ms. Makeup Guru Extraordinaire, I knew she had a point. Whether she was rocking her natural hair, braids, or a lace front, Loraine kept her hair done and laid and her makeup neat. She also had a great fashion sense and she could do no wrong with what she picked out. Honestly, I could've had it a lot worse in the help department. Loraine *was* gorgeous.

"Fine, but don't make me look too eager."

~

"Come on, Cree, get out of the car." Troiann tried to coax me as we sat in her mom's car down the street from DeAndre's packed mansion. Music could be heard thumping from where we sat arguing about my postponing the inevitable.

"How do I look?" I wanted to know. Why I was nervous, I wasn't sure. Loraine had put together a cute 'fit for DeAndre's party. A long-sleeved half tee, black ripped canopy jeans, and supercute booties.

Troiann clicked her tongue, making a stank face. "Some of us don't have a nice ass, you do, and if I have to drag you out of this car so you can show it off, I will."

Feeling slightly better and encouraged, I opened the passenger door and got out of the car. The feeling of being weightless lasted all the way up to DeAndre's front door, where I fought the urge to renege on the whole ordeal.

Troiann's familiar hand found mine as she opened the front door and walked me inside where a loud R & B song by H.E.R. blasted throughout the house. Unlike those teen drama clichés, no one noticed me as I stepped inside and was face-first in DeAndre Parker's private world.

Troiann looked around at our surrounding peers and possibly DeAndre's neighbors, and shrugged. "Eh, it's okay."

I loved my best friend. "Yeah, it's all right."

We were both lying. There was no denying the beauty of DeAndre's large house with all its high ceilings and large rooms filled with expensive things I would have to work my life away to afford. It was immaculate, and I was almost positive our entire school could fit inside, population-wise at least.

The perks of being an NBA player's kid, no doubt.

"I always wondered why Mr. Parker made the boys go to public school instead of private," Troiann said as she admired their home.

It was thought provoking.

I could still remember seeing one of the people I followed on Instagram reposting one of Devonte's stories when they won the state championship this past March.

Devonte had had his arm slung around DeAndre's neck in the video. "*Talk to me nice. Talk to me nice. How you feelin', twin?*"

DeAndre tossed the camera a humble yet tired smile. "*Victorious. You?*"

Devonte had turned the camera on himself and held up DeAndre's wrist, flashing the shiny, expensive watch on it. "*Piguets or nothing else!*"

DeAndre leaned into the camera, puffing his chest up. "*Unless it's a Richard Mille, feel me?*"

The brothers laughed and I couldn't help but smile at the memory.

"Probably to keep them humble," I said, as I came back to Troy.

Troiann scrunched up her face. "Humble? Riiight. You seen that ride DeAndre pulls up in at school. My mom's car isn't even *this* decade."

Together, Troiann and I advanced to the large kitchen to find something to drink. The place was abuzz with conversations trying to be heard over the music and people serving and mixing drinks at the island. The patio doors were open, showing a glimpse into the large backyard where a fire pit was set up. Peering closer, I found that the Ballers were outside. The boys all stood around the fire, having a private toast and looking like four kings, laughing about things we couldn't hear.

Looking on, I studied DeAndre and his nonchalant stance. Cool, calm, and collected.

A little research had me seeing the much bigger picture that was DeAndre Parker. Ten million Instagram followers, half a million on X, and we couldn't forget TikTok had him coasting at a cool six million and he hadn't even posted anything there. DeAndre was only good to post about his 'fits, shoes, and of course, basketball. Still, there was no denying how he was a god to our peers and our city. He hadn't even touched an official NBA court and yet everyone was looking on as if he was one of one. A phenom in the making.

I turned away, only to find Troiann gone, leaving me by myself.

While I walked around DeAndre's place, admiring the décor and the upkeep, I had to admit I felt the feeling of something missing. I wasn't able to pinpoint what until I was standing in the hall where there were a few photos hung up on the wall. There were shots of each of the Parker boys and their father. There were group photos, photos from outings, and even a photo of DeAndre's eldest brother at his high-school graduation, standing next to their father. There was no sign of Mrs. Parker anywhere; the whole house seemed more like a bachelor's pad the more I stood and thought about it.

Through the glass windows on the sliding doors that led to the living room, I found DeAndre standing with Tremaine having some conversation. The longer I stared, the more it dawned on me; he was just like me. We *both* didn't have mothers.

Before I could stare any longer, I felt myself nearly lose my balance as someone bumped into me. Turning, I saw that it was Armani and a pack of her friends, all equally as pretty and as stuck up.

"Watch it," Armani snapped.

"Excuse me, *you* bumped into *me*," I told her.

Armani lifted a brow, questioning my audacity to talk back. It was three against one, making me a little upset Troiann was nowhere to be seen. "Say what?"

Alone or not, I wasn't backing down. "You heard me. You should watch where *you're* going."

One of Armani's friends whispered something in her ear and she flat out laughed, at my expense, no less. Together they all carried on, leaving me standing by myself as they went into the kitchen.

I turned around and froze as I found DeAndre watching me. I made a gesture, as if to say *I'm here.*

DeAndre responded with a bob of his head.

Cool, we were even.

I stepped back, accidentally bumping into the shelf behind me, sending something to the floor and breaking.

Universe, just swallow me whole now.

It was a trophy, a golden basketball on the ground and the diamond-encrusted silver basketball net it had once sat on was lying next to it.

"Oh shit." I sighed as I bent over to pick it up.

Two hands beat me to it and together they gathered the trophy and stood before I could. Naturally, it was DeAndre.

He stood examining the two separated pieces.

"I'm so sorry. I wasn't watching where I was going and—"

DeAndre shrugged. "It's okay."

He was kidding, right? "No, it's not. I'll get it fixed. I'll pay you. I'll do anything I can—"

"Cree, it—anything?" DeAndre asked, a brow perked up.

"Well, not *any*thing, but—"

DeAndre laughed. "Nah, we good. It was already broken to begin with."

My eyes fell to the trophy. "It was?"

He nodded. "Devonte's dumb ass broke it when we were kids. He superglued it together and it's been cool ever since, well, until now. Let's just go into my dad's office and see if we can fix it again, okay?"

I didn't argue as I followed him through his house and into the back office.

DeAndre entered the room and flipped a switch before going in search of some superglue.

He found some in his father's desk, and he then had me hold the trophy's base while he restored the ball on top of the net with the glue.

I took the opportunity to look around.

God. There was no missing the gigantic portrait of Darrel Parker sitting in a leather chair in an expensive-looking suit and staring straight into the camera while twisting his pinkie ring—emphasizing his *fifth* NBA title, as all of his fingers held rings.

In the photo he looked mean; intimidating yet still handsome. A trait his youngest definitely possessed.

On another wall hung a large dry-erase board filled with running times. Geez, Mr. Parker had his kids time themselves when they ran?

"How often do you run?" I asked.

"Every morning at five, the goal is two miles, sometimes three or four," DeAndre replied.

I felt bad for him, obviously this wasn't his choice. "It must be a lot of pressure being Darrel Parker's son."

DeAndre squinted, studying me. "That's funny you say that."

"Why?"

"Usually people would say it must be dope being his son."

"I just figured there would be a lot of pressure to be as good as him, or to live up to some standard, that's all." I gestured to his father's portrait. "I mean, talk about intense."

DeAndre was indifferent to it. "Or inspiring."

"Think you'll get that many rings someday?"

He shrugged. "If I'm on the right team with like-minded individuals, it's a possibility."

He sounded so humble. "Would you ever want to play with one of your brothers?"

DeAndre thought over the idea. "I'd rather play with them than against them. To win as a family would be lit." A small smile made his lips curl up. "Besides, Darnel's pretty tough on the court."

Aww.

I looked around more, finding more photos of the boys and none of Mrs. Parker. "Where are the pictures of your mom?"

DeAndre focused on the trophy as he shrugged coolly. "I don't have one. She left when I was three."

A feeling of being able to relate sliced through me. I had been the cause of my mother's leaving, but still, I knew what it was like. "I'm sorry."

DeAndre looked at me as I looked at him. He snorted and rolled his eyes. "Yo, we not about to have some heart-to-heart and cry over bullshit, Cree. It's whatever."

Having your mother walk out on you wasn't "whatever," it was everything. At least it would've been to me.

I let it go. "No stepmom?"

DeAndre shook his head. "My father's got too much money to lose."

"I see." His father didn't trust women with his money and didn't want to risk losing any of it in a divorce. A lot of NBA players ended up losing big-time when divorced. It was partially smart and partially sad that the Parker boys had no mother figure in their lives.

"There," DeAndre said as he set the trophy aside. "I'll let it dry. Come on, let's get back to the party."

He wrapped an arm across my shoulders and led me back out to his party. Soon, we were in the entertainment room where the music blasted the loudest and people migrated to the most.

I went and sat on the couch with crossed arms, taking in the atmosphere and trying my best not to text Troiann and beg her to take me home.

DeAndre came and sat next to me, resting his arms across the back of the couch. "You say you dance, why don't you get up and show me somethin'?"

And have him look even more like a king than he already did? "No, thank you." I scooted away, only to have DeAndre scoot closer.

"Why don't you go and put the moves on some other girl?" I suggested.

"Who says I'm puttin' the moves on you?"

"Why else would you be all up on me and not giving me space?"

DeAndre looked like he wanted to say something, but then he stopped and looked around, mumbling something to himself before turning back to me, scanning me over quickly.

"Let me tell you something, Cree," he said, leaning over to get a good look at me. "My boy is fuckin' ya friend, so I don't know why you act like you're not the only one not down with the Club, 'cause you are."

No. "You're lying."

DeAndre shook his head. "Nah, go and ask her, she and Marcus been getting it in for a minute." He gestured past me. "Matter of fact, take a look and see for yourself."

I followed his gaze and to my epic surprise, across the room stood Troiann . . . with Marcus. He had his hand on her hip and he was making her smile and laugh, and I could just tell by the way she was leaning into him that it wasn't their first interaction.

My best friend was involved with a Baller.

My mouth fell open as denial evaded me.

Shit.

DeAndre was watching and gauging my reaction to the scene before me. "Told you, so stop with the attitude and just chill."

I could've told myself that Troiann was just talking to Marcus, but then it all fell into place. At After Hours DeAndre had warned me, saying he knew something my eyes weren't ready to see, and here it was my best friend had been messing around with a Baller for who knew how long.

I swallowed my pride and put on a brave face. Even if Troiann had fallen into their web, there was no way I was going to follow suit.

I peered at DeAndre. "You're acting like this whole getting me to become a fan of your little club is going to be easy."

The corner of DeAndre's mouth turned up. "Well, it won't be hard."

I eyed the crotch of his pants. "I bet it won't be."

He chuckled. "Still think you're above us?" DeAndre was in my ear, and then he was gone.

Troiann was by herself when I found her standing by the Parkers' extensive movie and video game collection.

I tapped her shoulder. "Troy, can we go?"

Troiann faced me, but not before searching around us. "What's wrong?"

I looked at my supposed best friend, unable to believe she could keep such a secret from me. I didn't want to get into it; I just wanted to go home and fall into bed and work it all off with some dancing in the morning before work.

I put on a mask and pretended, just like how Troiann was pretending to be against the Ballers Club. "Nothing, I've just seen enough. Let's just get out of here."

6

DEANDRE

Drake was in my ear, rapping about no new friends, and, as I looked around, seeing Marcus to my left and Tremaine and Chris to my right, I knew Drake's words to be true. It wasn't usual for them to wake up early just to join me on a run, but as I stepped out of my house at exactly 5:00 a.m. on the dot, I found my three best friends waiting to run with me.

I never had to question their support or loyalty, because time after time they showed me that they were down for whatever. And with friendships as good as ours, what was the point of building new ones?

I lived in one of those nice neighborhoods shown on reality TV shows or in suburban pamphlets; big houses with clean brick driveways, healthy green manicured lawns, and perfectly trimmed hedges.

We were all running side by side down the street. "I can't believe you do this shit every day, Dre," Tremaine was saying as he slowed his pace.

At this point, my mind and my body were used to it. "Gotta keep in shape somehow."

"But still," Tremaine continued.

"That's why Coach is always wildin' on you, you never wanna work," Marcus cut in.

It was a known fact that if Tremaine didn't care, he didn't put in effort. But even when he slacked off, he still dominated on the field. He had an arm crafted by God.

Tremaine smirked. "I put in work last night, though."

That caused all of us to laugh. After failing to bed Ari, he'd moved on to a friend of hers.

I was partially happy Trey hadn't succeeded with Ari. She was one of the finest girls in our junior class. She was bad, tatted, and built to perfection with her pretty face and slim shape. But that was the thing, Ari knew everyone was checking for her, and she made it hard for anyone to succeed. I had yet to try with her, but I knew it wouldn't be too much of a challenge. Word on the street was that she had a crush on a Baller, and I was MVP.

"Looks like Dre ain't get any play from Cree, though," Chris joked. By now we were all walking instead of running.

I shrugged. "It ain't even about that."

I meant it when I said I didn't want Cree. She was the good girl, and I didn't do good. I was down for one thing, and that was something Cree wouldn't give up until "love" or some other shit. Besides, her mouth was just as bad as Troiann's—how Marcus put up with it was beyond me.

"Shit, then let me holla at her," Tremaine replied.

If Cree didn't like me, she sure as hell wasn't about to fall for Tremaine—even if he was a good talker.

"Yeah, right," I said.

Tremaine frowned as he looked my way. "I know you don't think she ugly."

Cree was far from ugly, attitude and all.

Shrugging, I let her and the topic go. "She's okay."

"Man, whatever." Tremaine waved me off. He looked over at Marcus. "When you gon' let me talk to Troiann?" He rubbed his hands together, licking his lips lasciviously.

Marcus glared at Trey. "Never."

Tremaine frowned, taken aback. "*Never*, why not?"

Marcus didn't admit to being whipped, but he said, "No-Fly Zone."

He'd thrown down the flag, then. Our No-Fly Zone list was an exclusive list of girls we'd hooked up with and refused to let any of our friends get with next. None of the girls on the list had been our girlfriends, but we'd liked them to a point where we didn't want to see them hooking up with our boys. I wasn't surprised Marcus was putting Troy on the list, especially if he liked her enough to hassle me about how I was treating her friend.

"Get outta here, you gotta at least let me know if—"

"Yo, Trey, let me talk to Dre alone for a minute," Marcus interrupted.

Both Tremaine and Chris went ahead of us, beginning to run again as we were a few blocks from my house.

I turned to Marcus, wondering what was up. "Yeah?"

"So last night Troy took Cree home," Marcus began, "and then she came back and she was complainin' about Cree being all down." Marcus looked at me, studying me. "Mind filling me in? I saw you talkin' to her."

When it came to my boys, I didn't lie, period. "The truth hurts, I guess."

"*Truth?*" Marcus repeated.

"I told her you were messin' with Troiann."

He sighed, taking in a sharp breath upon doing so. "Why?"

"Have you ever talked to Cree?"

Marcus shook his head. "Not really."

"She got a smart mouth." Things were going fine, even if she had rebroken my father's trophy and had been cornered by Ari and her friends when I laid eyes on her. But then she took my kindness for me trying to get with her and again she insulted me and my dick—what was up with her obsession with it? "I was proving a point, and you made it even better by standing close with Troy."

Marcus scowled. "Man."

"Did you still hook up last night?" It couldn't have been that bad if Troiann hadn't brought up Cree saying something about our conversation. Maybe she was in denial.

"Yeah," Marcus said. "But still."

I threw Marcus a bone, because in the end, I didn't even feel right about what happened. "Look, I'm sorry. It's done with Cree. You just focus on your ball and chain."

Marcus pulled a face. "Never that."

Together we shared a laugh as we raced back to the house.

⌒

Darnel came home around noon on Sunday, and it felt just like old times as he, Devonte, and I went out to the backyard and played ball on the court our dad had installed. When it came to basketball, no one could beat Darnel; after years of playing he was just as good as our father. After Darnel, I was the next best, and then Devonte, and as we played against one another, I couldn't fight the feeling of how much I missed my oldest brother since he'd been down in Columbus for school.

"Damn, it's like you've gotten better." Devonte huffed as he leaned over, planting his hands on his knees to catch his breath.

Darnel spun the ball around on his index finger, grinning. "Or you two have gotten sloppy."

I smirked. "Shit, you ain't been to our games this past winter. I owned that court."

Devonte shoved me. "You mean I did."

We could argue all day about who was the better player. We were all cocky that way.

"I'd say you're all about the same, not nearly as good as your pops." From behind us, our father stood on our back patio, holding a cigar in hand, apparently watching us play.

Devonte waved him off. "You're rusty."

It wasn't true—at forty-three our father could still play as well as a twenty-year-old. He loved the sport too much not to stay in shape for it.

Darnel tossed me the ball then headed over to the hoop and scooped up his water bottle to take a swig.

"Nice to have you home, son." Our father spoke up. "How are things at school?"

Darnel barely looked at our father. "Good, I've been busting my ass in chemistry, but I think I'll finish the semester with an A."

My father narrowed his eyes for a moment as he took in Darnel's words. "Put in twice as much effort on the court as the books, that's where your future lies."

Darnel gazed down at the ground, picking at the label on his water bottle, not responding.

Before an awkward silence could set in, our father turned to me next. "I see you recently had a party here, Dre."

There were two of us at home and still I was caught for being responsible for the party? I snuck a peek at Devonte. *Snitch.*

"Yeah," I answered. "I threw a little something." We had a

housekeeper, so it wasn't like the house was a mess when he came home Saturday afternoon.

"And you was all up on that girl too." Devonte spoke up, elbowing me with a sly grin as he stole the ball from me.

My fists balled up and I squeezed my eyes shut, wanting to calm myself before I released my fury on Devonte for bringing up Cree.

Just as I'd feared, I found my father watching me when I opened my eyes.

"What's this?" he asked.

"Nothing," I said. I knew his rules about dating. He didn't care if we messed around, but we were not to get caught up with a girl. Our focus was basketball. His rule didn't bother me. I hadn't the interest or the patience for a relationship, and I couldn't help but be pissed that he was looking at me like I was going against his word.

"Come again?" he asked.

I forced interest at the squirrel that was eating a nut by our pool. "I'm not repeating myself."

"Oh, you not?" My father chuckled with a hint of sarcasm. "Well, it appears I'm missing a few cigars. The box cost me quite a penny, too, so to make up for it, how about you run an hour before bed every night this whole week, starting today."

It would be a bitch getting up, but I had no choice. "Yes, sir."

Devonte was doing a terrible job of hiding his laughter beside me.

"Same goes for you, too, Devonte, don't think I didn't measure my Henny, and I didn't see your times on the board for Friday and Saturday. I'm disappointed, I leave for a day and this is what you do?" He shook his head before placing his cigar back in his mouth and retreating into the house.

Devonte tossed the ball to the side and sighed. "Man, this is bullshit."

"What the fuck was that?" I snapped, getting in his face.

Darnel was quick to get between us before I could take a swing. "Easy, Dre," he warned.

"Nah." I shook Darnel off, going and getting back in Devonte's face. "What was that?"

Devonte smiled at me, not at all intimidated, knowing he could take me if need be. "I was just joking, relax. She was fine, anyway."

I had talked to Cree for all of a minute. It wasn't even something for Devonte to bring up, unless he purposely was trying to stir up some trouble. "That shit wasn't funny. Now I gotta get my ass up and run in the mornings *and* nights thanks to you."

"Didn't you hear him, I do too," Devonte shot back.

Darnel stood off to the side, staying out of it as he stared at the both of us, shaking his head.

"What?" I asked, tired of his judging.

"You mad at the wrong person, Dre," said Darnel. "You talk to a girl and Dad flips out? Why doesn't that bother you?"

It did, but not in the way Darnel was getting at.

I shrugged. "Why should it?"

"Because you're seventeen, why should it be a big deal if you talk to a girl?"

"He knows I get around, he doesn't care."

"But if you brought that girl home and said she was your girlfriend you know he would trip."

Of course he would, because then I'd be losing sight of what was important: basketball. "Because it's not what's important right now."

"Not what's important? Do you hear yourself? When are you supposed to do something for yourself, then?"

Darnel was reading too much into things. "I do things for me,

Darnel. I don't want a girlfriend. That shit is for people who don't like being alone anyway."

He took a step back as if I'd just hit him in the gut. "I can stand being alone just fine, Dre."

What was he saying? "You have a girl?"

He looked away from me. "I met someone, so what? Was I supposed to tell her I can't be into her right now because getting drafted's more important? What if I don't want to get drafted? What if I don't want to play ball?"

Now he wasn't making any sense. We'd all wanted to play ball for as long as we all could remember. It was a dream to someday go pro like our dad.

I shook my head. "What are you talking about right now? You make no sense."

Darnel smirked. "I'm just thinking for me now. You're still being controlled by Dad. Think for yourself. *Do* for yourself."

Devonte waved him off. "You got PMS or something?"

Darnel shot Devonte a mean look. "Sooner or later sleeping with girls you don't remember in the morning and going to parties gets old. I'm just trying to open your eyes. Parties, ball, girls, it's not the world."

It was to me. "Don't let Dad hear you talking like this, he'll—"

"What? Disown me? Let him, or maybe I should disown him if he can't accept the fact that maybe I'm tired of *just* basketball," Darnel said. "Maybe it's time someone else walks away from him, or else he'll never know what effect he's having on people."

His words were scaring me. Darnel was always the brother I could go to for advice. When I started having crushes, Devonte gave me condoms, and Darnel gave me words of wisdom. It was how it always had been. Devonte was the fun brother, and Darnel was the serious one. He couldn't abandon us for some girl and quit ball. It was disloyal. It was traitorous. It was wrong.

"What are you saying?" I grew the strength to ask.

"I was five when Mom walked away. Five, Dre!" Darnel snapped. "Why do you think she left?"

Our mother leaving was something I barely thought about. I was too young to even remember what she looked like or how she was.

I shrugged. "Because she was too caught up in her emotions."

Darnel frowned, shaking his head in disappointment. "Like it or not, one day you're gonna realize you've got a chip on your shoulder. We *all* do, and we get it from him." He pointed to the house before walking away, leaving me in the backyard with Devonte, without so much as a goodbye.

7

CREE

"How was the party?" Loraine asked Sunday as I sat eating leftover pizza while reading *Cosmo* magazine at the island.

I wiped my greasy hands on a paper towel and flipped a page, scowling at the sight of a recipe for bacon-wrapped chicken breasts. Bacon wasn't parsley, it didn't go on *every*thing.

"It was," I began, searching for a word to describe the event, "revealing."

Loraine appeared confused. "Say what?"

I resisted the urge to laugh and turned my eyes back to *Cosmo*. "I saw a lot of things, no body parts included, if that's what you're wondering." *Just my best friend's secret life being thrown in my face, if she was my best friend to begin with.*

Okay, dramatic much?

Troiann had been calling me all weekend, and thankfully, heading to the dance studio Saturday morning and then working that evening had made her calls easier to ignore. I was not in the mood to face her. I hadn't any idea how to look at her, let alone speak to her. How could I trust her after she'd lied to my face?

"Cree?" Loraine was at my side. "Is everything okay?"

I wished my father was home to talk to. I shrugged away from her and nodded. "Yeah, it's all good, Lori."

Loraine sighed and placed her hand on her hip. "Cree, it's been two years, do you have a time in mind for when you're finally going to cut me some slack?"

I wanted to yell and scream and say things that would purposely hurt her, but deep down, I knew I was just being a spoiled brat. Loraine wasn't the person responsible for my father's lack of TLC—*he* was.

Sighing, I looked down at our tiled floor. "I'm sorry."

"Don't apologize because you think you've hurt my feelings."

"I'm not, I know how much you want me to like you, and how much you try to be nice. I'm sure I don't make it easy."

Loraine came around the island and went to touch me. Instinctively, I moved away. "We don't have to—" I cut myself off and let her place an arm around me. Everything was upside down already, why not make up with Loraine and have less stress in my life?

"The party was okay, but it was too real," I said.

Loraine pulled away and examined me. "What do you mean?"

"It was just—" What did I mean? Everyone else was having a good time, Troiann included, so what was I whining about? I was the only one sitting to the side sulking, with the big *L* tattooed on my forehead. Maybe DeAndre was right, I should just lighten up and relax. Or maybe he was wrong, who knew? I just wanted things to go back to normal.

—

Sitting in Mr. Ventura's class on Monday, I decided to ignore DeAndre once and for all. I had approached Troiann that morning as though nothing happened, acting like I hadn't a clue she was seeing Marcus. I wanted things to be the same again, and if it meant playing dumb about her stupid fling with a Baller, so be it.

Class was almost over and Troiann was beside me rambling on about her previous period when some girl had been flirting with Marcus and Tremaine. Troiann appeared to be nonchalant about Marcus, but the more she talked, the more her feelings came out.

"I mean, no shade, no hatin', but that girl had a moustache, CJ," Troiann was saying. "That shit was thicker than a snicker."

I blinked to stop from rolling my eyes. True, I was her best friend and she was mine and I wanted her to be happy, but with a Baller?

I shook my head and changed the subject. "So, Loraine and I are getting along now."

Troiann stopped complaining and sat up. "For real?"

"She's been trying for so long, and she isn't that bad, why not stop being a brat and meet her halfway, you know?"

Troiann smiled and reached out, taking my hand. "Good, Cree, this is good for you. I know she's not trying to replace your mom or anything, but you do need that maternal influence."

I thought to shake her off. I hadn't had a "maternal" influence my entire life—I was seventeen; it was a little too late, wasn't it?

Instead, I just bobbed my head as the bell rang.

Everyone stood and gathered their things, and the hairs on my neck stood as I felt him even before he circled around me and stood at the opening of the aisle.

DeAndre.

Tremaine was beside him, looking between us curiously.

Troiann scowled. "What now, DeAndre?"

DeAndre heaved a sigh, eyes focused on me. "Can we talk? Alone, please? I promise I come in peace."

I should've just walked away, but the earnest look on his face made me pause and nod for Troiann to leave us be. "I'll meet you in the hall."

Troiann looked like she wanted to say something but she conceded, still managing to glare at DeAndre as she passed him on her way out.

DeAndre let Tremaine leave as well as he crossed over to me.

He was right in front of me, too close. "Well?"

"I wasn't lying about your girl and Marc, Cree," DeAndre said, even appearing sympathetic.

I didn't care about that. I would cross that bridge when I got to it. "I know. But that's not what this is about."

"Right," DeAndre agreed. "I don't want any static with you. Let's just agree to be cool, okay?"

"Cool?"

"Yeah, you and me, friends, *cool*," DeAndre repeated.

He was kidding, right?

I took a step back, hugging my books to my chest. "What?"

"I mean, we gotta be friends. I like you too much to not have you around." DeAndre shrugged. "That snarky shit you're always on, it's grown on me."

My lip curled up. "Um, you 'like' me, and you want to be friends?"

"That's what I said."

"You tried to humiliate me in front of our peers—"

"I wanna move past that."

"—and then you rub it in my face that my best friend isn't really my best friend, that she's sleeping with your best friend," I went on. "Your idea of being cool sucks, Dre."

DeAndre stepped closer, invading my personal space. "Troiann is your friend, she's just got a secret. Nobody's perfect."

"Still. It's probably best to just leave each other alone."

A smile washed into the corner of DeAndre's mouth. "Have lunch with me and the boys."

Was he hard of comprehending?

"I—"

He held his hands up. "I just wanna be cool, Cree."

It was just another mind game, it had to be. "You can't have me at all."

DeAndre smirked. "All right, now that that's been established, you gon' join us or what?"

He wasn't giving up as he stood waiting patiently in front of me.

"If I say no will you do anything else to me?" I asked.

DeAndre shook his head.

"No," I said loud and clear. I went to leave, but he caught my arm, pulling me back. Annoyed, I shook him off. "Enough! No means no, so leave me alone."

The grin on his face ignited my anger more. "I think despite how irritating it can be, I can't let you go because I'm amused by the smart things that come out of your mouth." He placed a hand on his chest. "I'm sorry for how I've been. It was disrespectful and insulting, and I'm sorry."

I crossed my arms. "Fine."

"I don't know why I told you about Marcus and Troiann the way that I did. It was kinda mean."

"Not kinda, it *was* mean."

DeAndre hung his head, bobbing it in agreement. "I used what I knew about them to bother you. It wasn't worth it. I don't know what made me do it. Maybe it was my ego."

"No, not 'maybe,'" I said, standing firm. "Either you are wrong or you're not, either you're sorry or you're not. Black and white, yes and no."

DeAndre blinked, and slowly, he smiled. "I *was* wrong and I'm sorry, Cree."

I swallowed, satisfied. He hadn't had to come and apologize or try to clear the air. He didn't owe me anything. He was DeAndre Parker, popular athlete and son of a great. Who was I to him? Something had made him see the error in his ways, and that couldn't be ignored.

Unlike his friends, DeAndre showed humility in this effort to squash our beef.

I looked into his eyes and saw sincerity. "Maybe I . . . misjudged you, and you're not a bonehead after all."

DeAndre chanced a step closer. "*Maybe?* So, we're back to that word now?"

I bit my lip. Okay, to be fair, I said, "I misjudged you based on observations that weren't studied closely."

DeAndre cracked a grin, and I tried my best not to smile too. "Wow, I knew there was something about you."

I wrinkled my nose. "Stop."

"I'm for real. Look, last week was lame. You were bein' a know-it-all, and I was bein' arrogant," DeAndre admitted.

I humbled myself and agreed. "I was. Our egos and pride clashed."

"I only wanted to show you that not all girls feel like you do about us, that even your best friend was cool with us, that's all, Cree. I'm not up to anything. I'm not attracted to you and you're not attracted to me, what do we have to lose if we decide to be cool?" He seemed honest and sincere.

"Fine, we'll try."

DeAndre looked away and rubbed the back of his neck. "If we're really gon' try, I gotta come clean. I blackmailed Troy into getting you to come out to After Hours. I just wanted to try to be nice before . . . you know, the reveal."

Troy was my best friend, yet she'd gone and fed me to the opps?

"She's just into him. She *is* your friend, don't doubt that. My boys have done some fucked up shit in the past, too, it's how people are. Trust me, it doesn't mean she isn't down for you."

I blocked it all out and focused on his maroon jacket. I blinked. "Can I ask you a question?"

DeAndre stood back, arching a brow. "What?"

"Why the jackets?"

DeAndre studied himself as he smoothed a hand down the material. "I seen this old picture of my uncle posted up with his crew back in the day once. They had these jackets on and they just looked legit. Like nobody was touchin' 'em on some gang shit. Reminded me of my friends. People thought it was lame at first, but now look, girls be geeked to borrow our jackets and dudes be tryin' to jack the style."

At first I'd thought their jackets were stupid, but really, it made their little group that much more appealing. Some even went so far as to buy their own jackets, but they couldn't measure up to the Ballers. They couldn't wear them like them, walk with the attitudes like them, make it all look so easy like them either.

I sighed. "So, you really want to be 'cool,' huh?"

DeAndre nodded. "You talk back to me." He gave a helpless shrug, like that was it. "I guess *maybe* I like that."

"Ah," I said, nodding as if I suddenly understood him. "A degradation kink, I'm sure there's a fix for that."

DeAndre snorted, fighting a smile. "*See*. No one gives me shit like that—well, outside of my brothers or the guys."

Maybe in a weird way, I'd grown on him. Who knew? "I guess we should get to lunch, then, huh?"

DeAndre gestured at the door. "After you."

I walked past him and headed out to the hall, where Troiann was waiting.

"Mind telling me what's going on?" she asked.

"I'm going to have lunch with the Ballers, join me?" I wasn't really asking as I walked past her and headed for the lunchroom. She was seeing a Baller, why would she front like the idea would bother her?

"Um, Cree, do you hear yourself?" Troiann asked as she followed close behind me.

"What's so wrong with the idea?" DeAndre was behind us, Tremaine at his side.

Troiann narrowed her eyes. "We can't stand y'all."

DeAndre lifted a brow, gaining a cocky grin. "Word?"

Troiann didn't want to argue. She didn't want it to get out about her and Marcus, so she backed down. "Whatever, do we really wanna sit with these clowns, Cree?"

I made a power move, feeling like DeAndre as I said, "Why not, Troy? It's just lunch, how hard could it be?"

Troiann didn't argue, and we entered the cafeteria without another word.

After we gathered our lunches, DeAndre led the way out to the quad to his usual table, the royal table, where Marcus and Chris were waiting and discussing something before they looked up and noticed us.

"Uh, did we miss something?" Chris asked, sitting up and moving down on the bench to make room.

DeAndre had the seat at the head of the table and Tremaine took a seat on the bench; Troiann and I took seats on either side of him.

And the awkwardness set in.

"We're all cool now," DeAndre announced, like the leader that he was.

Chris shook his head. "This won't end well. Females ain't nothing but drama."

"Which explains why you're still single," Troiann mumbled.

Chris peered across the table at Troy. "I got plenty of girls."

Troiann glared at him. "Basic ones if they dealin' with that attitude and rudeness."

Not at all offended or really bothered, Chris waved Troiann off.

DeAndre rolled his eyes. "Cool it, Chris."

Chris backed off. "Fine."

Troiann managed to take a spot across from Marcus, not even smiling or looking his way.

As odd as it was, we all managed to sit and eat civilly.

"It's Ventura's fault there ever was any issue. All that love shit he be talkin' about is getting weak," Tremaine was saying. "Ain't nobody tryna fall in love at seventeen. It should be illegal for him to teach that stuff."

"Maybe you're just afraid." I spoke up.

Tremaine's forehead adopted a crease as he faced me. "Of what?"

"Of falling in love, duh."

All the boys at the table smirked in sync, and I knew I had World War III coming my way.

Tremaine turned so that his whole body was facing me. "Let me tell you something, Cree, love isn't real at this point in our lives."

Marcus agreed. "It's all financial."

Not letting me get cornered, Troiann stepped in. "You're damn right it's financial," she said, taking me by surprise.

Tremaine chuckled. "For real?"

"Hell, yeah, I'm not letting a guy use and dismiss me so freely. It's not even about money, just respect and some time."

Tremaine held his fist out and I watched as they bumped knuckles.

"And love?" he asked.

Troiann wrinkled her nose. "Maybe in college or after. I'm all about figuring things out right now, who knows about love?"

Marcus sized Troiann up. "Yeah, right, you'd fall as soon as you got used to all the special treatment."

Troiann gave him a clever look. "Who's to say I don't have more than one guy buying me things? Life's too short for feelings, Marcus, you should know that, being a Baller and all."

They stared at each other, a challenge in their eyes, and the chemistry was tangible.

I didn't get their take on the subject, so I stood from the table and excused myself to go buy a bottle of water instead.

Troy could talk all she wanted. We both knew she stayed up watching romance movies in the hopes of it someday happening for her. She was bluffing, probably trying to play off her feelings for Marcus in front of him.

She shouldn't have had to do that. If he liked her and she liked him, they should be upfront, and not play games instead of playing hard. Playing hard got you nowhere but alone, still bluffing like you had it when you didn't.

"Don't be that girl, Cree." I jumped, turning around and finding DeAndre in line behind me.

"What girl?" I asked.

He looked past me through the cafeteria windows, where Troiann and the boys were still talking. "That girl who's constantly givin' relationship advice yet never has a dude of her own. That shit is pathetic."

"She deserves better," I argued.

DeAndre disagreed. "Nah, she being real with herself, at least she's smart enough to not think she and Marcus are headed for love."

"Why can't they be?" I challenged, tired of them all acting like the idea was so impossible.

DeAndre rolled his eyes. "Life is all about the buying and sellin' of dreams, and any dude who's gon' tell you he 'loves' you and wants to be with you forever right now is sellin' you a dream. I hope you keep the receipt."

"You're all just afraid."

"We're bad, we couldn't please you in the long run. We're not out for feelings, but fun. At least we're willin' to admit we can't commit instead of leadin' you on."

"You don't wanna try, that's the issue. You could meet your high-school sweetheart and let her go because you're too caught up trying to be this hard guy who doesn't do feelings."

DeAndre shrugged. "Maybe, maybe not, who knows if that shit is real or not?"

Shaking my head, I said, "One day you'll learn what type of love I'm talking about, Dre."

"And one day you'll learn what type of reality we're livin' in, Cree."

We'd reached an impasse, and I decided to let it go. We didn't have to debate about love forever.

"So, we're working on our friendship, right?" DeAndre brought up next.

I nodded. "Allegedly, yes."

DeAndre grinned, chuckling and repeating my words. He paced in front of me momentarily. "Listen, I have an idea for us."

"You do?"

"Mm-hmm." He nodded. "Ever since our little disagreement in class I've paid attention to you."

"Please tell me I can be creeped out by that."

"And," DeAndre went on without missing a beat, "I was

thinkin' you have something not a lot of people have." He stopped pacing and stood in front of me, staring me down, making me feel exposed.

"And that is?"

DeAndre lifted his eyes to mine. "An argument. You go against the norm, against the crowd, against *me*."

I wasn't following. "Yeah?"

DeAndre's lips twitched, revealing a small smile, as if he enjoyed my nervousness. "I can make a lame joke and ten people will laugh because of who I am and who my father is." His eyes measured me, peering into my soul. "But not you."

"You're not really funny."

He cracked a smile. "See, you don't give a shit, and I like that. I like your self-esteem. You real, Cree."

DeAndre stumbled saying this, letting me know he wasn't buttering me up. Interesting.

"Okay . . . ?" I waited for the shoe to drop, for him to get to his point.

"I think you and I should write that paper on culture for Donatelli's class. We could write some real shit together."

I paused. He wanted me to write a paper with him? "Wait, what?"

DeAndre took in a sharp breath through his nose, almost as though he was holding back saying something. "Do I really have to repeat all that?"

"I heard you, but I was thinking about taking the exam, and besides, no one wants to hear my opinion on the self-deprecation of our culture."

I went to head back to our table, but DeAndre caught me. "*I* do," he said. "There's so much I love about our culture, our people, but also things I hate." He took a step back and checked his watch.

"I'm not aimin' to win a Pulitzer, but I'm a real dude, and you, you're a real chick, so let's get together and write something real."

If DeAndre Parker were running for president, he would've had my vote, because for some reason I found myself saying yes.

He nodded, satisfied with my concession. "Good, how often do you work after school?"

"It varies, I'm off today, but I planned on catching the bus downtown so I could put in some dance time. I could cut that a little short if you wanted to do something."

DeAndre was looking across the cafeteria at Armani Young's table, where Armani was sneaking peeks back at him, and I wasn't sure if he'd even heard me. He turned back to me and again nodded. "Yeah, sure, we'll work it out."

8

DEANDRE

She moved like an angel, becoming one with the melody as it played loudly in the background.

Cree was oblivious to my observing her as she danced in the studio while I watched from the next room through the two-way mirror. She'd said she would be dancing after school, and seeing how she'd given me permission to watch her, I followed her. I just wanted to see if she could really dance, and as I stood tracing her movement to some song by Tinashe, it was unanimous, she could.

Cree was incredibly flexible. Her moves weren't explicit, but art. Her dancing was a motion picture.

I was so caught up watching her dance that I nearly missed Marcus calling me.

"Yeah," I answered, continuing to watch Cree.

"Workin' hard or hardly workin'?"

"It wouldn't work unless it was hard."

"What?"

I shook my head, dazed. "Nothing. What's up?"

"Nothing, where you at?"

"Right now? Watchin' Cree dance."

There was a pause on Marcus's end. "Do I wanna know why you're being creepy?"

"She said she danced and I wanted to see. We're just friends."

Marcus sighed. "Don't do it, Dre."

Really? It wasn't like I had the urge to mess with every girl I came across. "I don't want anything, Marc. She's not my type."

"Doesn't matter, you start off friends and the next thing you know it just happens."

"Speaking from experience?"

"Something like that."

"Please don't act like our being friends will result in something more. It is possible for a boy and girl to be friends."

Marcus snorted. "No, it's not."

"So you're saying you couldn't be friends with Cree?"

Marcus took a moment to think, but I already knew he would say he could due to Troiann. "Eventually I'd get curious."

Or maybe I was wrong. "Even though Troy's a factor?"

"Troy's not my girl, Dre. Cree's got that attitude." Marcus stopped to chuckle. "Plus you said she's a dancer, most dancers are good in bed. That mixed with the attitude is a sign that the sex would be fire."

Watching Cree dance and wind her body, I knew he had a point, but still. I just wanted to write the paper together, to see what we could do if we set aside our differences. I liked the way she stood her ground and how she thought.

"Either way, I'm not out to do anything," I said.

"Is she going on the No-Fly Zone?"

I had no right to declare such a thing. "No."

"So I can ... ?"

It was beyond fucked up that he was willing to do that to Troiann, but in the end, it would be Marcus's mess to clean up. "Do you."

There was a pause before Marcus responded. "I guess you don't want her. Just checkin'."

I rolled my eyes. "So you don't want her?"

"I gotta share a lunch table with Troy, could you imagine what things would be like if I slept with Cree?"

Incredibly messy. "She's my friend, Marcus, or at least we're workin' on it. So do me a favor and don't make this awkward by trying to hook up with her."

He grumbled something, but I knew in the end he'd accept and fall through. If I was really going to be Cree's friend, then I had to look out for her, and I couldn't have her getting her feelings hurt by one of my boys. But knowing Cree and her need to read between every fucking line, I had a feeling she wouldn't be fooled by Marcus or any of the others.

Marcus and I hung up and I looked back through the two-way mirror, finding Cree now dancing to some classical number.

She was wearing a gray sports bra and black leggings, making it easier for her to move fluidly with the music. Her hair was on top of her head in a bun, and for a moment, watching her like I was, I could've sworn she was a real dancer, a professional.

"She's good, isn't she?" A woman stepped out from behind me, taking me by surprise as she stood beside me watching Cree dance as well.

I nodded. "Impeccable."

The woman smiled, following along with Cree's moves. "Just like"—she took a moment to think of an appropriate word—"a professional."

She turned to me, staring me up and down. "Now, do you have a reason to be trespassing and watching my niece, or do I have to call someone?"

Trespassing? "Isn't this place public?"

"Yes, when it's open."

"Oh, I was just comin' to watch Cree dance. We're going to be working together on a project when she's done."

She didn't lighten up. "Uh-huh, and you're just working together on a school project?"

"Yes, ma'am."

Again those steely dark eyes scanned me over. It was hard to miss the disapproval on her face as she gazed at the tattoos covering my arms. "And you have no other reason to be bothered with Cree?"

I hoped she didn't think I liked Cree, or worse, was stalking her. "We're just friends."

She looked over to where Cree was in the dance studio turning off the music and hydrating herself. "Well, it looks like she's all done . . . " She waited for my name.

"DeAndre."

"DeAndre what?" she persisted.

"Parker."

A brow shot up speculatively. "Parker as in *Darrel* Parker?"

Parker was an ambiguous last name, but not when it came to our family. It was a known fact that my father had a spot in Akron and that his kids went to public school. Plus our names often littered the sports page of the local paper and evening news because of ball.

I kept my mouth shut, but nodded.

"That's even worse." She glanced over at Cree again, an almost motherly look crossing her eyes. "Cree will shower and then she'll be right out for you two to go and study."

"All right."

She turned to me, narrowing her eyes and assessing me. "Now, I hope you mean what you say when you speak of not being interested in my niece, because I don't want your lips anywhere near hers."

She walked away, disappearing just as quickly as she'd appeared.

She must've overheard me talking to Marc. I could've been offended that she didn't find me good enough for Cree, but it was a truth I knew to heart, and it didn't bother me.

"DeAndre?" I looked over, finding Cree standing in the doorway with her gym bag on her shoulder. Sweat glistened on her body as she stood looking at me curiously. "What are you doing here?"

I ignored the brief conversation I'd just had with her aunt and went back to the thought of Cree's dancing. "I wanted to see you dance."

Cree looked around. "Now?"

"If I had told you I was comin' you would've been nervous, instead you were perfect."

Cree appeared thoughtful as she looked on at me silently.

"What are you doin'?" I asked when her quiet stretched on.

Cree shook her head, moving on. "Just wondering how much mace costs, and if it's easy to use."

My lips twitched to smile. "Anyway."

"Anyway," she repeated, letting loose a smile of her own.

"What are you doin' Friday night?" I asked as I got an idea.

Cree regarded me suspiciously. "Working, why?"

"After?"

"I don't know."

"Friday night is initiation into my circle, Cree. No discussion about it."

She rolled her eyes. "Anything else, Your Highness?"

Moving along, I said, "You're really good. You find a lot of people who say they can sing or dance, but you're the real deal."

Cree fought a smile. "Thanks." She fiddled with her water bottle. "So we're going to go work on our paper now?"

"That would be the plan."

"Okay, just let me go get showered and dressed."

I checked my watch, finding that it was already four thirty. My father was probably out—hopefully he was—and that gave me a window to have Cree over. She would be the first girl I'd ever brought home with my father around, chancing a lecture, but if her aunt was down my back about my just being friends with her, there was no telling how her mother and father would be.

"Just do me a favor," I said.

Cree turned back to me. "Yeah?"

"Make sure your aunt knows that we're just friends, only that."

"Oh god, yes." Cree hurried off to talk to her aunt and shower, and I stood back and waited.

———

She sat at the far end of the dining room table and I sat at the other. There was nothing but space between us—it was safe that way, in case my father came home.

Cree set her things on the table while I set up my laptop to type notes. I was just opening up a blank document when I noticed Cree leaving the table and looking along the walls of the dining room, where our family's decorator had placed family photos. Cree looked around the room, face void of emotion until she stopped and stood in front of a photo, her mouth forming into a frown.

"What?" I asked, peering past her to some photo of my brothers and me as kids.

Cree faced me curiously. "Why don't you guys ever smile?"

In none of the pictures of us did my brothers or I smile. It wasn't something we often did in front of a camera, except if it was school related.

"I don't know," I said, shrugging.

Cree's brows pushed together as she appeared confused. "Weren't you happy?"

Of course we were happy. *Weren't we?* "Why wouldn't we be happy, Cree?"

She stood staring at me, some gears turning in her head. I didn't like it. Neither that nor her audacity to silently judge me.

At that moment, I wanted to take down every single picture that hung on the walls of our house. It was as if some message was being displayed, and I didn't want it to look that way. I didn't want Darnel to be right.

I didn't want to think of his words about our father. Our father had only guided us our whole lives. Stuck by us when our mother left. We were family, the only family that mattered. Darnel was just trippin', plain and simple.

"Dre?" Cree was sitting down again, watching me with concern. "Are you okay?"

"I'm straight."

Cree nodded, but I could tell she wasn't buying it. What gave her the right to question me?

She looked like she wanted to say something, but then Devonte stepped into the room. He buzzed past her as if she wasn't there and came over to my end, planting his hands on the tabletop as he leaned toward me to talk. "Yo, where've you been? I've been blowin' up your phone."

My phone sat on the table beside my laptop. I noted I hadn't missed a single call or text.

"Really?"

Devonte grinned. "Nah, I was just at the library and I ran into

Ari. She was askin' about you. That's way too much for you, bro."

"Nobody wants you, Devonte." He had his own troubles with the two girls he was two-timing.

Devonte appeared doubtful, and then he suddenly noticed Cree. "'Sup? I see you're back."

Cree looked over at me, lifting a brow.

I rolled my eyes. "You pay him any attention and he'll make you regret it, Cree."

Cree returned to Devonte and smiled politely. "Hello to you, too, Devonte."

He grinned at her, checking her out, before turning back to me, questioning me with a funny look. "You've got some nerve bringing her here."

"We're just friends."

Devonte smirked. "Like Dad'll care."

He stood away from the table and eyed Cree one more time. "Well, I'll let you two kids get back to whatever it was that you were doin'. I may just go out back and shoot around. Unless—" He faced me. "Do you think Dad'll give me credit for runnin' an hour now?"

Our father hadn't been that pissed about the party. "I don't know, run and find out."

Devonte scowled. "And waste an hour and *still* have to run tonight? Nah, I'm good."

He left us alone and I faced Cree, not surprised to find her watching me.

"What's your other brother like?" she asked.

I could only stomach enough strength to say one word, but it was a word that described Darnel perfectly. "Different."

But I didn't want to think of Darnel, not after the way we'd left things Sunday. I'd woken up Monday morning with a text from him:

I meant what I said last night, Dre. One day you'll open your eyes and see what we've been subjected to, what we missed out on, what we don't know because of him. When that day comes, I'll be here for you, always

It sounded like a goodbye, and I wanted to break my phone. He was overreacting. He was the one who needed to open his eyes and realize what was at stake. He couldn't turn his back on us, we were his family.

Cree didn't pry, sensing it was a touchy subject. Instead, she opened her notebook and started scribbling things down, spouting off about what topics we should discuss in our paper while I hurriedly went to typing on my laptop to catch up.

"So, where do you want to start on our paper? How should we open it?" I asked as I looked over at Cree once more.

"I want reparations for every *Step Up* movie after the first," Cree declared, in a tone that said she was serious.

I snorted, cracking a grin. "Think I seen the first two with a cousin."

"Two was enough. Okay, we get it. Pretty White people with problems can dance too. Hell, they even had your obligatory Black side characters to make the culture vulturing less harsh," Cree reasoned. "I'm just saying, if there's going to be a dance movie influenced by hip-hop and the culture, then it should be cast and led by the people who created it."

She definitely wasn't wrong there.

"You tryna be in a movie, Cree?" I teased. Really, I could see her going that far with her dancing. With the little I'd seen, I could tell she was going places.

Cree blushed, shrinking a little. "I need to better up my skill. I just . . . I don't know, it'd be nice to see a pretty Black ballerina fall for a handsome Black boy who's more urban and street with his dancing. *Step Up* meets *Stomp the Yard*."

I made a note of that idea, because it did sound interesting.

"Okay, I think we should do the stuff we *dislike* about our culture first to get it out of the way, that way it's easier and more fun to get into the positive later," I suggested.

Cree shrugged, bringing out a little packet of doughnuts she must've gotten from the vending machine at the dance studio. She hadn't wanted anything when I'd offered her refreshments. "Sure."

She grabbed a mini glazed doughnut and nibbled on it.

"So healthy," I teased as I typed in the words *Things We Want to Improve On* as a topic point in my document.

Cree made a face. "Don't tell me you're one of those health freaks."

"Nah, I just watch my junk intake. Gotta stay A1 for the league."

Cree snorted. "You know, between you and my father, I'll be fortunate not to get an eating disorder before I graduate."

"Don't tell me he thinks you're out of shape."

"Quite the opposite, actually."

I could only see her from the chest on up, but it was still enough to know that she was definitely fit. "You're fine. He has nothing to stress you about."

"He's just strict about—" Cree caught herself and shook her head.

For a moment I wondered if he was on her about her dieting habits and she had to sneak and enjoy sweets. "About what?"

Cree waved me off. "Never mind."

"Nah, what's up, Cree?"

Cree sighed, pursing her lips for a moment and shaking her head. "My father's real funny about dancers and their weight. He doesn't want me shrinking due to some disorder, which is why, according to him, dance can only be a hobby."

A hobby? When you had raw talent like us, me with basketball and her with dancing, it should be taken to the next level. Hobbies were for amateurs, something neither of us were.

I sat up in my seat. "You don't plan on takin' it further?"

"I'd need more training for that, not that it'll ever happen. Dad wants me to do something else with my life. Even if I don't make it as a professional dancer, I'd like to study it in college, but . . . yeah." She shrugged dejectedly, as if it was no big deal her father was getting in the way of her apparent dream.

"He shouldn't hinder you from doing something you're so good at."

Cree looked up at me, a sad smile on her face. "We have very different fathers, DeAndre."

I could've laughed at her statement. Our fathers' viewpoints on our dreams were different, but their stressful input on us felt similar. Her father was strict about her dancing and her body, mine was strict about everything if it got in the way of basketball.

"You'd be surprised how much they have in common."

Cree left it at that and we soon got to work. We were going to write about it all to fill those ten pages. From our community, to our music, books, films, and art; the good, the bad, and the ugly.

"Music?" I suggested as I made a new bullet point.

"Okay, I don't like how *accepting* we are of other races coming into our culture," Cree began.

"What do you mean?"

"Like, you have these White artists who grow up influenced by other White artists and their White roots, or something that's far from Black culture, but when they want to branch out to truly sell records, they grab the latest It rapper or R & B singer. They use our slang, our style, and yet everyone in their music videos is White. They use us for the monetary gain and then it's back to their original style. When something racist happens out in the world, they don't speak up at all because we're dust now," Cree explained. "So, I just wish Black artists were more selective and protective of our art and who they allow to use our magic in their music."

I understood her point loud and clear about certain musicians riding our wave for a check, but as soon as shit hit the fan, they were dead silent. I typed Cree's words and added in my own take.

"What about our side of things? The things we say in our lyrics? I hate how when something goes down in the Black community rappers want to use their platform to discuss and try to unite us, yet in their lyrics a lot of them speak about killin' or shunnin' people out. Black people committin' heinous crimes against each other is just as important to actively eliminate as any other crime against us. You can't talk about givin' back to the community on the radio or in an interview, and then rap about the shit you're sellin' out of your duffel bag or how many opps you're smokin' on.

"I mean, I know I listen to a lot of these songs and they're played at After Hours or one of our parties, but sometimes I get sick of that shit. Two-faced rappers are the worst."

"Yeah, and their idea of love songs always includes sex. I'm pretty sure the best love there is doesn't involve anything physical, you know?" Cree wrote down her thoughts. "I don't want the guy of my dreams telling me how good my sex is, or how wet I can get, or something private like that. That's not romantic. How can they have daughters and expect the best for them yet they can't even give the best to these girls' mothers? Women are so disposable in hip-hop music."

That I couldn't deny and added, "Some guys can't love."

This set Cree on another topic that got her heated, and I had my hands over my keyboard, ready to go. "That's another thing, do you know what this generation of Black people is missing?" she asked.

I shook my head.

"Love. Pride to be one's color. I hear it all the time in school or on the radio about how light skin's the right skin, or how it's shocking that some dark-skinned girl is pretty." I could tell her blood was boiling. "Sometimes it just makes me so sad. What if one day I have two girls, one my color and the other ebony. What am I supposed to tell my darkest child, that she's not as beautiful and won't be accepted because she's not light or brown like her sister and me? What kind of shit is that?"

Cree was brown skinned like myself, an in between of being light or dark in tone. I loved that she cared to speak up about it.

Cree wiped at her eyes, getting emotional over the thought of the hypothetical. "I think we should focus on loving each other for who we are rather than the shade of our skin. What happened to 'Black power' and 'Black is beautiful'? You have people who would rather run to another race than sit down and try to rebuild our people and teach our youth. You have girls who want to date outside their race to have light-skinned babies with 'good hair' or guys who only like girls of different races because Black girls are 'too much.'"

I couldn't relate to that. "Girls of all colors can be beautiful to me, but I'm only interested in my own—light or dark, it don't matter. I'm not like that."

"But a lot of Black guys *are* these days. There's so much self-deprecation within our race and it's sad. I can go online and watch interviews or music videos and I'll see Black men talk bad about Black women, saying we're too thickheaded or act too ghetto and that's why they date White, Spanish, or Asian women."

I knew some guys like that, so I understood Cree's grief. But she couldn't fault everyone for the few guys who hated their own.

"Okay, but for the paper, you might want to dial it back a little bit and be more open minded. Sayin' the wrong thing could make everything go left, and that's not what we want."

Cree smirked, crossing her arms. "Oh, I'm not racist, my dog is white."

One glimpse at her found that she was dead serious.

I shook my head and went back to typing. That snarky shit was getting cute.

"I guess you're right, though, maybe we should cancel all that. If I say that people will be all over me and—"

"No, you know what?" I spoke up. "You can say whatever the hell you want. If you wanna start a new generation of Black Panthers, say it. If someone has a problem with you, they've got a problem with me, because my name is goin' on the paper too. I'm goin' to stand by what you say, and no one wants to have a problem with me."

Cree's eyes grew big, but she said nothing. I could sense that she knew I wasn't playing around.

I could help her word her angst better if need be, but she and I were going to speak our minds. It was the sole purpose of my choosing her, to see what we could do if we just stopped beefing. Cree was passionate about something that wasn't mundane like partying or doing basic shit. She had things she wanted to say, and I'd be damned if I let her fear of the backlash censor her.

Cree peered down at her notes. "You don't have to do that for me, Dre."

"You're my friend, I take up for my friends."

My words made Cree smile, and seeing her lighten up made me smile.

And then my father stepped into the room.

He noticed Cree almost instantly, stopping and staring at her for a moment, as though he'd never seen a girl before.

"Hello, Mr. Parker," Cree said as she looked at my father and offered him a smile.

He didn't return the expression for a moment as he looked at me before turning back to Cree. "Hello, Miss . . . ?"

"Cree Jacobs."

My father put on the charm, smiling at Cree after assessing her for the third time. "How nice to meet you, Cree." He turned to me and the smile dropped. "I was just in a meeting and I came home to tell you boys the big news."

"What is it?"

After deciding that it wasn't a big deal that Cree was sitting in the room, my father shrugged and went on. "Some sports magazine wants to do an interview with athletes whose offspring took after them in their sport. And looking at stats, I argued that we should get the cover. I've got five NBA titles, my sons will have five or more titles. No one has bred winners like me."

I was fine with winning one ring, but five? Talk about pressure.

"What'd they say?" I asked.

My father grinned. "We're in talks, but I'm sure we'll get it. They'll be here Saturday morning to talk with all four of us." He turned to Cree, sizing her up. "Impressive, huh?"

Cree faced me, forcing a smile on her face. "Yeah, exciting, I guess."

My father took a step back incredulously. "You *guess*?"

"I'm not really into the whole sports or athletes thing, but it's cool that DeAndre will be in a magazine," Cree went on.

My father chuckled. "Everyone is into athletes."

"Not really," Cree argued. "It's not my thing."

No one went against my father. The only one brave enough was

Darnel, yet Cree sat unafraid. Seeing her so unaffected by the news of my being in a magazine made me like her more as a person. Plus she was standing up to my father; it was almost comical seeing the mouse stand tall against the lion.

"It's getting late. We'll pick back up when you're free, Cree." I closed my books. Studying wouldn't go well with my father home. "I'll take you home."

Cree nodded and closed hers as well. "Yeah, Tremaine said he wanted to do something later anyway."

"My Tremaine?" I asked, wondering if he was pulling a Marcus and making a move.

"Yeah, I think we're just going to the mall or something," Cree said.

I didn't worry about it; she was smart enough to ignore Tremaine's games.

My father reached out and grabbed my keys from the table and handed them to Cree. "Would you mind letting me talk to him for a moment?"

Cree accepted the keys and gathered her things and left us alone.

I was already annoyed by the time I glanced at my father.

"She's interesting," he said as he came closer, pocketing his hands in his trousers. He suddenly laughed a taunting laugh as he rocked back on the heels of his feet. "All girls like athletes, son, and if they don't, they're the ones you have to look out for."

"What are you talking about?" I shut my laptop and stood from the table, ready to go as quickly as possible.

My father shrugged as if it was simple. "You can't get a girl like that, son."

Even my own father? "Excuse me?"

"I know her type. They're untouchable, they get guys like you hooked, make you focus on useless things and think you're close to getting with them. They play you, son, they just want you to lose it all."

"Cree's not like that." Besides, we were just friends.

"Either way, she doesn't like basketball and that's all you're about."

I didn't say anything. I wasn't into Cree and I didn't want to put up a fight against my father for a lost cause.

"Yes, sir," I said as I walked past him.

He grabbed my arm, stopping me, but I didn't turn around as he spoke again. "This is the last project you're doing together, right?"

It was April, school would be out in less than two months. More than likely there weren't any other projects to be assigned in any of my classes. "Yes."

"There and back, Dre," he instructed from behind me as he let me go.

I went out to my car and got in, finding Cree listening to one of those rap songs we'd both put down as a negative for our culture. The song and the irony made me lighten up enough to shake my head with a chuckle and buckle in.

"He seems nice," Cree said as I backed out of my driveway and drove to her house.

I snorted. If she only knew. "Don't worry about him."

"Was I rude for not being excited? Because I think it's cool, but you know, I'm not into sports and—"

"No, you were all right. He's just used to people kissin' his ass." When I looked at Cree, I couldn't miss the resilience in her eyes when she was pushed. I'd seen it the day she'd called me out in

Ventura's class, I'd seen it the night at After Hours, at school when I apologized, and at my party, and I saw it tonight at my dining room table.

"Gosh, you must be freaking out over there. Do you remember when everyone swore they were LeBron James's cousin? I bet it's the same way with you Parkers."

My father was an entity in the NBA world. Five-time champion, popular sneaker line, entrepreneur, my father had it all. And people wanted their piece as well. There were a lot of guys who used to try to get in good with my brothers and me, but we didn't play that shit.

For me, I was only down with Tremaine, Marcus, and Chris—the only three guys besides my brothers who didn't give a fuck about my father or where I came from. Chris would come over swearing Michael Jordan, LeBron James, or Kobe Bryant were better players, and for that I liked him, for being able to see past the image of Darrel Parker and all his majesty, and just see him as a player with some comparable stats. And Marcus and Tremaine played football, not really giving a shit about basketball altogether. We all came from money, but in the end we were friends based on common interests and meshing well together. They weren't fake and neither was I, which was why after all the years I'd been in school I only rocked with them in the end.

Truth be told, it was one of the reasons Cree stood out to me. *She* didn't care about any of that shit either.

I shrugged. "Every now and then you get the person who's only interested in meeting your dad and acting all hard because of our popularity. It's cool for a while but then I get annoyed."

Cree nodded. "I get it. Sometimes you just want to be a normal person, huh?"

"Yeah, exactly."

"Still, I feel terrible after telling him I wasn't into athletes, I probably sounded so stuck up."

"Nah, you were fine. I'm sure when you go home and tell your mom she'll freak out for you," I said. Women loved my father, and he definitely loved them back, if only in a physical sense of the word. He wouldn't bring them home, but he was known for hotel room romps every now and again.

Silence was her response, causing me to look over to find Cree biting her lip.

"What?" I asked, wondering what I'd said wrong.

Cree folded her hands in her lap. "I don't have a mother, Dre."

I nearly hit the brakes. "What?" Everyone had a mother. I had a mother, even if she'd walked away from my brothers and me.

Cree looked absentmindedly out the window. "She died giving birth to me. It was always just me and my dad, until he got married my freshman year."

I didn't know what to say. It wasn't often I met someone else who was motherless.

She looked over at me. "Yet another thing we have in common, huh?"

I didn't want to respond but I had to. "It's not something people should have in common, Cree."

Another sad smile came to her lips. "Yeah, good thing we have such great dads to make up for it, right? I don't know much about my mom, but my dad's been enough, you know?"

I didn't want to relate to her on that level.

I felt . . . I *felt*. What, I wasn't exactly sure of.

She sat calmly beside me, yet I felt an unrelenting urge to do something to offer comfort. I couldn't figure out why until it hit me. *Empathy*. Something I wasn't used to. It was a foreign feeling swirling around inside me, and as soon as I realized what it was, I wanted to flush it out.

Still, I reached out to pat her shoulder, but I never got the chance; the ringtone assigned to my father's number rang out, interrupting us.

9

CREE

It was Friday and I'd only became cool with the boys Monday, yet it hadn't taken long for things to fall into place. One minute I couldn't stand guys like Tremaine, the next I couldn't stop laughing with him in class. I wasn't okay with the way he chewed through girls, but I was getting used to him; enough to where we could have full conversations over the phone.

People definitely noticed that there were new additions to the Ballers' lunch table and entourage. Guys looked at us strangely and some girls appeared to share the sentiment.

I didn't let the hate faze me or ruin my mood as I headed for the den where my father and Loraine were watching TV. My father was sitting back in his chair and enjoying a cold beer while Loraine sat beside him in her own chair, grading papers.

My father turned, noticing me. He checked the clock on the wall and looked back at me. "Where are you going?"

I briefly glanced down at the small black tee and denim jeans I was wearing. The small peek of skin between the hem of my tee and the top of my jeans must've alarmed my father, not to mention the way my jeans hugged my curves. "I'm just going out with Troiann and the guys."

"Oh—wait, what *guys*?" my father demanded. Alert set in on his face and I now had his full attention.

So I hadn't exactly told my father that I was now best buds with the Ballers Club. I hadn't ever brought boys up period, but now I knew he was that type of father. The "no boys allowed" type of father.

"Just Troy and a few guys from school, they're on the sports teams and they do a lot of volunteer work around school," I explained vaguely.

My father narrowed his eyes. "And you're going out like that?"

I shrugged innocently. "What's wrong?"

Loraine glanced up from her papers and faced my father. "She looks cute, Mack, let her be."

My father pouted. "Have you eaten today, Cree? You're getting a little on the skinny side."

I gritted my teeth. There was nothing "skinny" about me. My father was just saying that because he was about to get on me about dancing again. "Yes, Dad, I ate a whole dinner at work, fried chicken oughta fatten me up."

He smirked. "How much dancing did you do this week? I think it's been enough. You don't want to overexert yourself."

Loraine sighed and put her papers aside. "Mack, please, let her have her fun. She doesn't dance too much, she spends just as much time at school, work, and with Troiann as she does dancing."

Loraine was straight up going for the Best Stepmom Award. Before it would've bothered me, now I didn't mind so much. She just wanted to bond with me and move forward, so why not?

My father didn't get a chance to reply before the doorbell rang, causing my stomach to drop.

Here it goes.

My father stood and set his beer aside. "Must be the *boys*."

Frowning, I had no choice but to follow him out of the room and over to the front door.

To make matters worse, only DeAndre, Tremaine, and Chris stood outside. There was no way my father was letting me out of the house with a gang of boys drenched in tattoos, muscles, and the gorgeous Baller grins that sent panties dropping.

"Hello, Mr. Jacobs." DeAndre took the initiative to speak first as he stepped forward to shake my father's hand.

My father stared at DeAndre's outstretched hand for a beat before reaching out and shaking it.

Tremaine, being the knucklehead that he was, reached out and did a little handshake with my father before pulling him into a hug in that way that guys often did.

He peeked in at our foyer, observing Loraine's décor and the overall layout. "Nice place, Cree."

My father looked back at me before turning to the boys and pocketing his hands. "So."

I had to hand it to the Ballers, none of them seemed intimidated.

"Did you all decide to wear black and not tell this one?" my father asked, pointing at Chris, who stood sporting white jeans and Lebrons, and a graphic white tee under his olive-green bomber jacket.

Tremaine grinned. "Nah, we just like to remind him that he's not one of us."

DeAndre snickered and that made me laugh as well, easing my nerves.

Chris rolled his eyes, pretending to snort. "Black people."

Yet he stood in a room full of us, making us chuckle at the remark. Gotta love Chris Casey.

I went and stood beside Tremaine, feeling comfortable. "So, we'll just be going, Dad. We won't be out long." I looked over at DeAndre. "Right?"

He nodded. "Right, we're just seein' a movie and grabbin' a bite to eat."

My father wasn't convinced. "Where's Troiann?"

Not missing a beat, DeAndre said, "She's meetin' us there. She carpooled with some other friends."

My father loved Troiann, and having some peace of mind that she would be with me, he gradually eased up. "Well, I guess I'll let you go. Don't be out too late, Cree."

I obeyed. "Yes, Dad."

I followed the boys outside to where an all-black Escalade was sitting in front of my house.

DeAndre stepped out in front of us and went for the driver's side.

"So what movie are we going to see?" I asked curiously.

Tremaine and Chris laughed.

I stopped in my tracks. "What?"

DeAndre shook his head. "We're not goin' to a movie, Cree. We've got more excitin' things to do to get you initiated."

If he had lied about that, where was Troy?

"And Troiann?"

He shrugged. "Take a wild guess where she is."

"Or who she's under," Tremaine joked.

None of it was funny to me, and I was irritated that DeAndre had lied and hadn't told me all week about his plans for the evening.

"Where are we going?" I demanded.

DeAndre wouldn't let up. "I'm not tellin', just get in and find out."

"No."

He paused, coming back around the car and stopping in front of me. He looked from my black sneakers all the way up to my eyes, arching an eyebrow. "No?"

"I'm not going anywhere until I know what's going on."

For a moment his upper lip twitched, and he barely covered his scowl. "Cree, stop bein' a pain in the ass and just get in the car."

I stood my ground. "No."

DeAndre stared at me as I stared at him, both of us unwavering.

It wasn't until Tremaine came over and placed his hands on my shoulders that I pulled away from our intense stare down.

"Before you two start fuckin' on your lawn—"

I took a moment to laugh dryly at Tremaine's comment, and DeAndre did the same.

"He could never," I muttered.

DeAndre rolled his eyes. "Sure, Cree."

His sarcasm ate at me. I sneered at him, feeling haughty. "You couldn't get in this castle if you had the key."

DeAndre eyed my body, shaking his head as he checked the time on his fancy watch. "Cree, I could own that castle."

The way he said it, so laid back and at ease, like it was a simple fact, made me unable to respond right away.

"I—"

Tremaine cut into my line of vision, giving me his attempt at a charming smile. "Cree, trust me, I wouldn't let Dre take you any-where you couldn't handle. We cool, right?"

"Yeah."

"So just get in and have some fun tonight. We only wanna celebrate, okay?"

For some reason—probably due to all the talking we'd done in class and out of it since Monday—I found myself able to trust Tremaine. He was transparent with me and didn't try to hide who he was.

"Okay," I said, giving in.

DeAndre got in the driver's seat and we all climbed into the Escalade. My nerves were still jumpy as to what lay ahead for the evening, but I allowed myself to trust that we weren't doing anything that I couldn't handle.

But it left me wondering about what I could handle.

❧

Nearly half an hour—and a few too many sleazy rap songs and TMI stories from Tremaine—later we arrived at our destination: some nondescript building that housed several other vehicles in its parking lot.

We got out of the Escalade and the boys circled around me before we could advance to the entrance.

"It's a hookah bar," Tremaine explained. "And before we go for the first half of our evening, we gotta break you in."

Why didn't I like the sound of that?

"Break me in?" I repeated, nervous.

"Of course." DeAndre dug around in the back of the Escalade. When he came back to our group my jaw hit the ground. In his hands was a small mauve bomber jacket. The earnest smile on his face caused my heart to flip-flop around in my chest. "For you."

The others stood back as DeAndre helped me into my jacket; my very own official Ballers Club apparel. "For me?"

"Yeah," DeAndre said with a bob of his head. "You was askin' about mine, and I just figured it was the perfect way to invite you in."

I was touched as I ran my hand down the satin material. "Thank you, Dre."

"Besides, it's not every day someone applies pressure," Tremaine joked. "Had my boy big bothered."

They all laughed, even DeAndre, as Chris reached into his own jacket. He furnished a small pack of cigars and handed one to each of us.

I held back a giggle as I examined the cigar. "What's with you guys and the cigars? I'm surprised you don't smoke weed."

"All kings smoke cigars," Chris informed me.

"Plus, Coach would flip if our piss came back dirty," Tremaine added.

DeAndre took the lead and lit each of our cigars and stood back. "We gotta break in our first ballette."

I giggled at the phrase. *"Ballette?"*

DeAndre shrugged. "What else will we call you?"

I wasn't a Baller, so I supposed it fit. It was still a little weird, but I let it go as I did something completely lame. I curtsied, making the boys laugh, before we all held a toast with our cigars before taking a drag.

One intake was all it took to send me into a coughing frenzy. A rancid flavor coated my mouth as I choked. The boys instantly laughed at my failure.

Tremaine reached out and patted my back. "Easy, girl."

The boys enjoyed their cigars for a few more moments before stubbing theirs out and tossing them in the trash. I would've done the same but I wanted to keep mine. I'd only been friends with Troiann, and now here I was joining links with the Ballers Club, and it felt special that they were inducting me and deeming me a "Ballette" in the process.

The hookah bar was small and intimate, and groups of people sat around on couches sharing a hookah. The room was dim and the music was familiar as I recognized Rae Sremmurd playing loudly. A few blondes were up and dancing to the song, embarrassing themselves as they were out of sync. There was a fruity smell in the atmosphere, making me feel better about smoking from a hookah rather than the foul cigar Chris had given me.

We looked like a group of college kids, so when Tremaine was carded and handed over his fake ID, it was no hassle. I sat in awe watching the boys decide on what kind of hookah to get.

I shared a chair with Tremaine and watched as the boys gathered hoses and prepared to take their first hits.

"Don't inhale too much, you'll get light-headed," DeAndre instructed.

I nodded and took a small pull from my own hose, much more pleased with peach flavored tobacco than the cigar.

The boys all settled down and soon I got used to the hookah and the scene around me.

"Why you keep looking around?" Tremaine asked, placing his hand on my knee to get my attention.

I turned back to my group. "Just making sure no one from school is here. After that little thing in class with Dre some people have been slick and shit."

Tremaine smirked, as did the other boys. "Man, fuck that."

Before I could question what he was doing, Tremaine whipped out his cell phone and tapped on his Instagram app. Soon, he was going live. Even more, he held me close as he recorded. "Ayo, this the big homie with the little cute homie. I got a message for anybody with a problem wit' it. Cree's good with the squad, and if something needs to be addressed, come through *me*."

Chris leaned over and slung an arm around my neck. "And me!"

Tremaine almost broke character and smiled before he glanced at DeAndre. "Anything to add, Dre?"

With his eyes locked on me, DeAndre said, "Don't let it be a problem."

Tremaine returned to his camera. "Hear that? Baby girl anointed now."

I snorted at that remark. "Gee, what was my life like before the Ballers graced me with their presence?"

Tremaine shot me a mean mug. "See, we was tryna help your goofy ass." Tremaine turned back to his camera. "She canceled now."

I broke into a laugh and they all followed as Tremaine ended his live.

It seemed safe to say that the Ballers *were* my friends.

The thought made me laugh. "This is so weird, we're so different and yet here we are."

Tremaine shrugged and threw an arm around me. "Not really. Basketball's just full of skinny-ass dudes runnin' back and forth chasin' a ball, and yet I support these guys." He gestured to Chris and DeAndre. "It's not so bad."

DeAndre rolled his eyes, turning to me. "And football is a bunch of dudes who enjoy bein' tackled by other dudes, but we accept Tremaine and Marc for who they are."

Tremaine made an impressive muscle and I admired how his tattoos complemented it. "It would take a pretty big dude to pin me down."

"Is that what you want, Trey?" Chris teased, causing us all to laugh.

"Is it true you guys don't cut your hair for most of the season?" I asked.

Tremaine nodded. "Only when the season starts to get really good and we win a lot. Now Chris doesn't wash his hair, but he be on some White boy shit with that."

I looked at Chris, feeling sorry that he was repeatedly the odd one out. "You shouldn't let them pick on you, you know."

He shrugged as if it was nothing. "It's whatever, it's not that deep. These are my brothers, at the end of the day it's all love."

Aww.

"Here he go with that soft shit." Tremaine snorted, making us laugh.

Boys.

"Yo, when you gon' finish my playlist?" Tremaine asked me.

"What playlist?" DeAndre poked in on our conversation.

"Troiann says Cree makes good mixes, and I've been waitin' for her to hook me up."

I looked at DeAndre and made a face. "He wants me to pick a set of slow songs and I have no problem doing it, I just feel like an accomplice when it comes to the bullshit he's going to say to the poor girls he's going to seduce with the list."

Tremaine elbowed me. "Just mind your business and make the playlist, Cree."

DeAndre looked thoughtful for a moment. "Make me a playlist sometime?"

I shrugged. "Sure, what do you want?"

"Whatever comes to mind at the thought of me," DeAndre said simply. "You know, anything that reminds you of a king."

I rolled my eyes as I felt my upper lip curl up. "Clown shit, got you."

DeAndre cracked a handsome grin. "Nah, for real, you pick whatever you think fits."

I smiled, liking his trust in me to make him a good mix. "Okay."

A couple of girls walked by and Tremaine wasn't shy about admiring them.

"Are you guys boob men or booty men?" I asked curiously, as I watched some other guys check out the attractive duo.

Tremaine and Chris looked at each other simultaneously and

nodded, confirming some unspoken code before turning to me and saying, "Booty."

I faced DeAndre. "You?"

He shrugged. "I prefer proportion, can't have one without the other."

I liked his answer; it was fair to girls who hadn't big asses or amazing boobs.

I sat back and took another drag from the hose, blowing smoke toward the ceiling. I was enjoying myself and the hookah bar, and, for a lack of greater words, I felt *cool*. "This wasn't so bad as initiation."

Tremaine chuckled as he reached into his pockets. "This is only the *first* part, wait till you see what else Dre had in mind." He reached out and handed me a roll of twenties, and then he reached into his pocket and pulled out another thick wad.

I gathered the money, not sure what was happening. "What is this for? A tip?"

Chris laughed. "Not for here."

I glanced at all the boys, hoping someone would clue me in. "I don't get it."

Tremaine slapped my back, too hard, causing it to sting. "We're going to Inferno."

Why did that name sound familiar?

It hit me. It was a strip club; the same strip club I'd heard some guys at work talk about, the same strip club the Ballers brought up. A strip club as in topless dancers and—god forbid—possibly bottomless dancers as well.

Turning to DeAndre, I saw that he appeared expressionless as he sat watching me.

I rolled my eyes and stood up. "Screw you, DeAndre."

I couldn't have gotten out of the hookah bar quick enough. We weren't in Akron anymore, so getting home wouldn't be easy, but I had a cell phone and a means to call—

An arm wrapped around my waist, and before I could turn around, I found my back meeting the wall of the building and me coming face to face with DeAndre as he crowded all of my space.

I pushed him away with a hard shove. "Don't touch me."

He held his hands up. "I just came to sort this out."

"Sort this out? You're trying to take me to a strip club. Do I look like one of the boys to you?"

He opened his mouth.

"Don't answer that!"

DeAndre sighed, looking around and remaining calm. He reached into his jeans and pulled out something and handed it over. "Here. I found it when I was in my dad's office."

I was still angry, but I took the photo he handed me. It was of a smiling toddler being held in someone's lap; by the red fingernails I could tell it was a woman.

"Is this you?"

DeAndre nodded. "You said we didn't smile a lot when we were young, and I found that. Thought I'd show you that we did smile."

Curiosity got the better of me and I came out and asked. "Is this your mother?"

"Could be, I don't know."

It bothered me that he stood before me so indifferent about the fact that he possessed a picture of his mother. The only picture of his mother, it seemed. Didn't he care? Wasn't he curious to know what the woman who abandoned him looked like? Sure, the photo only showed her from the waist down, but it was closer, a step in the right direction.

But then I realized he was distracting me from the reason I'd stormed out of the bar in the first place.

I jabbed him in the chest with the photo. "I hate you right now."

DeAndre got a goofy grin on his face as he poked me. "I'm smilin'."

Against my anger, I loosened up and laughed at his silly side. He was infuriating.

"Come on, Cree, you can handle a strip club. It'll be fun."

My idea of fun did not involve nude women. "How will we get in?" A hookah bar was one thing, but a strip club?

"Chris has connects."

This was something I just did not want to do. "Do they . . . show *every*thing?"

DeAndre smiled and I cringed. "Tremaine wishes. Just breasts, you can handle it, trust me."

His words made me look down at my own chest. "Seeing my breasts is one thing, but these are other people's."

"Come on, Cree, it's no big deal." DeAndre did something cute and pouted. "Please, for me?"

I hated the way it softened my unease.

"Just fuck already." Snickering caused DeAndre and me to tear away from each other and look over at Tremaine as he stood with Chris.

"Nah." DeAndre backed away from me. "It's already been established. 'I can't have her.'"

I wasn't sure if he was mocking me or being sincere.

"Whatever, let's just go to the stupid strip club," I mumbled.

"Yes!" Tremaine came and handed me the money.

I started to follow Tremaine, but then I felt DeAndre catch my hand.

"Wait."

We all turned and faced him.

Perplexity masked his face for a moment, and finally he settled on Chris. "Ay, Chris." He tossed Chris his car keys. "You and Trey hit the club, Cree and I'll do something else. We'll text you when we're done."

Chris lifted a brow. "But she just said—"

"The lady doesn't want to go." DeAndre brought his attention to me, regarding me impassively. "Do you?"

"I—it's okay," I said.

He shook his head. "We'll meet you guys later."

Tremaine made a face but didn't argue as he climbed into the Escalade beside Chris. Soon the two took off, leaving me with DeAndre.

I felt shy, and grateful. "You didn't have to do that."

"Yeah, I did. You said no, and your no meant no. It's not about what I want, and I'm sorry it took me a moment to realize that." DeAndre massaged the back of his neck awkwardly. "You wanna see a movie? There's a theater down the street, we can even grab something to eat afterward if you want."

Biting my lip to contain my joy, I felt happy. Just like before at his dining room table, he was standing up for me. Looking out for me.

It was nice to know he had a sweet and considerate side.

"Yeah, let's do that," I said.

Just like before in the car, DeAndre reached out to offer comfort, hesitating and unsure what to do.

I felt bad for whoever he ended up with, because there was no telling what the girl would go through teaching DeAndre how to offer affection.

It seemed like with his father calling the shots in his life, he was only happy when he let loose and did things with his friends. If we were going to be friends, then I would make it my job to see to it that he was always genuinely happy. It was what I'd do for Troiann, and DeAndre was no different.

I looped my arm around DeAndre's and walked with him to the parking lot's exit.

"Havin' a good time?" I asked.

DeAndre nodded. "Yeah, you?"

"This is definitely a night I won't forget." I couldn't wait to tell Troiann about it. "Even if I wasn't fun enough for Inferno, I loved the hookah bar."

"I don't think you're boring, Cree. Guys like us"—he pointed in the direction his friends had taken when Chris drove off and then to himself—"don't deserve girls like you. So we just stick with what we're used to."

"I think you deserve whatever makes you happy, Dre."

"I have that."

"Do you?"

"I have my friends, my family, and basketball, what else matters?"

He didn't get it, and it pained me to think that he never would.

I didn't allow myself to think of a future for DeAndre like that, instead I dwelled on the present. "Tomorrow's the big interview, nervous?"

DeAndre stared off ahead of us. "Nah, not really."

Being corny, I elbowed him. "Don't be afraid to shout me out."

DeAndre chuckled. "Yeah, sure."

"Your other brother is going to be there too?" I knew Darnel was away at college, but this seemed like such a momentous occasion to pass up. A whole spread dedicated to the legacy that was the Parker brothers.

DeAndre stared down at the ground, silent for a moment. "Yeah."

There was a sense of complexity in his voice, and for that I clung closer to him, trying to reach him somehow. "You guys pretty close even though he's away?"

He shook his head. "He's busy with school, and other things. We play ball every once in a while, though."

I ached for him, and I pushed out every negative thought I ever held for DeAndre at that moment. "I'm sorry."

DeAndre peered at me, and seemed to be searching the depths of my soul the longer he looked. "Don't pity me, Cree. It's fine, everything's cool. He just has school and I've got my own shit, it's not that big of a deal, really. We text a lot."

The smile that came to my mouth was forced, but I wasn't sure DeAndre could tell. He wasn't as simple as I'd once thought. He wasn't some arrogant, asshole basketball player. He had his own issues, issues he didn't seem capable of acknowledging.

I kept a firm grip on him as we continued on our own adventure, determined to make good on my promise of being the friend who kept him genuinely happy.

10

DEANDRE

It was show time.

The journalist, Susan Thomas, sat across from us in our living room, occupying the chair by the grand fireplace. She was sitting with her legs crossed. They looked delicate in her pinstriped skirt, oiled to perfection and appearing smooth and toned. Her dark-brown skin complemented her beauty, that and the bun she had her hair pulled up in. She wore glasses, and they topped her look off even more.

We sat like ducks in a row on the sofa. Darnel, Devonte, and then me. Our father, dressed in an impeccable three-piece suit, sat across from Susan in the other chair, leaning back comfortably. Darnel wore a sweater, a stupid bow tie, and pressed pants. Devonte had on a designer polo and jeans, and I'd gone for a simple black tee and sweats. Aside from my father's Doc Martens, we all wore various editions of Parker sneakers on our feet.

Susan had taken a moment to just stare at all four of us, jotting down notes like we were specimens in a lab or something.

I wasn't too excited about the interview. The only benefit was my father letting us all skip our morning run.

"Let me start off by saying to the brothers that you guys are a pretty big deal with *three* back-to-back state titles at Moorehead High. Congratulations," Susan commented.

Together my brothers and I bobbed our heads, holding back smiles as we thanked her. Winning state three times had earned us our own segment on the local news even.

"Before we get into the nitty-gritty, I have a fun icebreaker, if you will." Susan smiled between my brothers and me. "Cut, bench, or start. LeBron James, Michael Jordan, or Darrel Parker?"

I cracked a grin as I exchanged looks with my brothers. That was one way to kick this off.

Devonte swung his attention from me to Darnel. "We goin' unanimous, or one by one?"

Darnel appeared thoughtful. "What you think, Dre?"

Rubbing my jaw, I shrugged. "I mean, we probably all on the same page anyway."

Devonte rubbed his palms together deviously. "A'ight, who we cuttin'?"

"Remember where you gotta sleep tonight." My father cut in from his position in his chair.

The room filled with laughter at his light joke. Really, his stats and position in NBA history couldn't be denied.

Darnel spoke first. "Gotta cut LeBron."

I winced alongside Devonte. It was tough but fair.

"Really?" Susan challenged.

Devonte shook his head and sighed. "I mean, you really can't mess with that three-peat."

Of my father's five NBA titles, three of them were won back-to-back. But . . .

"And Jordan did it *twice*," I added.

"Which means?" Susan prompted.

Devonte folded his lips, backing off. Darnel chuckled softly.

Guess I had to be the one. "Start Jordan. Bench Parker."

"But you still on the team, though," Devonte added, looking at our father. "Even the water boy get a ring."

My father laughed along with us, able to take a joke.

"See, not so bad. That was probably the hard one," Susan said as she settled back into her chair. "Now, to the good stuff. Did you all decide to play basketball on your own, or did your dad just shove a ball into your little hands and you had no choice?"

"I grew up watching my brothers play and seeing my dad teach them. It made me want to play too," I said truthfully. "He taught us how to play but we became good on our own. Or maybe it's just in our blood. I know a lot of guys who know how to play basketball but suck at playing. Our father taught us the rules and mechanics, but we make it our own when we step on the court," I concluded with pride.

"He definitely was an influence," Devonte said. "But as far as playing now, we became good at it and we like playing on our own."

"He gave us the ball and we just ran with it. It's definitely a family thing," Darnel added.

"Speaking of family," Susan began. "Let's be real, this is history in the making here, a one-of-a-kind legacy. What's it like being Darrel Parker's sons?" Susan held her hand out in a placating motion, a soft smile spreading across her face. "No pressure." Her face softened at the cheeky comment.

I snorted. Pressure? "Nah. It's just inevitable. My dad's an NBA champion—our bloodline is anointed. It was destined for us to ball and to conquer on that court. Not that it's easy, but I look forward to the challenge every game."

My father tipped his head my way, impressed with my lack of fear.

Darnel went on, adding, "There are definitely perks. You're easily popular around here and people tend to gravitate to you, but not just from relation—from the work you put in on the court too. There's a lot of attention being related to my father. Now, there's also the downside. There's a ton of pressure to be just as good as him and there are a lot of fake people who come with the notoriety. People who just wanna mooch off of our supposed 'wealth.'"

Those types of people were the worst. Our father gave us a healthy allowance when we did something substantial, but every dollar was hard earned. People looked at Devonte and me and assumed we were drowning in cash since we actually owned Piguets. If it wasn't for winning the state title back in March, proving that the remaining two Parker boys at Moorehead High still had it, we wouldn't have gotten shit but extra running from our father. We worked our asses off, and every luxury we had was earned.

"It's interesting that you say that, Darnel. You take after your father in that your position is also shooting guard. You've been the talk of the city for years, and a lot of us are curious about your take on the upcoming draft."

My father glanced at Darnel, and I could only imagine the amount of pressure on his shoulders. I wasn't too worried, though; Darnel was the strongest out of all three of us.

He leaned over, propping his elbows on his knees and looking Susan in the eye as he spoke. "I've played ball for as long as I can remember. It's always been about basketball, and it's what almost everyone wants to talk about when they meet me. Now, I'm trying to take college seriously and build toward something outside of the sport. Basketball's always come first, but right now I wanna put learning ahead of that. The NBA will always be there."

My father was not pleased. The hard look on his face made me sink into my seat, grateful that it wasn't my question.

It also pissed me off. When did Darnel get so damn soft? He was top ten in the country and rumors were constantly going around that he was going to be the number one draft pick. He was willing to throw it all away for school? Didn't he want to go pro as bad as the rest of us?

Susan perked a brow. "So no NBA?"

Darnel shrugged. "I've got all the time in the world. They want me so bad, they can wait to see where I'm at in a few years."

We all looked at my father.

"How do you feel about that, Darrel?" Susan asked.

My father observed Darnel, appearing calm. "He's coming from a position where he was the best high-school athlete as far as basketball goes, now he's in college full of guys who were the best in their respective schools. If he wants to wait a year or two to really train himself, it's better that than rushing into something he's not ready for."

Susan turned to Devonte and me. "I've seen the work you boys put in this season, and a lot of sports fans are proud to see the Parkers *all* have it. It seems like you two are just in your own world on that court, almost like you challenge each other on who can score the most points per game. I remember I saw the Arlington High game and it felt that way."

Devonte and I pounded fists, both appearing cocky at her remark.

"Some teams we just know we're gonna beat, so we go out and just do our thing," Devonte said.

"Arlington's team is pretty hit or miss, some years they have it, others they don't. We knew we had that game, so we just felt like entertainin' after a while." I almost laughed, remembering how Coach had scolded Chris for doing a little dance when he'd scored a perfect three.

The crowd was in hysterics that night. Between us Parkers scoring and Chris showboating, it was one hell of a game.

Susan bobbed her head and jotted down some notes. She then looked up, smiling big at each of us before turning to our father. "I must say, Darrel, it's amazing how handsome all of your boys are. They're like three variants of you."

My father barely acknowledged the comment as he simply nodded his head. "Sometimes it feels like I cloned myself three times."

Susan turned back to us, reassessing us shrewdly. "So no one resembles their mother?"

I was only three when my mother left, so I couldn't remember what she looked like. From the photo I'd found of myself in her lap, I knew we took her skin tone, so we had some of her, even though we had none of her.

"I'm lucky they all look like me," my father replied, giving a forced smile. "I hear I'm quite good looking."

I watched as Susan blushed and pretended to roll her eyes. She was a goner.

"What was that like, growing up without your mother?" Susan asked. "Did it affect your playing in any way?"

"We're kinda in an era where some kids only have their moms. Some of them be at the games just wildin' out on the refs and just bein' into the game. Sometimes I wonder if my mom was around if she'd be that turned up for us," Devonte admitted.

My father sat up, observing Devonte with eyes ablaze. "Discredit that, Miss Thomas."

She regarded him questioningly. "Excuse me?"

"Discredit his comment," he said, authority in his voice. "Let's ignore their mother."

"With all due respect, Darrel—"

"With all due respect, Miss Thomas, you never know *who's*

going to read this article, and I'd like for that chapter to be excluded. She left when they were five, four, and three. They grew up just fine without her and needn't have reminders of her absence."

Susan didn't back down. "No offense, *Mr. Parker*, but I'm conducting the interview, and you want the feature story. I want to have a lot of great material and write something good, please let me do my job."

She had bitten back.

Darnel was impressed, and his small smile showed it. He probably would've liked to have seen Cree nearly argue with our father on Monday. It was such a rare sight.

Susan went back to her notes. "Now I'll refute the mother question if you *all* think it's too personal and irrelevant." She looked over at us, asking for a response.

"I don't think about my mother. She was never there and my father always has been. He's our biggest supporter in basketball. He's more important than someone who just left," I said to end the whole thing.

Devonte agreed. "Facts."

Darnel shook his head. "It still would've been nice having her around or at games. But we don't have to talk about that."

Still, Susan scribbled something down, and I knew we were all wondering what.

"Now, I gotta ask, Darrel," Susan began, as she switched gears and faced my father. "Why a public school?"

My father shrugged as if it was simple. "Why not?" He pressed a hand to his chest. "*I'm* from a public school. It was important to me that I didn't separate the boys from the people—not that private schools don't hold good people, but I wanted them with their roots. Moorehead High is a good school, top of the line, their academics are something I'm proud of."

"So, you wanted them humble?" Susan pressed.

"In a way. I look at it like this, a lot of times people make it big and put their kids in these fancy schools and move into these sophisticated neighborhoods full of people who don't even look like them, don't even want 'em around—don't understand them, which isn't good for their kids in the long run socially or mentally. I'm from Akron and proud, and I wanted my boys to be proud of this city and its people. Just because I played in the NBA don't make my boys any better than a kid on this block."

Susan smiled, impressed as she wrote down another note. "That why you make your sneakers so affordable?"

My father nodded. "Absolutely. Kids look up to people in my position, they watch every game, know every stat, get teary eyed just asking for a picture, and who would I be to turn around and charge them an arm and a leg for shoes?"

He wasn't feeding her bullshit. My father actually was into giving back and not overcharging the community. He'd donated anonymous funding to Moorehead High before Darnel even touched down, ensuring there were new textbooks or whatever else was needed at the time.

Susan gushed as her smile broadened.

Gone.

"So, who in here has a girlfriend?" Susan asked a moment later, grinning as she looked at each of us.

"My boys tend to stick on track as far as basketball is concerned. They—"

"My girlfriend's my support system," Darnel spoke up, interrupting our father. "When I need to make a decision, I go to her first before anything. The best part about her is that she hates sports. It would be nice to have a fan as a girlfriend, but then again, it's nice knowing I have someone who loves me for me and doesn't expect anything out of me."

This girl didn't even like basketball? Of course he was losing it, she was pulling him down.

"Aww, what's her name?" Susan asked.

"What she look like?" Devonte asked next.

Darnel got this stupid smile on his face as he reached into his pocket and pulled out his phone and scrolled through his photos. "Her name's Ashley." He held his phone out, showing Devonte and me first. It was just a photo of some brown-skinned girl blowing him a kiss from a selfie shot. Her hair was natural, long and curly, framing her cute face.

Susan admired the photo with a smile. "She's certainly pretty." She looked over at Devonte expectantly.

"I haven't found anyone yet." *Except his two girlfriends.*

She sat up. "Oh, we've gotta fix that, I'm sure tons of girls are in line for you. What do you like?"

"Real eyebrows, real eyelashes, real baby hairs." He stopped to ponder some more. "The hair on top of their head doesn't have to be real, but those other three should be. Um, good credit is a must. Maybe one or two kids I'll accept, but no more than two. At least a GED if they dropped out, no bullet wounds—"

"Devonte." My father cut in.

Devonte grinned. "I'm just kiddin'. A good personality and actual conversation, nothing pretentious. But I'm kind of focusin' on basketball right now, so who knows what the future brings."

Susan sat blinking, no doubt questioning where the hell Devonte had come up with his list.

Darnel patted Devonte's back extra hard. "He's definitely the comedian in the family. Too funny for his own good."

She shook her head, coming out of her haze as she held her pen out, pointing at Devonte. "You're the funny one." She turned to Darnel. "You're the wise one." And she turned to me. "And you're the mysterious one. I see it now."

It was my turn. "I kinda just like to keep it solo. Besides ball, friends, and school, I don't really have time or interest to be pursuing anyone."

"Mysterious indeed." Susan scribbled down some notes.

I wasn't mysterious. I just didn't care about dating or catching feelings. Darnel had, and now he was soft and wasting his potential. It was a shame too—he could've been one of the best, and now he was going out a chump. All because of a girl. That would never be me. Never.

—

"Last question," Susan said forty-five minutes later. "And this is an interesting one, seeing how Darnel answered the draft question. Is basketball a 'now' thing or is it something you plan to take to the next level as far as career goals go? Do you have a backup plan?"

The answer was easy. "No," both Devonte and I said together.

Devonte went on, "This is in our blood. This is our passion. This is who we are. We want this, there is no room for second options. I wanna go pro and I wanna get as many titles as my dad. I want my own sneaker line. I wanna go to the Olympics, hell, I wanna be on a box of Wheaties."

I agreed with him 100 percent. "We've worked too hard to just give up and start planning another life for ourselves. We're Parkers, we were born to ball."

Darnel spoke up as the final voice to answer. "I'm actually

studying sports medicine. If I don't go pro I'd like to be involved somehow. I don't want to just put it all on basketball, because if I get hurt, I'm going to need other things."

What fucking planet was he on?

My father came over and patted Darnel's shoulder, reaching past him and touching Devonte too. "I'm raising winners, Miss Thomas. It's loser mentality to sit and think of another goal in life. I wouldn't be here if I'd thought about basketball not going well for me. These boys are going to make me proud, just you wait and see."

Susan ended the interview, citing that she'd had a nice time chatting with us and to look out for the photo shoot that was in store next. My father saw her out and my brothers instantly stood, stretching their legs after sitting down for an hour and a half.

"Dad's so about to smash," Devonte stated crudely as he went through his phone, looking for missed calls or texts.

Darnel seemed skeptical. "Nah, she has some backbone in her. I see this as a challenge."

Devonte smirked. "Let him buy her a Hermès bag and see how fast she folds."

Darnel didn't reply. He shook his head and still held with his contention.

Devonte tapped Darnel on the arm as he headed out of the room. "Ay, let me see some of Ashley's pictures."

"Hell no."

As soon as they left a call came through on my phone. It was Troiann.

"Yeah?" I answered.

"Um, why didn't I get an invite to the strip club?" she asked, no doubt standing somewhere with her hand on her hip.

"Because you were too busy with Marcus."

"You could've told me and I would've came through."

"Would you?" It was clear that my best friend was nearly whipped, was Troiann as well?

She clicked her tongue. "Hell, yeah, Marcus ain't that special."

"Sure."

"Anyway." I could hear her rolling her eyes in her tone. "I want a jacket too. I want mine in light blue, don't be stingy."

"I'll make it happen." Troiann was cool, outside of Marcus, and what was one more added member to our group?

"I also heard you and Cree didn't even go to Inferno."

"Wasn't her speed."

"I appreciate you doing that for her. Almost makes me trust you."

I chuckled. "I'm not up to no good, Troy. We're just cool, okay?"

"Mm-hmm, you better be." She hung up, leaving the unsaid threat hanging in the air.

Cree texted me next.

I dialed her number, unable to contain my laugh. She took things too personal.

Cree answered immediately. "I oughta knock you upside your head."

I leaned back into the sofa. "Which one?"

There was a pause and then she said, "Eww, we are not talking about your little friend."

Her words made me smile. It was so easy to get a rise out of her. "You're always the one to bring him up first, and there's nothing 'little' about my friend."

"Enough flirting, geez."

"Cree?"

"Yeah?"

"When I'm flirtin' with you, you'll know it. Got it?"

"Noted. Now, how was it?"

"It was okay. She was pretty cool."

"And your dad?"

The only plus was that Darnel lived in the dorms at school, but come time for summer when he moved back in, shit was going to hit the fan.

"He was okay too." I didn't want to think about my father. Darnel had blatantly rebelled the whole interview, saying and admitting to things my father wouldn't approve of. Yet he sat calm, just listening and watching Darnel, and that made it worse. I could only imagine what was coming now that Susan was gone.

"You okay? You sound kinda sad or something."

"I'm fine. What's work been like?"

"Oh my gosh, today we got to fry tortilla chips, Dre!" She sounded excited about the task. Usually she complained about work and her co-workers.

"Yeah? Bring me some."

"I can't, as soon as I get off I'm going home to shower and then Tremaine and I are going to hang out."

I wondered if my best friend was trying to get Cree. Tremaine had been hanging around Cree more often since we'd made good. Cree wasn't his usual type, but who knew how things would play out.

"So you just texted me to see how the interview went?"

"Yeah, I'm on my lunch break and I was just curious."

"I bet you're sittin' there eatin' some junk food, too, huh?" In the background I heard the crumbling of wrappers and her swearing under her breath. "Your dentist must hate you, Cree."

"Whatever, I indulge a little, sue me," she said. "But I am off on Tuesday, do you wanna get together and work some more on our paper?"

"Yeah, we can do that."

"Great, and Dre?"

"Yeah?"

"In the fall, am I going to have to come out and support you guys at your games now that we're friends?"

"That would be the *friendly* thing to do."

"If you guys want me there, I'll come and support."

"I'd support your dancing if you ever had a show." And she did have a show.

"Really?"

"You're good, Cree."

"I'm okay."

I rolled my eyes. "You got some weak-ass thinkin' goin' on over there. You're the shit and you gotta get that in your head."

She giggled. "Gee, thanks for the motivation. I gotta get back to work. Tell your dad I said I hope you score more *home runs* next season."

I couldn't fight my smile as I hung up.

Darnel stepped back into the room, Devonte behind him, talking about something Darnel clearly didn't care about.

He looked at me, noticing my phone in hand. "You tell the boys about the interview?"

I shrugged. "Nah, that was just Cree."

"Cree?" he repeated.

"She's just this girl DeAndre's been hanging around," Devonte cut in.

"The one you told Dad about?" Darnel asked.

"She was over here on Monday, and I bet Dad wasn't too happy about that," Devonte went on.

Darnel scowled. "So what." Devonte fell back and slumped on the couch next to me, going through his phone quietly. Darnel turned to me. "It's good to see you stepping up. I bet she's nice."

He was getting the wrong idea. Cree was just Cree.

"What's she like?" Darnel asked me.

"She's into dancin'. She real cool and simple. Plus, we can argue over the dumbest shit. She's just different."

"Different?"

"She don't look at me and get all starstruck or caught up on my last name. She could walk away tomorrow and not bat an eye at the thought of me. She just is. Besides, I think she has something goin' with Tremaine. They've been hangin' out, and I think they'd be good for each other." Cree could teach Tremaine some things and he could definitely teach her some things. "I've got my eye on Ari Young."

"That girl with the attitude?"

"Her attitude ain't that bad."

"Nah, that girl is stuck up, and she ain't even all that," Devonte said as he stood from the couch. "You can't be actin' like that when you work at McDonald's."

"You're just mad she wouldn't give you any," I shot back.

Devonte waved me off and left the room, leaving Darnel

standing before me just watching. I thought to cross my fingers in the hope that he wasn't about to lecture me, but I knew it would be to no avail.

I sighed, resting my head against the soft cushion and eyeing my oldest brother. "What, 'Nel?"

He frowned. "Please, please, don't be like him. He's miserable and alone and he's trying to make us just like him."

I was sick of him talking shit against our father. "You done?"

"No, I gotta be honest, Dre, one day you're going to fall in love, and it will be the death of you." Darnel shook his head. "Dad didn't teach us how to feel and love, and when you meet that one girl you fall in love with, you're going to lose your shit and not know what to do. I can only advise you not to fuck it up by letting her go."

I wasn't in the mood to talk about soft things such as "love."

"Whatever you say, Darnel."

He stared at me for the longest time.

"What?" I demanded, letting irritation leak out in my voice.

"I just think you deserve fair warning, that's all."

"Noted. One day I'll settle down, you happy?"

"No."

Of course not. He wanted me to swear I'd give the girl my nuts in exchange for our relationship. Like he had done with Ashley.

"And why not?"

"Because you're not going to know how to love her back, and that's what scares me. Question, what's your favorite thing to hear from a girl?" Darnel prompted, lifting his chin at me.

"It's yours." I loved hearing those two words, even if I didn't want it long term.

"Okay, say you meet a dope-ass girl, she's just perfect for you. She makes you happy and vice versa, and she tells you it's yours, Dre. That she's in love with you, and she'll do anything to make you happy, that she doesn't care whether you go pro or keep playing ball or not, and that her heart is yours. What would you say back to that?"

I hated this line of conversation. I hated how thought provoking it was and how it required me to sit and be all in my feelings. Even more I hated the one-worded answer that made me feel weak for realizing its strength.

Because there was only one thing to say to such a girl if she existed and told me those words.

Stay.

11

CREE

Just before lunch Monday afternoon Troiann caught me in the hall at my locker. She had a clever but nervous smile on her face.

I eyed her cautiously. "What?"

"I've got a confession to make. I've been messing around with Marcus Hamilton." She said his last name like there was some other Marcus who would come to mind at the admission.

DeAndre had beaten her to the punch, but I played along for the effect anyway. "Marcus 'The Dog' Hamilton?"

Troiann rolled her eyes. "I'm just hooking up with him, Cree. I don't even let that boy cuddle with me. But I do wanna make it up to you. I feel bad for leaving you in the dark about it."

"You want to make it up to me?"

"I've set you up on a date this weekend."

I couldn't have heard her right. She hadn't just said she was setting me up on a date with a complete stranger. No, my best friend wasn't stupid.

Seeing my reaction, Troiann went on. "Oh come on. It's about time you get out there and try."

"But I—"

Troiann went on, touching my hair and spouting off about her plans for the date. "Friday you'll go home and shower, figure out your hair, paint your nails—and ooh, I'll get you the outfit."

Touching a strand of my hair, I took a step back. Usually I wore my natural 4C hair down on my shoulders or sometimes up in a puff. I straightened my hair sometimes, but when I knew I would only sweat it out at the studio or stuff it in a hairnet at work, I would just leave it as it was.

Looking down at my jeans and sweatshirt, I wondered what was so bad about my choice of clothing.

"What's wrong with how I am?" I dared to ask.

Troiann waved me off. "Nothin', girl, it's just fun to get all dressed up for a night sometimes. That's all."

Despite being all things apprehensive, a tiny part of me was curious. Maybe—

I lurched forward. *Hard.* Someone had walked into me, too forceful for it to be a mistake.

Whirling around, I saw Armani and a couple of her girls walking by.

Troiann spotted her, too, and took off before I could stop her. She wasted no time catching Armani by the arm and cornering her in front of a locker. "Um, excuse you."

Armani snatched her arm back. "What? Your friend should watch where she's standin'."

I really hated Armani Young.

Thankfully, Troiann did too. "Uh-uh, see, you not about to play with her like that."

Armani laughed, looking at her friends as if Troiann was a joke. "Or what?"

Surprise peppered Troiann's face briefly before a mean smile washed across it. She pointed a finger in Armani's face, about to say something foul, I could already tell by the look in her eye and the balled fist at her side. Troiann was a loose cannon when pissed, and for that I attempted to grab her.

I held my best friend back as much as I could. "Stop it, Troy. I got this."

"That's right, hide behind your friend!" Armani shouted over to Troiann, trying to stir up some more drama.

Shoving Troiann out of the way before it could get worse, I replaced her in front of Armani. "Just stop it, Armani. You don't like us, and we don't like you. Stay in your lane and we'll stay in ours."

Armani snorted, eyeing me from head to toe. "And what lane is that, Cree?"

I almost, *almost*, felt tempted to sic Troiann on her, or better yet, handle her myself. But girls like Armani weren't worth the negative energy.

"Let's be real. This shit ain't cute," I said.

"Is that right? It's crazy how almost every boy in school would say otherwise, includin' the Baller you followin' around like a lost puppy."

A Baller? "Who?"

"DeAndre Parker."

I frowned. "It's not like that."

Armani rolled her eyes, walking past me. "Got that right."

I should've gone after her, but I was frozen in my confusion. I hung out with all the Ballers, more with Tremaine than DeAndre. Did people think I was following DeAndre around like a puppy?

Troiann stood beside me, reaching up and removing her earrings, prepared to throw down.

"Troy." I reached out and grabbed her arm.

"I just wanna talk to her. Her, me, and the ground."

The fact that she was serious made me laugh and calm down. Armani was nothing to get upset over. I wouldn't let her win by getting on my last good nerve.

Instead, I led my best friend down to the cafeteria where we gathered our lunches. It was too cold outside, so we found a seat with the Ballers in the far corner of the lunchroom where all the other athletes seemed to migrate.

The Ballers were by themselves at a long table, leaving enough space for Troiann and me to sit on either side of Tremaine.

"Okay, Troy, tell me more about this date you're forcing on me." I gave in as we sat at the table.

"Well, he's cute, really sweet, I met him at the library, and he's just looking to find the right girl," Troiann replied.

How was I to know if I could trust her judgment; she was messing with Marcus after all.

The Ballers stopped their line of conversation and poked in on ours.

"Cree's got a date?" Tremaine sat up and looked over at me and then at Troiann.

Troy appeared proud of herself. "Yes, I found a nice guy who's perfect for her."

Tremaine frowned. "We should've gotten a say."

"Um, what?" Now he was acting like my older brother or something.

"We know dudes, and we can tell who's tryna play you," Chris cut in.

Not only had the Ballers become my friends, they had turned into four variations of my father.

Troiann waved him off. "I know what type of guys my best friend likes. I wouldn't set her up with just anybody."

Chris wasn't deterred. "What type of guys you like, Cree?"

They all turned to me like a spotlight. "Uh, honest, smart, hardworking—follows the rules?" I said uncomfortably.

Tremaine laughed, as did the other Ballers, except for DeAndre, who didn't seem to be paying us any attention.

Tremaine reached out and patted my shoulder. "You know what your problem is?"

"What?"

"You've got a bad taste in dudes, which explains why you was never feelin' me."

I focused on my lunch, poking at the school's version of macaroni. "I just want a good guy, Trey."

"And you can get you one, you just gotta be a little more fun and open. Live a little, Cree, try new things."

I loved my father because he was all those things I listed that I wanted in a guy, and even if in the beginning I didn't like him with Loraine, I admired the way he treated her as an equal rather than falling into some archaic gender role.

Thanks to my father, I wanted a boy who would see me as his equal. A boy who would consider my feelings and opinions before making decisions for the both of us. A boy who was respectable and wouldn't pressure me to be anything that I wasn't. A boy who accepted me for me. A boy who didn't deem the idea of love as something to avoid because of our age or place in life.

I felt like laughing. I wanted a boy who didn't exist.

DeAndre hadn't uttered a thing. I looked his way to find him texting on his phone.

"Don't you have any input?" I wanted to know.

He shrugged indifferently. "I'm cool on relationships, but I feel like at the end of the day, just be honest. Don't commit to anyone you're not really tryin' to be exclusive with, and let them know. I'm not tryin' to date a girl, cheat on her, disrespect her, and then potentially have her doin' wild shit to my car or clothing. It's not worth it."

DeAndre went back to texting on his phone and I again felt confused. He was such an enigma. The king of the Ballers on the surface, and yet the more I got to know him, the less like them he seemed. They were all smart, but DeAndre seemed to have it more together. He hadn't ever "exclusively" dated anyone from my knowledge. There was no trail of broken hearts in his wake.

Tremaine tapped my arm. "Yo, if the date goes well maybe ol' dude can come see you in the talent show."

Talent show? "I'm not in the talent show."

The boys and Troiann all appeared confused.

"I saw your name on the list by the guidance counselor's office." Chris spoke up.

"I didn't—" I stopped, looking at the only person who hadn't said a thing. DeAndre didn't even have the nerve to appear apologetic. "What did you do?"

"If I'm going to sit through that boring shit with a bunch of basic people showing their 'talent,' I might as sit through it and see you saved for last. You can win if you do some dance routine."

Wasn't it *my* decision to decide if I wanted to go to the damn show in the first place, let alone be *in* the show?

"You'll be fine, Cree," DeAndre went on.

My fist was shaking, and I had half a mind to knock the nonchalant expression off of his face. "You can't just go doing shit like that, Dre!"

He rolled his eyes and went back to his phone. "Scared?"

And now he was challenging me?

"Dre says you're a good dancer, but we haven't seen a thing," Tremaine said, gesturing to the rest of the Ballers.

It was just dancing, something I enjoyed. Plus, DeAndre had a point; it was either the talent show or being stuck in class.

Still, I wanted to kill the asshole for signing me up without even speaking to me. I knew he'd done it from a good place, and that was the only reason I calmed down as I faced him.

"Fine, I'm going to give you my trust on this. It's yours."

At those words DeAndre's eyes darted up from his phone, his pupils tripling in size. He peered at me quizzically. "What?"

"My trust," I repeated. "It's yours. I trust you with this talent show thing because I know you did it from a good place."

DeAndre stared at me longer before shaking his head. "You're weird, Cree."

Tremaine tugged on my arm. "You should do it because you'll be better than the rest of these guys singing terribly."

"You know you can outdo half of these people," Troiann added.

Having my friends' support, I shrugged. "Fine."

Lunch ended and I was about to stand and head for my next class when I felt a hand rest on my thigh.

DeAndre held his hand up, signaling for me to wait while the others left.

"Yeah?" I asked.

He waited until Chris walked off with Marcus before he spoke. "Nervous about your date?"

I looked down at my floral print sneakers. "Is it that obvious?"

"Just be yourself, Cree. If anything goes wrong, call me."

"Seriously?"

He held his hand out, nodding. "Definitely."

I shook his hand. "Okay." Not knowing what else to say, I added, "Thanks."

DeAndre jabbed my shoulder. "You'll be okay, you're cute, you've got talent, and you're a nice girl. Like I said, you're too good for guys like us, don't let what they say get to you."

His words caused me to stop walking. "But 'cute' isn't the same as 'bad.'"

DeAndre stopped too. "No, it's not."

"But 'bad' is what boys like."

DeAndre didn't respond right away, knowing his attempt to make me feel better had just failed. The longer he took to find something to say the more hurt I felt.

"I gotta get to class. I'm sure Troy's already there waiting for me and planning my date. I'll see you."

I didn't wait for him to respond or catch up. I tugged on my messenger bag strap and headed for class, feeling completely plain, basic, and, worst of all, undesirable.

✎

Troiann had it all set. Friday night, I went over to her father's condo. She figured if we got ready at her father's, or, *Mr. Jackson's* place we could hide my date from my father, and if it didn't work out, the boy would have no clue where I really lived.

I sat in a robe at Troy's vanity while she set out makeup along the tabletop, preparing to fix me up. "Your eyebrows aren't bad, but it's been two weeks, time for a touch-up." Troiann arched my eyebrows first before applying lashes and doing my mascara and eyeliner. She then stood back and stared at my hair.

We only had so long before my date showed up. My twist out from a few days ago was still holding up and presentable otherwise.

The top I was wearing underneath my robe made me feel very bare. Hair down it was.

"Just leave it down, Troy. Just in case he keeps sneaking peeks at my boobs all night."

My father would've grounded me into the next century for

attempting to leave the house wearing a bustier top. As soon as I'd developed breasts my father had barred me from wearing tank tops. Now at seventeen and with a C-cup, my father was still quick to tell me to put a T-shirt on.

The studded black bustier with spaghetti straps definitely called attention to my breasts and exposed navel. The long pale-pink maxi skirt at least hid the curves of my legs and butt.

Troiann conceded and went about styling my hair to her liking.

"He's not a total dork, is he?" I wanted to know.

"Of course not. He's no Baller, and that's all that matters. Elija's in college, though."

A college boy? "Really?"

"A freshman, but yeah."

"Oh wow. Do you think I've got what it takes?" I had never had a real boyfriend or a serious suitor. The guys who hit on me were usually old and drunks traveling from the liquor store in Henry's. Or assholes who catcalled to me on the street.

"Uh, duh, Cree."

"But I'm not *bad*." Oh, how I'd grown to hate that word.

Troiann took a step back. "My best friend is not basic. And tonight you are going to be the baddest bitch in town. Believe that."

Mr. Jackson poked his head in the door, eyeing Troiann as she lined my lips with lip gloss. He shook his head. "You girls have so much to learn. You should want nothing to do with a boy who sees you as a 'bitch.'"

Troiann scowled and ran her fingers through my hair, a little too hard, showing her anger. "We don't need your advice, Howard."

Mr. Jackson shook his head and vacated the room.

She huffed, tossing the tube of lip gloss on the desk so hard it bounced and rolled onto the floor.

She made no attempt to pick it up.

"So, you and Marcus, huh?" I said, to change the subject.

Troiann rolled her eyes and backed away, going and sitting on her bed. "It's not like that, Cree. We just hook up."

"So it's just sex?"

"He wears a condom and I'm on the pill. It's nothing. I know better." Troiann stood and came over to me and undid my robe, urging me to stand up and model myself for her. "Though DeAndre doesn't seem so bad if I was looking for something real."

My best friend was beautiful. Gorgeous. A "baddie," if I was being on the Ballers' level. DeAndre and Troiann would make sense, but I got the feeling it wasn't that simple with Marcus.

"Really, you and Dre?"

Troiann smirked. "You know how it is, Cree. They can sleep with both of us and get praised, but on our end it's like we're nothing but hoes. Besides, Marcus would probably cry or something."

"Anh would probably like you and Marcus."

"Oh, you know my mom would love that boy, with his muscles and good looks."

The thought made me sad suddenly. "Yeah."

Troiann stopped fussing over my outfit and paused, examining me. "What?"

"Nothing."

She wasn't fooled. "No, what?"

"I wish that my mom was here to talk about boys and dating and how relationships should be. I'm just now letting Loraine in, but . . . forget it."

Troiann frowned. "You can have my mom too."

My eyes watered. "But it's not the same."

"Don't cry. Do not ruin your makeup." Troiann tried to joke as she waved her hands in my eyes. "Hey, what's the first thing I told you when we became best friends?"

I couldn't fight my smile. "That your mom had two daughters, Troiann Ciara and Cree Michelle."

"Right, we're sisters, Cree. My mom is your mom and your dad is my dad, and we also have Howard."

My best friend was the best.

Mr. Jackson poked his head in the room. "A boy's out here waiting for Cree."

Butterflies blossomed and fluttered in my belly.

Here we go.

Together Troiann and I walked out to the living room, where a boy stood with a flower. He was tall, a couple of shades lighter than me, and staring right at me.

"People say he looks like J. Cole." Troiann leaned over and whispered in my ear.

He did not. But that was okay, because he was still handsome.

"You must be Cree. I'm Elija." He came over and shook my hand with a nice, firm grip. "It's a pleasure to meet you."

Elija peered into my eyes, making me feel small and unable to hold eye contact for too long. The tone of his voice and the way he was looking at me let me know he meant business. Everything he said was to the point and serious.

"You won't have her out too late, will you?" Mr. Jackson asked, exposing those muscled arms of his as he crossed them.

Elija wasn't intimidated. "No, sir. Ten at the latest."

I hoped we were going dancing. It was such a carefree activity, and no pressure like the clichéd dinner and movie.

As soon as Elija and I stepped outside into the late April air, regret at letting Troiann dress me in such a light and revealing top flooded me.

At his car, Elija opened the door for me and then closed it as I buckled up. He got in beside me and my nerves increased a notch.

It wasn't just because it was my first date; it was his whole vibe too. I knew he was older, but everything just felt odd.

"So you're almost done with school, are you excited?" he asked as he began driving.

"Yeah, a little, but it's not really over. I mean, there's college."

"What are you going for?"

That was a good question. "Secretly, I wanna do dancing, but my dad won't have it. I guess I'm undecided."

"He has a point," Elija responded. "I mean, you have to be a bit realistic in this day and age."

Ouch.

"Right. Dancing is a reach that's too far out of my grasp." *According to everyone else*, I thought bitterly.

"You should spend your senior year looking at a lot of schools and seeing their different programs. Maybe join a few organizations. I work with the NAACP and I campaigned for the president. That's good stuff to have on file, Cree. My older brothers never did that—they have no degrees and are both working jobs they don't really care for."

I smoothed my hand down my arm as I inched toward my door, doing my best not to frown. "I'd still like to study what I love."

Elija smirked a little, playing it off with a smile and bob of his head. "Of course."

He was being dismissive.

This time I did frown.

Elija pulled up to a quiet little restaurant downtown I'd only heard adults talk about. House of Solé was one of the few Black-owned businesses downtown, and was highly praised in newspapers and magazines all across the state. The family-owned restaurant went back for many generations, and it was the spot to go to get some good soul food and listen to old-school music.

We were seated across from each other at a table in a quiet corner. Elija stared at me as I concentrated on the menu. Whatever I decided on, 7 Up cake had to be for dessert.

"So," he began. "This is nice. I'm glad Troiann hooked us up. You're a beautiful girl, Cree."

Did beautiful beat bad?

With my eyes glued to my menu still, I blushed and said, "Thank you."

"Look me in the eyes when you thank me."

The tone and the authority in Elija's voice made my heart jump like I was a child getting in trouble. He sat waiting and watching me across the table. An eerie chill ran down my spine as I peered into his hard eyes. "Thank you."

Satisfied, he moved on. "Troiann tells me this is your first date."

Why had she mentioned that? "It is."

"I doubt I'm the first person who's ever been interested in you before."

"I don't know, I guess it's because I never really want to date any of the guys who usually approach me," I said.

Elija's brows furrowed and he sat back. "Why?"

"What do you mean?"

"Why would someone want to be alone?"

"It's not about wanting to be alone. It's just about not feeling those guys who approached me."

"You never know until you give them a chance."

"I'm pretty positive the right guy doesn't approach you with a 'Hey, ma.'" That was the ultimate turnoff. My name wasn't "ma" or "ay" or even worse "baby girl."

"Some people just don't know any better. I hope you can give me a chance. I'm pretty sure this can all work out."

He looked sure as well. Something about his optimism turned me off.

"Let's hope so," was all I could say in return.

Again, he looked so assured. "I *know* so. I feel from your vibe that we can take each other to the next level."

Did he really just say that . . . on the first *date?*

"Wow. Levels, huh?"

"Yes, maybe I can teach you some things and you can teach me a few things."

"What if I don't want to be taught and just want to ride out this wave as time goes on?"

Elija shook his head. "You gotta open your mind. I'm not like those other guys. I have a good paying job, I help the community, I'm getting a good education—trust me, I know what I'm talking about."

"And you think together we can go to the top?"

"I think I can help you be where you need to be, and you can help me."

And he got all this from my vibe? I could've sworn I was coming off nervous and shy, not in need of assistance.

"With me, Cree, you can just be yourself. You don't have to make yourself out to be anything you're not. You don't have to dress that way or wear makeup. You don't need it."

His words ticked me off. I *liked* wearing makeup every once in a while. I liked spicing it up sometimes and wearing cuter clothes than what I wore on the usual.

"I like how I look right now," I said.

Again, Elija shook his head. "We're gonna work on you."

And there it was. Elija wanted a project, not a girlfriend.

Rage boiled inside of me, and I almost bit my tongue off to

keep from cussing his ass out. Because he had to be fucking kidding me.

I blinked, composing myself as best as I could. "Excuse me, I have to go powder my nose or whatever." I made sure to smile nice and act friendly before standing up. Elija stood as well, tipping his head at me. But it only served to make me feel like he was giving me permission.

Hell no.

Thank god our table was in the back corner and Elija's back was to the front of the restaurant. Instead of the women's restroom, I headed straight out the door and down the block, pulling my phone out of my pocket and calling Troiann.

"Please, god, pick up," I prayed into the phone as I kept walking, waiting for Troiann to answer. It was rude to abandon my date, but dude was coming on way too strong and way too assertive for me.

It went straight to voice mail, twice.

"Shit." I hit End and tried Tremaine, but of course his phone did the same.

I stopped walking and leaned against a brick building. I didn't want to call Loraine, and I couldn't call my father. The only person left for me to call was the last person I wanted to see, ever since that whole "bad" mishap after lunch.

Tilting my head back, I stared at the sky. "Why do you hate me?"

DeAndre answered on the second ring. "What's up?"

"Can you come and get me?" I pitied myself for sounding pathetic.

"What's wrong?" I could hear him sitting up in the background and something on TV going mute.

"I can't do this date, Dre. I need a ride, but if you're busy I can just—"

"Nah, where you at?" The jiggling of keys could be heard next. He was coming to save me. Thank god.

Wanting to put enough distance between me and that creep, I went and waited at the university fountain a few blocks away. I sat scrolling through my phone, anything to distract me from what had just occurred.

A sleek black car pulled up a few yards away, and soon DeAndre was getting out and coming over to me.

I stood up from the fountain and kept my distance as DeAndre stood in front of me. He didn't look amused by my failed date or annoyed that I'd called him. He looked sympathetic.

He spoke first. "Hi."

"Hi."

"I know you don't want to see me."

"I don't."

"And I know you need space."

"I do."

"But I'm glad when you needed someone you called me."

I kept my focus down at the ground. "Troiann didn't answer and Tremaine was MIA."

"I was with Marcus before he left to hang with Troiann, and Tremaine's with Chris."

"Okay."

DeAndre took a step closer and looked around. "Where is he?"

"At House of Solé, probably just figuring out I ditched him."

"Do I need to . . . ?" He let the threat hang in the air.

I blinked. "No, no, he was just . . . no."

DeAndre came closer and stood in front of me. "You look nice, Cree."

I started to walk past him. "Sure."

He grabbed my arm, forcing me back. "I mean it."

The look in his eyes let me know he wasn't bullshitting me. It annoyed me when I thought of what had happened between us earlier in the cafeteria at school.

I waved him off. "Don't try to be a nice guy now, Dre."

"I didn't say I was a nice guy. I said we'd be friends, and that's why I'm here. When Tremaine fucks up with me, I can't stand his ass, but I know if he needs me or vice versa, I'll be there. You needed me tonight, and here I am. What I said at school—"

"It's whatever." I shook my head. "Cute girls like me only get weirdos and egomaniacs to ask them out. 'Bad bitches' like Armani Young get the good guys. That's just how it is. Good guys are too busy trying to save the baddie, and the bad guys aren't any good. I can deal."

"Cree—"

"Is it so much to ask to want to feel special?"

DeAndre frowned. "You *are* special."

I snorted. "Yeah, right."

Now DeAndre looked annoyed. "Don't compare yourself to Ari Young, Cree."

"I'm not, because I don't compare." She was a bitch, but a pretty one.

DeAndre rolled his eyes. "You're a great girl, you're smart, you're pretty, you're talented, you're not afraid to stand up for yourself. If any guy doesn't see that, then *he's* the problem, not you."

Against my angst, my heart throbbed deep in my chest. Why did those words make this night better?

"Yeah?" I asked softly.

DeAndre bobbed his head. "Hell, yeah. Those are the qualities I want in a girl. When I'm ready."

I calmed down. "You think about that?"

"Sometimes, yeah."

"And you plan on being good to her?"

"I'm used to seeing guys all around me cheating and all this drama, and I don't wanna hurt anyone when I make the official step. Getting into a relationship is going to be big for me. I'm a boy now, but when I connect with that right person, I aim to be a man and respect her."

DeAndre was an enigma. It was entirely frustrating.

I punched his arm. "Do not keep doing that."

DeAndre took a step back. "Doing what?"

"That mysterious thing. One minute you're this dick and the next you're showing you may actually have it together."

He cracked a grin. "I'm not so simple, Cree."

I looked down and kicked at some stray trash. No, he wasn't.

"You okay?" DeAndre asked gently.

It wasn't the end of the world. "Yeah, I'll survive."

He gave me a crooked smile. "Friends?"

As much as he could annoy me, I felt okay with him enough to agree. "Friends."

Then he shook his head and clarified. "*Best* friends."

"'Best friends,' huh?" I questioned, taking a step back.

DeAndre bobbed his head, appearing serious. "Friends is casual, and ain't nothin' casual about you, Cree. You solid and real. We gotta be best friends."

My insides were turning to mush, and I couldn't stop smiling and blushing.

DeAndre opened his arms, and just when I thought he was about to hug me, he reached out and patted my arms in an awkward attempt to show affection.

It was all messed up.

I shook my head and led the way to his car, and together we got in.

We weren't on the road long before DeAndre glanced at me, concern peppering his face. "You cold? How long were you out there? I could turn on the heated seats."

A smile touched my face at his gesture. "No, thanks. Heated seats always make me feel like I peed my pants," I admitted, and laughed at myself for voicing *that* confession.

DeAndre chuckled beside me huskily. "Heard you."

"So tell me, what happened at the restaurant?" DeAndre asked.

I sat back and rolled my eyes. "He was too much, you know? He told me that together we could take each other to the next level. That he could enhance me and vice versa."

DeAndre snorted, slapping the steering wheel as he drove. "My dude was a supreme hope dealer, sellin' dreams by the ounce."

I laughed. "I don't think he's ever sold a dream in his life."

Elija was a huge red flag.

"And then he got on me about my wanting to take dance in college and how I dressed and wore makeup."

"Dude sounds lame as hell. I don't care if a girl wears makeup or none, has a weave or real hair, that doesn't equate to her personality."

That was nice to hear. "Exactly. When I'm at home I just wanna wear sweatshirts because my dad makes me feel ashamed about my body. When I get around Troy, I can breathe a little easier, and then that asshole says I'm dressed all wrong."

DeAndre glanced at me. "I like your body, it's nice. But whether I do or anyone else does, you have to be comfortable with it. If you want to wear formfitting clothes, do it. Don't let anyone stop you from seeing yourself, Cree."

I felt a smile break across my face. "Thanks." At least DeAndre wasn't psycho like Elija had been. "Plus he told me how he's 'not like those other guys.' And how he had a 'good' paying job and was getting a 'good' education."

"Frontin' 101: never brag about your money. You might as well take your dick out and show how small it is."

"You've never bragged about your money?"

"I'm Darrel Parker's son, it's kinda assumed. I'm not into braggin', I'd rather show you than tell you. And FYI, if a guy has to tell you he's not like those other guys, chances are he's exactly like them."

"Oh, is that true, Mr. 'I'm a Real Dude'?"

DeAndre lightened up and smiled. "You got jokes."

"I'll get past this. Never let your friends set you up on a date, *ever*."

"My boys know better than to pull the shit Troy pulled with you."

His words piqued my curiosity. "Why are you so against dating?"

"I'm not. The way I see it, I'm seventeen years old, and right now my focus should be on maintaining my grades, training for basketball season, and keeping my eyes on the prize. We're young, we do not have to date seriously right now."

"When you put it that way, it makes sense. But how could you speak about love in class when you clearly haven't ever dated."

"Love isn't just something you feel for a significant other. I love my father, I love my brothers, I love my friends, and I love basketball. That love is an entity—it's more than my showing them and vice versa."

No, DeAndre wasn't so simple at all.

A familiar song came on the radio and just as I was going to reach down to turn it up DeAndre beat me to the punch. He had one hand on the wheel as he leaned back, snapping his fingers on the other and bobbing his head.

"This shit never gets old." He turned to me, seeing if I agreed.

"I'd Rather Be with You" by Bootsy Collins never got old. Of course, none of the classics I heard growing up ever did.

"Hell, yeah," I agreed, digging the iconic tune. "You weren't busy when I called, were you?"

"Nah. I was watching *Barbershop*."

"I haven't seen that in ages."

"You wanna come through? Or do you have to go home?"

"I could fangirl over Michael Ealy and Eve." I quickly agreed.

DeAndre changed the direction he'd been driving, going for his house instead. "I oughta stop and get something. I could kill for a sandwich right now."

"You got some turkey at your house?"

"I think so."

"I'll make us a sandwich, I'm starving too."

He laughed. "Damn, Cree, you should've at least eaten first before dippin' out."

I should've.

DeAndre pulled into his driveway ten minutes later and killed the engine. He faced me and jabbed my arm. "You'll be all right. You just need a good dude who's gonna treat you right."

"And you need a freak for the sheets who knows when to leave in the morning."

"Damn, you right." DeAndre held his hand out and we high-fived, sharing a laugh.

We got out of the car and I followed DeAndre to the front door. He let us in, and up ahead of us Devonte passed by on his way to the staircase, stopping and noticing my presence. He looked at DeAndre and grinned. "I told you not to listen to Darnel, Dre."

DeAndre sighed. "I'm not."

Devonte's eyes shifted to me. "'Sup, Cree?"

I waved. "Hey, Devonte."

He angled his head, blatantly checking me out. "I see things were blossoming underneath those heavy sweatshirts of yours. Not bad."

"'Te!" DeAndre snapped at him in my defense.

Devonte shrugged and jogged up the dual staircase, disappearing onto the second floor.

We weren't in the door a full minute before my phone went off. With a look down I saw that it was Troiann calling me back.

"I'll be in the kitchen," DeAndre told me as he left me alone for privacy.

I sat down on the bottom step of the staircase and answered the call. "Hey."

"Hey, what's up?" Troiann sounded worried. "Marcus took me to get my nails done and I just seen you called."

My best friend's boyfriend was sweet. "Things didn't work out with Elija. I bailed and DeAndre got me."

"What?" Shock lit Troy's voice and I found myself nodding even though she couldn't see me.

"That guy was an asshole, Troy. Where did you find him?"

Troiann sighed over on her end. "He was so sweet when I met him at the library. Tell me he ain't try anything. One word and Howard will—"

"Relax," I cut in. "I skipped out on the date and Dre came and got me. *Never* again, Troy."

We promised to link in the morning to go over the full, gory details, and I hung up and went and found DeAndre in his kitchen. He waved a hand at their expansive pantry and large fridge.

I gathered the ingredients for turkey sandwiches and assembled them at the kitchen island. My mind drifted back to the date. Maybe I had agreed to the date just to taste what everyone else was experiencing. I once heard a girl say being a virgin past sixteen was just lame and unacceptable, let alone graduating as one. But I was fine with my virginity, and okay with my single status, so maybe DeAndre was right.

"You're cool, Cree. The right one will get you without forcing it." DeAndre sat on top of the counter farther down from me, observing. "Basically, don't rush it."

"You're right."

He tapped his temple. "Love is not just a verb, it's more, remember that."

I couldn't help but laugh. Now he was educating me about love?

I finished making the sandwiches, turning and just studying DeAndre until he caught on.

"What?" he asked.

"You don't know how to love romantically, do you?"

He looked down at his shoes, shaking his head. "No."

This poor boy. "Maybe you just need to be taught."

"Maybe someday I'll meet someone who will teach me." DeAndre agreed. "But until then, I know I love basketball."

I handed him his sandwich on a plate. "Word of advice, I hope you know the chances of finding real, true love, when you're in the NBA are slim."

"Then I'll aim for college."

"Yeah?"

"Someday, Cree."

"She's going to have to be really patient," I joked.

He squinted, opening his arms as if to gesture to himself. "Yo, what are you sayin'?"

I headed past him to the rec room. "Oh, nothing, let's eat."

12

DEANDRE

Darnel wasn't picking up. It had been two weeks since we'd last spoken or seen each other. I blamed Ashley. I blamed college. I blamed everything that was getting in the way of him speaking to us. It was unlike him to turn his back on his family. He always came home or at least called.

I sat at Chris's house up in his bedroom, waiting to get in contact with Darnel, but so far, it was a no go.

I wanted to leave a voice mail calling 'Nel out on his shit, but he suddenly picked up. "What do you need, Dre?"

No *Hello, how are you?*

I pushed past his irritated tone and answered. "You've been MIA."

"I've been busy. Do you need anything?"

Yeah, my brother. "Too busy for us?"

"I've got a lot on my mind right now." Darnel paused before adding, "I just need some space."

"Space?"

"I just need time away from the family. There's a lot on my

mind and I don't need any bias distractions, plus with finals coming up I just need all the space I can get."

I had the biggest feeling Ashley wasn't getting space. But I didn't bring it up.

"So we're a distraction?"

"I'm not saying that—look, I gotta go. I'ma call in a week or two, okay?"

I didn't respond, my hand was too busy shaking. Was he abandoning us? He wouldn't do that. He couldn't do that.

"It's going to be okay. I love you, Dre."

"Yeah." I hung up and set my phone aside.

Fuck him.

Chris came back into the room carrying two bottles of water. He handed me one before retreating to his bed and scooting back until he was sitting against the wall.

We were supposed to play basketball, but I had to pick Cree up from the dance studio and I didn't want to do it all sweaty.

"I need a favor," Chris blurted, rousing me from my thoughts of Darnel fucking up.

"What?"

"Your dad's going to take Devonte to Miami after graduation, you going?"

I shook my head. They were going for a week and it was tradition for it to be one-on-one.

"My dad's going to chew my ass about geography, and I know he's going to be bitchin' for the first week of summer about it . . ."

He was stalling. "What, Chris?"

"I can't use my house, so I was wonderin' if could throw a party at your crib. A big blowout to celebrate the end of the year and the fact that we're now seniors."

As amped up as I felt, I didn't even think before agreeing.

"Fuck it, let's do it. Just don't play no more of that rock shit you be listenin' to."

"I know what to play. The new Playboi Carti album is dope."

I rose to my feet. "No."

"Carti is—"

"Overrated," I finished. "Nobody wants to party listenin' to a dude be demonic or the other weird shit he be on."

Chris clicked his tongue. "Stop it."

We would be here all day if he wanted to go there. I went for the door. "Pick a better artist."

"We're playin' Carti, Dre!" Chris called to me as I left his room. *Note to self: keep AirPods on me.*

"I'm takin' a Gatorade from your fridge for Cree," I shouted back up the staircase. "And you better play only the hits." I grabbed the hydrating drink from his fridge before getting in my car. But before I could start it up, I saw a call coming through from my father.

With my phone paired to my car, I answered and backed out of the driveway. "What's up?"

"I just got home from a meeting. Devonte's tutoring some girl at the library and I was wondering where you were," said my father.

Devonte had ditched his two girlfriends and had been on the prowl ever since. I prayed for his sake this girl he was tutoring wasn't next on his list, because sooner or later the shit he got into would catch up to him.

"I was at Chris's house."

"Oh, you two shoot around?"

"We were supposed to, but I have to go and pick up Cree."

The tension was there even if I wasn't in the same room with my father. I knew he was shaking his head in distaste at the mention of Cree.

"You need to hurry up and handle that and get back on track so you'll be ready for the scouts next season," my father urged.

"I'm not interested in her," I said as I tightened my grasp on the wheel.

"Good, I've already got one boy out here acting stupid, I don't need two."

He had that right. Darnel had lost his damn mind and needed someone to set him straight.

"Not happening, Dad."

"So you're studying?"

"We're meetin' up to finalize our paper for class. Is that okay?" I tried to keep the irritation from my tone, but his constant questioning about Cree was getting annoying.

It was then that I decided not to bring Cree over to my house. While part of me viewed the idea of the two of them debating as humorous, I wasn't in the mood for him to chastise me or walk around, conveniently taking interest in our paper and spying on Cree.

"Your tone, Dre."

"You're diggin', trying to see if I like her or something, and I said I didn't. How much clearer do I have to make myself before you get it?"

"I don't want you losing sight of what's important."

"I've been playing basketball for as long as I can remember. I wouldn't let anything get in the way of that. You should know that by now."

"That's what I like to hear. You better work hard, I want all A's on your report card." He hung up with a joke. We both knew I'd be bringing home a few B's as well, but nothing lower.

I pulled into the studio's parking lot and got out of the car and went over to the entrance. It was four thirty and Cree should've been done preparing her routine for the talent show. Not that many people had signed up for it, which gave Cree more time for her set, which she was thrilled about.

She wouldn't let me see her dance or let me know what she had planned. She wanted me to wait and see with the rest of the school. It was her way of getting back at me for setting her up in the first place. With the talent show a week away, I had a strong feeling Cree was going to kill it.

Cree met me in the lobby with her gym bag on her shoulder, dressed in a tank top and yoga pants, ready to go.

"Hey." I held out the Gatorade for her.

She accepted the sports drink and smiled up at me. "Thanks."

I led the way out to my car. "How's it going?"

"I think I just about nailed it down," Cree replied. We were walking side by side but she stopped and turned to study me. "Something wrong?"

"No. Why?"

"You seem irritated. Is everything okay?"

Not with Darnel. Not at my house. No. But I wasn't about to get into all that. "Everything's fine."

Still, she looked skeptical. "You sure?"

"Yes, Cree."

She shook her head and reached out, taking and holding my hand. "I'm here if you need to talk, okay?"

I dropped her hand and went to the driver's side. "Noted."

Cree rolled her eyes and joined me in the car. "After this I'm taking a good break from dancing."

"So, it's going well?" I asked.

"Yeah, I've made my mix and my routine is pretty solid so far. My aunt loves it."

"Okay, I've just been hearin' things out in these streets about you bein' nervous."

"*These streets?* DeAndre, you live in an affluent suburb."

"Whatever, you better kill it."

"I'm sure I will. I heard Ellis Thornberry is singing, and you know she can blow."

I nodded. "You got that right."

Cree elbowed me and laughed.

I pulled into her driveway behind her father's or Loraine's car and parked.

Cree looked at her house and frowned. "Here?"

"My place is gettin' played. We gotta switch it up." I wasn't in the mood for my dad to chastise me anymore today.

Cree made a face and got out of the car, obviously not loving the new plan. I wondered if it had anything to do with the fact that maybe her father was home. According to her, they had been close before Loraine, but barely did anything one-on-one anymore. She said it wasn't intentional on her father's part, but it bothered her—that and the fact that he wasn't supportive of her dancing.

Mr. Jacobs met us at the door. He took one look at me and faced Cree, an eyebrow raised in curiosity.

I held my hand out to shake his. "Hello, Mr. Jacobs."

He shook my hand but said nothing, still eyeing Cree.

Cree reached out and patted her father's chest. "Oh, Daddy, knock it off. DeAndre and I are just going up to my room to practice making grandbabies for you."

He took in a sharp breath through his nose. He didn't like her sense of humor.

Mr. Jacobs had nothing to worry about. When Cree was around my eyes never lingered below her neck, if he was watching.

He stepped out of the way and allowed us into the house. "You dancin' too much, girl. You losin' weight."

Cree grimaced and said nothing as she led me to the staircase.

I got the feeling she was relieved when he didn't follow us. Her letting out a breath confirmed it.

I tapped her arm. "You okay?"

She shrugged like it didn't bother her, but I knew she was lying. I had a father who could be as much at times, and for that I didn't push her.

"You invite him to the talent show?"

"The talent show you forced on me?" She countered with a raised brow.

I chuckled. "Yeah, that one. The one you're goin' to dominate."

For just a moment Cree's shoulders sagged and she bit her lip. "I didn't invite him . . . *yet*. I want to master my routine first, get more confident before I ask him. It would mean a lot if he sees me at my best and really likes it."

From the little I'd seen, Cree was a phenomenal dancer. I couldn't imagine her father thinking otherwise. "I'm sure he'll love it," I told her, to ease her anxiety.

Her room was the paradigm of innocence. The color scheme of the room was pink and white. Along one wall she had built-in cupboards and a wardrobe. The panels of the cupboards were pink while the borders were white. Her pink and white bedding sent warning signs through me. Everything about Cree's room screamed *soft* and *nice*. In a corner was a toy chest with CREE on it, its panels also pink with white borders.

When she'd been in my room for the first time she'd explored, and I did the same thing as I moved over to her toy chest to see what she had inside.

She had an old baby doll that was Black, just like the rest of her Barbies and Bratz dolls. I wasn't surprised. When I was younger and would go to my grandmomma's house to play with my cousins, she and my aunts would only buy my girl cousins Black dolls, stating that if their White friends didn't have Black dolls, why should they have had White dolls?

There were a few kid's books in her chest, one called *Me and My Period: The Girl's Guide to Learning About Her Body.*

I frowned as I held up the book. "Eww."

Cree clicked her tongue. "'Eww'? There's nothing 'eww' about what's natural."

"Natural or not, I'd rather die than bleed from my dick every month."

Judging by the way her lip curled up, I'd obviously offended her. "If you can't handle what happens naturally to the female body, you oughta get with a boy then."

I shrugged and sat at her desk. "Maybe."

Cree scowled and sat on her canopy bed. She grabbed her backpack and sat cross-legged as she dug through it for her notebook.

I set my laptop on her desk and opened the document I was typing our assignment on. It was pretty much finished; we just had to go over it for a few disagreements we had on each other's takes.

Cree had proven me right about my decision to bury the hatchet and write a paper together. Her opinions and writing style were amazing. She may not have been super popular at school, but she was passionate about our people and culture. And when Mr. Donatelli read our paper he would see it.

"Ownership is something I love seeing in our culture and community," Cree was saying as she sat across the room from me on her bed. "For so long Black people owned *nothing*. A rapper or singer would come out with a clothing line, perfume, cosmetics line, or a full 'empire,' but in reality they only got a small percentage from it. We were nothing but a sticker corporations used to make money."

There were a lot of rappers who did interviews talking about publishing and how the record labels owned all of their work. Now people were flipping the script and pushing for change.

"We may not all be billionaires, but I love seeing more of us owning things," Cree said. "I mean, look at your dad, he's a staple in the NBA, and he's built malls for god's sake."

My father owned a mall, a barber shop, and a sneaker store in Cleveland, and a few other businesses in major cities like L.A. and New York. He hadn't lusted for diamonds and gold chains in his early days, but for equity.

Cree raised her pen to illustrate another point. "I also love that we're getting more creatives in film and TV. I grew up watching *Roots*, *Boyz n the Hood*, and I don't mind watching those old movies now, but there was a point where year after year we were getting constant slave, butler, maid, or race-based movies. It drove me mad.

"I love seeing people break that mold because we need more normalized and healthy Black films. Films where we're the star, the spies, doctors, scientists, lawyers—we can do more than act out another history lesson or perpetuate stereotype filled with trauma. *Black Panther* was the shit."

I chuckled and typed up her point. There were a lot of sports or music movies regarding Black people; seeing different topics was always a plus.

Cree sat on her bed bringing up points we had missed and I typed them in and changed things around as I looked at our work from top to bottom. When I felt like we were done and made a mention of emailing her a copy, I dreaded what came next.

"I think we're done," Cree said.

Not yet. "There's just one more thing I wanna talk about."

"What?"

"Your view on interracial dating." Her stance on this nagged at me, and I felt the need to discuss it more before turning the paper in on Monday. I looked over and caught her appearing surprised.

"Oh?"

"What you say about Black men dating out of their race may read some type of way, Cree. I get your point, but I don't think you should feel that way."

I could tell she was about to go on the defensive. Whenever Cree felt a certain way or was frustrated, her brows would knit together in a frown and she'd either have a hurt or a determined look in her eyes. But she would never back down, no matter what the challenge. It was that zeal alone that made me respect her no matter if I agreed with her views or not.

At the moment the look in Cree's eyes was one of irritation.

"But it's how I feel about our culture."

"And I think you should be a little open minded about it."

Cree bit her lip and looked away, breathing hard through her nose, causing her nostrils to flare.

"So I'm not supposed to talk about how I feel about the disrespect Black women get from Black men when they choose other women over us?"

"I'm not saying you can't say how you feel, but I'm saying you shouldn't say you dislike *all* couples of that variety. I understand what you mean, but I don't agree with all of it. You do know that we don't *have* to date Black women, right? I could have an apple tree in my backyard, but I can still eat other fruit."

Cree huffed, throwing her hands in the air. "Okay? I'm not saying a thing against *genuine* love. I just feel increasingly that Black women are alone."

"Why do you think that?" I wanted to know.

"The most disrespected person in America *is* the Black woman, and no one is defending her. When something goes wrong and a

Black man is wrongfully imprisoned or murdered, we all band together and support him, but when it's a Black woman, who's standing up for her? We're the ones who bring you into this world, we hold you down, we listen to you complain about injustice, we let you rest your heads on our chests, we're your support, and when we get hate hurled at us, who has our backs? Nobody. A lot of Black men are quick to bash Black women just as much as the rest of them these days."

I almost wished we could present our paper in front of the class. Hearing Cree's grievance made me glad I'd reached out to work with her. She brought so much perspective to the argument. It was easy being a male in America, but being a *Black* female was ten times harder.

"I have to straighten my hair, be super educated, speak eloquently, dress properly, and good is not enough. These mediocre White girls who are famous for nothing get all the accolades, but as a Black girl I have to fight for even one. People can say we're all human, but that's bullshit, this is America, the land of hate, not equality. You know there are little Black girls who won't play with a Black doll because they don't think she's pretty or important?" Cree shook her head. "So you can't tell me I'm wrong for feeling the way I do. When you go online and watch interviews of your favorite female singers or actresses and you see people in the comments saying she's ghetto trash, ugly, or that her hair's a certain way and they could never date a Black woman, then you can get back to me on how I feel. The internet—"

"The internet's irrelevant." I got what she was saying, but she shouldn't let the people online get to her. They were cowards who wouldn't say the same thing in the light of day.

"No, it's not. The internet is the real world, it's where people take off their masks and say what's really on their mind. In person they can smile to your face, but in their mind they see you and me as just another 'dumb nigga' or something. And when it's Black men who see Black women this way, it hurts." Cree hung her head and continued, "I like Black guys, DeAndre, I can't help it, not that I want to either. Now how am I supposed to feel when more and more they would rather date some White girl or a girl who's exotic because I'm 'not pretty enough'? It's like the world's a pageant stage and we come in last every time."

She fiddled with the bracelet on her wrist. "I just want to be beautiful. I just want a Black boy to look at me and see beauty and not all those awful things out there. I want to feel important and to be told that I matter. And romance aside, I just wish we loved each other more, valued each other, fought for each other, and really meant it."

Her voice broke and her eyes started to water. This was deeper for Cree. She was truly scarred from all the hate she'd seen against Black girls. Fuck. She was my best friend, or else I wouldn't have found myself doing something I wouldn't do for anyone. I stood from her desk and went and kneeled before her. Looking up at Cree from this angle, I could see the unshed tears in her eyes.

I licked my lips, finding the words that I needed to say. "You're beautiful, Cree. You matter way more than those sellouts who judge you based on bullshit. Your beauty is more than skin deep. I'm not impressed with aesthetics or any of that other vapid shit out there. You have more to you than just looks, and that's why I wanted to be friends. I think your mind's the most beautiful thing about you. You are smart, talented, kind, passionate, and worthy. You are not a stereotype and they are wrong."

Cree wore her hair long, thick, and natural, or what some people deemed "nappy." It hung just past her shoulders. Some days she'd wear it up in a bun, others she'd wear it secured behind a headband or in a ponytail. Her brown skin tone mixed with her prominent Black features made her all that she was. Cute. Pretty. Cree Jacobs.

Cree sniffled at my words. "You're not just saying that because of what happened before?"

She was talking about when I'd said she was cute and she felt as though *bad* was better and beyond the compliment. "Nah, word is bond, I mean it."

Cree bit down on her lip and looked away as she wiped at her eyes. "Thank you, Dre," she said in a soft voice that let me know I had touched her.

"No matter what, I represent your father wherever I go. If tomorrow I get desperate and go rob a liquor store, people are gon' look at your father different. It doesn't matter if he's a good guy or not. One of us does something fucked up and we all get shit for it. Is that fair?"

Cree shook her head dejectedly. "No."

"I feel your pain on these guys out here dogging Black girls as a whole, but it's not fair to judge those guys who genuinely fall for White girls, Asian girls, or whoever." I tapped her calf to gain her attention. "Hey, I get it, as a Black girl you're dealt a bad hand in the world sometimes. But you can't fight hate with hate. You're a queen, Cree, and no matter what these wack dudes are out here sayin' about girls your color, it doesn't make you any less. Shine your crown and stunt on them, you're far too talented to let them shrink you."

Slowly the corner of her mouth curled up. "You're good at this."

"Good at what?"

"Empathy. You're learning, Dre."

"What good is a friendship if we're not learning from each other? We good, Cree?"

"Yeah, we're great."

"So tomorrow if I go out and try to wife Emily Gardner you're not going to stop fuckin' with me, are you?"

Cree narrowed her eyes. "Now you're pushing it."

I stood and shoved her. "Come on, what's your answer?"

Cree rolled her eyes, offering a tight-lipped smile. "It's Christian Wednesday, so I can't say no. I always try to be one with the Lord on Wednesday."

Her smart mouth never got old. "Cool, come on. Let's go watch *Save the Last Dance* just for the occasion."

Cree scowled and pushed me away. "For the record, that wasn't my point. My best friend's mom is Vietnamese and her dad is Black. I love Anh and Howard to death, and wish they'd fix their issues. I'm not against interracial, DeAndre, I just think it should be cosmic and not based on fetishes and wack-ass 'preferences' because you have unhealed self-hate."

There was no hatred there, and I could understand that point versus being completely against it. "Fair enough." Thinking deeper, I decided to throw her a bone. "My dad wants to read our paper too."

Cree turned from her TV and faced me. "Yeah?"

"And he'll probably kill me for this, but I was thinking, how about for the paper we discuss the pressure for a Black boy to grow up to become a rapper or an athlete? How come parents aren't encouraging their sons to become librarians, nurses, or teachers?"

Cree smiled. "I like that, and I'm sure Poppa Parker will too."

My father would have my neck if he thought I was speaking out against going pro. But for Cree, I was willing to take the heat over the argument.

13

CREE

Troiann was acting funny. It was fifth period Monday morning and she sat with posture and attitude as Mr. Ventura droned on about the themes in the assigned reading.

She hadn't said anything all morning, and from the way DeAndre and Tremaine kept looking at her I knew something was up.

While Mr. Ventura rambled on about something I didn't care to hear, I gathered my phone in my lap and texted Troy.

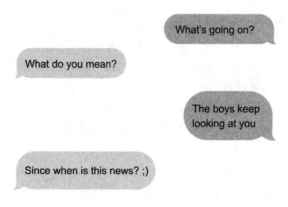

What's going on?

What do you mean?

The boys keep looking at you

Since when is this news? ;)

Troy

I ended things with Marcus

The bell rang somewhere in the background. What?

Troiann gathered her things and I had to rush to gather mine to catch up.

I met her in the hall, huffing for breath.

"What happened?" I wanted to know.

"Nothing." Troiann watched as DeAndre and Tremaine walked by, looking at her with judging eyes, at least on Tremaine's part. Tremaine whispered something to DeAndre and DeAndre simply shook his head.

"Then what's going on?"

"Nothing, Cree. I was just done with Marcus, that's all. The rest of the Ballers are just acting like a bunch of babies." Troiann led the way to the lunchroom with a sway in her hips. "We're not sitting with them anymore, by the way."

"Why not? They're our friends."

Troiann snorted. "Yeah, right. They're nothing but a bunch of assholes. We were never friends."

"That's not true. They look out for us."

Troiann stopped as we made it to the cafeteria entrance. The scent of tacos wafted around us.

"*Friends?* DeAndre blackmailed me into convincing you to go to After Hours that night. He knew I was messing with Marcus and held it against me."

She said it to hurt me. To turn me against DeAndre and the boys. But what had hurt more was that DeAndre had told me first to prove that he was genuinely trying to be my friend.

Blinking, I took a step back. "You're only saying that to turn me against them. DeAndre already told me everything."

Troiann appeared impassive. "So is that your decision?"

"My decision? Troy, we can still sit with them."

Troiann rolled her eyes and headed into the cafeteria. "Fine, be that way. When something bad goes down and you need someone, we'll see who's there for you."

"Just like you were there for me with Elija?" I shot back as we got in line.

Troiann faced me, ignoring our small audience. "Grow up, Cree."

"He came off controlling and aggressive!"

"Wow, one bad date and you act like you can't go on another one."

I took a step back and squinted at the person standing in front of me. It wasn't the Troiann I knew. "What's wrong with you?"

She stepped closer. "You're what's wrong with me. You're supposed to be *my* best friend but no, you're standing here defending them. I ended it with Marcus thinking maybe we could all still be cool, but the first thing I see this morning is Tremaine looking at me some type of way. Why? Because he's a Baller and they stick together. I bet if it was Marcus who ditched me Tremaine wouldn't see a problem and would be eyeing me like he was next in line. They look out for each other, and I thought we had the same thing. They're judging me, and you don't even have my back!"

I was at a loss for words as she turned her back on me.

I wasn't hungry, and I wasn't in the mood to sit with the Ballers either. Troiann's words had sunk in deep and I couldn't shake them off. Instead, I found myself alone at a table, sulking.

Troiann went and sat with a couple of football players, eyeing me before shrugging and smiling at Brandon Karter. Brandon was big, buff, and the total package when it came to looks. He wasn't a Baller, but by the way he got girls, he could give them a run for their money.

Troiann was very social and people gravitated to her. She was more worldly than I was, and seemingly the only person besides DeAndre who kinda got me. Next to DeAndre, Troiann was the only one with the patience to see things my way and still try to set me straight. It seemed like Tremaine was becoming like that, but with the way he was looking at Troy, I wondered if we were through too.

A chair screeching against the floor pulled me out of my thoughts and I saw DeAndre taking a seat across from me.

He set a pack of Reese's and a bag of my favorite Rap Snacks on the table and slid them my way as some sort of peace offering.

I couldn't help but smile since he was always picking on me about my sweet tooth.

"Thank you," I mumbled, as I slid the candy into my purse.

"What's wrong, Cree?"

I shook my head. "Nothing."

"Nothing?" He cocked a brow. "Nothing involves you sitting over here and Troy over there?" He nodded in Troiann's direction. She really was hitting it off with Brandon, who seemed to be enjoying her company as well.

Across the cafeteria Marcus had his gaze locked between Troiann and Brandon. If looks could kill, Brandon would be annihilated.

"We had a fight," I confessed.

DeAndre nodded. "That's what most friends end up doing at some point."

"She says you guys aren't really our friends. She threw the After Hours incident in my face."

"I told you all that."

"Yes, because you're really trying to be my friend."

"Your *best* friend," he corrected.

I didn't want to smile when I was upset with Troiann, but dang it, if DeAndre didn't have impeccable timing. "Stop it, I wanna be mad right now."

"What for?"

"I'm fighting with Troiann."

DeAndre rolled his eyes. "Friday is the big day and I'ma need you to be mentally focused. Cut the shit."

Anxiety bloomed in my gut at the mention of the talent show. In the beginning, when it was sprung on me, I had no idea what I'd perform. But as time went on and things at home were, well, *things at home*, I found my theme. I found my message and my voice, and part of me was terrified to actually go through with it. I shivered involuntarily at the thought of asking my father to attend. I would do it, though; I had to.

"Why do you care so much?" I dared to ask as I got back to DeAndre.

He shrugged. "I'm being a best friend. Besides, it's practice. Next winter I expect the same treatment when it comes to basketball if I'm ever stressed."

"You guys won the state title this year."

"I had Devonte, and it's gonna be even more pressure to do it again next year on my own. Being a Parker's tough shit during basketball season."

I could only imagine how hard Mr. Parker rode him every winter.

"I'll be here for you, I promise."

He nodded as he stood. He passed by me, squeezing my shoulder and saying, "Get to the right table, Cree."

DeAndre headed over to Troiann, no doubt to smooth things over with her like the mediator he was.

My mood wasn't completely restored, but I felt good enough to go grab lunch and join the Ballers' table. I took my place beside Tremaine and started with my Reese's.

Tremaine nudged me with a friendly smile, but I looked elsewhere. Troiann was my best friend, and it wasn't right that he was treating her funny because of Marcus.

Troiann came over to the table escorted by Brandon. Together they were laughing about something, causing tension to set in quickly.

Brandon set Troiann's tray down and handed over her backpack before going back to his own table.

Troiann took her seat and immediately looked my way. Her upper lip curled up and she made a face, but soon she rolled her eyes and smiled.

I smiled too. We were too close to let anything really get in the way of our friendship.

"Oh, Cree, before I forget. Howard wants me to spend the night today, can you please come over with me?" Troiann asked.

"She can't." DeAndre spoke up for me. "We're doing something."

We were?

He gave me a look as if to challenge him.

Troiann rolled her eyes. "She's never going to let you hit, Dre."

"Never say never, Troy."

"By the way," I cut in, looking at the both of them, "I'm right here." I turned to DeAndre. "And she's right, you couldn't. You could *ask* me before making plans too."

DeAndre conceded. "Can we hang out later?"

"Brandon's one of the sorriest dudes on the team," Marcus muttered, causing everyone to stop what they were doing.

We all knew it was a lie. Brandon often got compliments on his playing skills. In fact, he, Marcus, and Tremaine were the top three football players at our school.

Troiann went on as if Marcus hadn't even spoken. "I think Brandon's perfect. He's cute, probably the best on the team, and he's tall, dark, and handsome. I just hope he's packing or else I'ma be really disappointed."

I had the grace not to let my mouth fall open in shock. I couldn't believe Troiann had said that. Apparently, neither could the rest of the Ballers. All eyes were on Troiann as she obliviously focused on her tray.

"Shit, I forgot my milk. Be right back." Troiann stood, ignoring the glare Marcus was shooting her.

Marcus sat watching Troiann walking to the line, burning a hole in her back. The aggravation on his face and the fact that his leg was bouncing had me worried what was about to happen.

Five seconds went by before he shot up from the table and went after her. We all turned and watched as Marcus grabbed Troiann by her arm and led her from the cafeteria.

Tremaine whistled. "They about to fuck."

"Do you think this means they're together?" I asked.

Chris gave a lazy shrug. "They need to be after all that."

"He likes her, he's just letting his ego get in the way," DeAndre said. "I gotta hand it to Troy. I never saw her pulling the plug."

Five minutes went by, and soon ten, and then fifteen. By the time lunch was over there was no sign of either Troiann or Marcus. It was safe to assume that they'd ditched together.

⁓

Loraine was out getting takeout when I got home and discovered my father alone in the den.

"Where have you been?" my father asked from behind his paper.

"I was with DeAndre. We hung out after school." I had been over at DeAndre's house watching a couple of movies and avoiding Troiann. He said I should give Troiann space so she could spend some time with Marcus to hash things out. I was glued to my phone, but there hadn't been a call all afternoon.

"He seems nice and respectable," my father said matter-of-factly, sneaking a peek from behind his paper to smile at me. With DeAndre's tattoos and status, I was surprised my father wasn't deeming him unfit to be my friend.

"Yeah." I tugged on the bracelets on my wrist. A bubble of anxiety swelled in my chest and I swallowed a few times, getting the courage to speak. "So Friday is the talent show, you coming?"

I waited with bated breath for his response. If he said no, then it would all be for nothing. I bit my lip, mentally crossing my fingers he'd come and see me.

My father let out a frustrated breath. "What time?"

I managed a calm breath. "Just the last two periods of the day. Around one o'clock."

"All right. Lori and I will be there."

At least he was coming. "Thanks, Dad."

"Mm-hmm." He was lost in the news and so I left the room.

The talent show wasn't that big of a deal at school, but it was the first time I'd be front and center. I was a little nervous, but mostly excited. DeAndre thought I was the shit at dancing, and the more I nailed my routine during practice, the more I was starting to feel that way too.

My cell phone rang on the way up to my bedroom, and I was elated to see it was Troiann.

"Hey," I answered as I stepped into my room and went and sat on my bed. "What's up?"

Troiann sighed over on her end. "Nothing. Did I miss anything in school?"

Were we really going to beat around the bush? "No. I've got your stuff by the way."

"Thanks, you're a doll."

"Troy, where are you?"

There was a pause before she answered. "In Marcus's bed."

"*Oh.*"

She chuckled. "Don't worry. He's downstairs getting some water. Trey called him, so he'll be a minute."

"Troy—"

"Am I crazy? I told him I was done and he says he doesn't want to be done. I don't wanna fall in love, Cree. I don't want to give him all of me and get hurt like those other girls. I don't wanna end up like my mom and Howard."

Her vulnerability pulled at my heart. "Then talk to him. Either you're all in together or you're out."

"I don't think he's willing to accept being out. He wants me to be his and no one else's."

"That has to be a mutual thing."

Troiann was quiet, and after years of knowing her, I knew she was fighting back being emotional and crying.

"Troy?"

"Yeah?"

"I'm here if you need me, always, no matter what."

"Cree?"

"Yeah?"

"I'm sorry I never told you about Marcus and that I tricked you into going to After Hours."

It had been messed up, but I couldn't hate her for it. "It wasn't right, but I forgive you."

"I hated the Ballers like you, you know. It wasn't like I faked it the whole time. Things just happened."

"How'd you even meet Marcus like that to begin with?"

"I was having problems at home," Troiann admitted.

Immediately I sat up, concerned. "Where was I?"

Troy sighed on her end. "Sometimes I like to get out and deal with it on my own, Cree. No offense."

"It's okay." I'd been there too many times when her parents were fighting and she felt embarrassed and overwhelmed.

"I was at that twenty-four-hour mini-mart, Quik-N-Serve, and Marcus pulled up one night. He noticed me sitting out on their picnic table and tried to be nice," Troiann began. "I shooed him away at first. And then the next night he came back and tried again. A total week went before he decided not to walk away and sat next to me. I guess he eventually broke down my walls and here we are."

"You're my best friend," I let her know adamantly. "I wish you would've come to me."

"I know. It's just, we used to clown the people who fell for their mess, and I didn't want you to clown me."

The Ballers usually were full of crap with girls, but sometimes you couldn't really blame someone for having hope, for putting faith in others to do the right thing.

"You can't help who you fall for," I reasoned. "And I'm sorry if you thought I would judge you for this. Just be careful, okay? Your feelings mean a lot to me."

Troiann sounded like she was sniffling on her end. "Thank you. I didn't plan for this to get this far. One thing led to another and the next thing I know we're hooking up on the low. It wasn't about feelings, just a physical thing. He's only the second boy I've ever been with, and it feels way better and real than with Jalen. I get scared sometimes that it'll get deep and I'll fall for his shit."

"Don't be, just talk to him."

"Can you stay on the line, just until he gets back?"

"Yeah, whatever you want."

I lay down with my phone to my ear and listened to her breathing, being there for her for as long as she needed me to be.

14

DEANDRE

Mr. Donatelli stopped me in the hall as everyone was entering the auditorium for the talent show. My boys were grabbing front-row seats for our group.

"Yes, sir?" I asked as I stuffed my hands into my shorts's pockets. May was bringing the sunshine after several months of freezing cold and rain, and with only a few weeks of school left, summer felt like it was close.

"I just wanted to talk to you about the paper you and Miss Jacobs turned in," Mr. Donatelli said. "It was the best essay I've read in a long time. I learned a lot. I'm actually thinking of taking it with me tonight and showing a few colleagues from college."

I had thought our paper was brilliant, but not *that* brilliant. "You're showing professors?"

Mr. Donatelli shrugged. "Just a few friends, a couple of them teach at KSU. My good friend Byron teaches African Studies and I think he'd like what you and Miss Jacobs put together."

I made a mental note to rub it in later when my father was around. "I'll make sure to tell Cree the good news."

Mr. Donatelli reached out and patted my arm. "Easiest A plus

I've ever given out. You and Miss Jacobs make a great team. I only wish I could see what else you two could do when you put your heads together. Enjoy the show."

I went inside and found my spot next to Tremaine. We were in the middle row of seats sitting up front. The end seat next to me was empty as Tremaine, Marcus, Troiann, and Chris all sat down to my right.

Marcus had his arm across the back of Troiann's chair, his hand playing in her curled hair, and together they were lost in conversation. He had yet to claim her, but each time she tried to pull away there he was, pulling her back. As far as I could see, Troiann wasn't trying to change Marcus or herself, and that was what made them work so well.

I leaned over to get Troiann's attention. "Yo, Troy, we should get into something later to celebrate."

Marcus glared at me, pulling Troiann into him. "Get your own girl, Dre."

"My *own* girl? Is that your way of sayin' you have a girl?" I feigned ignorance as I asked the simple question that had the rest of the guys instigating and waiting for Marcus's response.

He faced the stage. "Enjoy the show."

The lights in the room dimmed as the seat next to me filled. Looking over, I found Ari sitting beside me, sucking on a sucker.

She watched me watch her, a cocky grin taking her lips. "Hey, DeAndre."

I lifted my eyes to hers. "'Sup?"

Ari crossed her legs, her short skirt exposing how long and toned they were. "I hear you're throwing a party in a few weeks."

"Chris is, I'm just supplying the location."

"Can I come?" she asked in a voice that held more meaning than the question really called for.

"When have you ever missed one of our parties?"

Ari smiled. "Things seem . . . different now."

"How so?"

"I heard you're seeing that one girl."

My jaw twitched uncomfortably. *"Cree?"*

Ari nodded, playing coy, as if she hadn't known Cree all that well. "Yeah, that's the one. I mean, I do see y'all together a lot."

Her mouth was better when she had the sucker in it.

"I'm with my boys a lot as well," I countered. "Cree's the homie, as is Troiann."

Ari looked past me and her upper lip curled up at the sight of Troiann. "Since when does DeAndre Parker have *girl* friends?"

I already got enough of this kind of interrogation from my father. "Since I do whatever the fuck I want."

If it was too harsh she didn't let it register on her face. "Anyway, I'm hopin' this party is gonna be lit."

"Chris is throwin' it, expect the unexpected. We might see some barn animals and shit."

Ari laughed. "He is a wild boy. Do you like to get wild, Dre?"

"Occasionally."

There was a twinkle in Ari's eye as she placed the sucker back in her mouth. From the row behind, Ari's friend tapped her shoulder and whispered something in her ear, and they began to carry on a conversation.

A nudge from my right drew my attention to Tremaine.

"Careful, Dre." He looked over at Ari and back at me.

"Jealous?"

He smirked. "Just sayin'."

The talent show had begun, but I didn't give a shit about the kid up on stage singing "Weak."

The show went on for another hour, and it was just as basic as we all would've guessed. When Nelson Edmonds poured baby oil on himself and danced to Jacquees I looked elsewhere, finding Troiann dancing along in her seat—clearly enjoying the show—until Marcus pushed her, knocking off her groove.

"What?" Troiann laughed as she fanned herself. "Shit, that's gon' be tough to beat."

"Cree hasn't gone yet." Tremaine spoke up. "And I'm hopin' they saved the best for last."

They had.

The curtains closed for a few moments, and when they opened Cree was sitting on a chair in the center of the stage. Two girls I recognized from a few classes, Kianna and Ariel, were dressed as ballerinas with their hair and makeup done, sitting off to the side of the stage pointing and whispering at Cree. We were all surprised to see Coach Booker taking part in the performance, standing to one side of the stage with his arms crossed. Cree had straightened her hair and had it up in a bun and was wearing baggy pants and a black top that exposed her belly button.

From the speakers in the room, a man could be heard asking what someone's aspiration in life was, and soon I recognized Beyoncé's voice as she answered that it was to be happy.

The music began to play and Cree stood up from the chair and pushed it to the side. She stood in the middle of the stage, allowing her body to become one with the music and find the melody. She went to leap but fell, and Kianna and Ariel laughed and mocked her.

Cree sat on the stage pretending to cry as Coach Booker stood off to the side shaking his head. She got up and tried the move again and fell once more as Beyoncé sang about how it hurt to be pretty. No matter how hard Cree tried she couldn't stick the move, and the girls continued to tease her and Coach Booker kept on shaking his head and scowling at the girls. Kianna and Ariel then gathered their things and gawked at an upset Cree as they walked past on their way off the stage.

Beyoncé faded away and was replaced by a piano instrumental that led to vocals that I didn't recognize. Whispers from behind me told me it was some Britney Spears song. Her lyrics somehow seemed to flow with Beyoncé's as she sang about not being a girl and not yet a woman.

On stage Cree and Coach Booker mimed an argument, both seeming more and more upset. As he tried to reach for her, she fought against his hold. Cree pushed him away as she went back to the center of the stage. This time, as she went into her routine, she successfully landed each move. She moved fluidly with Britney and I could hear the crowd's applause as she danced smoothly without messing up. She was just as graceful and angelic as she'd been the first time I'd ever seen her dance, and hearing the rest of the school applaud and agree made me proud.

Britney faded away and a new song came on as Cree stopped dancing and pointed to Coach Booker, demanding he leave the stage. He made an angry face, to which Cree cocked her head to the side and challenged him back.

Coach exited the stage and joined Kianna and Ariel standing against the wall on the far right side of the auditorium.

Cree was back in the center of the stage. She reached up and removed the bun and let her hair fall past her shoulders as she wiggled her hips to the song. It was old school. Janet Jackson's "Control" was playing as Cree went from ballet to something modern and sexy. She played with her hair, shook her hips, and imitated the moves of classic Janet. And then she grabbed a chair. All eyes were on Cree as she ground her hips into the chair, turned it around, and straddled it, repeating the motion and making it look sensual.

"I think I might want that," Tremaine leaned over and whispered to me.

I leaned forward in my seat, just to get a better view of the show before me. Beyond the sex appeal and even the dancing, I could see the story she'd written to go along with her skit.

Mr. Jacobs had to notice—he had to see her anguish over failing, her determination to make it, and her triumph as she succeeded at doing the one thing she truly loved: dancing.

I watched as Cree finished dancing and the whole auditorium stood up and clapped for her. She had the biggest smile on her face and I couldn't help but smile as well, knowing exactly how it felt to do something you were good at and to kill it.

No one was surprised when Cree was handed the cheap-looking trophy and sash from the judges. When the show was over we all bolted to find her.

Troiann hugged her tight, smiling just as big as the woman of the hour was. "Oh my gosh, girl, you did it! I for sure thought Nelson was taking it home, but you showed him."

Marcus rolled his eyes. "Nelson was wack."

Cree and Troiann shared a look, both agreeing on something we couldn't decipher from their faces.

I reached out and patted Cree's arms. "Nice job, you did that."

Tremaine shoved me. "What the hell was that, Dre?" He pulled Cree into a bear hug, picking her up and making her laugh. "*This* is how you congratulate her."

"Trey! I'm all sweaty, put me down," she demanded.

Her long hair was matted to her neck, and her exposed stomach and small amount of cleavage held a warm glow from all the perspiration. Disheveled or not, she looked good showcasing her exertion and hard work.

Tremaine set her down. "Nah, I like it. Damn, you were sexy. Took me by surprise."

Cree flashed Tremaine a smile and patted his chest. "That's the point, right?"

Knowing Tremaine, he was about to say something inappropriate just as her father came over with Loraine.

Cree smiled over at her father, who only stood studying her. "Did you like it, Daddy?"

We all looked his way. He had to have liked it; she'd done it for him.

"We'll talk about it at home, you ready?" Mr. Jacobs avoided the question altogether as he stepped to the side to make room for Cree to walk by.

Cree's joy burst instantaneously as her shoulders sagged. She glanced between our group and me before leading her father and Loraine out of the auditorium.

Troiann sighed, shaking her head. "I swear, one of these days he's gonna fully push her away." She looked over at Marcus. "Come on, let's get out of here."

Marcus nodded over to Tremaine, Chris, and me. "I'll catch y'all later."

Chris gathered his car keys from his pocket. "I gotta go too. I've got this little study sesh set up."

"I can't believe he didn't even congratulate her," I said as I thought of the way Mr. Jacobs barely lit up at Cree when he'd come over.

"I'd be mad, too, if my daughter was shakin' her ass like that on stage," Tremaine pointed out.

"It wasn't even like that."

Tremaine's phone chirped and he held it up and smiled. "Gotta go, fun's waitin."

Everyone was leaving the auditorium and still raving over the show and Cree's dance. To my surprise, my father was in the room and heading my way after signing a few autographs.

"Dad?" I asked, unsure what he was doing at the school.

"I was at the club with Greg and he said Mitchell's son was about to embarrass his family's name, so we decided to stop by to get a few pictures," my father explained. "I'm glad we did, that girl was quite impressive."

"Cree's amazing," I said.

My father actually nodded. "Definitely the best out of the bunch. I know people in case she's interested in doing something with that dancing."

"I'm not sure she's takin' it seriously like that."

"Why not?"

"Her dad's not really supportive."

"That was him who escorted her out of here?" My father shook his head. "He should be proud. She could have it a lot worse."

I shrugged. "She's a dancer and I'm a baller, we only got one direction in life and that's the top."

My father patted my shoulder. "Who was the girl sitting next to you?"

He'd seen me during the show?

"Ari," I answered. "She's in some of my classes."

My father gestured toward the exit. "Be careful with that one, Dre."

I smirked, happy he couldn't see the expression on my face. "Yeah?"

"I know her type. You don't want any trouble."

Right, because all girls led to trouble in the long run.

"You said the same thing about Cree, remember?"

My father reached out and squeezed my shoulder. "Stick to the goal, boy, you don't need anything holding you back. Like you said, you've got one spot in life, and that's the top. No distractions."

15

CREE

I should've been happy. I should've been running around squealing that I'd gone through with the talent show and won. I wasn't Cree Jacobs, that girl from class. I was Cree Jacobs, the girl who could dance and put on an amazing show. That should've put the biggest smile on my face, but instead I was kind of bummed.

I couldn't even bring myself to be happy about the text DeAndre sent me telling me about how Mr. Donatelli was raving about our paper.

After the talent show my father took me out to dinner, but even if the gesture read as loving, it wasn't. It was just face-value nice. He spent the majority of the meal focusing on cutting his steak while Loraine kept going on and on with her praise.

It wasn't Loraine's praise I wanted; it was my father's. Weeks of preparing my routine just to have him barely acknowledge it and brush it aside? It hurt so much.

Needless to say, I barely ate, and when we got home I immediately went upstairs to shower and lounge around. After changing, I pulled my hair up into a bun and scrolled through social media aimlessly. It wasn't really fun, but it beat being around my father, who'd barely looked at me since the talent show.

I let out a breath as my phone rang. I picked it up.

"Hey, Troy," I answered.

"What's up? How'd Mack take it?" I could hear the fear in Troy's voice, and that only caused me to roll my eyes.

"Oh, Mack barely took it at all."

"What do you mean?"

"He's been ignoring me since we left the school. We went to dinner, or really, he accompanied Loraine and me to dinner while he mostly sat staring at his plate." I lay on my back and stared at my ceiling. "I give up, Troy."

Troiann groaned. "I swear, our daddies suck, Cree. I'm sorry he didn't like it."

Blinking back tears, I let it go. "Forget it." I was embarrassed at the sound of my own voice breaking. "At least Nelson Edmonds really liked it. He said he'd like to get together and do some dancing sometime."

Nelson Edmonds wasn't my type. He played basketball with DeAndre and Chris, and after becoming friends with the Ballers, I wasn't too sure about ever really dating one.

Troiann clicked her tongue. "Eww, nah. He's mad corny, Cree."

I couldn't breathe due to how hard she made me laugh.

"Anyway, Cree," Troy went on. "Don't even waste your time. Nelson ain't nothing but a heartbreaker. He *does* play basketball."

"Yeah, maybe next year I'll bump into someone and we'll hit it off or something."

"Next year? That's too far away. I've got a plan."

"Yeah?"

"We gotta get our hair braided soon for the summer. I'm

thinking box braids and I may even get some honey blonde, you think that'll be cute?"

"I don't know, your hair is too fine for braids that thick and wouldn't the blonde clash with your skin tone?"

Troiann sucked her teeth. "Nah, maybe I'll do a few that color and not my whole head. We just gotta get a hair braider. Since it's summer you know we get to show more skin, and more skin means more boys and—"

Her line cut off and I could only assume Marcus had crept up behind her and ended the call.

I shook my head. Those two were a trip.

My cell phone pinged and I looked at the screen to see that Tremaine had sent me a text message.

You should be out celebratin'

Then come get me and we can celebrate

Can't, I'm w/ someone

Of course

2moro tho, we can do something. Tonite, call up Dre, I think he's alone too

One pity party coming right up

With everyone busy hanging out, I only had one option left to salvage this night, and I hoped DeAndre wasn't busy with Armani Young. I didn't want to be alone, not in the same house with a father who didn't care about a performance I'd put on specifically for him.

"What's up?" DeAndre asked as he answered my call.

"Nothing, I'm bored. We should get into something," I said.

"I guess that explains the text I just got from Trey. You should be celebratin' with your family."

I picked at my sweats. "Trust me, I already did the whole awkward dinner thing. I'm cool on that."

"So what do you wanna do?"

"I'm thinking movies, ice cream for me, for you a nice turkey sandwich and cherry Coke."

"Cut diagonally?"

I laughed. "Of course, there is no other way to eat a sandwich."

"You're speaking to my heart. I'll be there in a few."

We hung up and I stood from my bed, slipping my feet into some sneakers. I grabbed my phone and headed down the stairs, hesitating about whether I should just leave versus telling my father I'd be going. I knew I'd get in trouble if I snuck out, so I sucked it up and headed over to the den, surprised to hear Loraine and my father arguing.

"I am a member of this family, I have a right to say something," Loraine said.

"Not in this case," my father replied, sounding pissed.

I rounded the corner and came into the room, finding Loraine standing with her hands on her hips and my father seated in his chair with the TV on in the background. They both looked livid, which was a first for them.

Because my father had ruined my evening, I decided not to

care as I faced Loraine. "Loraine, since you're the only one in the house speaking to me, I'm just letting you know I'm going to a friend's house to watch movies."

My father glared at me. "Cree."

I looked his way, feigning curiosity. "Is there something you wanted to say, Dad?"

Loraine crossed her arms. "Say it, Mack."

He gritted his teeth and looked as though he wanted to strangle her. He returned to me. "You were good tonight, Cree. You were truly the best in show."

His tone of voice, the lack of care on his face, his stiff posture, it all sliced me open. His words meant nothing when they were merely forced out due to Loraine.

Loraine rolled her eyes at her husband and turned back to me. "Your mother would've been proud."

That hurt even more—the reality that I would never know how my mother would've viewed my dancing compared to my father's austere approach to it. I stared down at the carpet. "Yeah, well, who knows if my mom would've even liked my dancing?"

The silence that met that remark caused me to look up. My father was visibly wincing while Loraine stared at him.

"What?" I asked.

"Mack," Loraine said.

"Loraine, no," was his reply.

"What's going on?" I wanted to know.

Loraine looked at me. "Your mother would've supported your dancing, Cree."

"Why do you say that?"

Loraine sighed. "Because your mother *was* a dancer."

It felt as if the wind had been knocked out of me. I could barely breathe, let alone speak.

"What?" It took everything to turn and question my father instead of sinking to the floor and vomiting at the reveal. "My mother was a dancer?"

Slowly my father nodded. "It's what killed her."

It . . . *killed* her.

"And you never told me?" I couldn't believe it. No, it wasn't true. He wouldn't have kept something so vital from me. Not when I had been dancing for all these years. Not when I knew nothing of my mother.

"Cree, it's been hard for me." My father tried to reason as he took a step closer.

"You told Loraine but you couldn't tell me?" I shouted. "She was *my* mother!"

I backed away and shook my head, heavy in denial at the treachery before me.

"Cree." My father reached for me but I dodged his grasp.

"You kept this from me my whole life? And then when I started to dance you hounded me day and night about my body, making me feel like shit, and it's all linked back to her? How could you do this to me? The one thing I had besides you, and you just ruined it!"

My heart was racing. I had to get away. I had to leave.

Tears clouded my vision and I tripped as I made a run for the front door, ignoring my father's pleas from behind me, but I kept going, out into the night.

My whole life I'd wanted to know about my mother, but when my father had said it was hard for him to talk about her, I kept quiet. When we barely brought up my mother's side of the family, I kept quiet. When my aunts said I looked more like my mother every day, I kept quiet. Apparently, keeping quiet was the Jacobs family trait, because not only had my father kept me in the dark my whole life, so had my aunts, especially Kathy, who worked with me to perfect my dancing. And Loraine knew before me, and that just made me cry harder.

I was a few blocks from my house before I realized my phone was ringing.

"I don't wanna talk to you," I shouted into the phone, knowing my father would try to get me back.

"Um, Cree, it's me," DeAndre responded. "I'm at your house and it looks like something's wrong. Your dad's on the porch right now. Everything okay? You did call me."

I stopped walking and wiped my face. "I left. Can you come get me?"

"What?"

"I'm at the corner of Bertha and Madison, please, DeAndre."

"I'm on my way."

I sat down on the devil's strip and buried my face in my palms and tried to calm down. It was to no avail, though, because the tears kept coming, and I knew eventually I'd really break down when it all caught up to me.

DeAndre pulled up in front of me in his Escalade. He got out and helped me up, even though I was more than capable of standing on my own.

"What's wrong, Cree?" He leaned down to look me in the eyes, reaching out and wiping away my tears.

I shook my head. "He hurt me."

"Your dad?"

I nodded.

Understanding and not asking any more questions, he led me over to the Escalade and helped me in before going around and claiming the driver's seat.

He kept quiet the whole way back to his house, and I kept trying to stop crying, but the faucet was on and the tears kept pouring out of me. My phone rang the entire time DeAndre drove but neither of us budged to answer it. I wasn't sure I ever wanted to see or speak to my father again; I was that hurt by his betrayal. It wasn't just about my mother, it was about how our relationship had suffered due to his withholding, and I wasn't sure I could ever get past that.

When we made it to DeAndre's house, he led me up to his room and shut the door behind us.

Standing in front of him, I knew he was curious as to why I was breaking down and had run away from home.

"You can tell me, if it's okay," he said.

My eyes watered as I stared down at the floor. "My mother." I breathed out. "She was a dancer, Dre, and it's what killed her."

"You never knew?"

"My dad never told me. Loraine just did." My throat swelled with the hurt and I knew the full breakdown was imminent. "He never told me."

And then it happened, I started to sob and moan and I couldn't stop. DeAndre stood before me like a helpless child, not knowing what to do and how to offer affection, and it all just made me more upset.

Then his hands were on my waist, steering me closer to him, and in a moment he was pulling me against his chest, allowing me to soak his T-shirt with my tears. He pulled me into him slowly, as if he had to think about how to touch me. His grasp was loose and unsure. It didn't feel natural at all, but I appreciated the effort.

A knock came on his door before it opened.

Devonte stepped into the room, eyeing our embrace and holding out a phone. "Uh, Darnel's on the phone."

DeAndre looked over at his brother. "Tell him to call back tomorrow, okay?"

Devonte studied me and nodded before retreating from the room and closing the door behind him.

I pulled away from DeAndre and stepped back, wiping my face. "You should get that."

He shook his head. "You need me right now."

I looked into my best friend's eyes as mine began to water once more. "I just wanna go to sleep, is that okay?"

DeAndre gazed at his bed and then over at me, appearing unsure. "Yeah. You can have the bed. I'll sleep on the floor."

I reached out and held onto his shirt. "I don't want to be alone."

Beyond the fact that I was hurt when it came to my own father, I found room to curse Darrel Parker for how he'd raised his boys. On any other day DeAndre would've been confident and sure of himself, but as I sat there crying and upset in front of him, he truly looked as though he had no clue what to do.

I removed my shoes and climbed into his bed, waiting for him.

DeAndre stood at the foot of the bed, staring at me, assessing the situation. In that moment I wondered if he regretted befriending me, a girl who was susceptible to emotions.

After turning off the light, DeAndre came and got into bed with me, lying on his side and facing me. I knew he was calculating his every move by the way he was looking to gauge my reaction. He knew nothing about affection and how to console a girl. His touch wasn't right, but it didn't matter to me in that moment because he was trying, for me.

My world was tumbling down around me and when I let out a whimper, indicating another breakdown, DeAndre didn't shift away from me. He pulled me closer, allowing me to rest my head on his chest as he wrapped his arms around me.

He told me it would be okay, but I could only doubt him. I could only hold contempt toward my father for what he'd done. I could only know and feel in my heart that dancing would never be the same again.

When I'd grown weak and tired from all my crying, I lay in DeAndre's arms, feeling inexplicably safe from any more havoc. DeAndre was there, holding me tight.

16

DEANDRE

Cree fell asleep on my chest, and soon after I was asleep as well. I had never fallen asleep with a girl before. It was one thing to have sex with a girl because I knew how to move and what to do, but comforting one was a whole other ball game. There were levels to touching girls, and with Cree, I was clueless. I wasn't used to girls like her or girl *friends* in general. If she had been just some girl, I would've pushed her away and ditched her, but now that we were friends, I knew I had to be there for her. What her father did to her wasn't right, but I was sure he had his reasons, and sooner or later she'd find them out.

Saturday morning, I woke up alone in my bed. It was nine thirty and I'd slept through my morning run, making me wonder if my father would later reprimand me. To my surprise, I found Cree down in the kitchen eating breakfast with Devonte.

Cree looked over at me and smiled. "Dre! Come and eat, Devonte made me breakfast!"

She seemed to be in a better mood, making advancing toward her easier.

I looked at my brother as I took the seat farthest from Cree. "Breakfast?"

Devonte shrugged. "Girl's gotta eat, don't she?"

Plates of bacon, eggs, toast, waffles, and potatoes covered the table, along with cold bottles of orange juice and milk. It was a lot of food for just three people.

I grabbed a plate and fixed myself a little of everything. "Dad here?"

"Nah, he stayed downtown. He's really trying to get that reporter," Devonte said.

"'Te," I warned. Cree had enough hearing the boys talk shit. She didn't need to be hearing it so early at the breakfast table.

Devonte appeared clueless. "What? This is the longest he's ever chased a woman." He looked at Cree. "It's all the more fun when you let them think they're in control."

Cree's brows rose. "Really? Do you think Susan will give in?"

They'd talked about Susan?

Devonte shrugged. "She's smart and determined, but this is my father, so she'll fall eventually. No woman can resist a Parker for too long."

True or not, I wasn't interested in talking about my father and Susan. It was time to change the subject. "I didn't do my run," I said.

"Me neither. He says he's letting you off the hook for the summer, it'll be up to you to keep up with running, but in August he wants you back on it."

It was a test to see how committed I was. Either way, I'd get up and keep with the routine. Running made sense, just like basketball. In a lot of ways it helped start my day and clear my head. Something I wanted to do especially after the previous evening with Cree.

I faced her. "What do you wanna do today?"

"I was thinking about sitting back and keeping up with annoying women who disrespect their mothers."

It took a second to catch her drift. "Cree, you hate the Kardashians."

"And right now I hate my father just the same."

I gazed at Devonte, urging him with just one look to keep quiet.

"You don't really mean that," I said. There was no way she really felt that way when her father had raised her and had always been there for her.

"I remember when he first saw me dance, and the look of instant disapproval that flickered in his eyes. I never got it. I always thought it was because I wasn't good enough." Her eyes watered and she quickly wiped them. "I spent all this time trying to get better so that one day he'd look at me and say I was good. Little did I know that that day would never come, and that the reason he doesn't approve of my dancing is because it's what killed her."

I could understand her hurt and feelings of betrayal, but there had to be more to the story. It was obvious Mr. Jacobs wanted to protect Cree in his own way. Sure, it maybe wasn't the best way, but he had his reasons. Reasons Cree needed to go and learn.

"Cree, you have to talk to him. Or else you'll never know the truth about your mom."

Cree sighed, hunching her shoulders and picking at her plate. "I guess you're right."

"I'm not forcing you to go, but—"

"No, I should just hear him out." Cree stood from the table.

She turned to me on the way out of the room, stopping and peering up with glassy eyes. "Thanks for last night and letting me stay here, DeAndre. I know it wasn't easy and I was a wreck, but it means a lot."

I reached out and smoothed some of her messy hair back out of her face, admiring its softness as I shrugged at her comment. "Would you have done the same for Troiann?"

"Of course."

"For Tremaine?"

"Yes."

"For me?"

She nodded.

"Then it's nothing."

Cree stretched up on her toes, kissing my cheek and wrapping her arms around me anyway. "Still, it means a lot."

All of the hugging was beginning to take a toll on me. I patted her back, wishing for things to go back to normal.

Cree pulled back and scowled. "God, Dre, you are *awful* at hugs."

"I thought I did okay last night."

Cree looked over at Devonte. "Hey, can you come here for a sec?"

Devonte was confused as he came over to us. Cree disappeared behind me and soon I felt her breasts on my back as she was up against me, grabbing my arms and making me hug my brother.

Devonte took one look at me and twisted up his face. "If you don't get the fuck off of me." He turned and peeked at Cree. "Unless you wanna get in between us."

Gone were Cree's breasts and her grasp on my arms as she took a step back. "Fine, I was just trying to help."

She went upstairs and left me with Devonte.

"Nice of you to make breakfast," I said as we got back to the table.

"Same to you in letting her spend the night. Since when does my little brother spoon with a girl?"

"We didn't spoon." I only held her to my chest until she fell asleep.

Devonte wasn't buying it, but he let it go. "Darnel was annoyed. I don't think he's going to be calling anytime soon."

I dropped my fork, ignoring its harsh echo of clattering against the tabletop. "Why not?"

"He said you've been trying to reach him and when he finally calls you were too busy."

Only on a rare occasion did I ever get mad. Darnel was pushing my buttons. Did he not have the sense to figure out I'd avoided his call because something came up?

I shoved my plate away and tried to think of anything irrelevant to keep my fists from clenching so much. It wasn't working, and Devonte could see it.

He shook his head. "He's fuckin' up."

I stood from the table. "I need to run."

"You want me to take her home?" Devonte offered as he cleared the plates from the table.

Cree was my friend, and the least I could do was see her home.

"I've got it." Thinking of the situation at hand, I wondered out loud, "Do you ever think about our mom?"

Devonte took a moment to digest the question. "Sometimes. You?"

I shook my head. "What's the point? She left."

Devonte looked down at the floor. "Still would like to know why sometimes, you know? Was it us? Was she too young, overwhelmed, was it basketball? Sometimes ignoring it doesn't do anything but push it back for later."

I let it go.

Cree came back downstairs wearing a T-shirt of mine and her sweats. Her hair was in a tighter bun, but still a little messy from her sleep since we didn't own a bonnet she could borrow.

"I figured this was a great way to rub it in about where I stayed last night," Cree said as she gestured to her clothes.

The last thing I wanted to do was crack a smile or laugh or feel anything, especially not after the game Darnel was playing, yet Cree managed to lighten the mood with her smart-ass sass.

I gathered my keys and led the way out of the house. "Let's go, Cree."

We listened to the radio the entire drive over to her house. She didn't say anything and neither did I. I was too busy thinking of ways to calm down and not go off on my oldest brother. It almost seemed like he'd been looking for any excuse to distance himself further from me and the family.

Fuck him.

I pulled up in front of Cree's house and killed the engine. Together we sat in silence while neither of us budged to leave the car.

"Are you okay?" Cree asked after a while.

I nodded, not taking an eye off the street ahead of me. "I'm fine."

"You sure?"

I didn't want to talk about it. Looking past Cree, I saw her father outside. He stood on their porch with his arms folded. "He's waiting."

Cree looked over at her father and quickly averted her gaze to her lap. "Can't you take me to Troiann's?"

I shook my head and placed my hand on her thigh, gaining her attention. "You need to do this."

"He's probably more mad than sympathetic."

Gazing at her father, I could see that she was right. Mr. Jacobs seemed to be practicing patience as he stood on the porch instead of coming down the path and yanking Cree from the car.

"I'll talk to him." I doubted he'd really listen to me, but I could at least buffer the situation before Cree and he went at it on their front walk.

Cree blew out a shaky breath, peeking back at me. "What are you going to say to him?"

"I'm just going to soften the blow and get him ready." I patted Cree's arm. "Hey, you don't really hate your dad. Not when he's the only parent you have left. My dad can be a pain in the ass sometimes, but he's the only one I have. My mom bailed, but my dad stayed. Your mom died, but your dad didn't check out mentally, he was a man and raised you. Yes, he fucked up by not tellin' you about your mom, but he was there, Cree, you can't forget that."

She took her bottom lip into her mouth as her eyes watered. "I hate you right now for making me understand him."

Sensing she needed to be held, I leaned over and took her into my arms. "I know. I'm goin' to go prepare him."

I got out of the car and headed over to Mr. Jacobs, who wasn't happy to see me at all.

"What are you doing here?" he asked, his tone threatening.

I looked back at my car, finding Cree watching us. "Bufferin' the situation," I said. "Cree's upset and she needs answers."

Mr. Jacobs snorted. "I'm not talking to a seventeen-year-old about my private matters. Get back in the car and send out my daughter, now."

He was right about that. I didn't expect for us to talk and for him to lighten up and things magically get better. I just wanted to try to lessen his anger before he and Cree really got into it.

"I'm not tryin' to talk all heart-to-heart, sir, but I do want to say something about Cree." I gestured back to her. "She's hurt, and she feels betrayed. I know as her father you're pissed that she ran out and stayed out all night, but I think the bigger matter is the situation at hand about her mother bein' a dancer and you not tellin' her. You're the only parent she's ever known and you kept her in the dark about her mom this whole time. Not to mention she loves dancin'. I have a strong feeling she'll never see it the same way again. You have no idea how happy she looks when she's talkin' about dancin'—the passion, the vigor, the zeal—and that's going to suck if she gives it up. I'm not sayin' you shouldn't be mad, but I do think you have to put yourself in Cree's shoes and understand you withheld something from her that's a major part of her life." I backed away and held my hands up. "That's all I wanted to say. I'll go get her now."

Cree was already out of the car and standing against the passenger door by the time I made it back over.

"I can take over from here," she said.

Not knowing whether to give her a pat goodbye or if I was obligated to hug her again, I stood there for a moment beside her, feeling unsure.

Cree looked over at me. "Thanks again, it means a lot."

She must've sensed my confusion and reluctance to make a move, as she went past me toward her father.

I let out a breath of relief. There was just too much going on.

～

Troiann was at my house when I got back, pushing my appointment with running back further. She was sitting in our rec room watching TV while Devonte sat opposite her in a chair, texting.

Once Troiann noticed me she sat up and appeared concerned. "I was coming over to hang out and Devonte said Cree spent the night and was crying. What's going on?"

It wasn't my place to say so I kept quiet. "Call her later and ask her."

Troiann wasn't happy with that response. "I'm her best friend and she goes to you?"

"We were already meetin' up." I looked around and noticed she was alone. "Where's Marc?"

Troiann sat back. "I ditched him."

I sat beside her and looked at the TV, seeing that they were watching *Next Day Air*.

Troiann elbowed me. "I'm serious, I hope you took care of her last night, Dre."

"I did all right."

Troiann chewed on her lip, still unsure. "I hope it's okay."

Cree never really spoke about her mother, and judging from her tears, I knew the confession had hit her hard. We were both in the dark about our mothers, but unlike Cree, I wasn't sure I cared to know why my mother left.

Devonte stood up and pocketed his phone. "I'm going out, I'll catch y'all later."

I faced the TV and let him leave.

Troiann's phone rang but she didn't answer. It rang again and she still ignored it.

I sighed and glanced down at the phone sitting between us. "Don't hurt my best friend, Troy."

She scowled as she turned from the TV. "Would you be saying this to Marcus if he was sitting here and I was calling him?" She crossed her arms and didn't wait for me to finish. "Of course not."

"You're different." And she was. No other girl had ever had Marcus so consumed and captivated. It was beyond them messing around, because he was genuinely spending time with her as well.

Troiann rolled her eyes. "Come this summer I'm over it."

"Troy—"

She held her hand out to stop me. "What? Why should I stay with him? Hmm? I'm so different yet he doesn't even claim me? Only a fool would stay with a guy like that."

I had nothing to say. Marcus was fucking up a good thing by letting his ego get in the way. He was into Troiann, and he was playing it off for either our benefit or his own. She'd tried to let him go and he'd chased after her. It was obvious to everyone that they were together; there was no use in pretending.

"He won't say it, but he shows it. When you tried to cut him off, he chased you down. He's givin' you all of him, Troy," I said.

Again her phone rang and she rolled her eyes as she grabbed it and answered.

"What ... I told you I was at the library. ... Well, there's more than one library in Akron. ... Why are you looking for me anyway? ... You sound like a stalker. ... I'll call you whatever I want to call you. ... I wish you would. ... Uh-huh—"

"What's going on?" Marcus stepped into the room and pressed a button on his phone and shoved it into his pocket. He was staring at Troiann and she merely grimaced.

"I'm fuckin' Dre on the side," she said in a lazy tone. "What are you doing here? Did you track my phone?"

Now it was my turn to roll my eyes. All I wanted was some peace and to enjoy the weekend. If I wasn't comforting Cree, I was playing therapist for Marcus and Troiann.

Marcus glared at her and I stood up from the couch. I really needed to run.

"No, I was comin' to see Dre. What are you doin' here?" Marcus said.

"Getting away from you."

I was in the middle and I couldn't even use the TV for a distraction because the tension was too much to avoid.

"Why are you playin' games, Troy?" Marcus demanded.

"What games? I'm free to hang out with whoever I please, and I do not have to answer to you."

Marcus frowned. He looked at me and I merely shrugged,

staying out of it. He focused back on Troiann, and I knew the jig was up. "You're my girl, okay?"

There she had it, he'd officially claimed her.

Troiann was stubborn as she crossed her arms and faced the TV screen. "Oh, *now* I'm your girl. Too late for that. I'm good."

Marcus crossed the room and I backed away to the doorway.

There was way too much shit going on and I couldn't deal.

I thumbed a finger over my shoulder as I watched Marcus whisper things in Troiann's ear that caused her to blush. "I'm just goin' to go run now."

They were lost in each other, oblivious to my existence.

I needed to run.

17

CREE

It didn't happen right away. As soon as DeAndre drove off my father inspected me, taking a very long look at my T-shirt—DeAndre's T-shirt. It was big on me and hung to my thighs, and it smelled incredible. After my father practically memorized every detail of the plain black tee I was wearing, he led me into the house.

He went straight to his den where I followed his lead, prepared to face this.

"I don't want any grandchildren right now, Cree," my father stated.

So he suspected I'd slept with DeAndre.

"Don't look at me, I know nothing about mothers," I responded.

My father visibly winced. "I'm sorry. I should've told you, especially when you took up dancing." He peered down at the carpet, shaking his head. "But it's an ugly truth."

I hugged myself, taking a moment to look around the den at all the photos on the wood-paneled walls. Photos of my father's side of the family and me hung, illustrating only *part* of my family. For so long I'd respected my father's sensitivity regarding my mother, but as I came back to where he was sitting in his chair with guilt in his dark eyes, I had reached my limit.

So I stood my ground. "I have a right to know."

He nodded. "I blame her family for what happened to her."

"Was it an eating disorder?" I asked gently, inching closer now that he was opening up.

"Yes," my father answered, leaning over in his chair, his shoulders taut with grief. "It was an ugliness that took over her entire life. We didn't even think people in her condition could get pregnant. It's rare. And then you happened and you were our miracle; I thought you would be the reason she would get better."

"She got that way because of dance?"

My father nodded once more. The sadness in his eyes made my heart clench as I tried to be strong and hear it all. "She used to make a fuss about her weight and being perfect. Her momma ain't help it either. She said 'Black girls don't get eating disorders, that's for White girls.' Her own daughter was shrinking in front of her eyes, and she thought it was just stress. That's the reason I never let them around you. I couldn't forgive them for ignoring the obvious signs."

"How'd you guys meet? How'd *you* know she was sick?" I asked.

My father clasped his hands, his eyes staring out of the room as if he was peering at the memory. "I noticed *that* over time. We met in college. Kathy was taking dance classes and she and your mom, *Michelle,* met there. Kathy used to talk about her all the time, and I got so annoyed I just had to see who this Michelle girl was, and then I saw her, and it was over." His eyes glazed for a second with unshed tears, and I bit my lip to keep from trembling. "Her illness wasn't clear at first. The more I got to know her and started seeing her, the more I gradually picked up on a few things. Moving food around her plate during dinner, picking apart her body, and focusing on how many calories or how many carbs were in things."

I'd never heard the story of my parents courting before, and I hated to have to hear it under the current circumstances. "I noticed her size from the beginning, but she was just so beautiful and graceful." He paused, looking at me. "You look just like her. You even walk like her, Cree."

I'd heard several times growing up that I looked like my mom, but hearing the pain in my father's voice as he said it, seeing the way he was looking at me, tore me apart. I wiped my eyes, trying to keep it together.

"She wanted to make it as a dancer, do shows, and be one of the greats. There was this competitive dance school she wanted to get into in Cleveland, and I remember hearing her obsess about how small the other girls were, how their forms were tighter and perfect. She always used to stress over being *perfect*, and it killed me."

"Did she get into the school?"

My father shook his head. "Kathy and I watched the audition, and we both agreed it was flawless, but they thought otherwise. They thought her moves weren't fluid enough and her weight wasn't being distributed with balance. They said she needed to lose a few pounds to work on her pointe."

I could just imagine my mother's dreams being crushed by people telling her she wasn't good enough to get into the dance school. With my full chest and hips and thighs, I knew I was nowhere near as thin as the many dancers I'd seen in flyers or on TV commercials. But I was okay with that.

"She'd skip meals and spend hours dancing, and she wouldn't listen to me. She was obsessed with her body. It was a mental disease. She'd even lie about eating and how often she worked out. She came over for dinner once and I heard her purging in the bathroom, and we argued about it. We'd spend hours arguing about her weight and her body and her obsession with dancing, and she always swore she'd quit worrying so much about either.

"When we got married she put on a few pounds. We weren't sure she was able to conceive a child, but somehow you were meant to be." My father sighed. "I can honestly say I never saw her put off eating while she carried you. She was happy, she wanted you more than anything, and I think she saw you as her second chance. I think the pregnancy saved her."

"But how did she die?" I needed to know.

His voice broke as he answered with the hardest thing I could imagine he had to say. "Right after she delivered you her heart stopped. Just when I thought she'd beaten the disease and it was a thing of the past, it crept up on us and gave us one final blow. The anorexia and the bulimia had taken their toll on her heart, and after having you her body just . . . gave up."

My shoulders shook as I began to cry, and it didn't feel like I'd ever stop. I leaned over, covering my face and my sobs as my heart poured out of me.

I went through all five stages of grief at once, and I couldn't fight back my pain, even when my father came and held me to his chest.

"It's okay, Cree, she held on just long enough to give you to me. She stayed as long as she could, and you're here because of that."

But it didn't make it any better. If I hadn't been conceived she would still be alive and with my father.

I pulled back. "Do you ever regret me?"

My father's brows furrowed as he reached out and wiped my face. "If I had to do it all again, I wouldn't change a single detail as long as I got to have you in the end."

My lips trembled as I struggled to see through blurred vision. "You mean it?"

"Yes." He held me so tight against him it almost hurt. "I'm sorry for keeping it from you. I didn't want you to change your opinion on dancing, or to think of your mother in a different way. She was an amazingly gifted dancer and then she got sick. I don't want that for you."

In my heart I knew I loved dancing as recreation, but I wasn't sure about going pro like DeAndre talked about. I wasn't sure what my future held for me with dancing.

I spoke up. "You have to let *me* make my own choices, Dad. You have to let me decide how much I want to dance, or eat. You have to let me be a big girl and make my own decisions and form my own opinions."

I could tell he wanted to fight my words by the way he appeared so conflicted, with the worry lines seeping into his face and creasing his brows. "You're my baby girl, you're the only thing I have left of her. I don't want to see you go, Cree."

I wrapped my arms around him and buried my face in his chest. "I'm here, Dad, I'm not going anywhere, I promise."

He held me tightly.

—

I decided that it was best that I leave for the summer. My father didn't want me to go down south and visit my mother's family because he still held contempt against my grandparents, but he couldn't deny my request to spend my summer learning about my mother's side of the family.

It was the first Saturday in June and I'd be leaving in a week, once school was officially over and the summer before senior year began. To be honest, I was afraid of what truths awaited me in Florida. I'd never met my mother's parents and had only spoken to them on the phone when I was younger. I hoped they weren't mean and would accept me.

DeAndre and I were in his family's rec room, sitting in front of the TV. Well, he was sitting; I was lying on my stomach, snacking on cinnamon rolls while he finished off a turkey sandwich. We were watching one of our favorite movies. On screen Chadwick Boseman was competing to be King of Wakanda.

DeAndre's eyes dipped to the plate of pastries in front of me, and I could see the disapproval on his face.

"Stop judging me," I snapped as I wiped my hands on a paper towel.

"You ain't even offer one up and you used my oven to make them."

I narrowed my eyes and glanced at DeAndre. "Do you want some of my sweets, Dre?"

He perked a brow. "Depends."

"On what?"

"Are they hot and sticky still?"

My throat swelled and I looked down at my plate. I poked a roll, finding it just about hot. "Yeah."

DeAndre smirked. "Maybe later."

In the midst of our joking around his phone rang, and one look at the screen was all it took for the humor and emotion to drain from his face.

He stood up and barely glanced at me. "I'll be right back."

My own phone rang before I could question what I'd just witnessed. It was Troiann. "Hello?"

"Hey, what's up?" she asked as birds chirped in the background.

"I'm over at DeAndre's. What are you up to?"

"Wondering why we're not spending as much time together as possible before you abandon me for the summer."

Dramatic much? "I am not abandoning you, besides, you'll have Marcus."

"But I love *you*," Troiann whined. "I'm with Marcus right now, he's cool and all, but you're my best friend."

"I'll bring you back some cute clothes?" I took a stab at recovery.

"Deal!" Troiann squealed. "We gotta hang out tomorrow, promise?"

"Promise."

"Don't be a stranger, Cree, I know where you live."

Before I could challenge her threat she'd already hung up.

My best friend was a trip.

Twenty minutes had gone by and the movie was still playing, but DeAndre hadn't returned. I paused it and went to see if everything was all right.

He was sitting in the foyer on the last step on one side of the dual staircase. His phone sat beside him and he rested his chin on his fists, looking lost and angry.

I made my way over to him but was cautious not to get too close. "What's wrong?"

DeAndre shook his head. "Nothing, I'm fine."

He was far from fine. "You know you can tell me anything, right? That's what friends are for."

DeAndre drew his attention to me. "Yeah, I know."

I took a seat next to him and faced him. "And when things are tough for me you're the first person determined to help, so let me have a turn, and quit playing hard."

DeAndre sighed, running his hands down his face. "I just got off the phone with Darnel. He just talked to my dad and told him he wasn't goin' to play ball in the winter. My dad said he couldn't come home if he didn't play, and 'Nel says he won't then." His voice was eerily calm and hollow at the same time, revealing how hurt he was at the news. He didn't hide the fact as he faced me. "He can't not come home, Cree, that's my brother, that's family."

My heart ached as I reached out and hugged him. He had never allowed himself to be so vulnerable and open. Something had to be done.

Before I knew what I was doing, I was standing up and holding my hand out.

DeAndre looked at my outstretched hand. "What?"

"Come on, let's go *talk* to him."

"Talk to him?"

"How can he come home if he doesn't know he's wanted?"

DeAndre stared at my hand for a moment more before taking hold of it and getting up. "I guess we're takin' a trip down to Columbus."

18

DEANDRE

My stomach was in knots as soon as we hit the road. Not knowing how Darnel would react unsettled me.

Cree sat beside me in the passenger seat, humming along to the music playing. It was soothing, the only thing keeping me from really losing my shit.

"How's your dad?" I asked to avoid dwelling on Darnel.

Cree looked my way and shrugged. "Fine. I'll probably have to gain ten pounds this summer just to keep him off my back while I'm away."

"He's just goin' to miss you."

Cree brought her attention to her lap. "He's not the only one. Tremaine and Troiann are doing a great job of making me feel guilty for leaving, but this is something I need, you know?"

I thought it was important she go as well—not that I wouldn't miss her smart mouth—because she wanted to learn about her family.

"It is the *whole* summer," I pointed out. "Maybe you'll come back a week or two early?"

"I've got seventeen years to make up for. I doubt two months is enough, Dre."

Even if the news of her leaving was something I agreed with, I was slightly bummed she would be gone *all* summer. There were just way too many adventures to be had with all the free time on our hands.

"You're missin' out," I said.

Cree clicked her tongue. "Oh, I'm sure I am."

"The things we do, Cree, it could be a movie."

"Fast cars, fast women, fast life," she joked.

"Pedal to the metal, baby."

We had arrived at the university and my stomach sank.

"You can do this. Just tell him how you feel," Cree instructed, as I found a place to park at Darnel's dormitory.

It should've been easy to just say how I felt about Darnel's distancing himself from us, but I was honestly scared. What if he was to take a cue from our mother and leave us behind as well? I wanted to blame Ashley, but I knew this was more Darnel's doing than an outside influence.

"What if he doesn't want to come back?"

Cree did something I wouldn't let anyone but family do. She reached out and caressed my cheek. "Honestly, DeAndre, from what you and Devonte have told me, I don't think Darnel's an idiot. And only an idiot would walk away from you and your brother, especially when you need him."

Something about her words and her touch gave me the courage to get out of the car.

We were prepared to scavenge through the campus in search for him but luck was on our side as we bumped into Darnel at his dorm. The girl from the photo, Ashley was with him. They stopped in front of us, taking Cree and me in from head to toe.

Darnel sighed and looked around at all the people carrying bags and boxes from the dorm. Classes were out and people were moving. He had no excuse of class or exams to hold him back.

I shoved my hands into my pockets, feeling like a little boy. "'Nel."

"Must be my lucky day with all these visitors." Darnel looked over at Ashley and back at me. "I've got a lot of packing to do, Dre."

For a moment I was frozen, but then Cree spoke up for me.

"Oh no, we did not sit in a car for two hours just for that wack-ass excuse," she said. "We're not leaving."

Darnel faced Cree, lifting a curious brow.

Ashley stepped to the side. "Okay, I've had enough of this drama." She pointed to Darnel. "Enough with the bullshit, Darnel, you're going to talk to your brother and that's it. It needs to be done." She grabbed Cree's hand and pulled her away. "We're going outside to watch the football team load furniture and boxes. Maybe one of us will faint in the hopes of them lifting us up."

Cree's eyes grew wide. "I volunteer for that."

Ashley snorted as they made their way to the exit. Those two together were definitely trouble.

I faced my brother and broke the ice. "Nice to see who wears the pants in your relationship, not that I hadn't suspected already."

Darnel scowled. "Speak for yourself. Since when does my baby brother need a girl to speak for him?"

"I don't, and we're not together."

"Enough of all that." He let it go. "You didn't come all this way to talk about who you're not seeing."

We migrated over to the sitting area where we had full view of the girls through the large floor-to-ceiling windows. They were talking and watching the football team load furniture and boxes into vehicles. Together, Cree and Ashley looked like sisters, both with big, natural coily hair, slim figures, and matching heights.

"I don't know anything about 'wearing the pants,' but I love the essence of a Black woman, there's nothing like it. Their minds, souls, bodies, their faces, their hair, their attitude—nothing beats it." Darnel watched as Cree and Ashley talked, and I could see everything he'd said in both girls. "There's nothing sexier than a brown-skinned woman, especially when she's holding you down."

"I hear you," I agreed.

"Some days, I'm ashamed to admit I'm afraid of her." Darnel studied Ashley, but there was nothing but love and adoration in his eyes. "She's tough, quick to argue and state how she feels. She's honest, vibrant, and just genuinely strong. When I first met her, I was with my boys and she was ignoring us, twisting up her pretty little face, and I thought she was stuck up. She wouldn't even say hello to us when we greeted her." He tossed me a smile. "It's always the ones you don't think you want that you end up chasing after. Something about being told that you can't have them sets you off to prove some macho point, and before you know it . . ."

"Yeah," I said. "Except when they're tryin' to change you."

Darnel looked my way. "Every decision I've made thus far has been on me, not her. She doesn't like basketball but she's never told me to quit playing or second-guess myself. Ashley's not like that."

"Really?" So the decision to leave us behind really was all on him?

"Yes, really. You're too late, Dre."

"What do you mean?"

"Dad was just here," Darnel informed me. "And he tried his take at changing my mind and—"

"You're not coming home?"

He shook his head. "No, I'm not."

I hadn't expected things to go this way. I hadn't expected it to hurt so much. It was easy to not give a fuck about things in my life, but when it came to my family, my brothers, it was impossible.

I stood from the chair and faced him. "So that's it, huh? This is how you're goin' to end things between us?"

Darnel snorted, shaking his head as he looked down at the ground. "Stop being so dramatic."

"You're my brother!" I snapped. "What the fuck do you mean?"

"What about *me*?" Darnel shouted as he stood and got in my face. "All you care about is basketball, just like him. Open your fucking eyes, there is a whole world out there beyond ball. Why do you think I call Devonte more than you, why do you think I need space? You're just like him, and I don't need that right now."

I wanted to hit him, but my fist lay heavy at my side. He was blaming me and our father for his distance. He was saying he wanted space from *me*.

I backed away, holding up my hands. "So sorry I drove two fuckin' hours to talk to you. So sorry basketball is the reason why I worry you don't call so much. So sorry that basketball is the reason I don't want you to disappear like she did. So fuckin' sorry, Darnel!"

He winced and took a step toward me. "Dre—"

I immediately took a step back to keep my distance. "No, fuck you. Okay, I may care about basketball, but it has nothing to do with him. I love it on my own, just like we said in that interview. It's not the reason I'm here. I came to see you because you're my brother and I need you. For you to just back away from our family? Fuck you."

"You didn't give me a choice!"

"Don't blame me for what you're doin'. Just as easy as it was for you to go ghost, you could've picked up the phone and told me how you felt instead of hidin' like a little bitch."

Darnel stalked over until he was in my face, bumping his chest against mine. He hit the hardest. It would be either an ass-beating or a full-out brawl between us. "All I've heard from you this past year is the same thing I'm hearing for him. *How's ball, 'Nel? How many points did you average this year, 'Nel? How are the scouts, 'Nel? Don't forget about the draft, 'Nel. One day we'll all be in the NBA, 'Nel.* What about me? What about my classes? My day? My girl? But of course, in this family you're not supposed to care about anything or anyone not associated with basketball."

I didn't understand how he could go from being the best player at our school and loving every second of it to being the person standing in front of me, the person who looked sick of it all.

"I don't get it, okay? This is not the same Darnel who left for school last fall. You loved ball, you can't blame me or Dad for askin' about it. You're the one who pulled a one-eighty and said nothing. You're standin' here and actin' like you were verbal on your doubts, instead you said nothing and expect for us to just ride out with this sudden change."

"It wasn't sudden." Darnel dropped his attitude and sighed, taking a step back. "One day I was with Ashley and she asked me why I loved basketball, why it was so important, just to ask, you know? And the thing is, I didn't have an answer that was my own. I played through Dad, and then I got good, but it wasn't like it was all on me. I thought it was my passion, but then I wasn't sure anymore. People like me for basketball, not for me, and it started to take its toll.

"You're lucky. You've got your friends who genuinely like you. Tremaine doesn't even like going to games but he does because he's your friend. With me, it was all about stats and the girls and my image. When I got here I made real friends, people who like Darnel Parker, whoever that is." He ran a hand over his head, scratching. "I just need some time to really think about how I feel about basketball."

It would be different if he didn't play basketball anymore, but it would be worse if he didn't come around at all.

"Look, 'Nel, you're my brother, and for me, it wasn't about basketball, it was about you. When shit goes down, I know I can talk to you and you'll be there. If you don't wanna play ball, it'll be weird, but I won't hold it against you. Just don't shut me out. I didn't know our mom, but I know you, and I can't have you leave me too."

Darnel reached out and hugged me tight, patting my back and giving me a squeeze. "Never. Look, I'm sorry. I just thought you weren't going to support me on who I'm trying to be. I wanna find myself, and I just thought you only cared about the same guy everyone else cared about."

"I support my brothers, regardless."

Darnel furnished a smile. "I can't tell you how happy I am to hear that."

With things squared away, I couldn't help but wonder. "So, you're still not comin' home?"

Darnel shook his head. "No."

"But—"

"I need space, Dre. Time to focus on me and what I want."

"So you're movin' in with Ashley?"

"Nah, Dad may have been an ass and given me an ultimatum, but he's not ready to let me go. He said he'll pay for a place as long as I visit home often."

"I don't get it."

"Dad didn't think I'd stand this strong on quitting ball for a year, but I am. He's not really for it, but he doesn't want to lose a son, so he's agreeing to let me decide as long as it's solely my decision."

"Will you at least be in Akron?" I didn't want to endure driving two hours just to see him each visit.

"We talked about it and I'm cool with coming back to the city," Darnel said. "Doesn't hurt that Dad got me a nice condo there, too, as a means of a white flag."

Our father was being an asshole for trying to force Darnel into playing ball when he was unsure, but at least he wasn't really going to put him out on the streets.

"So what's Ashley like?" I asked as I looked back outside. Cree and Ashley were still gawking at the burly football players.

"Like I said, she's tough," Darnel noted. "Strong, opinionated. I swear, she wrote a paper on Black Power for English Comp II."

I whistled. "Sorta sounds like you're datin' Cree."

"Speaking of that, you sure you're just . . . ?"

"We're just best friends, 'Nel."

"Best friends?" Darnel stared out at Cree. "Not only does she hold you down and ride with you for two hours to see me, she argues for you when I try to brush you off. Yet you're just 'best friends'?"

"You act like one of the boys wouldn't have done it."

"It's different, Dre."

I rolled my eyes. "It's not like that. Besides, 'I can't have her.'"

Darnel lifted a brow. "Says who? From what I remember at Moorehead, there weren't that many girls you couldn't have."

"True, but I'm not entitled to Cree." I shrugged. "I don't see her that way anyway."

Darnel looked like he wanted to say something, but he didn't, despite the small smile appearing across his lips.

"We good, Dre?" he asked.

"Just as long as I get to see you more."

"I'll be better about that, I promise. And this doesn't mean we can't talk about basketball, I know it's important to you and you love it, we can still shoot around with 'Te too."

That made it all better. At least things wouldn't be too different. With the beef solved, we went outside to the girls. They'd clearly hit it off and were too busy to notice us for a moment.

"Oh, hey, they made up." Cree smiled over at Darnel and me, as did Ashley.

"About time," Ashley said.

Darnel went and pulled Ashley into his side. "I know." He faced Cree and stuck out his hand. "I'm sorry about my rudeness before. I'm Darnel Parker, Dre's oldest brother."

Cree shook his hand. "Cree Jacobs, DeAndre's personal bodyguard."

Ashley and Darnel found this funny, while I didn't.

"Ashley, this is my youngest brother, DeAndre," Darnel said as he introduced us next.

We shook hands and Ashley leaned into Darnel. "I promise I'm not trying to take Nelly from you."

Nelly. I almost snorted at the nickname. "I know."

Ashley tilted her head, taking me in. "He's not as scary as you made him out to be."

I frowned. "I'm disappointed my reputation doesn't precede me."

Darnel rolled his eyes. "He's a good kid."

"Definitely as handsome as the rest of the Parkers."

Cree looked at me and then at Darnel, probably judging the resemblance and forming her own opinion on our attractiveness.

"I'm kinda hungry. Does anyone want to get Chinese?" Ashley suggested, looking between the three of us.

Darnel nodded. "I could eat."

"We actually have to get back," I began to say. It was already late and I didn't want to keep Cree longer than I needed to.

"Actually, Chinese sounds amazing." Cree lifted a brow and gave me a look that read *Try Me.*

I never let anyone tell me what to do, but something about Cree's voice and her face told me not to push her.

I faced my brother and Ashley and shrugged. "I guess we're gettin' Chinese."

—

"Ugh, who let me eat all that food?" Cree asked. She had her hand on her stomach and was moaning a little.

"I told you we ordered too much. You ate like five forkfuls, and then that soda, and now look at you—oh, and don't forget the eggrolls."

Cree glared at me. "Why are you counting my food intake? Did my dad tell you to spy on me?"

"No, I'm just very observant." I kept my eyes forward as I drove us home. Even if girlfriends weren't my thing, I liked Ashley. Her attitude and demeanor were attractive, and she was beautiful. I liked that Darnel seemed happy with her and that she didn't really seem out to change him.

"I like Ashley," said Cree.

"Of course you do."

"What's that supposed to mean?"

"You guys are similar."

This fact didn't bother Cree. "Hey, your brother's got good taste."

"Hold On, We're Going Home" was playing, and Cree began singing along and doing a silly dance with it.

I shook my head. "You sound awful."

Cree stuck her tongue out. "Just hold on, Dre, we're going home."

She was being corny, helping ease the rest of the afternoon.

"Thanks," I said as I glanced her way. "For making me do that."

Cree gave me a goofy smile. "Would you have done it for Troiann?"

I rolled my eyes. "Shut up."

"Would you have done it for Trey?"

I didn't want to laugh, but I did. "Cree."

She laughed and shoved me. "No problem." She reached out and held my hand, squeezing slightly.

It was new to hold hands, but it was Cree, so I let it go. I held on to her hand, squeezing back gently.

19

CREE

Three periods remained on the last day of school day, but no one cared. The Ballers suggested we ditch the rest of the day and grab lunch at a diner, and we were all game.

As we all trekked across the student parking lot, Emily Gardner jumped out in front of our group with a video camera attached to her hands. "Wait! I'm doing a project for senior year. Any last words?"

"Senior year is going to be the best!" Troiann hollered, with an enthusiastic fist pump.

Emily turned, zooming in on Troy. "Think so?"

"Hell, yeah. It'll be the best year yet. New year, clean slate, new friends, new lovers—"

Marcus picked Troiann up and slung her over his shoulder, patting her on her butt. Troiann merely laughed as he carried her over to his car.

Emily giggled and turned the camera on me and the rest of the boys. "Well? Any predictions come the new year? Any plans to prepare this summer?"

Tremaine nudged me. "Some of us are runnin' away this summer."

Emily faced me. "Really?"

I decided to play into Tremaine's words. "Definitely. I gotta get away from these boys." I pretended to frown at the three remaining Ballers. "I can't stand them. Chris is clearly unhinged. Tremaine is a sadist, and Dre . . ." Shit, there was always a pause with DeAndre. He was too much of a conundrum to really pin down. "Dre Parker is a fake. Just look at him, no one is that calm about everything."

Emily laughed at my teasing and I gave in. I went and squeezed Chris's cheeks and smiled over at Emily's camera. "I'm going to miss these boys this summer," I told the camera. "I never thought I'd see the day that I was best friends with the Ballers. But it's going to be a long summer down in Florida without them."

Chris leaned over and hugged me tight. "And we'll miss Cree right back."

Tremaine did one better. He came up behind me and picked me up, causing me to squeal. "Cree Jacobs is my future baby momma, though."

DeAndre took that as his cue to speak. "And there you have it folks, Tremaine and Cree's private summer goals."

Emily smiled over at DeAndre with a blush on her cheeks. She tucked some of her blonde hair behind her ear and walked away to find more seniors to record.

"Let's go, I'm starvin'," Chris said as he and DeAndre took off for his car.

I followed Tremaine to his car. He opened the passenger door for me before rounding the car and climbing in next.

"For real, I'ma miss you this summer, Cree," he said sincerely. For once, he was serious, which made me feel special.

It was nice to know I'd be missed. "Aww, thank you, Trey."

"I mean it, you like a lil' sis for real. Anybody give you a problem, it's nothing for me to catch a flight."

My cheeks hurt from smiling so much. "I'll keep that in mind."

"I'm serious. I guess I'm really glad we're friends, Cree. You make me wanna be a better guy someday to get a girl as dope as you."

"You mean it?" I asked as he pulled into the diner's parking lot beside Chris's car.

"Yeah, just don't tell anyone, I got a rep to keep." He winked at me as he turned the engine off and got out of the car.

Ballers.

To celebrate the start of the summer Chris threw a party at DeAndre's house that night. With Mr. Parker down in Miami with Devonte, the house was clear for the mayhem Chris had in store. He'd promised pigs, strippers, confetti, and plenty of alcohol—only half delivering because as I maneuvered my way through the Parkers' packed house, I thankfully didn't see any roaming barn animals or dancers. Confetti littered the floor as red Solo cups filled the air and celebratory cheers echoed throughout the house.

I grabbed a drink and took a sip, taking a long look at my surroundings. I wasn't sure what Florida held in store for me, but I was pretty sure it wasn't anything like this.

"You owe me a dance," Tremaine whispered in my ear.

"Oh yeah?"

He pulled me into the room where everyone else was dancing. I took a big gulp of my drink and followed him onto the dance floor.

We danced closely to a few songs, and I drank more and more, wanting to swallow down my sudden sadness at leaving my friends behind for two months.

I was dancing into Tremaine when I looked across the room and saw DeAndre talking to Armani. She was wearing a black velvet dress that hugged her body in ways that my clothes never hugged me. She looked incredible.

"She's trouble, Cree," Tremaine said to me.

"When I'm gone, watch him for me?"

"Or you could not be gone for the *whole* summer."

I shook my head. "I need to go. This is my family. I've never met them before."

"Still, next summer we'll all be busy leaving for school and this is it."

"I'll miss you."

Tremaine squeezed me into him. "You better."

Some Jack Harlow song was playing and I went back to dancing into Tremaine, enjoying his hands as they held my waist.

Not long into the song DeAndre materialized in front of us.

"You ruinin' our dance," Tremaine groaned.

"Let me borrow your girl for a second," DeAndre pleaded.

Tremaine gave DeAndre a little shove. "She ain't my girl, Dre."

DeAndre grinned. "Whose girl would she be, then?"

Now I felt like an object to be toyed with. Hell no. The alcohol had me feeling less tolerant than usual. I gave DeAndre my own little push. "Why can't I be my own girl?"

He took a step back and eyed my body briefly. "With all that?" He shook his head. "You gotta be somebody's."

Even my thoughts came out stuttering. "What do you want?"

DeAndre tipped his head upward. "I got something for you, come upstairs with me."

"That sounds like Date Rape 101, Dre."

He smirked. "Shut up, Cree."

I turned to Tremaine as DeAndre began leading me away. "I'll be back."

We wove through the crowded house up to his bedroom and shut the door behind us.

I stood in the doorway, waiting on whatever it was that DeAndre wanted to give me.

He went over to his desk and retrieved a little black box and came and stood in front of me. "I just wanted to give you something. These past two months have been great, especially what you did for 'Nel and me, so I got you something to thank you. I've never bought a girl a gift before, so don't get mad if it's lame." He opened the little box, revealing a rose-gold analog watch. "Marc Jacobs for Cree Jacobs."

The watch was stunning and clearly expensive and he had gotten it for me, to show his appreciation for our friendship. I didn't know what to say; I could only revel in what I was feeling.

I stared up at him, taking in his handsome face and noticing his nice, full lips twitching to smile. "I—" Overwhelmed and a little tipsy, I stood on my toes and held his face in my hands and pressed my mouth to his.

A jolt hit me square in the chest on impact at the feel of DeAndre's lips.

Whoa.

DeAndre immediately took a step back. "What'd you do that for?"

I couldn't even believe I'd done it. "I—I just wanted to know what it was like to kiss you. Have you ever wondered what it was like to kiss me?"

He lifted a brow, as if surprised by my honesty and how cavalier I was to ask such a question. He angled his head, recovering fast as he licked his lips and stared at me thoroughly.

"Yeah, I've thought about it," DeAndre said, taking a noticeable step closer. "I thought about how I'd do it too."

"Yeah?" I backed up against the door as he came even closer.

"Yeah." His hand was on my waist, pulling me gently into him as he leaned down to reach my height. "I thought about how I'd do it slow."

"Slow?" My voice came out in soft breaths, and I feared I was doing something embarrassing like trembling.

"*Slow,*" he repeated, as he leaned closer and pressed his lips onto mine.

And it began slow, his kiss on me and my kiss in return. It was like he knew I wasn't experienced in much and so he took his time kissing me gently. At first it was soft and relaxed but when he slipped his tongue in my mouth, I was swallowing down moans at the feel of him. *Dre.* He kissed me until the heat from the slow burn became too much for him. In a moment he leaned down and picked me up, holding me against the door and going deeper.

I let out a whine I didn't care to be self-conscious about. Not with his hands on me and our bodies so close I could've sworn he could feel my heart beating hard in my chest.

I could hear the music blasting from downstairs, but it was no match for my erratic heartbeat.

My mind was bubbling over, I couldn't stop but realize DeAndre just looked so good in his signature black T-shirt and black jeans and basketball sneakers. The gold chains around his neck and the gold bracelet and watch on his wrists all just did it for me. The way he talked, the way he walked, the way he carried himself all made me dizzy, even if he had a firm grip on me.

"I gotta let you know something, Cree." DeAndre broke away.

"Yeah?"

"All that shit about my not being able to have you, it doesn't do it for me."

"No?"

He regarded me with a glance that let me know how serious he was. "Not even a little."

"Then tell me you want me," I demanded, bracing myself on his shoulders as he held me up against the door.

DeAndre took one look at my body and peered into my eyes. "I want you," he said with a look on his face that made me feel desirable, beautiful—*powerful.*

He held me tighter, a heavy look in his eye. "Tell me it's mine."

Something tingled deep in my belly at the request. Made me want to squeeze my thighs together if he hadn't been between them. "It's yours, DeAndre."

Our lips met again and did all the talking needed.

From the door DeAndre carried me over to his bed and laid me down, hovering just over top of me.

I was definitely more than just a little tipsy, because I felt bold enough to want to get a peek at DeAndre's body. I went to lift his shirt, but DeAndre was quick to swat my hand away.

Looking up, I found him shaking his head. He gestured down at me. "Shirt for shirt."

The temperature increased. Especially since I was barely wearing a shirt to begin with.

I shimmied out of my half sweater, but DeAndre still didn't look satisfied. "Shirt for shirt."

He wanted the tank top off. He leaned up just so I had enough room to remove it.

I stared into DeAndre's eyes, watching him watch me unzip and remove my top. Even though I was wearing a bra, I covered my chest, feeling shy. This caused DeAndre to smile that beautiful smile of his. Soon he was leaning down and kissing and biting my fingers until my hands were gone from shielding his view. A view he took a moment to really soak in as he peered down at me.

I licked my lips, staring at DeAndre's shirt. "Shirt for shirt."

"A deal's a deal." He leaned away and peeled the shirt from his body and tossed it to the side.

Oh fuck.

He'd been hiding a beautifully sculpted body underneath all those big T-shirts this whole time. Just like the others, DeAndre only had a few tattoos on his brown arms; his torso was naked of ink but was muscled to perfection.

As if someone hit Play, he was back to my level and kissing me all over again. Feeling his skin against my skin, him between my legs, I was ready to combust.

Our bodies tangled together, and I could feel the intensity of DeAndre's want for me. The hardness pressing against my belly.

"Dre," I let out.

He kissed my lips, my neck, and soon my chest, his lips lingering against my skin, driving me crazy. "You see what you do to me, Cree?"

Soon I felt his hands pushing my skirt up and disappearing underneath it. Then he had his fingers hooked around the waistband of my panties.

I stared up at him as he stared down at me, both of us breathless.

With his eyes on me, I felt myself nod, and then DeAndre slowly pulled down my underwear and I could immediately feel a rush of air at my bareness beneath my skirt.

My heartbeat intensified as he hovered over me once more. "Don't be shy."

I never thought I could trust him, but in that moment, trust was a heavy weight hung above us as I gave up my trepidation.

"Ohh." My voice came out breathy and whiny at the first contact of DeAndre's hand between my legs.

His lips returned to mine and his hand kept working what could only be described as magic, because I never knew anything in life could feel *this* good.

His cologne, his mouth on mine, his hands in places I deemed sacred—it was all so consuming.

"Oh god. Oh god." Something was bubbling up inside of me as my heart pounded itself against my rib cage. I didn't want DeAndre to stop. I didn't want the moment to end. I didn't want to miss a single second—

An explosion took over, sending me falling back against the bed as my chest heaved up and down. A whirlwind of pleasure washed over me and all I could do was smile.

That was amazing.

A look crossed DeAndre's face and he removed his hand from beneath my skirt. He suddenly pulled back, appearing incredulous. He looked at me as if he was really seeing me. "Shit." He closed his eyes and shook his head.

And the fantasy evaporated as reality set in.

I tried to sit up, and he must've seen the hurt look on my face because he tried pushing me back down.

"Cree, wait—"

I held my hand up as I got out from under him. "That was enough."

Solemnly, DeAndre agreed. "Maybe too far."

I swallowed down the first pitiful sob threatening to crawl up my throat. Nope. Not doing that.

We had just shared something special, but I'd be a fool to let it go further.

I deserved better than this. "I bet if we did more you would make it feel *so* good, but I want it to mean something, and I don't want you to pretend. I won't burden you with that."

He didn't love me and I didn't love him, and my first time was something I wanted to experience *in love*. Not some drunken sex in my best friend's bed.

DeAndre didn't say anything as he sat looking at me.

The clock on the wall glowed ominously, letting me know it was already one in the morning. I had to be up early to pack.

I grabbed his T-shirt from the floor and pulled it over my head.

"I think Troiann's going home with Marcus, if it's not too weird, can I ... ?"

DeAndre broke away from silently watching me as he nodded and moved away. "Yeah, get some sleep."

DeAndre stood from the bed and found another T-shirt to put on. "I just need to get some air. I'll be back."

He left the room and I lay down on my side, wondering what the hell had just happened.

20

DEANDRE

Funny thing about epiphanies, they could change everything. And once you had one, there was no going back.

I lay on my back, staring up at the ceiling in my living room. It was Friday morning and the party had ended a few hours prior to the sun coming up. I hadn't gone to bed; instead, I found myself alone in my father's office waiting for everyone to leave. When it was over, I came and lay in the living room, lost in thought.

She had soft skin.

This thought came to me more than once, and each time I winced at the memory of the feel of her. And then there was the look in her eyes when I'd been about to pull her panties down. The total trust and want. The look on her face when I brought her there after I touched her.

And that's when the fucking epiphany happened.

I hated it.

Chris came into view as he walked into the room, rubbing sleep from his eye. He yawned and slumped in the chair across from me.

"You hungover?" he asked.

"Nope." I didn't drink at all during the party.

Chris angled his head and studied me. "You okay? You look perturbed."

I managed to chuckle at his word choice. "Screwin' that tutor really worked out for you, huh?"

Chris smiled and lay back. "Hell, yeah. I got, like, a B plus in English."

It went silent again, and I was engulfed in the images of the previous evening. Cree underneath me, gazing up at me, trusting me, wanting me.

I squeezed my eyes closed.

Fuuuuck.

Chris tossed a throw pillow at me. "Hey, you sure you're straight?"

I wasn't. I was completely fucked up and there was only one thing I really wanted—needed—to do.

I sat up and faced Chris. "You should get cleanin'. This place looks like shit."

He smirked. "Don't you got a maid for that?"

"Yeah, and her name is Christopher Casey."

He waved me off. "I'm hungry. I think I'm going to go for a coffee and doughnut run, you in?"

"I can't."

"You look like you could use the caffeine, Dre."

I stood and ran my hand down my face. "What I need right now is to go for a long run. Maybe even call up Darnel."

"Then do it."

"Can't."

"Why not?"

"Because—"

"Hey." She was awake and in the room.

I thumbed a finger over my shoulder. "I gotta take her home." I glanced at Cree, and she glanced back, appearing normal. She was wearing her outfit from the party and her hair was a little messy from sleep, but she seemed all together.

Immediately I looked away. There was something different about her.

Chris was oblivious as he stood from the chair and peered over at Cree. "Someone had a good time last night. I saw you dancing all on Trey."

"You know how Trey likes to get down." Cree came more into the room until she was standing beside me. "I gotta admit, I'm upset he didn't try anything."

I studied Cree and she smiled at me, as if nothing had changed. "You guys were dancing close enough," I said.

"Still."

"So you remember last night?" Chris asked. "I thought you'd pretend to forget."

Cree gazed down at the carpet for a moment. "How could I forget? I wasn't that tipsy, Chris. Don't think I also didn't notice the lack of pigs you promised."

Chris frowned. "I tried, though."

I was over reliving the party.

"You hungry?" I asked.

Cree shook her head. "Nah, my dad's cooking a huge breakfast. He acts like I'm going to go down there and forget how to eat or something."

"You're leaving tomorrow." I said it more to myself than to her. As if to really see the bigger picture.

Cree smiled as if I were being silly. "Yeah, I am."

"Well, then, we gotta get you home. Mr. Jacobs probably wants to spend as much time with you as possible." I headed past her to locate my keys. I turned and faced Chris. "On second thought, I'll get the coffee and doughnuts, you straighten up."

"Where's your housekeeper, bro?" Chris groaned as he stalked out of the room.

Cree shook her head. "You guys are spoiled."

My tongue was heavy in my mouth, so I said nothing.

Even in my car I opted for an awkward silence. Thank god for the radio.

"You're not hungover, are you?" Cree asked as she examined me.

I shook my head. "I didn't drink last night."

"Oh." She kept quiet then.

I took the quickest route to her house as possible. I needed space. I needed to run. I needed to talk to Darnel. My head was all jumbled, filled with thoughts that wouldn't stop.

Cree didn't say anything when I pulled up in front of her house. Instead, she sat there for a moment, sighing and moving some of her hair out of her face.

She turned to me, giving me a lopsided smile. "Well, I guess I'll see you in two months?"

Unable to resist, I reached out and smoothed out her hair to straighten up her appearance. I focused on her hair rather than her face. I couldn't even look her in the eyes.

"Yeah, I'll see you in two months," I said.

Cree unbuckled her seat belt and opened her door. She froze for a second, as if contemplating something before leaning over and giving me a hug.

"Goodbye, Dre." Her voice was soft, and as she pulled back and looked at me one last time I inwardly flinched. The wind was blowing in her hair and the sun was shining down, nearly casting a crown on her head. I swallowed, having no words to say back.

As Cree got out of the car I could tell the smile and the wave she gave me were forced. I watched her as she headed up her front walk, her stride as graceful as ever. She never looked back once she made it to the front porch. She merely unlocked the front door and disappeared inside.

I sat back, staring at the vacant front porch, consumed with my thoughts.

Funny thing about epiphanies, they could really fuck up your whole afternoon.

No, Cree wasn't a "bad bitch" at all, but something deeper and more real. The MVP, the GOAT—something even better than all that, a friend, a companion, a partner, a rider, a supporter, the real thing, and I—

—let her go.

21

CREE

Two Months and Twenty-Seven Days Later

The first day back to school always made me nervous, but this was different. I'd been gone all summer and would be seeing some of my friends for the first time in months. I got to see Tremaine and Chris in Florida when Chris's parents had taken them down for vacation. We hung out at the beach and explored all that Fort Lauderdale had to offer. My grandparents were a little curious about our friendship, especially when Tremaine and Chris acted like, well, *Tremaine and Chris*.

My grandparents were loving people, though. They were big on hugs and kisses and asking about my day. Together they told me all kinds of stories about my mom, their family history, and how they fell in love. They hadn't had the perfect marriage and had dealt with tough times, but they always fought for their relationship and found a way to keep going.

I admired that about my grandparents. They'd lost a daughter and nearly a granddaughter, but they still managed to stand by each other. I looked at them and wondered if real love like that still existed; if people were willing to put that amount of work into a relationship and fight for each other and truly hold each other down. My heart ached with doubt.

Together we were a unique trio, but I loved every minute of it. In July things got even wilder when my two aunts came down to visit. My mother's sisters, Tami and Karen, reminded me of Loraine 2.0. They took me shopping and to the salon, where everyone encouraged me to do something different to my big, textured hair. They styled it to their liking—curls, Bantu knots, and braids—and dressed me as a lady. They fussed over me like I was their own breathing doll. I was just happy to be bonding with more women from my family.

I rarely danced, and I was okay with that. With each day spent with my family, I didn't feel the need to dance. It almost felt like there'd been a void my whole life and it was now filled.

The stories about my mother and the video footage I'd seen of her dancing were what put dancing in a real perspective for me. I wanted nothing to do with what it made my mother become. Dancing was the beginning and end of her. I loved dancing, but not enough to pursue it as a career. Not enough to let it define me. And that was okay.

It was a summer I'd take with me forever.

⌣

With one last look in the mirror, I considered myself ready for school, ready for senior year. I ran a hand through my long box braids, admiring my red ends. My aunt Tami had encouraged the endeavor. Grandpa Heath called me his little "Red Tail Girl," whatever that meant. My father and Loraine loved my braids.

I liked the enhanced Cree Jacobs.

Downstairs in the kitchen I found my father at the stove cooking what looked to be a heavy breakfast.

Some things would never change. My father would never stop overfeeding me and worrying about my weight, and I supposed it was just something I'd have to accept. He loved me, and in his own way he worried to the point where he'd always be cautious.

But other things had definitely improved. With the weight of the past lifted from his shoulders, my father was a different man. The days leading up to my departure were filled with more smiles than we'd shared in a long time. When he called me while I was in Florida he didn't worry me over my dancing or eating. He was just happy that I was happy. That my mother's parents were doing right by me. In a way, things felt incredibly whole now that I was back and felt complete as a person.

"About time," my father said as he came to the table and set down two heaping plates of eggs.

"Oh, Dad, I'm too nervous to eat," I said as I pulled a chair out and sat at my place.

My father looked up from making each plate. "Really?"

"Yeah, I don't know why I thought that would work." I gave up and covered my lap with a napkin. Even if I wasn't hungry, I ate anyway.

"What do you have to be nervous about? This is your senior year, you should be excited," said my father.

"I am, but I've been gone all summer. What if my friends replaced me?" I asked.

My father rolled his eyes. "I don't think Cree Jacobs is the least bit replaceable."

"Looks like Beyoncé was wrong, thank god."

My father cracked a smile and I did, too, easing up. It was just my senior year. There wasn't anything to worry about. Not much could've changed in the near-three months I'd been gone. Sure, I was a little different, but my friends had to be the same.

With my father's ease on the situation, I lost my nerves and ate my breakfast.

～

My father pulled up alongside the school and I could see the Ballers Club at their usual spot on the little brick wall just before the front walkway. Ever since freshman year, each group of "cool" kids sat on the wall and hung out before the bell. Freshman year, Troiann and I used to go to school early and eat breakfast in the cafeteria, and we'd always catch the popular crowd sitting out and kicking it. Each year there was a Parker boy in that crowd, and for each era of Parker, that boy was the main attraction.

Troiann was lounging there, too, chatting the Ballers up as I crossed the street to join them.

"Cree!" Troiann's loud scream drew my attention away from the homeroom listings I had paused to gape at where I saw them down on the cafeteria doors. Her tiny body collided with mine and nearly knocked me over.

I hugged my best friend back and tried to gain my balance. "Hey, Troy."

She pulled back and examined me. "You look so cute!" And then she smacked my arm, hard. "You barely called when you were down there, and you didn't call when you got back!"

I frowned. "Sorry, I was busy unpacking last night."

Troiann narrowed her eyes. "Don't give me that. I've been here all summer missing you."

"It's true," Marcus said sarcastically as he came over and gave me a hug. "She paid your dad to let her go into your room and sleep on your bed."

Troiann smiled and shoved her boyfriend. "Stop."

The others came over as well. Tremaine wasted no time picking me up into one of the massive hugs I'd missed when he'd left for the summer. Chris pulled me close for a brief hug, and DeAndre nodded.

"Glad to have you back," Tremaine said with a wink, and I blushed. "It was a crazy summer."

"What happens in Florida, stays in Florida, Trey," I told him playfully.

Troiann placed her hand on her hip and cocked her head to the side as she eyed Tremaine. "What the hell happened in Florida, Tremaine?"

He looked at me and wiggled his eyebrows. His lips were sealed, and so were mine.

Tremaine placed his arm across my shoulders and pulled me close. "Mind your business, Troy."

I knew she was about to go in on him so I quickly stepped in. "So, how was everyone's summer?" I turned to Troiann and Marcus. "How are you two?"

Marcus held Troiann closer and kissed the side of her head. "We had a great summer."

Troiann's smile read soft and shy, and I knew we were overdue for a major girl-talk session.

"Good." I turned to Chris next. "You?"

"I won this dunk contest at a college visit and smashed one of the judges." He seemed so proud of himself I couldn't find a reason not to smile.

"Way to go." I laughed and turned to DeAndre, who seemed to be keeping his distance. "What's new with you, Dre?"

Everyone turned to DeAndre and he nodded, prompting them all to leave us alone.

I watched Troiann wrap an arm around Marcus's waist as they

headed down the sidewalk, while Chris and Tremaine descended the steps to the cafeteria.

I returned to DeAndre and held my breath, searching for something to say. It had been so long since I'd seen him. We hadn't spoken over the summer, and I regretted that.

I had missed DeAndre, *deeply*.

It was getting to be too weird, and I had a feeling he realized it, too, as he cracked a smile. I relaxed and went and hugged him. DeAndre did something that took me by surprise: he engulfed me in his arms and held me, and it felt comfortable and right. As if he'd had time to practice the skill of hugging and holding someone.

I pulled back and smiled. "Wow, that's new."

He rolled his eyes. "I had a good teacher."

"So, everyone sort of left, what's up? Did I miss something?"

DeAndre lost his smile and scratched the back of his head. "Things kinda changed. Devonte went to orientation down at OSU and met a girl and they're together now."

"Oh wow, what is it with that school?"

He shrugged. "Hell if I know. I'm sorta having doubts about going now."

"Two Parkers down, one to go. Unless . . . you already found someone."

DeAndre didn't take the bait. "I got a dog, actually. I needed a running buddy to keep me company since Devonte was lazy all summer."

"Oh yeah? What kind?"

He pulled out his phone and showed me a picture of an adorable little black and white Border Collie. "She's a girl, and she's six months old."

"Aww," I gushed, as I took his phone and peered more at the photos he had of the puppy. "What's her name?"

"Moxy."

I looked from the photos to DeAndre. "Really, Dre?"

"With you gone I sorta missed someone bitching at me."

I narrowed my eyes and handed his phone over. "Ha-ha."

"I almost named her something else, but I like Moxy. She's energetic and fun."

"What else would you have named her?"

He didn't look at me as he shook his head. "Nothing, it was lame."

"Tell me." I goaded him.

He made a face and looked my way. "CJ."

I was at a loss for words. He would've named her CJ . . . like my initials?

"She's stubborn as hell, and there's only one girl I know who can't do things the simple way, and I was close to going with that name."

Biting my lip, I had to look away. It was just a name and a puppy, but it felt like so much more.

DeAndre touched my cheek. "I missed you, Cree."

"Me too." I breathed out. "I missed you a lot, DeAndre."

I dug into my messenger, searching for my cell phone so I could send him the playlist I'd curated for him. "Well, either way, I love her name. It's great."

One day over the summer I'd sat down and picked out all these songs that described what I was going through, how I felt, and how much our friendship meant to me. He'd asked me to make him a playlist when we'd first became friends, and he'd trusted me to pick a good mix for him. It was long overdue, but the timing felt perfect to me.

"So, tell me, what's really new with you? Did you meet someone *human*?" I fingered the phone at the bottom of my bag and reached for it. "If it's Emily Gardner I may be willing to accept this, it is Christian Wednesday, after all."

I heard DeAndre sigh and I looked up from my bag, finding his face crestfallen. "It's not Emily, Cree."

Nothing but dread covered DeAndre's face. Oh no.

"Then who?" I had a feeling, a sinking feeling that left me breathless.

"It's Ari," he said. "It's . . . she thinks she's pregnant, and it's mine."

I dropped my phone and pulled my hand out of my bag. "What? How can she *think* she's pregnant?"

"We hooked up back in June and she never got her period after."

He touched her. He'd slept with her. He . . . I didn't even want to think about it. "And you didn't wear anything?"

"I did, but I guess. . . . It's complicated."

"Oh wow." We were outside, but suddenly breathing wasn't easy and I felt light-headed.

Even more, my playlist felt very stupid and useless.

"Cree." DeAndre reached out and grasped my shoulder. "I'm—"

"I'm going to be late. I, um, I gotta go look at my homeroom listing, but we can talk later, in depth or whatever, okay?" I didn't wait for him to answer. I walked around him and darted down the steps and over to the sheets on the doors. Vaguely I registered that my homeroom was 115, and opened the door and went inside.

My mind was in a daze. DeAndre was probably having a baby, and I had come back bearing a playlist as a gift. I felt completely and utterly stu—I walked right into a wall as I came close to stumbling backward on my butt.

I looked up to realize I'd walked into a boy. Because life wasn't already beginning to suck. The boy turned around and I froze.

"Sorry about that. You good?" he asked.

He. Was. Gorgeous. He was exactly what Troiann would call a tall glass of chocolate milk. That, and the fact that looking closer I could see that he had some pretty brown eyes.

Shit.

I suddenly recalled him asking me if I was okay. Even though I had walked into him. "Yeah, yeah, I'm fine. Are you? I'm sorry. I should've been watching where I was going."

The boy waved me off and looked at some papers in his hands. "It's okay. I was just standing here like an idiot because I can't find where I'm supposed to be."

"Oh, you must be new."

"Senior year and I'm starting it off blindly placed in a new school in a new city."

And he was a senior. Hallelujah.

"That sucks, and here I am almost knocking you over."

He looked up from his papers to me, eyeing me from head to toe and lifting a brow. "Don't worry about it, I'm enjoying the view."

I felt my skin burn at the compliment. "Thanks," I said bashfully.

He continued, "Well, maybe we can work out a deal. I do need help getting to the senior office, and you did walk into me."

"Well, it's only fair then that I show you the way. Welcome to Moorehead High, by the way."

He held his hand out. "I'm Omari. Some people call me O."

"O?"

He grinned, exposing perfectly white teeth. "Like Oh." He said it making his mouth in an *O* shape, drawing my attention to how nice his lips were.

God, I was probably staring like a weirdo. *"Oh."*

He smiled again. "Right. And your name is?"

I nodded and then it hit me it was my turn to reply to the fine boy in front of me. "Cree, Cree Jacobs."

He shook my hand.

"Well," I said as I went around him to take the lead, "let's get you adjusted, Omari."

Omari grinned. "I'm beginning to think senior year just got interesting."

"Oh." I sighed. "You have no idea."

22

DEANDRE

There was once a time when I couldn't wait to get back to school. But that all ended two weeks before school started. Everything ended two weeks before school started.

I had just come back from a run and was about to work out when my phone rang. My caller ID said it was Ari. When I didn't answer, she called again. There was no avoiding her.

We'd hooked up back in June but nothing had happened since. I could barely remember if the swim had lived up to expectation. I'd been out of it all summer, focusing on my routine: running, working out, and playing basketball. The boys said it was unhealthy, but there was no thinking involved with my routine, and I didn't *want* to think.

Ari called again, and a look at my screen highlighted a missed voice mail as well.

This was getting irritating.

What did she want?

When she called yet again I lost my patience and picked up the line.

"What?" I snapped.

There was a pause, and I could've sworn I heard her catch her breath.

"Ari?" My tone wasn't the nicest, but I wanted to get to the point. Whatever she needed wouldn't matter anyway, in two weeks—

"I was just letting you know I—I think I'm pregnant." Her voice was heavy, as if she'd been crying, but her words came at me loud and clear. *Pregnant.* "Sorry to be a bother."

She hung up and my arm fell to my side, my grip on my phone almost loosening.

Pregnant.

Goose bumps prickled across my sweat-soaked skin, and I felt dizzy enough to pass out.

Pregnant.

No.

This type of thing wasn't possible. I always used a condom, to avoid situations like this—to have fun and not be stupid.

But yet still . . .

Pregnant.

I didn't want to be a coward, I didn't want to ignore her and pretend that the phone call hadn't happened, because it did. Her words kept echoing in my ears, taunting me.

As soon as I showered, I forced myself to bullshit with two of Ari's annoying-ass friends on Instagram in order to get her address.

I had to see her, because running away wasn't going to stop the inevitable.

Of all my friends, and between Devonte and me, I was the responsible one, and yet I'd gotten a girl pregnant.

The word *think* kept popping up in my head. She'd said she thought she was pregnant, as if she was unsure.

Hopefully a quick test would alleviate our issue and set us straight.

To my surprise, Ari didn't live too far from me. Just a few blocks away in a nice Cape Cod–style home. Something about the sight of her house took me by surprise.

Still, I used all the courage I had to walk up to the front step and ring the doorbell.

A moment later a woman dressed in a blouse and slacks, like she'd just gotten in from the office, came to the door holding a basket of laundry on her hip. Tiredness hung in her dark-brown eyes, and one look inside her spotless foyer told me she ran a tight ship.

"Yes?" she pressed, when I didn't speak up.

"Hi, is Ari home? My name's—"

The woman rolled her eyes and leaned back into the house. "Armani!"

"What?" I overheard Ari shout back.

Ms. Young mumbled something under her breath as her fist squeezed the door handle tighter. "Get off that phone and get down here."

In seconds Ari came down their dual staircase. She stood in the doorway beside her mother. One look at me and she shrank, bowing her head.

Ari at home was nothing like Ari at school. Before me, Ari looked dejected, dressed in a T-shirt and pair of gray sweats. Her hair was in a ponytail, and on her feet were Minnie Mouse slippers. She looked less like herself, less confident, less happy.

Her mother made a face as she dug into her laundry basket. "Tell me you weren't out here wearing makeup again? If I told you once, I told you twice, you shouldn't be wearing it, especially if you don't know how to apply it without it staining your clothes."

Ari frowned, looking down at their polished hardwood floor. "Yes, Mom."

Ms. Young heaved a sigh and shook her head, turning and disappearing down the hall.

Embarrassment hung off of Ari's shoulders; she could barely look me in the eye as she walked past me down the steps and to my car.

Watching Ari cross her front walk to my car, hugging herself, made me feel like an asshole. I hadn't needed to be so rude on the phone.

I beat her to the car and opened the door for her, an act that caused her to smirk.

In the car I contemplated sitting there to talk, but then the vibe was all off with the not-too-far presence of her mother.

I started the car up and drove us to the nearest drugstore.

Beside me Ari sank in her seat, eyeing the building with dread.

Maybe this was too much of a push.

Silence fell upon us like a thick and suffocating blanket. My thoughts were running at me a million miles per minute.

The first thing I could really comprehend was the fact that my father was going to kill me. This all meant one thing: goodbye basketball, hello part-time job.

For the first time in my life I had truly fucked up.

The worst part about it, I wasn't the one who would have it bad.

It was evident that Ari's mother was as strict as my father.

The thought made me regard her with sympathy.

"I haven't eaten, you hungry?" I asked.

Ari shook her head as her eyes remained down on the floor.

"Are you sure you're pregnant?"

Beside me she flinched. "No."

I raked a hand over my head, feeling uneasy. Trying my best not to panic. "I just want you to know I'm here for you, okay?"

Ari faced me, a gleam in her eyes. "So you want me to have your baby?"

"Do I want to be a teen father right now? No, that was never the plan, but if you're pregnant because of what we did, then I'm willing to take responsibility."

Ari peered out the window, nibbling on her bottom lip. "Good to know."

The whole thing felt bizarre. Even if I couldn't remember enjoying the act, one thing was certain. "I wore a condom."

Ari flinched again, as if I'd accused her of something. "I only slept with you, DeAndre."

Okay, that wasn't the best approach either.

I reached out and placed my hand on her shoulder. "Let's just go in there and get a test, you can take it at my house and then we'll know."

Her eyes doubled in size at the idea. "No! I'm not pregnant, I just . . . maybe I'm just late. I've been late before."

"*This* late?"

Ari looked scared—I *was* scared, but I needed to know.

"Ari—"

"You don't understand! I can't, I can't," she sobbed. "She's gonna kill me. I have nowhere to go. And I can't be pregnant." Ari's shoulders shook as her lips trembled. She quickly covered her face as she began to cry.

For a moment I watched her break down in the passenger seat, rocking back and forth as she kept repeating that she couldn't be pregnant.

The sight tugged at me.

I crossed the space between us and took her into my arms, allowing her to soak my tee. I held her close, as gently as I could. "Hey, it's okay, I'm here."

Truly, I didn't know what I could do. My father would kill me and possibly worse, blame Ari for the whole thing.

I wanted to believe she was just late, but an entire summer without her period didn't really seem to be in our favor.

I was scared, disappointed in myself, and not prepared to be responsible for another human being—but I wasn't going to place the entire thing on Ari. My mother hadn't been there for me or my brothers. I couldn't live with myself if I did the same thing for a life I'd created. I didn't feel anything about my mother's absence, but Darnel and Devonte did, and it made me sick to think of doing the same.

I reeled back and met Ari's eyes, trying to be strong enough for the both of us. "I'm not letting you do this on your own."

Her eyes watered once more. "I'm scared, Dre. My mom's going to be so disappointed."

I didn't know what to do. Taking a pregnancy test seemed logical, but peering at Ari let me know she wasn't ready to face the truth for what it was.

I swallowed.

Fuck.

"Okay, let's say you're late. When do you usually get your period?"

"At the end of the month."

It was only the thirteenth; maybe we'd get lucky and she wouldn't be pregnant. "If you don't want to take the test right now, let's just wait and see if you get your period this month, okay?"

This last shred of hope was the only thing that made Ari lighten up as she bobbed her head. "Okay."

Once more I took her into my arms and did the only thing I could do. Hope for the best.

I held Ari close and promised her she wasn't alone, all the while knowing everything had changed, and what could've been no longer mattered.

It was the end of August and my stomach was in knots at the thought of Ari finally getting her period any day. Really, the picture wasn't looking too good for either of us.

Senior year may have been off to a chaotic start, but at least the majority of my classes were shared with a mix of my friends, and as we grabbed a table in the senior lounge for fourth period lunch, I was grateful to still have our free period together. Our senior lounge was a large hangout space that housed several large tables on one side of the room and a recreation area on the other, complete with a foosball table, lounge chairs, a coffee table, vending machine, and a massive flat-screen TV.

Ari sat by me next to Tremaine, while I occupied the head of the table. We weren't officially together or trying to be a couple, but I didn't want Ari to feel alone during this time.

The others thought Ari didn't belong, and it showed in how they barely acknowledged her. Troiann acted as though she wasn't there, and Tremaine practically scowled at her when she'd sat beside him.

It all annoyed the fuck out of me.

"Hey, guys." Cree was standing at the table, looking around at all of us. She was right by me, and I caught sight of the watch on her wrist.

Her hair was different, she had new clothes, and even her skin radiated in a special way. She wasn't the same Cree Jacobs from junior year. But the watch I'd gifted her remained on her wrist. I looked down at my lunch tray, not wanting to think or feel too much on it.

Tremaine glared at Ari. "You're in her seat."

Ari looked at Tremaine and scrunched up her face. "There's only so much room at this table, Trey."

"Troy could be sitting over here, but she playin'," Marcus said as he shot Troiann a look.

Troiann had always sat next to Tremaine, as had Cree, just like I always sat at the head of the table and Chris and Marcus sat on the other side. There was room for Cree, just not next to Tremaine.

Cree waved them off. "Oh, it's okay. I'm going to sit with Omari, I was just saying hi. I'm glad we all have the same lunch period."

Tremaine's face twisted. "The new dude?"

Cree nodded while Chris appeared clueless. "Who?"

Troiann got this devilish grin on her face. "The new boy. He's fine as—he's okay, really." She quickly changed her tune with one swift look from Marcus.

I shared two of my morning classes with Omari. Troiann was definitely not the first girl to gawk at the new senior.

Cree went bashful. "He's okay, Troy."

Troiann smirked. "Really, Cree?"

Cree laughed. "I gotta play it cool, leave me alone." She looked around the table once more and avoided me. "I'll see you guys later."

Cree walked away and tension set in. Tremaine made a show of scooting away from Ari and Troiann flipped some of her hair as she looked elsewhere.

Enough was fucking enough.

"Trey," I said with more edge in my tone than I'd ever really used before. "If you don't like Ari sitting here, why don't you go sit with Cree and Omari?"

Tremaine sucked his teeth. "Nah, I ain't cockblockin'."

"Still," I went on, "if you have a problem with who's sittin' at this table—"

Tremaine wasn't hearing it. "*You* got her pregnant, not us. Don't make us have to deal with her."

Troiann was quick to step in, coming and ushering me away

while Tremaine shrugged as if his words weren't that big of a deal.

We sat at the other end of the lounge by a window that overlooked the side of the school.

"Calm down, Dre," Troiann instructed.

I let it be known. "I'm not going to have any of you disrespecting her."

"Trey's right. None of us liked Ari before this happened, and you can't expect us to start liking her now that she's trapped you."

Leaning over, I planted my elbows into my thighs and took a deep breath to calm down. Whether Ari was pregnant or not, there was no way in hell I'd let anyone talk shit about her. That was the difference between Tremaine and me; he'd sleep with a girl and not give a shit as soon as the deed was done. I may not have ever wanted a relationship, but I still kept it respectful.

I focused on Troiann. "She didn't trap me."

"Oh, so you went in raw?"

"No."

"Her box is made of lava and it melted the condom?"

"Troy."

She held her hands up. "You know what, I'm leaving it alone. That's not why I wanted to talk to you."

I looked her way, finding her appearing soft and friendly. "It isn't?"

She gave me a lopsided smile and reached out and patted my shoulder. "I'm proud of you."

"For?"

"Doing this." She gestured across the room where the boys were making clear amends with Ari. Tremaine had his arm around her as Chris was saying something. They may have not cared for Ari, but my boys cared for me, and we stuck by each other no matter what. Marcus would bring Troiann along if we were supposed to hang out, and none of us cared to complain. We'd all been friends for too long to let the littlest things get to us. I didn't want to force Ari on any of them; she was just emotional and wanted to sit with me. It wasn't permanent. It didn't feel right to kick Cree out of the group.

"Takin' responsibility for my actions?" I asked as I got back to Troy.

Troiann snorted. "You don't know how many boys would bail on Armani if they were in your shoes. Half of these fools would've denied the actual hookup or called her all types of hos. A year ago, being on the outside, I would've expected a Baller to bounce too. If this was Marcus and me—" She stopped and shook her head.

Marcus had this thing he'd do. If Troiann was in the room, he'd stop and peek at her every moment or so. If we were talking and someone said something funny, he'd look at her just to watch her laugh. He had a thing for looking at her and being proud of her, as if she was the most perfect girl in the world. It was scary, because being around Darnel and Ashley, I knew without a doubt that Marcus had fallen.

Troiann had her guard up, I could see it each time she inched away or played off their relationship. I couldn't really blame her. Marcus used to be an asshole with girls prior to Troiann. We'd all hung out at Troiann's house a few times over the summer, and I could tell she was extra guarded due to her parental situation. She referred to her father by his first name and rolled her eyes each time her mother brought him up. I knew Troiann was scared, but I was willing to gamble that Marcus wasn't going to fuck up what they had.

I patted Troiann's back. "Marcus would be doin' the same thing, Troy."

Her bottom lip trembled. "I think you're right, but sometimes I still wonder."

"He's not that guy anymore."

"It's hard to believe guys like that can really pull a one-eighty, you know?"

"He found the right one, Troy."

"At least Cree's year is off to a good start, huh?" Troiann nodded toward the table where Cree sat alone with Omari. They were smiling and talking about something, and even if she wasn't with her friends, Cree seemed to be enjoying herself. *Good for her.* I wished the same could be had for Ari. She was in a bad spot and needn't the extra stress.

"He seems like a cool dude," I said. I'd briefly overheard him say he was from Cleveland and ran track, and maybe wanted to play basketball while at Moorehead. If he was down to ball, he was cool in my book.

"About time she got some action."

I cracked a smile. "I have a feelin' she's going to be fightin' a lot of girls to get to him."

Troiann smirked. "Look at the way he's leaning into her as they talk and the way he smiles; he only sees Cree Jacobs, Dre. She has no competition and neither does he. I'm for it."

I continued to look at the pair, noticing all those things Troiann had stated.

Nothing mattered anymore.

"Maybe it's for the best," was all I could say.

23

CREE

Rap videos played in the background as Troiann and I sat up in her bedroom Wednesday evening discussing the first day of school.

Troiann and the Ballers had grown closer while I was away and she had nothing but adventures to fill me in on. Midnight streaking with Chris, egging an annoying teacher's house with Tremaine and Marcus, and watching movies with DeAndre were among the many shenanigans she had gotten into.

I looked around Troiann's bedroom. It had changed over the summer. Her bed was moved, her old box TV swapped out for a flat screen, and there were pictures hung up everywhere.

On her nightstand were a cluster of photos, some from our youth and others from recent years. There were a few new ones I hadn't recognized that I had to grab to get a good look at.

One frame held a photo of the Ballers and Troiann at After Hours, another of Troiann and Anh in bikinis at some lake. I gravitated to a photo of DeAndre that was sticking out. He was sitting on the hood of a black Rolls-Royce Phantom, his legs open with the hood ornament between them. DeAndre was holding up three fingers on one hand and an O on the other, representing our area code. Marcus was posted at the grill of the car with a snapback on, giving an adorable little mean mug that had me smiling.

"They looked so good I had to take a picture," Troiann said.

I ran my thumb over the image of DeAndre. He was wearing a gray T-shirt with the word *Jefe* on it along with camouflage shorts and some Parker sneakers. *Yeah, they did.*

There was another photo of Troiann under DeAndre's arm, doing her impression of a duck-face pout. The last photo was of her and Marcus kissing with the moon shining down on them.

"Mr. Parker got DeAndre the car for senior year, because he knows this season is going to be hard without his brothers on the court. We went driving and just started taking pictures," said Troiann.

"Sounds like you guys had fun while Chris and Trey were away."

Troiann side-eyed me. "Not as much fun as you and Tremaine, apparently."

I knew I had that coming.

"Yeah," I let out.

Troiann crossed her arms. "Okay, spill, Cree. What happened?"

I thought of the midnight swim Tremaine and I'd shared, knowing it was staying in Florida. "Nothing. It was barely PG-13."

Troiann's eyes bugged out and she swatted at me. "Y'all skipped the G rating?"

I laughed and shook my head. "Do I know everything about what *you* do with Marcus?"

Troiann scoffed. "What do you want to know?"

I didn't really want to know the gory details of what she did with Marcus. Besides, it wouldn't compare. "Trust me, Troy. It's not what you think. It's nothing."

Troiann went back to watching videos. "You suck, Cree."

"Anyway," I said, changing the subject. "This year's off to a good start, don't you think?"

"Oh yeah, I saw you at lunch. You barely ate."

Omari and I had been talking a lot, barely giving either of us time to eat, not that I minded. I had really enjoyed his company.

"We were caught up," I explained.

I watched as my best friend sat cross-legged and faced me. "Okay, Marry, Fuck, or Kill," Troiann said with a mischievous grin. "Omari, Tremaine, or DeAndre."

Ugh. Those were my choices? No celebrities? "Really?"

"I'll give you mine and you can think of yours, deal?"

I rolled my eyes. "Sure."

"Kill: Omari because he seems boring so far. Fuck: Tremaine because I wanna see all the shit that he's been bragging about. I'd marry Dre because he's quiet, mysterious, but I just know one-on-one he's gotta be more."

He was. He so freaking was. "What about Marcus?"

Troiann waved me off. "That's a safe bet."

I thought of my choices, feeling shy at the meaning of my options. "Um, I would kill DeAndre because he hooked up with Armani and the last thing I need is her sloppy seconds. Screw Trey because I'm not sure he's marriage material. Marry Omari because he seems nice and genuine."

"Dang, Dre gotta die?" Troiann laughed. "But for real when his dad finds out he's gonna kill him."

"He doesn't know?"

Troiann shook her head. "Dre found out two weeks ago. If his dad knew . . ."

She didn't have to elaborate. If Mr. Parker knew there'd be a storm.

I didn't want to think of DeAndre at all, so I let it go.

"How are things with Marcus?" I asked.

My best friend sighed, picking at her comforter. "Oh, we're fine. Sometimes I get iffy, but that's just because Howard and my mom are trying again, and you know how that goes."

I sympathized with her, placing my hand on her thigh. "Marcus isn't Howard, Troy."

She gave me a lopsided smile. "I know. He tries to be there for me and understand. My guard's not as high as it used to be, which is good."

It was. Together they were chaos, but as dramatic as they were, it was love all the same.

As if we'd spoke him into existence, Marcus entered the room carrying fast food.

"Hey," he said to the both of us. He handed Troiann a bag and stood back, looking proud of himself.

Troiann dug into the paper bag and soon procured a burger. She unwrapped it and inspected what was beneath the bun. She looked up at her boyfriend and smiled. "No tomato and no pickle. You're the best."

Marcus grinned. "I know."

Troiann rolled her eyes. "You all right."

Marcus went and grabbed Troiann, holding her tight as he buried his face in her neck.

"Ahh!" Troiann squealed before laughing. "What was that? Did you bite me?"

"You just look so damn edible," Marcus cooed.

I could only look on at the two of them for so long before something ugly bubbled up inside of me. It wasn't long ago a part of me thought I'd be coming home to be able to do the same thing with a certain Baller.

Sensing the intimacy of their moment, I took it as my cue to go, despite Troiann's pleas for me to stay. I stood up and backed out of the room and headed downstairs. Anh was watching TV on the sofa with their dog, Bugs, lying next to her.

"Cree, baby, something wrong?" Anh asked.

I shook my head, feeling ashamed for what I was really feeling. "I just have something I need to do. I'll call Troy later, okay?"

"You sound upset, come here."

I couldn't, because I knew I'd cry and confess things I shouldn't have been feeling or thinking. Especially with reality being so cruel.

"I have to go."

Anh shook her head. "Well, at least let me take you home."

"I'm not going home."

"Where are you going?"

"A friend's house."

Anh stood and turned the TV off. "Come on, I'll give you a ride."

Anh enjoyed looking after me, so it was no surprise she insisted on driving me all the way to DeAndre's house.

"So you like this boy?" Anh asked as we sat in the car. Up ahead of us the Parker estate appeared ominous, as if total doom awaited me up the driveway.

"I can't," I said as I turned to Anh. "He's got someone."

Anh reached out and squeezed my knee. "Doesn't mean they're the right someone."

"It doesn't matter now," I said defeatedly. Armani was pregnant, and there was no way that could be forgotten.

"Then why are you here?"

I looked down at phone clutched in my hand. Something about seeing Troiann and Marcus made me want to go to DeAndre and show him the playlist I'd worked so hard to make. The twelve-track mix held things I couldn't put in words and could no longer attempt to say. Twelve songs to match his jersey number. It wasn't supposed to be how it was, but there was no denying the present.

"I don't even know," I confessed.

"You've always been an outspoken girl, Cree. Don't change now, go and tell him how you feel."

"Thanks, Anh, I'll be sure to get a ride back home," I said.

Anh hugged me, and I got out of the car and started up the long driveway to the front door. I rang the bell and stood back, feeling my stomach flip-flop inside of me. The door opened and there it was: reality.

Armani was standing in the doorway, looking past me and then at me. "Yeah?"

It took me a moment to find my words. "Um, is DeAndre here?"

Armani shook her head. "No, he went to get some food."

"And Mr. Parker?"

"Is not here either. He's staying with some chick." Again Armani peered past me. "Did you need something, Cree?"

My hand shook. "I needed to give DeAndre something. A lot was going on at school and I forgot."

"So you came over late at night to give it to him?" Armani was eyeing me funny.

Pathetic. I was pathetic. "You know what, forget it."

Armani snorted. "Already forgotten. You can go now."

I stood, staring at her, unable to believe *this* was DeAndre's future.

"What else do you need?" Armani snapped.

Her attitude was uncalled for. I'd stomached it before, but I was over it.

I felt my upper lip curl up. "Just for the record, you're not pregnant in the face. You can still get knocked out."

Brief surprise crossed Armani's face, but then she snarled. "I would love to see you try."

I would've, but then I thought about DeAndre coming home to us fighting on his front lawn.

Plus, she wasn't worth it.

"Right, I'll be going, congrats on trapping him—I mean, *getting with* DeAndre."

Armani narrowed her eyes and glared at me. "Excuse me?"

"Nothing, just enjoy him."

Armani sized me up. "I will and I am. Problem?"

"Besides the fact that I think he can do better? No, not really."

Armani crossed her arms. "You sound jealous."

"Of what? I would never trap a guy because he's next."

My words set her off and she came off the front step and over to me. "Trap him? Is that all I'm good for to you people?"

"You just happened to miss your period after you slept with him?" I challenged.

Armani's nostrils flared. "Yeah, I did. Why would I get pregnant on purpose, Cree? I'm seventeen!"

I gestured to DeAndre's palatial estate. "Oh, I don't know, he's the son of a legend and is going places. Where are you going, Armani?"

Armani took a step back as if I'd struck her. Worse, I saw tears well up in her eyes. "That's all I am to you, isn't it? Out for a quick buck? You think this is easy for me? I see the way his friends look at me. I know for a fact that if it was you, they'd welcome you with open arms. But me? I'm the evil bitch who got pregnant on purpose. I didn't ask for this, Cree!

"He was just a boy I really liked, and now he's going to be someone I may have to spend the rest of my life dealing with. It's so easy to jump to the conclusion that I planned this." She shook her head and wiped her eyes. "Do you really think I'm so hard up for money I'd have a whole child? Do you think I want to be someone's mother, or worse, someone's baby momma?"

Seeing Armani break down and be genuinely hurt caused me to go and offer her a hug, which she quickly fought.

"Don't. I don't need your pity, not when you just accused me of trappin' Dre," Armani snapped as she wiped her face. "I just liked him a lot, okay? We hooked up, and it just happened one time, and now I'm pregnant. I can't tell my mom because she'll kick me out, I can't take a test because it'll be real, and I can't let it be real, Cree. I have no one."

Suddenly Armani wasn't just some girl I didn't like, she was just a girl who was in a bad spot.

"That's not true," I said. "You have Dre."

Armani took a seat on the front step and I joined her. "I didn't think he'd be here. I told him I was pregnant and he didn't even ask me to get rid of it. He just told me he was here and that we'd do it together. Like there was no other choice."

"His mother left him. I don't think he has it in him to abandon anyone."

"How are we gonna raise a baby together?"

"Do better than your parents, that's the best you can do." I reached out and patted Armani's shoulder. "One thing's for sure, DeAndre has a lot of great friends who are going to be here for him, no matter what."

Armani cleared her throat and sniffled. "Thank you, and I'm sorry for being so rude. It's just that you're always there. One minute it's DeAndre and his crew, the next it's you and Troiann always with them, and then there's you and Dre."

"We're just friends, best friends, it's nothing." It never would be.

"The truth is I was always just jealous."

"Jealous? Of *me*?"

Now Armani rolled her eyes. "The one boy I liked started

hanging out with *you*. Okay, I know I called you basic, but you're not. That talent show was amazing."

She didn't seem to be lying, which confused me more. "Then why are you so stuck up?"

"Because I have to be. You think it's easy being me? Growing up girls were so mean, they put gum in my hair, called me names, and boys would grab on me. You'd learn to put up a front if you grew up like I did. All my life I had to fight—"

"Okay, Sofia," I cut in.

Armani snorted and laughed, and then I laughed as she elbowed me. "Shut up, Cree."

We sat there together for a moment as the sun sank farther in the sky.

"I'm really glad we didn't fight," said Armani.

"Me too." Curious, I wondered aloud, "Are you and DeAndre still . . . ?"

"We're taking it slow, I guess."

"Right, you've got some time to really get to know each other."

"Wish me luck?"

I stood and prepared to go. "Yeah."

"I'll make sure he knows you stopped by. I promise."

The playlist wasn't important anymore. "Armani?"

"Yeah?"

"Be patient with him. He needs help with love."

She gave me a little smile. "Thanks, Cree. I'll see you around."

"Yeah, sure. Congrats on your little family."

Armani nodded. "Congrats on Omari."

Omari, right, the exact thing I'd wished for junior year. To walk into someone new and here he was. Maybe things would be okay after all.

"We'll see, fingers crossed." I waved to Armani, feeling like it'd be one of the last times I'd ever step foot on the Parkers' property. Things were different now, and as painful as it was, I had to accept that they'd never be the same.

—

I was back to work Friday evening, and as usual it was busy. Nola and I'd just served a huge dinner crowd and were running around trying to restock the hot case as the night was still young. Nola caught me up with all the drama of her love life.

"And I kept telling Sean that I'm not about to pay a bill. I got school to pay for and the little money I have left goes to me, as it should," Nola was saying before she looked past me and did a double take. "Who is that?"

I turned around and found Omari approaching the hot case. We'd spent the past three lunch hours of school together. The Ballers made room for us at the table and the boys were trying to make Omari feel included. But we mostly talked to each other when we were together, not really paying the group any attention.

I liked Omari, he was funny, smart, and charming—and okay, fun to look at.

I greeted him. "Hey, what's going on?"

"Nothing, you said you worked here, and I felt like stopping through," said Omari.

"Stalker," I teased.

He chuckled at my joke. "Maybe I am."

"Well, you gotta get something."

He peered down at the case. "I would, but my aunt's making a big dinner to welcome us down to Akron. Some other time for sure." Omari had started to tell me how his aunt was a great cook when DeAndre suddenly appeared behind him, and my entire mood shifted.

Omari noticed DeAndre and held his hand out. "What's up?"

DeAndre pulled him close and together they did that handshake-hug combo. "Nothing, you?"

"Was just visiting Cree," Omari told him. He eyed me as he asked Dre, "Be honest, the food any good?"

DeAndre glanced at me. "Only when she makes it."

Omari looked between me and DeAndre, who was still staring my way. "Did I miss something . . . ?"

DeAndre flashed Omari an easy smile. "Nah, you're good."

My fists closed and I lost all sense of happiness over Omari's presence.

A prick of rejection gnawed at my gut over DeAndre's words, and I frowned. It was always so easy for him to dismiss the idea of me. As if I never stood a chance. Considering the current dilemma with Armani, I shouldn't have cared, but the very fact that there was a dilemma only served to set the pain in deeper.

"Omari," I cut in. "Troiann was talking about a bunch of us going to After Hours tomorrow night to kick off senior year. You should come."

"Yeah? Save me a dance, or, *can* you dance?" Omari wondered.

Now I felt like smiling again. "I've been known to cut a rug."

Omari grinned at my corniness. "Cool, I'll be there."

"What are you about to get into?" DeAndre asked Omari.

Omari shrugged. "I've got a family dinner later, but nothing now."

"Wanna head to the park and ball? Chris and Tremaine are meeting me there in a few."

"Sure. Text me?" Omari recited his number for DeAndre before facing me one final time. "I'll see you tomorrow, Cree. Looking forward to *cutting a rug* with you."

With one last smile Omari was gone, and DeAndre remained.

I did my best not to glare at DeAndre, even if he was the last person I wanted to see.

He came closer to the case, to where we were looking directly at each other. He took me in, lifting a brow for a moment and shaking his head. "You've been avoidin' me."

I hadn't spoken to him since finding out he got Armani pregnant. He'd tried talking to me but I'd been brushing him off, avoiding his texts and calls altogether. Funny, it was only two days and he was already calling me out on it. "Yeah."

"Did I do something wrong . . . besides the obvious?"

"I just think you should focus on Armani and I'll focus on other things."

DeAndre's brows pushed down and he frowned. "So we can't be friends?"

It felt too different. "I just—"

He held his hand up. "It's fine." He chuckled a little, although he looked pained. "You know, you'd think I'd get used to these things happenin'. But I guess each time can take you by surprise. I'll see you around, Cree."

He walked away and I fought to control the tears that had stupidly pooled in my eyes.

Nola came and let me go on break.

I found myself in the restroom, locked in a stall. I needed space, but I couldn't just let him walk away like that. I knew how hurt he was by my actions. His mother had walked out on him, his brother had almost done it, and then there was me.

But things were different and I couldn't control how I felt about everything.

Finding some strength, I gathered my phone and sent DeAndre a text.

You're my best friend

Instead of texting back he called me.

"It didn't feel like that just now," DeAndre said after I'd picked up.

"This is a lot, Dre," I said, finding my voice had gone soft.

"If it was Troiann would you freeze her out?"

"It's different."

"How?"

"Because we.... It just is, I'm sorry."

"You're my best friend," he said.

"And you're mine."

"Don't go, please," he begged softly. "Stay."

I bit down hard on my lip not to cry. "I'll stay, I'm here."

"Promise?" He sounded unlike I'd ever heard him before, and for that the hurt sliced more within me.

"I promise."

"I missed my friend."

I had to hold the phone away to clear my throat and to get my voice in check. "And I missed mine more."

His chuckle was light. "I doubt that. Are you on break?"

"Yeah."

"Come outside, we'll talk."

I couldn't be that close to him. "I think this is better. I'm sorry."

He sighed and the line went silent for a while.

"It's okay," he said.

"So, tell me about your summer, Dre."

"I got a dog, I worked out, played ball, and got a girl pregnant. Not much to say beyond that."

My heart dropped to the pit of my stomach and my throat throbbed. "Well, my grandparents weren't what I expected."

"No?"

"No, they're so down to earth and funny."

"Tell me about them."

I sat there in the stall, telling him all about my summer, knowing it was a summer that had truly changed everything.

24

DEANDRE

Omari's basketball skills were decent—okay, I was being generous. We played two on two and even with Chris's help as a teammate, Omari couldn't keep up. He wanted to join our team, but it would take more than just wanting it to be a Bulldog. He belonged at Arlington High with his skills in basketball.

He wasn't the greatest player, but Omari seemed like a nice guy. I wanted to give him a chance. For Cree. "Good game."

Omari slapped me five. "Thanks."

"You like it down here so far?"

Omari took a swig of water and shrugged. "It's all right so far. Doesn't hurt to have met Cree, that's for sure."

Stiffly, I agreed with a nod.

Omari regarded me, a look of wonder etched on his face. "So, you're with Armani." He turned to Chris. "And you?"

Chris narrowed his eyes. "Single."

Omari looked at Tremaine. "And you?"

"I've got my eyes on someone. I'm going to make it known pretty soon too," Tremaine announced.

This was news.

Omari chuckled. "I'm not sure if I should wish you or her luck."

Tremaine glared at Omari.

Omari rolled his shoulders back, releasing tension. "Well, I've gotta head to my aunt's. Good game, I'll see y'all later."

He walked off the court and got in his car, pulling out and driving away as Tremaine, Chris, and I stood watching.

Tremaine shook his head, being the first to speak. "I don't trust him."

"Why?" I asked.

"He's just too squeaky clean to be true." Tremaine looked at me. "And now he's tryin' to get at Cree."

"I think he's smart enough to realize if he fucks with Cree he's fuckin' with us," I said.

Tremaine's upper lip curled up. "Whatever. He hurts her, I paralyze him."

I let it go. "So you really feelin' someone?"

He shrugged. "Yep, I hope they come to After Hours tomorrow night." He rubbed his hands together. "Would make sealin' the deal so much easier."

Chris chuckled. "Yeah, you 'like' someone all right."

Tremaine puffed his chest out a little as we all headed to the parking lot. "Nah, this one is different. It's goin' to take more to get her. I think I'ma have to work for it."

"I guess I'm lookin' forward to sittin' back and enjoyin' the show," I joked.

Tremaine got in his car and Chris got in mine beside me.

"You thinkin' what I'm thinkin' about Omari?" he asked me once we were on the road home.

"That he's never played a game of basketball in his life, at least not on an official team?" I replied.

Chris nodded. "That was ass. Yo, if you see Coach on Monday

before me, let him know that Omari is shit. Not all tall dudes can play ball."

I gritted my teeth, tightening my grasp on the wheel. *Right, basketball season with Coach.* I would've given anything to talk about the anxiety this season was bringing me, but I just couldn't find the words. This was my first year playing without my brothers. Newspapers and blogs were already talking about this upcoming season and what it meant for me as the final Parker at Moorehead High. I couldn't help but wonder if I could hold it down on my own.

"What's this?" Chris was scrolling through my Apple Music app on the car's touchscreen and had found the playlist Cree had sent me after we'd talked at Henry's. "Dre's Mix?" Without asking, Chris pressed Play.

The melody to an Alicia Keys song came on. Seconds later I recognized it as "You Don't Know My Name."

I hadn't listened to the playlist yet, and having Chris here definitely didn't feel like the right time either.

I reached out and turned off the song. "It's just something Cree put together."

"Y'all good?" Chris asked. "I barely see you two talk anymore."

The tension ached deeper, and I kept my eyes on the road. I didn't want to think about Cree at the moment, especially after our phone call a couple of hours ago. Hearing her voice and knowing she'd wanted to cry—

"We're just busy. Me with Ari and her with Omari."

Chris was quiet for a moment. "Hey, I just . . . what happened between you two?"

"What do you mean?"

"I remember stayin' the night at your house after my party, and Cree was there."

I swallowed, fighting being awash in the memory of that night. Her eyes. Her trust. Her soft skin.

Blinking, I let out a breath and focused on the reality in front of me. *She's already gone.* "Nothing. I think Marcus and Troy went home together and Cree just crashed."

I didn't like to lie, but I had to leave out the rest of it. It didn't matter anymore anyway.

Chris was quiet. When I dropped him off at his house he mentioned After Hours, and I agreed to meet him and the group there Saturday night.

Once I was home I took a long, hot shower, annoyed with the fact that my shoulders still ached with worry.

Upon going downstairs, I found Susan in the rec room watching some movie that starred Channing Tatum. She was sitting on the couch eating popcorn and scowling at the screen while Moxy lay at her feet eyeing the food with hope. I had seen Susan a lot since she'd interviewed us. We hadn't spoken about the status between her and my father, but I was beginning to think things were about to change. He had never brought a woman home or pursued one like he had Susan. He'd even smiled and whistled once, which was rare. Devonte was convinced she was holding out and keeping him chasing her, and I hoped it was true.

I petted Moxy's head before taking a seat on the opposite end of the sofa, leaving the bowl of popcorn between us.

Susan gave me a friendly smile. "Hey."

"Hey." I was wondering what she was doing in my house without my father home; they hadn't come out to my brothers and me, but then there was something natural about seeing Susan at my house watching a movie.

"Your dad stepped out to get some dinner for us. He wanted wings," Susan informed me.

I was starving. "Cool."

"Oh, I've got something for you." Susan reached over and grabbed her bag from the floor. She dug inside before pulling out a paper. On it was a shot of my brothers and me sitting in leather chairs in an arc with our father behind us, his hand on my chair and the other on Darnel's. It was a mock photo from a magazine with the title *Building a Legacy: How Darrel Parker Prepares the New Breed of the NBA*.

Only one of the boys in the photo was going to the NBA now.

"Nice," I let out, facing the movie.

"It hits stands in a week. Be prepared, the girls are going to flip!"

"Uh-huh."

Susan faced the movie and grimaced. "Ugh, this movie sucks. This is why I can't watch romance."

"What's wrong with it?"

Susan shook her head. "First of all, he's completely in love with her and yet he's giving her up so she can be with that guy." She pointed to all the characters on the screen. "All because he's got this job that requires him to be away for months. I know it's supposed to be this grand gesture of love, but I call bullshit. Being selfless like that is annoying, I want my man to be selfish and fight for me."

I looked at the screen, watching Channing talk to the couple before him. "Maybe sometimes you have to let them go. You have to give them up, for their own good."

Susan became skeptical. "You ever been in love, DeAndre?"

"I've never really dated any girl seriously like that."

"Doesn't matter. You can be in love with someone and them not know it or love you back."

I focused on the screen, feeling hollow inside. "I don't know."

Susan wagged her finger at me. "I don't know what your father taught you about love, but I will tell you this, love should be selfish. When you love someone and you're right for each other you don't let anything stand in the way. So many men play this macho role of being hard and not needing women or love, and it's all a game. Don't be like that, fight for the ones you love, fight harder for the ones you're in love with."

Her words sank in and I struggled to form a response.

The doorbell rang and I felt relieved and rescued.

Standing, I faced Susan, giving her a small smile. "If life's taught me anything, it's that sometimes love just doesn't work out."

I found Ari on the other side of the door in a basic T-shirt and jeans. She hardly ever really dressed up like her old self. Maybe this baby would change her as well.

We sat side by side on my front step, staring up at the night sky.

"How was your day?" I asked.

Ari let out a big sigh. "Work was super dramatic. Managers sneaking around with employees and then some rude-ass customers. I gotta get a new job, for many reasons."

I couldn't blame her, that shit sounded stressful. "Sounds like it."

Ari peeked my way with a smile. "Have a good day?"

I shrugged. "I'm sorta glad it's over."

She reached out and rubbed my back. Then she stood and got behind me and massaged my shoulders as she spoke. "Tell me about it."

As good as her hands felt, I knew starting off with telling her about Cree would ruin it. I knew she and Cree had talked and reached some understanding, so I didn't want to set her off thinking anything about Cree and me.

"Things just aren't going to be the same and it's hard to accept that," I confessed.

"You can still have it the same."

I shook my head. None of it was going to be the same. "I don't think so," I admitted. Silence flooded the front steps.

"Dre?" Ari tapped my shoulder. "What's up?"

"Nothing, was just thinking about the baby."

Ari chuckled and went back to massaging me. "I want a little girl."

I turned and faced her. "Yeah?"

"Mm-hmm." She nodded. "No offense, but I see the way your dad runs this ship and I don't want my son being forced into this strict basketball lifestyle. I want him to be happy above all. I think all kids deserve that."

Hearing her speak those words, I rejoiced. Maybe things wouldn't be so bad between us after all.

I smiled. "I want a girl, too, for the same reasons. I don't want to force my son into basketball. I'd rather he go off and do something that required him to think, like science or something."

Ari patted my shoulder. "I'm not entirely sure about everything, but I think we're going to handle raising this kid well."

It was easy to talk like we were, but still, I wondered if we should've been more serious about the situation.

"What are we waiting for, Ari? I'm going to be here and support you through this. Why are you so scared to find out?"

Ari frowned. "I know, I just. . . . It's easy to sit here and picture a future, but when I think about it being real when I'm around my mom—the reality of it is just too hard."

Being stuck in limbo was killing me, but I didn't want to push her.

I changed the subject to something lighter. "I played ball with Omari earlier."

"He any good?"

I shook my head. "Terrible."

Ari laughed. "Not everyone's a Parker, Dre."

The weight of my last name made all the grief rush back. "If I tell you something, will you promise not to tell anyone else?"

Concern crossed Armani's face. "What's wrong?"

"Basketball," I admitted. "Coach's talking about this new season and how important it is to him that I'm the last Parker on the team and that we win this fourth consecutive year and I just—" I shrugged and buried my face in my hands. "Who am I without my brothers on that court? What if I fail and can't measure up?"

I felt Ari's arms wrap around me and her body rest into mine. "You're DeAndre Parker, you're going to be fine. Your brothers weren't the biggest things on that court without you either. Freshman year I remember reading the school paper and them talking about the dream team of the Parker boys and Chris Casey. If anything, this is your chance to shine and show who the best Parker is out on that court. Or else in eighteen years maybe I'll be telling our daughter how much of a wuss her daddy was his senior year."

Instantly I eased up and laughed for real. Turning to face Ari, I reached out and held her hand. "Thanks."

She squeezed mine. "You got this."

"No." I shook my head. "We do."

25

CREE

After Hours was packed. Moorehead kids were everywhere mingling among the local university students. There was no drama. Everyone was in the mood for a good time. Chris sat laid-back at some table talking to a blonde. DeAndre and Armani were boo'd up in a booth talking by themselves. The music was decent, the crowd was dancing, and I was having a good time with my people.

Troiann and I were twins in our strapless dresses. Mine was navy blue and see-through at the sides, calling for no underwear on my part. It was something I wasn't used to wearing, but once I tried it on, Troiann said it was the one. She sent a pic to Tremaine and he'd immediately co-signed.

I got dressed at Troiann's house, knowing full well that one look at the mesh on my dress and the way it hugged my body would've sent my father into a conniption.

Out on the dance floor Troiann and I were dancing with Marcus and Tremaine. An old TLC song was playing and Troiann and I were singing the lyrics to "No Scrubs" at the top of our lungs. Troiann danced into Marcus while I wound my hips into Tremaine as he held on to my waist. Marcus had his face twisted up, not liking the diss, and I could only assume Tremaine's face registered the same expression.

"And we don't want no pigeons," Tremaine leaned down to whisper in my ear.

"Boy, 'bye, I got my own, I don't need you," I told him.

"I got a car, I got money, and I don't even have a job," Trey shot back.

I turned around, still dancing on him. "On second thought, I'll take all of that."

He laughed and his grasp on my waist tightened.

I loved Tremaine. I really did. What we had was something special. I didn't think I'd be where I was with the Ballers without him. His antics were what initially annoyed me that day I went against DeAndre. There were so many things I didn't agree with about Tremaine, but the one thing that made it tolerable was the fact that he owned who he was. I loved that about him. Despite how flirty we could be, we both knew at the end of the day that we were friends, good friends, and nothing more.

"You got two more songs then I'm taking you home, Troy," Marcus warned.

Troiann rolled her eyes. "I'll give you a song and a half and I'm taking *you* home."

Together they seemed extra-affectionate. She was even using pet names with him, and he couldn't keep his hands off of her.

Taking a quick peek across the club in DeAndre's direction, I frowned. At least some of us had things easy.

"Drunk in Love" came on, and I got into the groove of the record just as Omari came over.

"You look amazing," he said, standing back and admiring my outfit.

I got back to Omari. "Thanks."

"Dance with me?" he asked, leaning close to be heard.

Tremaine pushed him back a little. "Nah, bruh, I got this."

That was another thing; Tremaine had his big-brother moments. If a guy approached me and he wasn't a Baller, Tremaine was quick to send him walking. In his defense, half the guys at After Hours were just out to get it, but I didn't need Tremaine speaking what would've been my words.

"Stop it, Trey." I accepted Omari's offer and Tremaine found another girl to dance with.

Dancing with Omari was the polar opposite of dancing with Tremaine. Omari was respectful, never roaming his hands over forbidden parts of my body or groping me close. He kept it light, and I liked that.

By the time the song ended I needed to sit down and cool off.

Omari led me to the bar and bought me a soda, and we sat side by side, turned into each other, talking.

"How was basketball yesterday with the boys?" I asked, looking over and noticing Chris sealing the deal by getting the blonde's number.

Omari gave me a small smile. "I'm a little rusty. I didn't play as much as I should've this past summer."

"You said you ran track, so I'm guessing you're a better runner than a baller, huh?"

Omari agreed. "Yeah, but I wanna get better. I have something to prove. Your friends love talking shit, by the way."

I could only imagine which of my friends he was referring to.

I gathered my braids into a bundle, picking them up off of my neck and fanning myself. "They'll get over it soon."

Omari watched me, eyeing my hair. "I love the braids, especially the red."

"Thanks. New year, new me, right?"

"What color was it before?"

"I rarely braid my hair to be honest. I mostly wear it natural, it was easier to manage when I danced."

His brows rose with interest. *"Dance?"*

I gave a small shrug. "Yeah, like, contemporary dancing to R & B and hip-hop. I even won our talent show at school last year."

"Why'd you stop?"

"It's a long story."

Omari seemed to understand. "I'd like to know whenever you've got time."

Sweet, not pushy. "Okay."

I hadn't talked to DeAndre about my decrease in dance, something I knew we'd clash on. He was so into the idea of my going all the way with it in college or beyond. Unlike him, I didn't want my passion to be my career. I didn't want a critic telling me what I was doing wrong. I wanted it to stay a hobby, something I loved and did for fun.

Just thinking about DeAndre set me back, making me look over again, still finding him talking to Armani.

I forced my attention elsewhere, taking a big gulp of my soda.

"I like that," said Omari. "That you can do something like dance. Did you videotape the talent show?"

"I heard it's on YouTube somewhere," I admitted. He laughed as I made a face at the idea of it.

His eyes roamed over me once more, and I watched as they landed on my wrist. "That watch cold. Is it weird that I always think of them as obsolete since we're constantly in our phones?"

Feeling cautious, I held my wrist to my chest. "Yeah, but it was a gift. Or a surprise." A surprise that led to my first kiss, which led to my first orgasm, which almost led to my having sex for the first time. Not that any of it mattered anymore. The whole line of conversation was beginning to trigger me.

I didn't want to think about it or the watch. I wore it because the gesture itself made my heart swell.

"Well—" He wasn't able to get the words out before Tremaine came over.

"I need to talk to you," he said to me, appearing serious.

I started to stand up, wondering if we needed to go somewhere quiet to talk.

"Tremaine." Omari sighed.

Tremaine let out a breath through his nose before facing Omari, tilting his head to the side. "Problem?"

"Yeah, we were talking," Omari pointed out.

Tremaine didn't care. It was obvious as he turned back to me. "We gotta talk."

"Trey." I sighed, sitting back down. "Be nice."

"He can chill. It's not like I'm about to say I wanna pound your cervix or anything."

Tremaine Dickenson. "Really, Trey?"

He gave me a smile. "I have something to say, and you can't judge me on it."

"Should we be alone?"

Tremaine shrugged, waving Omari off. "Nah, he can hear it too. I need your help."

"With?" I prompted.

"It's not until later in the year, but I want your help gettin' in the school play."

I started to blink away my confusion, but then it hit me. "Sure, Trey, what's *her* name?"

He smiled as he knew he'd been busted. "Castidad Iglesias."

The name was vaguely familiar at first, but then an image came to mind. He was talking about a classmate of ours. Castidad was gorgeous with her golden tan face, soft brown eyes, and long, wavy dark hair. She kept to herself or her two best friends. She stuck to the books and avoided bullshit with boys as far as I could tell by seeing her around school.

"You just had to pick a tough one, huh?" I asked.

"She's been on my radar for a minute. I was hopin' she'd show up tonight, but nah."

If he was serious, it was going to take a lot more than his usual BS to woo Castidad.

"It's definitely gonna take some romance. Have you ever done anything sweet?"

Tremaine rubbed his chin. "I mean, I'm good to you, aren't I?"

He had his own way of being endearing.

"Do you like her or are you trying to bed her?" I needed to know.

Tremaine squinted. "I'm tryna to link up and have some fun. The last thing I need is to end up like Marc and Dre, out here lost in love and shit."

"Dre's not in love and Marcus is happy," I corrected.

"Dre's in love all right, Cree. Been like that for a minute too. But I like it for him, he's got good taste," Tremaine said, an earnest smile etched on his face.

I wanted to throw up. Even if I felt for Armani, I just didn't see the romance like I did for Marcus and Troiann.

I let it go. None of it mattered. None of it.

"I'm only helping you with the play, that's it."

Tremaine leaned over and kissed my cheek. "Thanks, trust, I can handle the rest on my own." He stood back and looked over at Omari, nearly frowning. "I'ma let you get back to ya boy."

Tremaine was gone before I could scold him about his rudeness toward Omari.

I faced him, frowning. "Sorry."

Omari was quick to let it go. "That's just the way he is, I just gotta get used to it." Omari leaned over to be heard over the music. "But you know you shouldn't encourage him, right?"

I wagged my finger. "Castidad Iglesias is never going to give him energy."

"What makes you so sure?"

"She's smart."

Omari appeared thoughtful. "Maybe he'll end up falling hard for her."

That was a rare possibility. "Fallin' hard or playin' hard, we'll see."

Omari ordered me another soda and we got back to talking.

"So, you liking Akron so far?" I wanted to know.

Omari looked around the room and came back to me. "It's an adjustment. Nothing beats home, but so far so good. I'm glad I'm connecting with you."

Same.

Time flew by with Omari. I could've talked to him all night it felt like, if it wasn't for my curfew.

"It's getting late." I stood from the bar. Troiann and Marcus must've made good on their word because they were gone.

"Need a ride?" Omari offered.

"Uh, yeah, if it's not an inconvenience."

"It's never an issue."

I was really starting to like him, a lot. "We should get together and hang out."

Omari placed his hand on the small of my back as he led us to the exit. "I'd like that."

Along the way to the door we bumped into DeAndre and Armani.

Armani gave me a friendly wave and smile. I was too busy

noticing her arm around DeAndre's waist to return the gesture. "Hey, Cree, you look amazing," she told me.

"Thanks, you too." I wasn't even sure what she was wearing, my eyes were locked on her touching him.

DeAndre looked at me, barely catching my gaze. "You should come over tomorrow night, we can watch a movie like old times."

I didn't want to, but remembering our promise, I nodded anyway. "Yeah."

DeAndre moved on to Omari, scratching his head. "And, uh, the boys are coming over tomorrow afternoon, you should come through. We won't be playin' ball."

Omari caught the joke. "I'm going to practice, Dre, and I will get better. Maybe even better than you."

DeAndre kept his cool while Armani smirked and leaned into him. "We'll see about that one."

Omari's expression changed as he eyed DeAndre. "Like I said, I'm not the best, but I will get better. Before you know it, I'll be taking your spot on the team and maybe even your girl."

That was a jab, even I could see that.

A cocky grin crossed DeAndre's face as he shook his head. He looked at Armani and they shared a brief smile. He turned to Omari and sized him up. "When it comes to this basketball shit, I'm the hardest. That's my court regardless of who comes to my school." He reached out and patted Omari's arm. "But if you're lucky, I'ma let you ride my bench." With a single wink, DeAndre was gone, leading Armani away.

Hours. I'd spent hours with Omari talking and getting along, and DeAndre just had to come and ruin it. Him and his easy, smooth, cocky words. Words that only he could say *and* back up. Because nobody did it like DeAndre.

Then again, of course they were being typical males, fighting over who had the bigger dick.

Ugh.

Omari loosened up, chuckling a little. "Motivation, huh?"

"'Steal his girl'?"

"I was just kidding."

I shook my head. "Tremaine can teach you a thing or two about shit talk, Omari."

"I'd rather be the nice guy instead."

"Good," I said, ready for the night to be over. "Because I like the nice guy."

26

DEANDRE

Darnel was home. He'd stopped by Sunday afternoon to hang out and the boys were more than willing to make room for him as we all chilled out in the rec room.

Darnel had his music playing. Some hip-hop song called "Truth or Truth."

Tremaine had been bobbing his head to the music until he looked my way, sizing me up.

"What?" I asked.

The smirk on his face read of trouble. "Let's play a game."

"What game?"

The devious smile etched on his face let me know I was in for it. "Truth or truth."

I wasn't surprised he'd gotten the idea to go that route. We weren't doing much anyway. "Sure."

Tremaine gestured to Marcus. "You first. Truth or truth?"

Marcus folded his arms across his wide chest. "Truth."

"You really tryna go to Kent State?"

Marcus and Troy had gone on a school tour and Troiann had been talking about how much they'd liked the school. For so long,

OSU had been our chosen school, and it was a wonder if Marcus was switching up.

He shrugged in the end. "OSU been the plan, but Kent is a good backup for now, just in case."

Marcus targeted Chris next. "Truth or truth?"

Chris sat back in his seat. "Numero uno."

"What *does* scare yo' wild ass?"

Chris took a moment to think, for once appearing serious. "Failure. Stagnancy. Not being enough. All of that."

Since Chris was closest to me, I reached over and slugged his shoulder. "You're enough, bro."

He gave a small smile and then it was my turn.

"Truth or truth, Dre?" Tremaine asked, rubbing his hands together mischievously.

"Truth," I said.

"Did you hook up with Cree?"

Everyone stopped what they were doing and looked at Tremaine.

His question was so left field, I had to pause and look at him sideways. "What?"

"You heard me. Did you hook up with Cree at Chris's party?" He leaned over to get a good look at me. "She never came back to me after you took her away, and I never saw her after that. And then you started acting weird all summer."

Now wasn't the time to push the topic of Cree.

"No," I answered. "You go."

Tremaine shrugged. "Truth."

"Did you hook up in Florida?"

He smirked and let out a chuckle. "No, I didn't."

"Then what happened?"

"What happened in your room?"

I stared at him as he stared at me. What had happened in my room was something I barely liked acknowledging, let alone something I wanted to put out there for them to dissect.

"I didn't fuck her."

"Ever think about it?"

"No."

"No?" Tremained challenged disbelievingly.

It wasn't that simple with Cree. "She's not the type of girl you fuck. You make love to her."

The boys erupted in blatant laughter; my brother included.

"What?" I snapped, annoyed at their hyena-like howls.

Marcus spoke up. "Nothing, you sound soft as hell."

I stared down at the hardwood floor, feeling more and more inadequate. I wasn't myself anymore.

"You ever think about *making love* to her?" Tremaine goaded me next.

Shooting Tremaine a glare, I controlled the urge to tell him to fuck off. "Why you on my back, Trey?"

He simply shrugged, leaning back in his chair. "Besides the fact that I can? Because you're in love with Cree, and I don't get why you're wastin' your time with Ari."

I didn't have the energy to laugh it off. I could only glower at my best friend.

He sat up, looking me dead in the eye. "One reason why I never allowed myself to get too deep with Cree or fall for her is because of you. Florida was fun, but I thought of you. It's been there from the beginnin'. The moment you first argued and she stood up to you. The moment we tricked her into going to the hookah bar, and almost Inferno, and she got pissed and stood up to you again. It's the way you look at her, like you respect her but won't hesitate to correct her when she's wrong. The way she looks at you says it all. The chemistry is undeniable."

Chris frowned as he faced me. "Plus, you *have* been weird since my party, since the morning after. You barely looked at her, and you barely look at her now."

Tremaine bobbed his head. "You're my best friend, and sometimes best friends gotta call each other out on bullshit. We all knew Marc was in love with Troy for a minute—"

"Ain't no one talkin' about love in our relationship," Marcus cut in.

Chris snorted. "Really? We're goin' to play this game?"

I dropped the whole topic, not feeling like getting into it. "Whatever."

"If you're not into Cree, who were you talkin' about the other day at the court?" Chris asked Tremaine.

Trey grinned. "Castidad Iglesias."

All at once Marcus, Chris, and I shared a look. Tremaine had to be high if he thought he could pull Castidad. She had her head on straight and wouldn't breathe in Trey's direction.

He appeared smug. "Laugh all you want, but Cree's gonna help me get in the school play. I heard Casi talkin' about joinin'."

The fact that Cree was helping him on this endeavor annoyed me. She was willingly helping him bed Castidad; that was low.

"You're joinin' the school play just to get some?" I hoped he saw how stupid this attempt was.

"I was goin' to go with the tutorin' route since she's cool with Michigan, but I'm smarter than her and my dad would kill me if my grades slipped. Plus, the school play will look good on paper."

"So you're joinin' the play to get some?" I repeated.

"I like a challenge."

"And Cree's helpin' you? That's stupid."

Marcus shook his head. "She probably thinkin' his ass gon' fall for Castidad."

"I wouldn't mind fallin' in love with Casi," Chris offered.

Tremaine flipped him the bird but Chris only blew him a kiss back.

"How is Cree?" Darnel wondered.

Tremaine's smirk was enough for me to want to just end the gathering. "Oh, Cree's got a new boyfriend, Omari."

Darnel looked at me. "Huh?"

"He seems nice, can't ball for shit, though," I said.

"You do know we only tolerate him because of Cree, right?" Chris asked.

It was true, without Cree, none of us would've bothered with Omari.

Darnel still appeared confused. "And you like Omari, Dre?"

"He's okay," I said. "Last night at the club he was braggin' about gettin' better in ball and takin' my spot on the team and my girl."

"He's already one for two," Tremaine replied.

He really was pushing it.

Buzzing sounded loudly in the background. Someone was at the door.

Thank god.

I went and got the door, finding that Omari had arrived.

Omari greeted me with a friendly smile. "Hey."

I almost felt bad for him, as I knew full well he was about to be eaten alive. "Hey, come in."

I led the way back to the rec room. Darnel studied him but kept quiet.

Tremaine patted the spot next to him on the love seat. "Park it here, Omari. We're playin' a game, join us."

Omari took the chair across from Marcus instead. "Sure." He looked at the TV. "What game?"

"Truth or truth," said Tremaine. "And you're up. If you a real dude, truth should be your native tongue. Truth or truth?"

Omari rubbed at his jaw. "Seeing how those are tough choices to choose from, I'll go with truth."

"What's up with you and Cree?" Chris asked, beating Tremaine to the punch.

Omari's eyes darted to Chris, sizing him up. Wrong move—he sized up one of us, he sized up *all* of us. "She's cool. I like her."

"That's what they all say," said Marcus. "What do you like *about* her?"

Omari came to me for help, which he wasn't getting. "Her personality." He again looked at me. "Can I ask you something?"

"Sure," I said.

"The thing is, Cree's—" Omari stopped and fished around for a way to describe Cree.

I threw him a bone. "Tough."

"Yeah."

"That's one of her perks. Things aren't so simple with her. Cree Jacobs is a big personality."

"I can handle that, I like challenges."

"Don't treat Cree like a challenge, treat her like a person," I warned. "She deserves it."

Darnel stood up. "Okay, Dre, can I speak to you in private?"

Chris sat back and oohed, teasing me as if I was about to be scolded. I tossed a pillow at his corny ass.

I left the room, following Darnel to the kitchen.

He stood in the doorway, staring at me as if he couldn't recognize me. "What was that?"

I didn't get it. "Some may call that tryin' to get along with the new kid."

"And you're setting him up with Cree?"

"He likes her and I think she likes him."

This caused him to squint. "This is what *you* want?"

"It doesn't matter, he's a nice guy."

Darnel stepped more into the room, studying me as if I were a puzzle needing to be put together. "Okay, you gotta ask yourself what's important here. At the end of the day, when you've made it into the NBA and are ballin', who do you want by your side? The girl who's always held you down or some random who came after?"

Two things I could never truly have anymore. NBA or the girl.

I didn't think it would hurt so much having my dreams laid out in front of me and my knowing I'd ruined my chances. I couldn't keep pretending anymore.

I sat down at the table, hanging my head. "It's over, 'Nel."

"What do you mean?"

"I mean, there's a reason why I hang around Ari all the time now."

"You're with her?"

"No." I shook my head. "I messed up and got her pregnant."

Looking at him I could see the weight of my anxiety transferring to his shoulders, causing him to sit down as well.

"Shit," he let out.

"She told me she *thinks* she's pregnant. We haven't told our parents, but how much longer can we hold it off?"

"Wait a minute, she thinks she's pregnant?"

"She's been too scared to take a test. We made a deal, if she misses her period again we're goin' to the doctor. Not that I need a doctor to tell me what's more than obvious by now."

Darnel refused to believe it. "You're the responsible one. I can see 'Te pulling this shit, but not you. Why didn't you strap up?"

I knew he'd be disappointed, letting him down made me feel worse. "I did, but I guess it broke or something."

"Damn it, Dre, this is going to change your whole life."

"You don't think I know that? I hated this summer. I waited two months for—and then Ari came and told me. This is my fault, I fucked up and there's no gettin' around it. So Tremaine can tease me all he wants, but that other guy is better than me." I pointed to the rec room where Omari sat. "I can't even play basketball like I wanted to now."

"You're givin' that up?"

"I can't go pro with a baby. I can't put that before my kid."

"I hope for your sake that this is just a scare because you don't deserve to punish yourself like this. Have you had sex since?"

I shook my head. Hanging with Ari was nice and all, but it wasn't there. I had no desire to go at it again with her.

"What did Cree say?"

"Cree doesn't even look at me the same anymore." Not that I looked at her the same, either, but I was sure our two reasons were far different. Every time she looked at me I saw sadness in her eyes.

"I'm sure that's not easy to deal with."

"I can't imagine how Dad's going to react. I'm sure basketball's goin' to be the biggest thing that pisses him off."

Darnel didn't deny this. "Maybe I can help with that."

I didn't catch his meaning. "What?"

"I didn't really play this summer, and I gotta admit, I missed it.

For so long I thought I was playing for him and everyone else, but then I realized I played for *me* too. I don't know, I like exploring who Darnel Parker is outside of basketball, but I'm lying to myself if I say basketball isn't me. I am going to play ball this winter, and keep aiming for the draft. Besides, Ashley was talking shit and said I probably would never get a ring anyway."

Gotta love Ashley.

At least my brothers would someday make it pro.

Darnel pulled me into a hug, one of the rare moments when we'd chosen to be affectionate. It didn't erase my problems, but it did make me feel a lot better.

~

Opening the front door for the boys to leave, I found Cree standing on the doorstep about to knock. A struggled smile formed on her lips and I had to look away because it was too much.

Tremaine greeted her with a nod, and Omari one-upped him, going and hugging Cree.

Darnel patted my chest and stepped around the hovering crowd of boys to get to his car.

Tremaine opened his mouth but Chris dragged him past them as well, with Marcus falling behind. Omari let Cree go and soon she was standing in the foyer with me.

"So I'm here, what are we going to watch?" She didn't sound or look excited.

"Anything you want," I said.

She bit on her lip, thinking it over. I watched her take the lead to the rec room, and then followed.

She fussed with Moxy for a minute before scouring our streaming services. In the end, she settled on *The Wood*.

Cree sat at the far end of the sofa, leaving a gap between us. She didn't even look comfortable as she stared ahead at the screen.

"Tremaine says you're helping him get in the school play," I said, ending the silence.

From the corner of her eye, she looked at me. "Yeah."

"You are aware of how messed up it is to help him bed her, aren't you?"

"He has no shot."

"Cree, it doesn't matter. You're helpin' him eventually hurt an innocent girl."

"Bossy DeAndre is Strict DeAndre," she mumbled under her breath.

I shook my head. "You're such a brat when you wanna be."

"You're right." She sighed. "I shouldn't help him. Castidad is a nice girl and Trey is . . . *Trey.*"

We managed to share a laugh, one that felt a little painful.

"So you and Omari are a thing now?" I asked.

Cree gave a small shrug. "We just met, but he seems really nice so far."

"Yeah? Good, I guess."

"I feel like I can talk to him about anything. He likes to listen and actually hold a conversation."

A slice of me fell off. "And I thought I was the only one who got you like that."

Cree smirked. "Jealous?"

Now I had to laugh. "I don't do jealousy."

"No?"

"No, and you shouldn't either."

Cree made a face. "Okay, Dre."

"I just think you can do better than a guy who gets possessive or jealous."

Cree shrugged. "At least it shows he cares."

Of course she thought that way. "Nah. That's the type of shit you find cute in books and movies, but it's not."

"So, if you had a girlfriend . . . ?"

"I wouldn't trip out if she hung out with a guy or gave one a hug."

"No?"

"No, it's about trust. If I don't trust her why should I be with her? And if it's the guy she should have enough sense to tell him what's up. At the end of the day, it's about us. If I'm doin' my job right, I don't have to worry about other guys."

Cree pouted. "I guess that's right."

"We're friends. It'd be pointless for a guy to get jealous of our friendship, right?"

For a moment Cree didn't answer.

"Look, I think your way is fine and all, but—" She shook her head. "I don't know, DeAndre, a little jealousy isn't a problem. If the guy I was with was nonchalant about me with other guys, I don't think I'd feel wanted."

"Why wouldn't you feel wanted? Look at you."

Cree threw her hands in the air. "What's that supposed to mean?"

"You're gorgeous, smart, and funny. You may be stubborn as hell but you have character, you can talk about anything—" I paused, thinking over all her accolades and cursing myself for feeling. "Maybe you do deserve to be with someone who wants you all to himself. You're special enough for any guy to want that."

Cree sighed, turning and giving me a sad smile. "You have a way with words, you know? You can make a girl feel beautiful and break her heart all in the same breath."

Sitting next to her, watching her, it both hurt and annoyed me.

I could see the watch on her wrist, the watch she'd worn every day at school.

It was too much.

It was like reaching for the moon but being unable to grasp it. Like admiring a star for all its beauty and willing to give anything to cherish it, but then realizing the desire alone was never enough to capture such a thing.

It couldn't be like before. One more glance at the watch that started it all and I knew deep down I couldn't fix it. What I had wanted before the end of the summer was unattainable now. And going forward as friends didn't seem so possible either.

I leaned over, gathering my thoughts and the words I had to say. I saw that my hands were shaking, but I did my best to calm down, despite what I had to do.

"This isn't goin' to work, is it?" I asked.

"I made a promise I'd stay," she said.

It would never be the same and there was no use in pretending. "What if I gave you an out?"

Cree's brows pushed together in confusion. "Why would you do that?"

Refusing to look at her, I said what was both true and a lie. "We can't be best friends anymore, Cree. I don't want to be."

It was silent for a minute and I kept forcing my gaze at the coffee table, as if I really cared about the fruit-flavored peppermint candies in the candy dish.

Cree stood from the couch. "Okay, I understand. I, um, I agree."

Her voice. Her fucking voice. She was about to cry, and it sliced me deeper than the decision.

One look at her and I found the tears had already started.

She was quick to wipe them away. "I guess I'll see you around. 'Bye, Dre."

"Cree—"

"I shouldn't have come." She left the room while wiping her eyes as I sat there, finding my hands shaking harder. I heard the front door close and shuddered at what I had just done.

Susan thought it was better to be selfish than selfless. But Channing's character had nothing on what I was going through.

The first thing I wanted to do was break everything in sight, and I would've had it not been for the last calm part of me telling me to run instead.

After going to my room and swapping my pants out for shorts and putting on my running shoes, I came downstairs and was about to head out when I saw that my father and Susan were entering the house with takeout.

My father had gotten the mail and Susan was carrying the food.

"DeAndre, hey." She smiled at me.

Now wasn't the time to face my father, not when I couldn't hide the stress of everything.

Leaning down, I focused on tying my shoes. "Hey. I'm going for a run, okay?"

"I like the effort," my father replied as he leaned against the wall sifting through the mail. "Do an extra mile for me and you can sleep in tomorrow morning."

"Yes, sir."

Susan stood there, watching me lace up my shoes. "Hey," she said. "I don't wanna pry, but I just want you to know that if you ever need to talk or need some advice from a woman's perspective, I'm here. We can't just leave you to Devonte."

Of course not, 'Te was hopeless; or at least he had been before college. "Yeah, sure."

Susan got a good look at me. "I mean it."

My father was sorting through mail and staying silent. Everything about this situation was new. "So I take it you're datin' now?" I asked them.

The smirk on Susan's face was adorable. "I'd say we were friends with potential."

My father scowled yet stayed silent. Darrel Parker, basketball champion, being shot down. Now that was a sight. No one said no to my father, and yet Susan had the gall to do so.

"I'm going to go set the table. I hope you're willing to stay for dinner." Susan squeezed my shoulder and disappeared down the hall and around the corner.

I looked at my father, feeling myself smile. "So, 'friends,' huh?"

"Don't."

I held my hands up. "Hey, I'm just sayin' how much I like your new *friend*."

My father sighed and stared me down. "Don't mock me, boy. She's playing hard to get right now, and I'm letting her think she's in control."

Despite Susan's strength, I had to hand it to my father. He was a go-getter, he never failed.

"Can I ask you something?"

He set the mail aside. "What's up?"

"Have you ever wanted something and had to give it up for the better?"

He thought to himself and ended up shaking his head. "I make wise decisions that lead to me getting what I want. Gotta keep your eyes on the prize. I try not to want things I can't have, not that there is much that I *can't* have."

It was hard to look my father in the eye and tell him what was really going on, that I had gone and majorly fucked up. That I could never have what I'd always wanted, or what I'd come to want.

I couldn't even ask my father for advice. My father had had us all in marriage, after he'd achieved his dream. All of my friends were seemingly more reckless than me, yet they weren't teenage fathers.

"I really need to run," I said, heading past him.

"What's going on?" Now he looked concerned.

Everything was going on. Mistakes. Watches. Truth or truth. Goodbyes. Broken hearts. Failed dreams.

"There's just a lot going on this new school year. Runnin' will clear my head," I said.

My father didn't get it, but he didn't appear annoyed at my wanting to leave. "Don't overdo it."

It was hard to promise that I wouldn't, especially when I wanted to run until my lungs gave out.

I made her cry.

I would run until there was nothing left of me.

I made her cry.

I would run until the image didn't burn inside my heart.

I made her cry.

I would run until nothing else mattered.

I made her cry.

I would run until I felt nothing at all.

27

CREE

They say it takes twenty-one days to break a habit. It had only been fourteen days since the end of our friendship, and I was praying it was possible to fall out of love in that amount of time. There was no denying it. This wasn't just a small, silly crush. What else but love could leave me feeling so intensely shook to my core where I couldn't eat, sleep, or smile. What other emotion could leave me feeling in ruin like this, unable to even utter his name? It was worse than a bad habit, and I was begging the universe to break me of this curse.

The verdict?

Only time would tell.

It was sixth period AP English and Mr. Ventura had us discussing the classic romance novel he'd assigned. We had to write a paper on it in a few weeks and I was debating on going rogue and just writing the truth. Love was nothing more than some redundant need cooked up by man that only led to heartache and pain, although I was sure writing *fuck love* would get me a detention along with a parent/teacher talk.

Sighing, I turned the page of my book and lazily read over its text, feeling nothing at all.

"Let's talk about Shakespeare," Mr. Ventura said as he leaned against his desk, crossing his ankles and his arms. "His interpretation of love is something that's lasted for centuries and is still relatable today. Wouldn't you agree?"

Castidad raised her hand and was called on. "At first, I thought he was weird, but now that I'm older I kinda like his style. *Romeo and Juliet* is such a beautiful story when you look at the idea of it. Two people who really love each other die at the thought of living without the other. That's sweet."

I rolled my eyes and could've sworn I was going to gag.

"Cree." Mr. Ventura called me out. "You don't seem to agree, care to explain?"

"*Romeo and Juliet* was a stupid story about a couple of idiots who were impatient and dumb. I like it only because they both die in the end and finally shut up."

"Girl, that's dark," a female classmate spoke up, looking at me crazy.

I shrugged it off. "People died over their stupidity and I'm supposed to cry at their 'love.' No thank you."

"Then let's talk about your favorite love story. I seem to remember last year you were very elaborative on this topic, causing a debate."

"I don't have a favorite love story. Love isn't important, not like knowledge and survival."

Mr. Ventura's brows furrowed. He faced the class. "Anyone agree?"

Castidad raised her hand, looking back at me with concern. "I think love is an important component of being a human being. We need love to survive. I think people in our age group barely grasp the concept."

Mr. Ventura got that look of excitement in his eye.

Tremaine spoke up next. "I disagree. We're in the prime of our lives. Knowledge should be our main goal. People our age have a whole lot of life to live." He glanced at Castidad. "Settlin' down now never works out. We should strive to achieve our dreams and to be successful in our careers and future endeavors."

Castidad turned and looked at Tremaine, who nodded at her. She shook her head and whispered something to her best friends, Lucia Muñoz and Michigan Hoover.

Tremaine held his hand back, waiting for *him* to high-five him, but *he* merely pushed his hand away.

"Interesting point, Tremaine," said Mr. Ventura. "I also think that that goes along with our reading. Can anyone relate this debate back to Percival telling Anna he had to go out on his own and leave her behind?"

In the book we were reading, *Winter's Knight*, Percival and Anna were two young lovers. Percival was poor and struggling, and Anna was high class. Percival's father had died, leaving his mother and younger siblings to tend to a farm all on their own. Percival wanted to go off to war and make money, and though he loved Anna, he was motivated to do right by his family. I'd read the entire book and felt nothing at the ending: he died.

At least his family got insurance and a new start.

I raised my hand.

"Yes, Cree." Mr. Ventura called on me.

"I agree with Tremaine. Love isn't important. We should focus on college and getting our dream jobs, and being the best that we can be. We barely know who we are on our own. How could we know another person right now and love them? Wu-Tang was right, it should be all about the C.R.E.A.M."

Everyone turned and faced me. Perhaps bringing Wu-Tang into it was a bit far.

Some blond kid named Trevor, who smiled way too damn much, raised his hand and agreed with Castidad. He also agreed with Tremaine, stating that we should focus on who we are now to be better lovers in the future.

Kiss ass.

Class ended and Castidad collected her things and kept talking to her friends, no doubt about the debate with Tremaine. A part of me wanted to warn her about wasting her time with him. The Ballers were all alike, luring innocent girls in with their looks, charm, and gold chains, only to smash their hearts. I couldn't believe I was going to help one of them procure another victim.

As I was making my way to the door, Tremaine stopped me.

We hadn't really spoken in two weeks. I no longer hung around the Ballers or shared lunch with them. Tremaine called it "the divorce," stating that *he* got full custody and I got nothing. I didn't care. I didn't care about any of it.

"I gotta go, Tremaine," I said.

"Just hold up, okay? Did you see that debate? I'm in there with Castidad, bro."

I shrugged. "Sure, I guess."

"You guess? I can tell she's talking about me."

"Why don't you just leave her alone? She doesn't need you or your shit, Tremaine."

His brows furrowed and he took a step back. "Okay, I'ma let that slide because it's been tough. I know the divorce was harsh, but I miss you. We all do. Come out tonight with us."

"I can't," I told him, as I hugged myself.

"Why not?"

"Because we've got plans," Omari said as he came up behind me. He pulled me close and I leaned into him.

"What? Organizing your *Star Wars* collection?" Tremaine mocked him.

Omari smirked. "It's comments like that that makes me glad we don't hang around you anymore."

"I bet you're glad you took her from us."

"Trey." I sighed, feeling tired and drained.

Tremaine reached out and held my arm, appearing concerned. "Cree, blink twice if he's hurtin' you."

For that I furnished a smile. "Come on, Trey. Stop."

"I don't get why you had to cut us off. We were friends. I thought we meant more than that. I thought I meant more than that."

I felt nothing.

"Maybe I regret all of the end of last year. Maybe I regret ever bein' your friend. What was the point anyway? Sorry, Trey, I just don't care anymore."

Hurt crossed his face for a moment before he stepped to me. "Okay, you need to chill out. I always kept it a hundred with you, and I wasn't the one who hurt you. So take some Prozac and get over it already."

Omari gently pushed Tremaine back. "She said her piece, let her go."

Tremaine sized Omari up, but then thought better of it. He shook his head and said, "Have fun fuckin' with Einstein here."

Tremaine left the room and Omari turned me to face him. "You okay?"

"I'm fine."

"You sure? What was that whole antilove spiel in class?"

After the divorce, I had gone back to the basics Troiann and I had come up with when we first got to Moorehead High:

1. Never date a guy with a tattoo on his face—because clearly it says that they'll do anything.
2. Never mess with athletes with egos.
3. Feel nothing until they make you feel something.
4. Guard your heart because no one else will.

And you know what? I discovered that Omari was everything I'd ever wanted and then some. It's funny that getting what you want is not often like what you expect. Omari was a nice guy and I felt safe with him. We weren't official—more still getting to know each other—and so far, so great.

"Sorry, sometimes Ventura can be a little hopeless with his romance stuff," I said as I led the way out to the hall.

Omari leaned down to my level, giving me a goofy smile. "You sure? I still see steam coming from your ears."

For that I managed to crack a smile. I liked Omari. "I'm good."

He nudged me. "Yeah? You free after school then?"

I was off work for the weekend, and the only plans I had was homework and continuing to feel sorry for myself. *Pathetic.*

"I'm free," I said.

"Good. If you don't mind, I'm taking you somewhere."

Nervous, I had to take a step back. "Where?"

Omari got this clever smile on his face. "A surprise."

⁓

Omari's surprise was exactly that, a surprise.

After school I found myself sitting beside him in his car outside of a local community center for boys and girls.

"Back in Cleveland, I found myself at the community center a lot to escape pressures to be out in the street or up to no good. Going to places like this when I was younger kept me calm, so

I like to give back by giving the young guys advice or guidance. Girls, too, if they'll have me."

A soft smile curved my lips upward. This was why I really liked Omari—call him a nerd, or a lame, but he was sweet and respectable. My father and Loraine absolutely adored him, though Loraine let it slip that she thought the other boy who used to come around was cuter.

The thought brought my eyes down to my right wrist, where the rose-gold Marc Jacobs watch remained. I fiddled with its band, feeling unwarranted emotions bubbling up. Not to mention, I *was* sporting my bomber jacket.

Focus, Cree. Enjoy this moment.

We got out of the car and Omari came and placed his hand on the small of my back as he led me toward the center's entrance. One step inside and I could already hear the riotous screams and cheers of the children in the nearby gymnasium. Omari flashed me a smile and I felt a wave of nerves hit me as I grinned back. My experience with children was lacking, but with Omari by my side, I felt comfortable enough to go into the unknown.

After we signed in at the front desk we went into the large gymnasium where twenty little boys and girls were running wild. Jump ropes and Hula-Hoops lay on the floor as girls chased boys or ran from them.

Some boys were shooting basketballs, and the sight caused me to pause at the door.

Three Black boys stood by a hoop, waiting on one of the boys to shoot. An image of a toddler flashed through my mind and I wondered . . .

No.

Omari came into my line of vision. "I know this isn't the best flooring or environment, but I was thinking maybe you could talk to the girls about dancing or something. I'm not the best ball player, but it's one of the easiest ways to connect with these guys."

I looked at the group of girls sitting on the sideline talking among themselves.

"Can't hurt to try," I said with a sense of peppiness.

I took off toward the girls and kept my head held high as I approached them confidently.

"Hey, girls," I said with a wave. "My name's Cree, and I was just wondering if any of you like to dance?"

One girl with thick braids in her hair eyed me sideways and lifted a brow. "Like twerking?"

Goodness, this generation.

"No, like art. Like power. Like Beyoncé, Ciara, and Usher."

The mention of the famous female dancing machines, along with the handsome and talented Usher, got the girls' attention.

An Asian girl stood up proudly. "Look what I can do. I saw it in a K-pop video."

She demonstrated a move where she rolled her shoulders and gave a cute little shimmy before dusting off her shoulder.

It was a simple move, but I loved the girl's bravery, so I clapped for her.

"Anyone else?" I asked.

The other girls weren't as brave. They all barely looked at me as they focused on the floor.

I looked back at the brave girl. "What's your name?"

"Hailee."

I went and stood by Hailee. "Okay, Hailee, can you show me that move again?"

Hailee did it again and I imitated her, causing her to reach up and high-five me.

Soon another girl stood up. "I can do something too!"

And then another girl stood and wanted to show me a dance move, and soon another and another.

It lasted for a good forty minutes before the girls got a little worn out. At first they were shy, but once they all loosened up we had a blast. I played some music for them and showed them a few moves of my own. There was something about their little smiles and faces as they learned the moves that touched me deeply. Going pro wasn't my dream, but maybe it wouldn't be so bad to help someone else accomplish it.

While the girls wound down on the sidelines and Omari was still off with the boys, I went and sat at a table off to the side and browsed through magazines. On the tabletop was a copy of *Vibe*. While I reached across the table I saw a sports magazine with a familiar family on the cover in the pile.

At home, under my mattress, was a personal copy of the same magazine signed by all four of the Parkers. It had come in the mail from *him*. At first I wanted to burn it, but then I felt like that was too dramatic, so I kept it tucked away instead.

My eyes fell upon *him* on the cover and I almost felt my armor crack, but I snapped my attention elsewhere.

Omari was approaching me and I smiled.

He eyed the sports magazine. "Pretty cool, huh? I'm not the biggest fan of Tremaine and the others, but Dre was always nice. I'm happy for him. How was your time with the kids?"

I blinked. "It was fun. I've never been the teacher before, except with Troiann, but this was something more."

"I'm happy I could help."

As we stood to go, I leaned into him comfortably. "Maybe I can return the favor?"

"Oh yeah, and what's that?"

I flashed him a genuine smile. "My house, I owe you a movie."

28

DEANDRE

It was Saturday night and Marcus, Chris, and I were hanging in my family's rec room playing *2K*. Naturally, Marcus was shit and Chris was beating his ass. It wasn't long before Chris dunked on his player and secured a solid win.

"WOO!" Chris leaped to his feet, controller in hand as he boasted arrogantly about his victory. "Take that shit!" He pounded his chest. "The GOAT is in the building!"

The exclamation caused me to chuckle and Moxy to jump from her doggie bed in the corner. This was Chris. Dude was a trip. He thought *he* was better than all of us Parkers on the court. So of course he was rubbing it in Marcus's face.

Marcus was acting salty as he threw his controller down. "Man, whatever."

Chris wasn't letting the win go as he continued to talk shit. "Aw, what's the matter? How's it feel bein' my bitch? How'd it feel havin' my nuts hangin' over ya head?"

Marcus shoved Chris as they began to laugh.

Chris shut the game off and faced me, appearing serious. "I heard Cree lost her shit yesterday in Ventura's."

I was sitting back on the sofa, zoning in and out of their game, my thoughts consumed by something else.

"So we're talking about the C-word, huh?" I said.

Chris chuckled. "Damn, fam, she's reduced to a letter now?"

Friday in Ventura's class Cree had lost her shit. She never got mad at Tremaine, let alone said harsh things to him. It wasn't right, it wasn't right at all.

I filled them in on the episode.

Marcus and Chris shared a look before turning and facing me.

"Well, I guess I should get to why I'm here," said Marcus.

"Which is?" I asked.

"I'm ready to tell Troy that I love her—that I'm *in* love with her."

It was a momentary surprise, one I sprang back from quickly as I was glad he was manning up.

"Proud of you," I told him.

Chris slugged Marcus's shoulder as Marcus stood from the floor. "We all knew he was whipped. I bet he's got a *Troiann* tat somewhere."

Marcus waved Chris off. "Whatever." He looked at me. "It's sorta freein' to think about tellin' her how I feel. Troiann's amazing, she deserves it."

She did deserve it.

"I'm happy for you."

"Ari go to the doctor yet?" Chris wanted to know.

"Her appointment's Monday." She was nervous but finally ready to face what lay ahead for us. I didn't know how to feel. We spoke on the phone every once in a while and she sat with her friends at lunch. We got along, but we knew it wasn't in the cards for us as a couple. Emotionally, I couldn't hack it, and thankfully, Ari didn't seem to be pushing for us romantically either.

"It's almost over," said Marcus.

Right.

Chris came and pounded his fist against mine. "Marcus is manning up, let that be a motivator for you. If you ask me, Dre, Cree wasn't yellin' at Trey after class yesterday, she was yellin' at you."

Together they left and I stayed seated, drifting into my thoughts.

When I said I didn't want to be best friends to Cree, I thought it would loosen up our friendship. Instead, she completely cut every one of my friends off. Yesterday at school she looked so tired and as if she didn't care. I wanted to grab hold of her and shake the nonsense out of her. Love wasn't important? Could she be any more dramatic? What the hell was she doing with Omari then? He was clearly into her.

Cree fucking Jacobs.

The silence was too much for me. I dug my phone out of my pocket and dialed Darnel's number.

"Hello?" he answered.

"Hey," I said. I took a breath, knowing what I was about to say had been heavy on my mind for months. "I was supposed to call you."

"You were?" Darnel sounded confused.

I bowed my head. "You knew everything Tremaine said was right, right?"

The line was silent for a moment before Darnel spoke. "How long have you known you were in love with her?"

I brushed my hand over my head, sighing. "Since I saw the look on her face after I told her Ari might be pregnant and watched her world get crushed. But even before I could admit it to myself, something happened that changed everything."

"What?"

I told Darnell what happened the night of Chris's party. How far we'd almost gone and how for the first time I felt *regret*.

"I got scared, 'Nel," I told my brother. "I realized I liked her and I got scared because I've never liked anyone, and it was Cree. I didn't know how to tell her, or look at her, and then she went away."

"Why smash Ari then?"

"Because I'm a fuckin' idiot who thought I was tripping. Do you know how hard this is? I can't even fall in love right."

"Nobody's perfect, Dre."

That was a piss-poor excuse for my situation. "I was goin' to call you, but I never did because I wasn't ready to face what I felt. I went to Ari thinking it would solve my problems, but it caused an even bigger one, and now look at me. I called you because you're the only one I could talk to about this. You're the only one who'll understand why I can't do anything now."

"Is she legit pregnant?"

"We're going to find out on Monday."

"You can't throw away how you feel because of a mistake you made."

I shook my head. "I realized I had feelings for Cree and so I went and had sex with Ari while she was away. Do you see how fucked up that is?"

"Yeah, it is fucked up, you fucked up, but this possible pregnancy has been punishment enough. I'm sure Cree will chew your ass out *once* you talk to her, but I bet she'll manage to forgive you."

She deserved better. "I just wanna be numb. I used to be this calm, cool dude, and this girl walked into my life and took all of that away from me. You gotta understand why I can't be with her, she has another guy who's better than me."

"I'm not going to sit on this phone and tell my baby brother some other guy is better than him. Want some advice? We all grapple with love, Dre. Dad never taught us to love and how to express our feelings, hence you having sex with Ari thinking it'd cure how you felt for Cree. When I was falling for Ashley, I was a wreck. My boys kicked it on me and I kicked it on myself, trying to deny it, but it only made it worse. You know what I did? I sat my ass down and wrote her a letter telling her how I felt. Write Cree a letter, and after you're done you can either give it to her or keep it, but at least it'll be out of your system."

"It was that simple for you?"

"I was scared, but sometimes you gotta just go for it. I gave the first girl I ever loved a letter and the key to my heart, and here I am today. The choice is up to you, Dre."

We spoke some more about him coming to visit the upcoming weekend and us hanging out. When our phone call ended I dragged myself to my bedroom and dug around for some lined paper.

Sitting back at my desk, I stared at the naked sheet for what seemed like hours before getting the courage to write down the first two words.

Dear Cree,

After that it didn't take long for the rest of the words to pour out. I folded the letter and placed it in an envelope and wrote her name on the front.

Would I give it to her?

What would be the point? Even if no one liked her with Omari, I would respect their relationship and not intrude. He'd gotten her fair and square.

A knock at my door soon revealed Devonte stepping in.

"Hey, figured I'd come up for the weekend. What's up?" he asked as he looked around and settled back on me.

I shrugged. "Nothing, you?"

Devonte sat on my bed. "I needed a break from campus. Sometimes I get homesick. I miss you and Dad. If it wasn't for Darnel, I'd drop out and go to school here."

I missed my brothers too.

At least Devonte had his girlfriend, Nique, now.

I faced him. "At least you also have Nique. What's she like?"

Devonte relaxed at the mention of her name. "She's the most well-rounded girl I've ever been with. When we met, I knew she was the one."

I had to sit back; this was so unlike him. "Go on."

"She was playing ball at the courts and I was watchin'."

"She any good?"

Devonte shrugged. "Not as good as me, which is what I told her. I was tryin' to help her and she got an attitude like I was insultin' her. She went her way and I went mine, and then I saw her again. I challenged her to a game and she agreed. I won of course, but then we became friends and started hangin' out and studyin' together. We would play ball a lot and then I realized that I wasn't just playin' ball for the win, I was playin' for her heart." Devonte paused and rubbed at his chin. "I should tweet that shit."

I rolled my eyes. "So she's into sports, that's cool."

"Hell, yeah, Nique is the perfect chick. She can ball and she got her feminine side. When we go out, she be lookin' sexy as hell."

He showed me a picture of Nique and him. In it Devonte had his arm around her and she was throwing up the west side sign. She wore her hair straight, and it was clear when not playing ball she dressed up and was into makeup. I liked the two sides to her already.

"She sounds nice," I said.

Devonte pocketed his phone and his face became serious. "To

be honest, Dre, she's a really nice girl. She knew I missed you and Dad so much that she forced me to come here. She considers my feelings and I don't deserve that. Shit, I just think different now. When you get someone like Nique, you gotta chill on all that playin' hard shit, because it's not worth it. It's not worth hurtin' the girl, and it's not worth wastin' your time over ego or pride either."

Devonte never got serious, and yet here he was, talking to me about true love. Darnel was far gone like that. Marcus too. I never thought I'd see the day when Devonte would be so normal and calm.

"Wow, you're really in it," I said.

Devonte smirked. "Two down, one to go."

"It's not so simple."

Devonte nodded. "It'll work itself out."

"Darnel told you, didn't he? About Ari."

Devonte didn't hesitate to tell me the truth. "Even big brother needs someone to talk to, Dre. He told me a while ago, and we're both pullin' for you and Ari. I mean, I imagine she has a lot of haters within your crew thinkin' she busy tryin' to make a come up or something. Plus you're into another girl. It can't be easy for either of you. This is a big lesson."

I nodded. "Lesson learned."

"I just hope you get your shit sorted out. Dad's got Susan, and I like her. She gets him and doesn't just yield. I'm glad he's not going to end up old and alone."

Moxy came into my room and over to me. She stood on her hind legs and set her paws on my thigh, whining before beginning to pant.

"I cannot believe he let you get that dog." Devonte shook his head and walked out of my room. As if to piss him off, Moxy left me alone and chased after my brother.

Shortly after, I walked downstairs for some water, finding my father home and hopping around to avoid tripping over Moxy.

He looked up at me. "You just had to get a pest, huh?"

"I like her, she's a pain in the ass," I said.

My father agreed. "Clearly."

I watched as he knelt down and petted Moxy, letting her lick his hand.

Thinking about the conversations I'd just had with my brothers, I wondered how my father and my mother had ever gotten together, and if she was the reason he was the way he was.

Noticing my staring, my father stood up. "What?"

I'd never been curious about my mother. I'd never allowed myself to care, but for some reason, I wanted to know. "Why did our mother leave?"

My father's expression went from nonchalant to on guard. "Where's this coming from?"

I shrugged. "Nowhere, I'm just curious. Why did she leave?"

"Why does it matter? You grew up just fine without her."

"That's subjective."

He lifted a brow. "Are you challenging my parenting skills?"

"No, I'm wonderin' why my mother walked out on me."

Annoyed, my father rolled his eyes. "You wanna know why she left? It was because she couldn't handle what came with being a baller's wife."

That was vague. "What does that even mean?"

"She didn't like my extracurricular activities. She had to whine about how long I was gone and how often I stayed out at night. I gave her a beautiful home, beautiful children, and she was ungrateful for all of it."

It became crystal clear just then. He'd cheated on her. She'd likely loved him, and he'd cheated and given her material things as a substitute. It was because of *him* that she'd left.

I took a step back, unable to even look at him. "You drove her so far away she didn't even care to save us."

My father squinted. "Save you from what?"

"You!"

My father took a step back, looking at me incredulously. "*Me?* Boys need their father."

Clearly that wasn't enough. "No, look what you did to us. You barely taught us to be *human*, instead we're like machines focusing on one fucking thing!"

Confusion covered my father's face and his hands were on his hips. "Are you serious?"

Couldn't he see? "You almost drove Darnel away and you won't stop until me and Devonte are gone too."

Now he was snarling, his nostrils flaring at my words. "Devonte would never leave, and Darnel was always the weakest link. He took after your mother, a bitch like her too." The menace on his face did me in, that and his audacity to insult my brother.

I didn't think. I just swung until I felt my fist collide with his jaw.

Silence erupted between us after the impact that left my fist burning.

For a moment I was terrified. I had hit my father. My fucking father.

I thought about running, but what was the point when I'd have to come back? Or maybe I didn't. Maybe I could pack a few clothes, get a job, and never come back. Maybe it was time for me to abandon him as well.

A hand landed on my shoulder and I found Devonte behind me, urging me away. He came and stood between us, standing up to our father, who was clutching his jaw and eyeing me like a bull taunted by red.

"Go pack a bag and get out of here," Devonte instructed me.

I expected my father to shove him to the side and tackle me, but all he did was stare at me as if he was calculating his move.

Scared and shaken, I did one better. I avoided packing any clothes at all and fled the house.

29

CREE

Save the Last Dance was playing on my TV. It was Saturday night and most people would either be out with their friends or somewhere lost with their significant other. Tonight, I just wanted to bask in my aloneness. Sometimes solitude was nice.

I liked Julia Stiles. I couldn't think of a single '90s or 2000s movie that she'd starred in that she hadn't killed. I especially loved the hell out of her and Sean Patrick Thomas in *Save the Last Dance*. From their strong personalities clashing in the beginning to their smoldering chemistry when they decide it doesn't matter that they come from different worlds, the movie was an honest classic.

My cell phone alerted me to a new text message. I expected to find Omari texting me, but to my dismay it was *him*.

> Can you come meet me at your back door?

I wanted to tell him to go screw himself and to lose my number. I wanted to also make note that he was trespassing.

Instead, I found myself marching downstairs to the back door, ready to tell him off to his face.

I opened the door, ready to say something foul, but then I caught sight of how he looked.

"DeAndre?" I was amazed at how easily and fluidly his name rolled off of my tongue after going for so long without saying it out loud. *DeAndre.*

He seemed jumpy. "Can I come in?"

No. Absolutely not. I should've told him to take his ass to Armani, or one of his "best" friends. But what came out instead was "Come in."

I found myself taking a step back, allowing him to enter my home. I had a right to be angry, but never had I seen DeAndre so frightened.

Together we stood there for a moment, too awkward to speak. DeAndre looked around and I just stood taking him all in. He was wearing a navy T-shirt with a pair of gray sweats. Sweatpants on guys was just all types of yes, yum, and—ugh.

I looked elsewhere.

"Why are you here, DeAndre?" I asked.

He ran his hands down his face, letting out a heavy, strained breath. "I got in a fight with my dad, and I hit him. I fucking hit my dad, Cree."

Shit.

Judging from the look of his handsome face, his father hadn't hit back.

Without asking for more, I grabbed his hand and led him up to my bedroom, closing the door behind us. We sat on my bed and I watched as DeAndre leaned over, bowing his head and drooping his shoulders.

I didn't know what to do. Instinct told me to touch him, caress him, but things were different now.

Reaching out, I hesitated before placing my hand on his back. "What happened?" I asked.

He shook his head, looking down at the carpet. "I just asked why my mother left us. He said it was because of his 'extracurricular activities.' He acted like it was her fault for leaving, that she overreacted to his cheatin'. And then when I threw it back at him about pushin' people away, Darnel included, he called my brother a bitch and I lost it."

It was both a surprise and shock. DeAndre didn't seem like the type to ever get mad, let alone mad enough to hit someone. In some ways, I'd always envied his calmness and nonchalance; in others, I found it irritating.

I leaned over and wrapped my arms around him, pulling him close. "I'm sorry, Dre."

It didn't last long before he fought me off and pulled away. "Don't," he said.

Right, he wasn't good about affection, let alone comfort when he was down.

"I shouldn't have come here," he said. "The best thing I did for you was end it. You don't need to hear all this bullshit. I'm sure bein' friends with Troy isn't *this* dramatic."

I snorted. "She did end up with Marcus."

DeAndre's mood didn't lift. "I'm sorry for intrudin'."

I hated this. I hated that things were so far gone between us that he had to be sorry for needing my help or company. Most of all, I hated that I'd given in and stopped being his friend.

I wanted to hold him but settled for reaching out and taking his hand. "No, I'm sorry for abandoning you when you really needed a friend. This friendship was never a burden, Dre. You were there for me, so let me be here for you."

DeAndre reached out and placed his hand on my shoulder. "Thanks for doing this."

I shrugged. "Yeah, no big deal."

He reached up and smoothed back stray hairs that had fallen from my loose ponytail. He seemed to be distracting himself as he kept touching my hair.

"Do you like it?" My braids were gone and I was back to my puff.

He lowered his gaze to me. "Your hair? I liked the braids, but this is nice too." He shrugged and touched my hair one final time. "I like whatever way you wanna wear it, Cree."

"So, if I got a fade?"

He pointed to his hairline. "As long as your joint was all straight, we'd be cool."

His silly comment made me smile. "Good to know."

"Most importantly, though, you shouldn't need the approval of a guy to wear your hair anyway. You shouldn't need a guy to tell you anything about yourself. You don't need a guy to tell you you're smart or beautiful, these are things you should come to know and learn and accept about yourself on your own."

I leaned back, studying him as I narrowed my eyes. "Are you a feminazi?"

He chuckled. "No."

"I'm sorry. I just picked up on that 'I don't need a man' vibe."

At that, we really laughed for the first time in what felt like forever.

"DeAndre, why did you come to me and not anyone else? We have to talk about it," I urged.

"It just felt right. I know you're mad at me, but when it comes to my dad and my family, you're the only one I've ever really opened up to about the stress. You're the only one it felt right going to."

There he went again, saying the perfect thing.

I pouted. "Damn, I wish we had a dog."

"Why?"

"So I can tell your ass to go and bunk with it."

DeAndre cracked a smile. "Shut up, Cree." He looked at the TV for a moment and back at me. "Do you mind if I stay here?"

"Of course not," I told him.

I looked over at my bed, wondering if its pink sheets were too girly for a Baller.

"On the floor," he quickly added. "With the way my luck's goin' Omari could come through here and then I'd have to punch someone else."

I opened my mouth to clear my status with Omari, but stopped, not wanting to go there. That was not *this*, and deep down I knew it never would be.

He stood from my bed. "I'm tired, I should get some sleep. He's goin' to beat my ass tomorrow."

"If you want I could—"

DeAndre shot me down. "Nah, I've got it. This is something that's been coming for a long time. I shouldn't have hit him, but he deserved it."

I turned the TV off and helped him make a pallet on the floor.

Long after I'd turned my lights off and could hear the sound of his breathing, indicating his slumber, I lay in bed, unable to sleep.

Nothing had felt right lately, and then fifteen minutes with DeAndre had made it all feel better.

A smirk crossed my face. Who was I kidding? My feelings had never left.

Being with Omari was nice, but being with DeAndre was polarizing in the best way. One minute I could knock him upside his head, the next I could kiss him. He made me hot *and* cold. But deep down nothing felt better than knowing he only wanted the best for me, that he believed in me. I'd always been decent in school but he'd made me feel like a genius when he championed my words for our essay. I always loved dancing and he'd made me feel I could truly take the stage by storm if I set my mind to it. He made me feel like I could *do* and *be* anything.

Knowing that he was fighting with his father made *my* heart break. Being unable to be there for him was impossible. After all that we'd been through it felt wrong to just let it go now.

Blinking back tears, I sniffled as my heart clenched in my chest.

The minutes were ticking by but I wasn't in the least bit tired.

Finally fed up, I gave in and just did what I wanted to do anyway.

30

DEANDRE

Before I opened my eyes I knew she was there. At some point during the night I'd felt her join me on the floor, but I'd drifted back to sleep. Now, the next morning, I awoke feeling her arm around me, her breasts against my back, and her cheek on my shoulder.

Cree was holding me.

I inched away, feeling too wound up inside to allow her to continue cuddling me. Only, once I moved, she moaned and moved with me, holding me tighter.

I gently and carefully got out from her grasp and stood. Cree lay there, her scarf loose and her arm stretched out from where she'd been holding onto me. She was beautiful.

I guess it was true what they said about love being friendship set on fire, because standing there, staring at her, knowing she'd more than likely move heaven and earth for me if I asked her to, I knew without a doubt that I was in love with her.

Fuck.

This was not the time to dwell on feelings. I looked at my phone and saw that it was 9:15 a.m.

In the bathroom connected to Cree's bedroom, I quickly and

quietly washed my face and brushed my teeth with a new tooth-brush I found on the bathroom shelf. A glimpse in the mirror found a rather pathetic and drained version of myself. It all used to be so simple, and now it was so fucked up.

There was no time to dwell on what was; I had to get home.

Cree was still asleep on the floor in her room, making my getaway easy. I stepped into my shoes and made my way to the bedroom door. I had just cracked it open when I heard a stir from behind me.

"You're just going to leave?" Her voice gave away how tired she was. Turning around and facing her, I found her rubbing sleep from her eyes as she leaned up on one arm.

"I really have to go, Cree," I said.

Cree nodded and stood up. "Okay, let's just wash up first."

"Let's?" I repeated.

"Yeah, me and you."

There was no way I was dragging her into my mess.

"No, I already did. You're goin' to stay here and I'm goin' to go."

Cree rolled her eyes. "Whatever, Dre. Just let me get ready."

She wasn't getting it.

Cree crossed over to her bathroom and I stood back while she freshened up. I listened to the sound of her as I stood there, taking it all in. Of course she wanted to be there for me, of course.

Cree came out of the bathroom and looked around for some-thing, probably her shoes.

"I don't want you coming with me," I told her.

Her lips parted as her brows dipped down. "You need me."

"No, I don't."

"Yes, you do."

"No, Cree, I don't."

"You did last night."

I pinched the bridge of my nose, letting out a sigh. "Last night was a mistake, okay? I'm sorry for comin' here."

Now Cree looked angry. "A *mistake*? No, it wasn't. You needed sympathy and I gave you that. That's what friends do. When my father and I fell out you were there for me, so let me return the favor."

"We're not friends anymore, remember? And frankly, this just proves how much better you can do. This is my problem, not yours."

Cree scoffed. "You're not perfect and neither am I, but together we make a perfect team."

Cree crossed over to me and wrapped her arms around me. "I'm no angel, so don't put that on me. Ride or die, that's what we do. You care about me and I care about you, so let's just cut the bullshit because I'm going to be here for you, Dre, always."

She was making it so much harder.

Between Ari and my father, I was too tired to put up with the strain of a friendship with Cree. Because I loved her, and she was with Omari.

I pushed her away. "No. Just stop, Cree. I don't want your help."

The way her face contorted, I feared she'd cry, and then that would really be my undoing.

"Why are you so afraid of me? I just wanna be here for you."

I wasn't afraid, just a whole coward.

I went to leave, but Cree was quick to get around me, shutting the door as I opened it and pressing her back to it.

"No," she said. "You tell me what I did to make it like this." She stabbed her finger into my chest, but she might as well have been puncturing my heart. "Tell me what I did wrong, Dre."

Leaning my arms against the door, I caged her in. I pressed my forehead to hers, staring at her mouth because her eyes were killing me. "You got in."

Her mouth dropped open, but I didn't wait for her to speak. I brought my lips to hers, just once, but that was all she needed to come forth, wrapping her arms around my neck. I pulled her close, kissing her deeper as I reveled in the sensation of giving in. It was just as good as the first time, the taste of her lips, the feel of her tongue, the thrill of it being Cree Jacobs.

I could pour my heart into her, but I couldn't shake reality.

Breaking away, I let her go. "I can't."

Cree's face crumbled. "DeAndre, don't."

There was no more discussing it, there was no hearing her out, I opened the door and left.

<hr />

I got out of my car and started up the front walk to my house.

The front door opened ahead of me, and to my surprise, Susan was stepping out of the house with my father following. He stood on the front step and Susan continued down the front path to where I was standing.

"Hey, DeAndre," she said with a warm smile.

Peering past her, I caught my father eyeing me and waiting. I turned back to her. "Hey, Susan. You should run while you still can." It was pushing it, but I was still mad at him.

Susan frowned. "Run from what?"

"Him."

Now she was chuckling. "Between you and me, he doesn't scare me one bit. Your father's nothing but a little boy who's always had his way. I hardly entertain him when he's pouting about something."

As much as I liked the game she was playing, I still wanted to spare her feelings. "No, you don't understand, you need to leave him alone. He doesn't have a heart."

Susan adopted another frown. "If that was true I don't think you'd be here. I don't think he would've taken care of you if he didn't love you. Most of all, I don't think he would've called me if he didn't love you."

She patted my arm and looked back at my father. "He's not perfect, but he's growing. I think it's time you both met each other halfway. Last night was a big night for the both of you, and it's up to you how you move forward. I'll see you later, DeAndre."

Susan headed to her car and I stood staring at my father.

He didn't seem angry, but he was probably covering it for Susan's benefit.

I went over to him to get it all over with.

He took one look at me and smirked, then turned to watch Susan get in her car and buckle in. Once she drove off, he began. "You've got some nerve, boy. Telling her to leave me when if it wasn't for her I would've gone to Cree's house and dragged your ass out into the street and beat you like you stole something." He drifted his gaze to me, appearing impassive but sounding serious.

"How'd you know where I was?" I asked.

"DeAndre you may come off as the mysterious one to a lot of these other people, but I know my sons. It wasn't hard to figure out where you'd end up after that." He took a seat on the step and patted the spot next to him. "Sit, we've got a lot to discuss."

"I would rather you just come out and hit me now."

He lifted a brow. "I've never laid a hand on you. Darnel and Devonte liked to push me when they were kids, but you were always the quiet one. As much as I wanted to get you last night, I don't feel like it." He looked out at the street. "What I said about Darnel and your mother was uncalled for and untrue."

I went and sat next to him. "I'm sorry I hit you, but you deserved it."

He nodded. "Darnel almost left me over my controlling habit. You're all I've got, you boys. I don't think I could handle seeing any of you walk away."

"But you let her go."

"I was young, completely foolish, and arrogant. I felt entitled to any woman I saw fit to have, and I felt like your mother should've respected that. I loved her but I didn't know how to treat her right once the fame hit. Fame ruins everything, DeAndre, remember that."

"If you loved her, how could anyone else tempt you?" It was something I'd questioned about myself when it came to sleeping with Ari. At the time I wasn't sure I loved Cree, but now that I knew, I had no interest in smashing a girl because she was interested in me.

My father regarded me honestly. "Some men can't pass on temptation. Some men know how to say no and how to stay loyal. At the time, I didn't. Your mother was beautiful, smart, funny, sweet, and all I could've ever wanted. I fucked that up so bad. My one biggest, truest failure was ruining what we had. I regret it because I see now that raising you boys on my own didn't quite work out."

"That's not true. I mean, we have our problems, but we stay on top of our shit. You and Grandmomma were all that we had and we made it."

My father disagreed. "If you had a mother, you'd all understand vulnerability. I bet it's hard for you to cry or to let your guard down, and it's because of me. You guys needed your mother. Her name was Devon."

Devon. Hearing it made her even more real, but a ghost all the same.

"Then why did you keep us from her?" I had to know.

My father sighed and leaned over. "I'm not sure you wanna hear this."

"I do."

"Your mother left on her own. I wasn't about to take full custody from her, but she didn't fight for it."

"What do you mean?"

"The last I heard about your mother was that she was in North Carolina with her husband and two kids, and she was happy."

I was surprised at how hurt his words made me.

I looked away, angry and ashamed at the fact that my eyes were watering. I couldn't even cover the fact that I was sniffling and clearing my throat.

"You okay?" he asked, reaching out and rubbing my shoulder.

"No," I admitted. I had gotten along fine not knowing anything about my mother, but learning that she didn't want me at all after the divorce hurt.

"I have her contact information. If you want I could—"

I shook my head. I didn't care to talk or ask her why she didn't want me. I faced my father and sniffled one last time. "Thank you."

His brows pushed together in confusion. "For what?"

"You sure as hell aren't the perfect father, but you're my dad and you've always been here for me. You could've shipped us to Grandmomma, but you were there for us. You got on us about grades, you told us to be careful with girls. I couldn't ever hate you, because you stuck by us and never left."

"I'm not perfect—"

"But you're here, and that's all that matters. You're my dad, you've put up with a lot of our crazy shit growin' up—"

"Like the fact that you all feel so comfortable cussing in front of me?" He gave me a funny look and I found myself smiling.

"Exactly. We throw parties, get tattoos, smoke your cigars, and you still love us and show your support. You're pushy as hell with basketball, almost to an annoying point, but I know it's because you see potential. We all have a lot to work on, but I'm glad we're at a point where we *can* work. I don't want anyone in our family walkin' away without fightin'."

He leaned over and pulled me into his arms and we shared a brief yet tight hug.

"I love you, you know," he said. "I may be tough about ball, but no matter what, I love you boys, don't ever question that."

I knew he loved me, which was why I felt safe to ask him, "If I didn't go to the NBA, would you still be proud of me?"

Not missing a beat, my father said, "You excel in all things you put your mind to, of course I'd still be proud of you. But you are going to the NBA, there's no question."

It was time to confess about Ari. "I'm not so sure that's going to happen now."

"That girl you've been hanging around with is pregnant, isn't she?" he asked, taking me by surprise.

"We're going to find out officially on Monday, but I think so."

He sighed, shaking his head. "You're in love with one girl and have another one pregnant. This is the type of messy shit I'd expect from Devonte."

I hung my head. "Am I that obvious about Cree?"

"You don't have girl friends, Dre. None of your friends have girl friends. I like Cree, she's got a good head on her shoulders and she's going somewhere in life. I wish you would've listened to me and left that other one alone. Now you're stuck with her and that'll be hard on Cree."

"There is no Cree," I said.

"No?"

"I don't wanna put her through this. If Ari's pregnant, how messed up would it be for me to ask Cree to be with me while I raise a baby with Ari? She's only seventeen, she has her whole life ahead of her. This is my life, I can't put this on her."

My father bobbed his head. "It's tough to give her up like that. But what if, by some miracle, the girl isn't pregnant?"

"I messed up, Dad. I can't even imagine her wantin' me."

"If Susan can want *me*, then I'm sure Cree can find it in herself to want you, despite all the bullshit."

"So you like Susan, huh?"

My father gave one of his rare smiles. "That woman is something else. I don't think I've ever been so captivated in my life. I'm thinking about asking to take this more serious. I'm getting old and I don't wanna be alone anymore."

"You've got us."

He shook his head. "The fall season makes me sad because my last boy will leave me."

"You still think I'm going to college now?"

"You can still have your dream."

"Maybe that's the problem, you pursued yours and our mother got nothing."

"Even if that's true, you're still going to college. You may want to be hands on with this baby, but you can't provide a stable future without a degree. I still know how to change a diaper and Susan likes kids. This will work out fine."

Surprisingly, I had faith in his words.

"Thanks, Dad," I said.

He patted my back. "I wanna do this more often. I should be the voice my sons turn to when in crisis. I'm sorry I haven't been."

Having his support and understanding made me feel whole. "I wanna talk more too."

"I think we're going to be fine, DeAndre."

I felt myself smile. "I do too."

31

CREE

I hated that girl. The one you always saw on TV and in films who lost who she was over a boy. The one who got her heart broken and completely lost her shit. The one who questioned if she was worth it all because some boy didn't love or want her back. I hated every ounce of that girl, and yet, for a second, that was me.

I couldn't be DeAndre's friend when he pushed me away. I couldn't tell him I loved him because he would likely plug his ears and start going *la, la, la, la*.

The last thing I wanted to do was be that girl any longer.

I called Tremaine and told him I was sorry for what I'd said in class and for abandoning him, and how much I missed his crazy ass. Before I could get too mushy, he immediately responded, "Fuck all that, we've got work to do on this romance angle with Castidad." To which I instantly shook my head and told him we'd meet up soon and discuss his idea of romance.

Wanting to keep my mind far from the DeAndre drama, I did what I hadn't done in forever and headed to Aunt Kathy's dance studio. It was Sunday so I knew it wouldn't be busy. Nothing cleared my head more than dancing and giving my body over to the music and getting lost in an effortless routine. Before long, boy drama and love would be nonfactors and I would be busy being happy by myself for myself.

When I got to the studio room I took off my watch, and something caught my eye I had never noticed before.

On the back of the watch was an engraved message I'd yet to discover.

To Cree,

Because our time together has meant everything to me

DeAndre

I set the watch aside and quickly turned my music on, not wanting to dwell on the surprise message I'd overlooked for so long.

By the time I got home in the evening and took a shower I felt rejuvenated. It had been too long since I'd last danced.

My father and Loraine were watching a movie in the den and I could hear Loraine offering up her commentary. Some things never changed, and this was one that I'd grown to love.

Loraine stepped into the kitchen as I was getting a glass of water from the fridge. She took in my appearance and offered a smile.

"Looks like you've found your way back to dancing. Good," she said.

"It felt good too."

Loraine studied me, a knowing look in her eye. "How are you, Cree?"

"Better."

"Better?"

"Better."

Loraine came and squeezed my shoulder in an attempt at affection. She was about to say something when the doorbell rang through the house. "We'll talk later, okay?" she said as she nodded to the front door.

I smiled. "Definitely."

I went out to the foyer and opened the door to find Omari standing on the porch.

"Hey," he said. He took in my hair, which I'd left in a puff after my shower. He touched it and smiled. "Poufy."

I was glad it was him. He was another point I had to get squared away.

"Can we talk?" I asked.

"Sure," said Omari.

I led him out to the front porch and we sat on our porch swing. I pulled my knees to my chest, thinking deeply about the words I needed to say.

DeAndre kissed me.

I liked Omari, but it would never work. Only one boy made me *feel*, and even if DeAndre was being ridiculous, it was only fair to be honest with Omari.

"So this is hard to say, but maybe we should just be friends," I came out and said.

Omari appeared confused as he sat beside me. "We are friends."

"And I think we should stay that way."

Having gotten my meaning, Omari nodded. "Ah, okay."

"It's definitely not you, it's just that I'm completely—"

"In love with DeAndre," he finished for me. He didn't sound angry, but simply like he'd already accepted the fact.

"Yeah," I admitted.

Omari sighed, shoving his hands into his pockets. "I'm not surprised. You were always weird around him, ever since school started. His friends always look at him when I talk about you. I don't think you've been happy for a while now, Cree. It feels like you settled with getting to know me because he had shorty pregnant."

"I wanted to get over him, I wanted to move forward." I stopped and shook my head at how stupid I'd been to use Omari in a sense, and to think I could replace DeAndre in any way. "It's just not the same. DeAndre told me we couldn't be friends and I felt like my world ended, I still feel that way. I feel destroyed because of him."

"You're too good for him." Omari frowned in pity. "DeAndre's a dumbass for letting you go. You deserve to be wanted and fought for. And from where I'm standing, he ain't fighting for you. I think you're a great girl, and I wish it could've gone further, but if we're meant to be friends, I can accept that."

His response made me want to cry. Here it was, an amazing guy who was into me, and I was turning him down because I couldn't let go of my feelings for someone who only let me down.

"I'm sorry."

Omari shook his head, reaching out and pulling me into a hug. "Don't be."

"If it's not too weird, I'd still like to help out at the community center with you."

At this, Omari lightened up. "I'd love that."

Omari and I would only be friends, and that was more than okay.

As for the rest, it didn't matter anymore. As painful as it was, for my sanity and peace, I was over DeAndre. For good.

32

DEANDRE

The future was uncertain. I didn't know what I was doing but I knew who I wanted to be with. And that was Cree. But I had a lot of wrongs to right with her.

Darnel, Devonte, and even my father had given me advice and it was time to put my pride aside and come clean.

But as I saw her in the hall Monday morning, I became tongue-tied. The only thing I could get out was her name.

"Cree." I said her name gently as I approached her.

Her back stiffened. The first sign something was wrong.

She slammed her locker shut with a loud bang and turned in the opposite direction of where I was standing.

"Cree!" I raced after her, not caring who was watching. Fuck it, let 'em talk.

Finally she spun around, glaring at me. She was almost a foot shorter than me, but one look into her fiery dark eyes and I shrank under her heated gaze.

"Leave. Me. Alone," she uttered between clenched teeth.

She was pissed, and what was worse, it felt like she hated me. Her energy had never been this cold before.

"Look, I'm sorry about the other morning. I fucked up. I've *been* fucking up, but—"

"That's right. And now I'm ready to end this cycle of nonsense. I'm sick of you, DeAndre. I'm sick of you making me feel like I'm not good enough. Like I'm barely second best. So fuck you and goodbye."

Her eyes glistened with unshed tears, and I knew this wouldn't be easy. I couldn't just string together pretty words to get her back.

Cree brushed past me and left me standing there facing the judgment of our peers. As much as I wanted to go after her again, I decided I'd let her cool down instead. I let her walk away. For now.

❧

Cree held onto her anger and avoided me all day. I didn't try to pursue her, figuring maybe we could hash it out after school at her house. Only, as soon as the final bell rang, she was like a ghost in the wind. I could just make out her single puff ponytail in the hall as I rushed out of my last class.

"Cree!" I shouted after her. Either she didn't hear me among our peers' chatter, or she ignored me.

Shit.

"Dre?"

The timing of Ari's soft voice couldn't have been worse.

A final glimpse down the hall found Cree paused, watching me where I stood with Ari. She simply shook her head and disappeared around a corner.

Getting to Cree was important, but so were Ari's feelings.

I turned and gave her my full attention. "Hey."

A sad smile had her looking down the hall and coming back to me. "Hey."

For privacy, I took Ari into the nearest empty classroom and sat down with her. With so much going on this past weekend, I had almost forgotten her doctor's appointment this morning. As we sat, she fiddled with her pointy nails.

"Everything okay?" I asked tenderly.

She slowly bobbed her head as she faced me. "Everything is great, DeAndre."

"What does that mean?"

"It means we're not pregnant."

Relief lifted from my shoulders, but it didn't take away the shock I felt. "What do you mean? It's been months without your period."

Ari nodded. "It turns out I have something called PCOS, where my hormones are imbalanced, and as a result I'm not ovulating like I should." She gave a lopsided smile. "My doctor's going to meet with me again to work on a way to treat my condition."

I didn't get it, but I understood the result. I just hoped she was doing better in all this. "But you *feel* okay, right?"

"Yeah," she said softly.

This moment was bittersweet, as were our smiles.

"I guess we're off the hook, huh?" I reached out and jabbed her shoulder, forcing myself to smile.

Ari gave me a sad smile of her own. "Yeah, you are. Now you're free to get back to normal."

"I think it's going to be a while before that happens."

"Dre," Ari said softly.

"Yeah?"

"Just, do me a favor, okay?"

"What?"

"Don't get a girlfriend."

I let out a sound reminiscent of a laugh. "Why not?"

Now Ari looked sadder. "Because she'll never be able to compete with Cree. I know I tried, and failed." I went to comfort her, but she only moved away. "In the beginning it seemed like we were going to be okay, but then I saw what it was doing to you and to her, and I felt in the way. And now I just feel stupid because you wasted all this time on me for nothing."

She started to cry and I got up and pulled her into my arms, holding her close. "It's okay. I got to know you and vice versa. Nothing can take that away."

Ari appeared serious among her tears. "I guess this is it."

I didn't want to end things like that. As if she was a burden. "What about a see you later?"

Bitterly, Ari gave me one last hug before getting up and walking away.

I watched her walk out of the classroom without looking back.

I was free, yet everything felt stale.

I went out to my car and bumped into Marcus and Troiann. These days, they didn't try to hide how much of a couple they were. Seeing Marc's arm draped across Troy's shoulders felt too natural and right.

"Do you know if Cree's headed home?" I asked Troiann.

She sized me up, obviously on Cree's side. "Where Cree is or isn't is private info, fool."

I hung my head, my shoulders sagging. "I fucked up and I'm tryin' to fix it."

"Yeah, you need to," Marcus chimed in.

"Or you could leave her alone," Troiann mumbled.

"Troy." I pleaded with the angry girl before me.

"You thought you could have her, and you were wrong," Troiann stated simply. "Your arrogance tainted this."

She wasn't lying, but I still wanted to try.

I heaved a sigh, trying to find the words to explain all that I felt. "I got love for Cree, beyond a friendship. That shit is scary as fuck, but at the same time, it makes the most sense. *We* make the most sense, and I'm tired of fightin' it and bein' an ass."

Troiann peered into my eyes for the longest time. I wasn't even sure if she'd lessen her resolve, but in the end, she shook her head and tossed up her hand. "She's spending the day at the dance studio. Make it right or I'll find you."

I threw an arm around her and hugged her close. "Say less."

It was all or nothing now.

I hopped into my Escalade and upon starting it up, I glanced at the Apple Music app on my touch screen. Instead of taking off, I pressed Play on Dre's Mix. I let Alicia Keys serenade me about not knowing her name. I rolled my eyes at Mary J. Blige singing about Mr. Wrong. I felt tired at Beyoncé singing about her flaws. And when Rihanna and Ne-Yo sang a duet about how much they hated how they loved each other, it just did me in.

Finally having enough, I clicked to see the entire list, and there it was.

In twelve tracks, I understood the message loud and clear. It was a love letter in song.

Leaning over against the wheel, I sighed. *Cree fucking Jacobs.*

33

CREE

As soon as I got off the bus and went inside the dance studio, I was greeted by a dozen little girls in tights, tutus, and hair buns.

"I did a switch up and Mondays are for the little ballet crowd instead of Tuesdays," Aunt Kathy explained as we stood in the hall and she brushed back one of my stray hairs.

"Oh."

Bummed out, I turned to go, but in my peripheral vision I saw the front door open and DeAndre walking toward me.

My nostrils flared and I took a step back, seething at his presence.

"What's he doing here?" Aunt Kathy wanted to know.

"Getting on my nerves," I mumbled, as I marched right over to DeAndre. "What part of leave me alone don't you get?"

DeAndre seemed to shrink at my reaction. "I would've gotten you flowers, but at the risk of being beaten with them . . ."

"There's a strong possibility that would've happened."

He snorted and shook his head. "Can we talk?"

"There's nothing to talk about," I insisted.

He stood over me, peering down at me with the most serious

look in his eyes. "I'm willin' to do whatever it takes to have you hear me out. So yell all you want, but I'm here to stay."

What was there to say anymore? I was tired of his back and forth, hot and cold need to get my hopes up just to let me down. I didn't know what game DeAndre was playing, but seeing him with Armani as I left school had put me in a bad mood. Enough to want some semblance of payback.

"You really mean that?" I smirked.

DeAndre nodded. "Anything."

I turned, glancing down the hall toward Aunt Kathy and her watchful gaze, before looking back at DeAndre. "How do you feel about tights?"

His face dropped and his brows furrowed. "Huh?"

You couldn't have paid me to believe DeAndre Parker would ever degrade himself to put on a pair of pale-pink tights and a tutu to learn ballet.

But he was doing it, for me.

It wasn't much at all, but it was a start.

Aunt Kathy was all too supportive of the humiliation. She dug around in the back and found a large enough costume for DeAndre to squeeze into, and the sight of his well-over six foot self in the black leotard, pink tights, and matching tutu with his muscular arms and tattoos had everyone laughing.

I took out my phone, filming this moment for proof. There was no way DeAndre was living this down.

As mad as I was, seeing DeAndre making a fool of himself with the littles warmed me up.

He had a *long* way to go to get back in my good graces, but at the same time, I couldn't deny what it all meant. Moorehead High's basketball MVP, *the* Baller of all Ballers, putting his ego aside to do this for me. He didn't even care if I posted it.

"You're doing great, sweetie!" I teased as I continued to film DeAndre in all his prima ballerina glory.

The girls giggled as DeAndre tried to balance alongside them on the barre.

No matter how difficult the task, DeAndre saw the whole practice through. By the end of it, he was loose and smiling as he stood among the girls.

"He's cute," Aunt Kathy said to me as we sat in her office after the girls had all filed out with their parents.

DeAndre was devastatingly handsome, and, infuriating, pushy, and rude—and supportive, caring, and *here*. I had told him to leave me alone and yet here he was, pushing as I pushed him away. When he kissed me Sunday morning my heart felt raw. Things were messy and complicated, and all I wanted was to go back and relive that moment and stay there.

"He's a pain in the butt," I finally got out.

Aunt Kathy hummed. "Looks like he's *your* pain in the butt."

If only.

"You like him?" she asked gently, a softness to her eyes.

I chewed on my cheek, embarrassed at the reality of it all. "*Like* is too small a word."

"Ah." She bobbed her head as she sat back in her chair. She looked around her office, her eyes floating from pictures of little girls in tutus to teen girls in leotards, before settling on an old family photo of her and my father. "I don't know what he did to make you upset, but he's here now." She gave me a smile that made me almost tear up. "There's nothing like those first-love jitters and feelings, Cree. Take care of yourself, but allow yourself this moment, this someone who is obviously special and important to you. Allow it and enjoy it."

I wanted to hate DeAndre Parker, but I couldn't if I tried. Not even a little.

Overwhelmed, I got up from where I sat on her desk and threw my arms around her. She wrapped me up good and tight, letting me breathe for a while as I collected myself.

The echoes of her landline going off pulled us apart.

"I need to get that. If you wait, I'll give you a ride home," Aunt Kathy said as she reached for her phone.

I shook my head. "Nah, the bus will be here any minute."

"You sure?"

"I could use the time to think."

I grabbed my messenger from the floor and left her office.

I heard the echoes of sneakers against hardwood and a basketball bouncing. Of course, he had found the gym room.

I stuck my head in the door and watched the scene before me. DeAndre had changed into his gym clothes and was at one with himself as he practiced shots.

He sank basket after basket. His focus and calm determination showed through every shot he made.

I guessed that came with being a Parker.

"It's late," I shouted loudly as I slipped inside.

DeAndre collected his rebound and stood under the hoop. "I was waitin' on you."

"I'm not entirely sure of the stalking laws in this state, but I think I have a good case," I said as I stepped farther into the gym. "Nice job today."

DeAndre made a face. "Yeah, sure."

"I'm serious, it takes guts to do that and not care I was recording." One upload would be his total undoing, and he knew it. For as long as I'd known DeAndre he'd always had a cool persona, a bit of an ego, and now, standing before me, it was gone.

DeAndre shrugged. "At this point, I have nothing to lose if I can't have you."

"*Have*, huh?"

DeAndre's eyes searched mine. He gestured to the hoop. "Come play with me."

"Like that's totally fair with your big ass," I pointed out.

A cute grin spread across his face. "It don't gotta be one-on-one."

One-on-one or not, I stood no chance of winning against DeAndre of all people.

"Let's play H-O-R-S-E," I suggested.

DeAndre shook his head. "Let's play *Cree*."

It was kinda corny, but I didn't miss the effort.

I peeled my bag from my shoulder and set it down along the wall by DeAndre's gym bag.

I turned and met him at the free-throw line and mortification set in. I couldn't make these shots.

DeAndre could read the fear in my eyes. He leaned down, giving me a rush of his cologne and sweat. I could feel his radiance, his body heat, the energy threatening to pull us closer.

"I'll go easy," he swore.

I made a face. "Since when has that been your style?"

He perked a brow and dribbled the ball. "Suit yourself. State your prize."

"If I win, I'm posting that video," I declared.

DeAndre smirked. "If I win, we have to talk. Ari isn't pregnant and as relieved as I am, it doesn't fix the mess I've made with you."

All thoughts of the game slipped from my mind at the news. "She's not?"

DeAndre shook his head. "It's complicated, but it's *her* health, and I'll let her tell you."

I admired the respect he had for her. "Still, are you both okay with all that?"

"Lesson learned, you know?" he said with a small shrug.

"I bet."

"Ladies first?" DeAndre held out the ball and I couldn't have cared less about playing just then.

Still, I took it and dribbled, staying planted on the free-throw line. I thought of all those rules I'd learned in middle school PE about how to throw a basketball, and did my best to cradle the ball with one hand and push through with the other.

The ball didn't even make it close to the hoop.

DeAndre whistled and took my place after grabbing the rebound. He dribbled once and took the shot. The orange sphere didn't even brush the rim as it dove through the center.

DeAndre turned to me, sympathetic. "C."

My next attempt was from out of bounds toward the wall of mirrors. I missed again and cursed when DeAndre made the shot and earned me an *R*.

By the time I'd spelled my name, I didn't even care. Basketball was stupid anyway.

DeAndre dribbled the ball as I stood off to the side sulking. "Need some water?"

While the game wasn't that rigorous, I took his offer and went and sat on the floor next to our bags. I scooped up his water bottle, my eyes landing on a white envelope sticking out of his bag.

"What's this?" I asked.

DeAndre's eyes turned to saucers and he dropped the ball. "Nothing."

I reached for the envelope and found my name on its front.

"Cree, don't!" DeAndre rushed over to get it.

I held my hand out, pushing him back before tearing open the envelope. Inside, to my dismay, was a letter written by DeAndre's hand.

Dear Cree,

For so long I've prided myself on being this "real" guy. This strong, tough dude. And then one day you answered a question about love and nothing's been the same since. I wanted to be your friend, and we were friends, but it didn't stop there. Gradually, or quickly for all I really know, I fell in love with you. It pains me to sit here and know without a doubt that I'm in love with you. I fucked up and now I can't even look you in the eye anymore, let alone tell you how I feel.

You're the first girl I ever truly let in, who I ever let tell me what to do, and talk as much shit as you do and get away with it. You're the first girl I've felt anything for. You've seen me in weak moments and didn't judge. You've held me down. There isn't anything about you that I don't love. I love all of you, flaws and all. I love you so much I know that the only thing for me to do is fall back and let you be happy, and there's no way you can be happy with me with where I'm at in my life right now.

Walking away isn't easy. For so long I acted as if I could have you whenever I wanted. The truth is, I never deserved you. I guess I deserve to see you with someone else. I wasn't right by you, and here we are. Though I'm saying goodbye, it doesn't mean I'm going to love you less tomorrow or the next day. Shit, I'll probably be one of those guys who ends up alone, loving that one woman forever and reflecting on all the mistakes he made to lose her.

Regardless of how I feel, I want to say I'm sorry. Sorry for hurting you, and sorry for not being man enough to just tell you how I felt in the first place. When I realized what I felt I got scared and ignored it. I'm a coward. Not "the man" at all. Not good enough for you. And most of all, I'm sorry I let you down. I wanna see you happy and if it's with him, I wish you the best of luck.

Dre

A teardrop ruined the ink in his name, but I didn't care.

I looked up from the letter at DeAndre, who looked worried. The stupid son of a bitch.

All the anger and hurt I had felt over the summer had me up on my feet, ready to draw blood.

"I hate you, I hate you," I said as I pounded my fists on his chest. "I hate you so much."

He grabbed my arms, stilling me. "Hate me all you want, but that stuff I wrote is real. How I feel is real."

I blinked back my misty vision and pushed on. I was so angry I was literally shaking, and all I wanted to do was hit him for making me this way. "You have a shitty way of showing it. You touched me in a way no one has before and then you pretended like it didn't happen. I tried to act like it wasn't a big deal so you wouldn't freak out, but I shouldn't have to bury my fucking feelings for you! Especially when all you do is hurt mine."

DeAndre didn't disagree as his shoulders sagged and his head hung low. "I know. I'm sorry. I didn't deserve to have that moment with you in my room if I wasn't prepared to handle the fallout. If I couldn't accept the feelings that followed. Truth is, my head's been messed up ever since.

"I fucked up and I just want to fix it. I'm sorry about Ari, about pushin' you away, and not ownin' how I felt. This shit ain't been easy. I can't eat, I can't sleep, I can't think about anything but you, Cree. It's been like that for months. I'm just tired of puttin' up a front. I just want you."

I let out a dry chuckle as I wiped my face. "What was so hard about telling me that? What was so damn hard you couldn't speak up last summer?" I demanded.

DeAndre stood toe-to-toe with me, unwavering. "I was scared. The only girl I ever loved turned out to be my best friend. Why risk losin' it all?"

"Risk," I repeated, seeing some truth in his words. We were friends, best friends; giving in to our growing feelings would've been a big risk.

"I have the utmost respect for you. You my closest friend. My confidant. And I trust you more than anything. Cree, I'm in awe of you.

"I've never been in love before. Never thought it was something worth believin' in, until you. I never knew how to handle my feelings until you. I didn't want to lose all that, but I fucked up and did anyway. So now I'm standin' here, tellin' you everything I feel because what else is there to lose if I don't have you?"

His pride had fallen and he wasn't hiding anymore.

Nobody made me feel like DeAndre did. No one pissed me off, challenged me, or encouraged me like he did. And despite how angry he could make me, I didn't love anyone like I loved DeAndre.

"Let's get one thing straight. I don't need you, and I'm tired of feeling like I'm not good enough. I hate you so much at times, but I love you even more. If I ever, *ever*, peep a lick of your 'you ain't shit' attitude again, I promise you won't be playin' pro ball after I'm through with you."

DeAndre wasn't fazed at all by my threat as he walked up and took me into his arms. "You *what* me even more?"

"You heard me," I snapped.

He coolly smiled, melting my angst and making me blush. "You what?"

"I love you," I told him. "But I still oughta kick—"

DeAndre pressed his finger to my lips. Slowly, he lifted his gaze to meet mine, giving me that cocky smile that I loved so much. "Just shut up and kiss me."

The order in his voice caused my heart to melt. I reached out and wrapped my arms around his neck, nuzzling him closer. "Yes, sir, Mr. Baller, sir."

DeAndre chuckled and shook his head. "You and that smart mouth."

"Yeah, but you love it."

He came closer, teasing my lips with his. "Yeah. Yeah, I do."

His forehead brushed against mine and soon our lips were entwined and all the mess of the past didn't matter.

After our lips parted, he went and grabbed the basketball from the floor, tossing me a wink. "What do you say? Best two out of three?"

Even though I'd lost the first round, I was so down for a rematch. I wouldn't have it any other way than playing my heart out with him. "You're so on."

ACKNOWLEDGMENTS

First, I have to thank every girl who read the Wattpad version circa 2013's conception and 2014's completion. When I got inspired to write this book I was just a twenty-year-old woman with something to say. Little did I know I wasn't alone. You all championed Cree and DeAndre's story from the start and I'll never forget. I'm forever grateful for my Wattpad readers, you made me feel heard when I wasn't sure anyone would listen. To the girls who saw themselves in Cree, I cannot thank you enough for making me feel important in writing her story.

To Wattpad, I thank you for always supporting this book and seeing its magic. From Rebecca for helping develop and structure the published version, and to Deanna, Fiona, Sun, and Delaney for overseeing its journey as well.

And to Uwe, for always believing in these two Black kids and their story no matter how many nos we faced. For loving them as is, unapologetic, unhinged, and uncensored. Without you loving this book I wouldn't have gotten where I am today. Thanks so much for supporting me through it all.

To the masterminds behind the hooks of Nicki Minaj and Cassie's "The Boys" as well as Kanye West featuring Big Sean and Jay-Z's "Clique," I thank you. Without ever hearing those records there'd be no Cree or DeAndre.

ABOUT THE AUTHOR

A lover of words, Whitney D. Grandison has been writing since as far back as she can remember. Outside of writing, she is a lover of Asian dramas, all things John Hughes, and horror films. Whitney currently lives in Akron, Ohio, with her cats. Visit Whitney's website, www.whitneydgrandison.com, and follow her on Instagram, @wheadee.

PLAYLIST

The Boys
Nicki Minaj + Cassie

Clique
Kanye West feat. Big Sean + Jay-Z

Playas Gon' Play
3LW

The Birds, Pt. 1
The Weeknd

Brown Skin Girl
Beyoncé + SAINt JHN + Wizkid feat.
Blue Ivy Carter

Forever
Drake + Kanye West + Lil Wayne +
Eminem

Bad Boy (Remix)
Ash K

Best Friend
50 Cent feat. Olivia

Pretty Girl Rock
Keri Hilson

Teach Me
Musiq Soulchild

Primetime
Janelle Monáe feat. Miguel

I Come Apart
A$AP Rocky feat. Florence Welch

Nobody Gets Me
SZA

Girls Like You
Miguel

Teenage Love Affair
Alicia Keys

Illest Bitch
Wale

Mixtape
Lyrica Anderson

Wu-Tang Forever
Drake

Adore You
Miley Cyrus

This Woman's Work
Maxwell

No Angel
Beyoncé

Differences
Ginuwine

I'm Going Down
Mary J. Blige

I Like It
Sevyn Streeter

Walked Outta Heaven
Jagged Edge

Poetry
Danity Kane

Hustler
Keri Hilson

How It Was Supposed to Be
Ryan Leslie

Sound of Love
Cassie feat. Jeremih

Playin' Hard
Trey Songz

Breakdown
Mariah Carey feat. Krayzie Bone &
Wish Bone

Letter
B. Smyth

Best I Ever Had
Drake feat. Nicki Minaj

My Boo
Usher + Alicia Keys

Hate That I Love You
Rihanna feat. Ne-Yo

Stay
Khalid

DRE'S MIX

You Don't Know My Name
Alicia Keys

Flaws and All
Beyoncé

Drew Barrymore
SZA

Angel of Mine
Monica

Body
Summer Walker

Sittin' Up In My Room
Brandy

Mr. Wrong
Mary J. Blige feat. Drake

Hate That I Love You
Rihanna feat. Ne-Yo

Shea Butter Baby
Ari Lennox feat. J. Cole

It's Whatever
Aaliyah

We Belong Together
Mariah Carey

It Won't Stop
Sevyn Streeter